Lucrezia Borgia
and the
Mother of Poisons

FORGE BOOKS by ROBERTA GELLIS

A Mortal Bane
A Personal Devil
Bone of Contention
Lucrezia Borgia and the Mother of Poisons

Lucrezia Borgia
and the
Mother of Poisons

Roberta Gellis

FORGE

A TOM DOHERTY ASSOCIATES BOOK

New York

LUCREZIA BORGIA AND THE MOTHER OF POISONS

Copyright © 2003 by Roberta Gellis

A Forge Book
Published by Tom Doherty Associates, LLC
175 Fifth Avenue
New York, NY 10010

www.tor.com

Forge® is a registered trademark of Tom Doherty Associates, LLC.

Library of Congress Cataloging-in-Publication Data

Gellis, Roberta.
   Lucrezia Borgia and the mother of poisons / Roberta Gellis.
        p. cm.
   "A Tom Doherty Associates book."
   ISBN 0-765-30661-1 (PBK)
   EAN 978-0765-30661-6 (PBK)
   1. Borgia, Lucrezia, 1480–1519—Fiction. 2. Italy—History—1492–1559—
Fiction. 3. Ferrara (Italy)—Fiction. 4. Women—Italy—Fiction.
   5. Poisoning—Fiction. 6. Poisoners—Fiction. 7. Nobility—Fiction. I. Title.

PS3557.E42L83 2003
813'.54—dc21   2003046845

Printed in the United States of America

09 8 7 6 5 4 3

To my beloved sister, Berenice,
and to my dear brother-by-marriage, Clint,
for the great pleasure their company gives me

Lucrezia Borgia
and the
Mother of Poisons

1

"POISON? Why? Why would anyone wish to poison so harmless and silly a woman as Bianca Tedaldo?" Lucrezia breathed, all the color fading from her face, leaving her skin like translucent alabaster.

"You wished to poison her," Alfonso d'Este shouted, "because she was my mistress!"

Lucrezia's mouth dropped open and her eyes widened with a shock that deprived her of the power to make any protest, for a moment of the power to think. Her husband's black eyes flashed. His expression was so filled with rage and hate that Lucrezia sank back onto the chair from which she had risen. She stared up at him, swallowing painfully.

"No," she whispered. "I have been away in the Convent of Corpus Domini since before Easter. I have not laid eyes upon Donna Bianca since I returned two days ago." Her voice grew stronger, angry, as the utter stupidity of such an accusation overcame the shock it had given her. "When was she poisoned? How? And why should I poison *her* when I never troubled any of the others? Why should I care about one more mistress—if she was your mistress?"

Frustration now mingled with the rage and hate in Alfonso d'Este's coarse face, and Lucrezia stared back at him defiantly. Alfonso was no cultured intellectual, but he was shrewd and had a most powerful sense of self-preservation. He was not really likely to harm the daughter of Pope Alexander VI and the sister of Cesare Borgia.

"I do not know how or why," he snarled, and then, as if he had read her mind, added, "If I did, you would be in the bargello with the other common criminals right now, and to hell with your father, even if he is the Pope, and that vicious mad dog of a brother with his armies."

For a moment Lucrezia almost believed him and her breath caught. "But it is not true!" she cried, tears rising to her eyes. "I never poisoned anyone in my life, and Cesare . . . well, he has killed, yes—"

She looked away and her voice trembled, as she recalled the beloved husband Cesare had killed, shattering her life just so she could be free to make a political marriage to this man who hated her and seemingly would do anything to be rid of her.

Alfonso apparently did not guess the reason for her distress and answered her words directly. "Killed, yes," he mimicked, sneering. "Among others his own brother, I have heard. So why should his sister hesitate to remove a lady I found attractive—"

Now that the shock of Alfonso's accusation had abated, Lucrezia detected the false note in his declaration. "You found Bianca attractive?" she echoed unbelievingly, rising to her feet again and laughing harshly. "I do not believe it. Light of mind and virtue Bianca was, but she was a lady. I never saw her behave like a street slut, and I know you care for no other kind of woman."

"So you say." Alfonso looked her over from head to foot and then met her eyes, sneering again. "Perhaps that I should court a lady is what you could not bear."

Lucrezia shook her head and lifted a shoulder contemptuously. "You are assuming you matter enough to me that I would be jealous."

A flick of Alfonso's eyes told her that shaft had hurt. Satisfied, she continued with a half smile, "but I tell you that even if someone had shouted in my ear that she was your leman—and no one bothers to gossip to me about you, since what you do is clear enough to all—I would never have believed it, so I still had no reason to kill Bianca."

Alfonso's powerful hands knotted into fists, but he did not step forward and strike her. Lucrezia wondered whether it was because he really did not want to hurt her or because he knew hurting her would infuriate his father.

"What does the reason matter?" he growled. "Perhaps it is no more than the Borgia urge to kill something. Certainly Cesare does not seem to need a reason to kill."

"But not with poison," she snapped. "Cesare uses a knife or a bludgeon or a sword."

Alfonso shrugged. "You do not have that option. And tell me, who else in my father's Court would use poison?"

Lucrezia stared at him for a moment and then laughed again, easily this time. "Do you want a list?"

He made a furious, wordless sound and snarled, "No one has ever been poisoned in the palace of Ferrara before you came."

Those words made Lucrezia pale and when he started to turn away she caught at his arm. "Wait!" she cried. "If you came here to tell me this, others must be accusing me also. I did not do it, Alfonso! And you know that. Will you not allow me to defend myself?"

"How? By proclaiming your innocence? My father is doing that already." His mouth twisted with an emotion Lucrezia could not read. "You may depend on his support."

"No," she said, "to say I am innocent would do about as much good as my father's friends pointing out that all those he is said to have poisoned are still walking about accusing him. You must discover who really poisoned poor Bianca."

"I? I must discover who killed her? Why the devil should I—"

He stopped speaking abruptly as if, Lucrezia thought, he had suddenly remembered that only a few moments before he had professed tender feelings for the dead woman. A lover would wish to avenge his lady. She raised her brows in silent, sardonic inquiry.

"My father would not countenance it!" he exclaimed. "Considering his determination to hold you blameless at all costs and my conviction concerning Bianca's death, it would be best for everyone that she be buried in decent silence and forgotten as soon as possible."

On those words, before Lucrezia could protest again, he was at the door, drawing aside the portiere and leaving the room. As the curtain lifted, Lucrezia heard the whispers and hisses of intense conversation. The sound was muffled into a barely perceptible murmur when the curtain fell, but Lucrezia stood staring at the hanging with burning eyes. The tapestry displayed a beautiful rendering of the Annunciation. The Virgin in her blue dress staring past a graceful pillar at the angel, whose wings glittered with thread of gold.

Lucrezia remembered when she had seen the tapestry on first entering this apartment a month earlier that she had hoped it was an omen, that she would soon be with child so her place here in Ferrara would be assured. That hope had been fulfilled; she was pregnant, but her husband seemed utterly indifferent. Or was he disappointed that she had conceived so readily? Was that the reason for his mad accusation? Was he so eager to be rid of her . . . No. Surely not. Surely he had been growing accustomed; twice not so long ago he had lingered after their coupling to say a few words.

Then, although her eyes were still fixed on the tapestry, her mind focused beyond it on those who waited in her public receiving room. The tapestry muffled whispers and low voices, but Alfonso's shouted accusation would have been easily heard. She could guess who was out there. The ladies her father-by-law had imposed upon her when he said her entourage was too large, too costly for him to support, and sent her own people back to Rome, those and the hangers-on who made themselves welcome guests to the less noble of the city by relaying the latest gossip and scandal.

What were they doing there so early? she asked herself. Her custom was to break her fast in private with the two ladies who had defied the duke and refused to leave her, then to respond to invitations or write letters until at least midday before she dressed and went into her public reception room. *Had they known that Bianca was dead,* she wondered, *and come to see what I was doing?*

She continued staring at the doorway, overwhelmed with bitter memories of similar accusations with as little cause. It had been mostly because she could no longer bear the hissing behind her back, the knowing winks, the significant smiles that she had welcomed the marriage to Alfonso, even while her heart was raw with the loss of her beloved. Of course, she had been afraid to refuse too, afraid of her father's displeasure and . . . of Cesare. Not that he would hurt her; she did not believe that. But God knew what else he might have done if she had not fallen in with his plans.

Marriage to Alfonso had promised freedom, freedom from the sickening rumors about her, freedom from being dangled like a ripe fruit in front of those who desired her father's favor, freedom from Cesare's dangerous notions of how she could be used to forward his purposes. Ferrara was far from Rome and a powerful state protected by an alliance with France. Being the heir, Alfonso could not be expected to live in Rome as had been demanded of her previous husbands.

She had known Alfonso was unwilling, that he had agreed to the marriage only under severe pressure from his father, but she had not cared. She had not wanted or expected love. She had come prepared to be a good wife in the face of her new husband's indifference, to be an ornament of the Court of Ferrara, to bear an heir to the dukedom. She had wanted only a haven—and thought she had found it. Until this very morning she had believed that all, even Alfonso, even the Ferrarese ladies who disliked her, thought well of her.

While she stared at the doorway and thought, Lucrezia had been increasingly aware of the sound of weeping behind her. Now she turned to face the companions who had shrugged off the duke's lack of welcome to stay with her. Her cousin, Angela Borgia, like herself blond and blue-eyed, was sobbing and shaking her head. Nicola la Sienese, dark-haired, dark-eyed, and olive-skinned, whose mind and sense of humor accorded more exactly with her own than any other companion she had ever had, looked more amazed than saddened.

"Who would kill Bianca?" Angela whimpered. "You said she was silly, and so she was, but she was also the kindest person in the whole world and the most obliging. She even parted from her old lovers on good terms. No one could have wanted to hurt her. I cannot believe it."

"What I cannot believe is what Don Alfonso said," Nicola muttered.

"Oh, you are quite right!" Angela exclaimed, wiping her eyes. "Bianca was *not* Alfonso's mistress. She had a new lover, and she was thrilled with him—"

"Hush!" Lucrezia said softly, looking over her shoulder toward the door behind the portiere. "Alfonso left it open—apurpose, I think. Come into my bedchamber."

Angela's hand went to her lips and Nicola took her lower lip between her teeth. Both stared at the doorway for a horrified moment and then turned to follow Lucrezia across the room toward a door at the back, which led to the innermost chamber of the apartment.

Before they reached it, a high, trembling voice said, "I know you did not do it, madonna, and I can prove it!"

"Lucia!" Lucrezia exclaimed.

"I was bringing the wine when Don Alfonso came in, so I stopped, and I could not help but hear what he said. But it is not *true,* madonna. There is nothing of yours that is private from your maid, and I know you have no poison anywhere. I will speak to the duke. I will cry it aloud to the whole world!"

"Why, thank you, Lucia," Lucrezia said.

She was much touched not only by the staunch support but by the reddened eyes and tear-streaked cheeks that displayed how frightened the maid had been. And she was not sorry that the girl had been so overset that she had spoken much more loudly than usual. It could do no harm if those gossip-greedy harpies in the public chamber heard Lucia's defense. However, before something was said that she was not as eager for the whole world to know, she had better obtain some privacy. Gesturing for Lucia to come, she led her ladies into her most private sanctum and softly closed the door.

She made a slight grimace of distaste as she stepped into the room and was nearly blinded by the gilding that highlighted the patterns of the blue walls. Even the moldings between the painted panels on the ceiling were gilded. She could only be thankful that the gold-embroidered blue bedcurtains hid it after she had closed them or the glitter reflected from her nightcandle would have kept her awake. She supposed she should be grateful that the room—actually all six rooms (if one counted the bathing room)—had been decorated afresh, but she could not help wishing someone had asked what she would prefer. Now it would be years before she could have all that glittering gold removed and the wood beneath it darkened to her favorite warm brown.

Lucia set the wine down on the side of her mistress's writing table and pulled out the chair. "Sit down, madonna. You are dreadfully pale. It was terrible to threaten you like that, terrible. And so unjust."

Lucrezia seated herself in the proffered chair with a rather tremulous smile. The maid poured a glass of wine, offered it to her, and knelt down before her. Seeing the fear shadowing the wide, dark eyes, Lucrezia sought for a way to comfort the girl, and then realized she could use the emotion to correct a behavior that she knew was common to many of the serving girls but was particularly noxious in her situation. So she fixed her kneeling maid with what she hoped was a reproachful and still stern expression.

"If you are afraid for me, I think this time you must forgo the profit or the pleasure you win from telling El Prete all the tidbits you see and hear in my chambers."

She expected the maid to blanch, to burst into tears, to deny she told tales or sold information and beg forgiveness. Instead the fear faded from Lucia's eyes and she grinned.

"Oh, no, madonna," she said. "I must tell him of this specially." She giggled softly, shaking her head as Lucrezia drew a sharp breath. "Not about what Don Alfonso said. Many will tell him that before I could reach him anyway."

"Then what will you tell him?" Lucrezia asked.

"I must tell him that I have secretly used every powder, lotion, cream, and perfume in my madonna's possession, and that none did me any ill. I must tell him of your devotions in the convent and that you invited none but Madonna Angela and Madonna Nicola to your table since you returned and that I spy on you every moment and know what you do, just as I know what gowns you wear and how gloriously golden is your hair and how beautiful and clever you are and how all the artists and poets flock around you and all adore you. I love to tell him such things." She lowered her eyes and giggled again. "Far as she is in Mantua, I can hear Madonna Isabella's teeth grinding as she reads his letters."

Lucrezia stared at the maid and then began to laugh also. "You mean you tell Madonna Isabella's spy what will make her fear even more that I will outshine her?"

Lucia looked contemptuous. "And right she is to fear it, for you do!" she replied. "She strives and struts and spouts fine words to overawe everyone. You smile and listen and reply so sweetly that everyone loves you."

"Except my husband," Lucrezia said with a wry smile.

"Ridiculous!" Lucia exclaimed passionately. "He cannot think you would harm anyone. He knows how gentle you are—"

"Does he?" Lucrezia asked, for the first time realizing how very clever Lucia was and seeing a path to learning what the servants said among themselves—and thus what the noble ladies and gentlemen did when they believed they were in private. "Or does he believe the terrible tales that were told of me in Rome?"

Lucrezia's eyes filled with tears, and that was no pretense. She had hated the whispering behind her back, the knowing smiles over stories of murder and baseborn babes, even incest. She had fled to this cold, gray north and a loveless marriage to escape the ugliness that surrounded her life in Rome. Was it to begin all over again?

The kneeling maid leaned forward and kissed her hand. "No one really believed those tales," Lucia said. "They only enjoyed whispering them to each other."

"But I did not enjoy it," Lucrezia snapped. "I have had great pleasure in the open way I am greeted here, in the ease of conversation, in the trust shown to me. There are a few who watch in hope I will do wrong, but most of the Court *liked* me. Now, after what Alfonso said, if no one finds out who truly killed Madonna Bianca, the whispering will all begin again. Lucia, will you help me?"

"Of course I will, madonna," Lucia breathed.

"Because you are a maid, no one sees you. No one thinks that you hear and see. Will you hear and see for me, Lucia?"

"Indeed. Indeed I will."

"Then go among my uninvited guests in the outer chamber. Bring them cakes and wine. All of them know I do not come out of my inner rooms until the nineteenth or twentieth hour, so what are they doing here at the fifteenth? Find out for me, Lucia. Did they already know what Alfonso would say?"

The maid's eyes widened with sudden comprehension. She kissed her mistress's hand again and scrambled to her feet. Then she nodded her head once, sharply, and slipped out. When she was gone, Lucrezia looked around at Nicola and Angela.

"But it is not true, that Alfonso does not care for you," Nicola remarked, her fine dark eyes narrowed. "Until this lunacy, I would have sworn that he was now well on his way to being satisfied—and more than satisfied—to have you to wife. If not, why should he continue to come to you every night when he knows he has already set a babe in your belly?"

Lucrezia's eyes widened at this telling remark. She had never considered that interesting fact. Then she frowned and shook her head. "But he hardly says a word to me."

Nicola shrugged. "He hardly says a word to anyone. Words are not Don Alfonso's strong suit. And it is true that mostly he likes his meat coarser. But still, I believe he is coming to know your value and respect you."

"I had thought so too," Lucrezia said. "And particularly just now. Not only am I, as you said, with child, but Cesare is about to come north—and he could easily come as far north as Ferrara if I were insulted. No, it is utterly ridiculous that Alfonso would accuse me of murder even if he had watched me commit the crime." She drew a long breath, then let it out, her eyes going from Nicola to Angela and back to Nicola. "So what was that all about?"

"Could *he* have—" Angela began, and then shook her head sharply. "No, that is impossible. I am sure Bianca hardly knew him. She never spoke of him, and I am sure she could not have resisted boasting if she had captured Don Alfonso's attention. . . . Unless . . . she was very kindhearted . . . she kept it secret so as not to hurt you?"

"But why make such a to-do if he were guilty?" Nicola mused. "No, if he were, he would pass the whole thing off as if it had nothing to do with him. He would not come here shouting aloud that Bianca was his mistress."

"Then was his purpose to besmirch me?" Lucrezia asked, her voice not quite steady. "Can he wish to be rid of me to make a French marriage?"

"Not with a baby in your belly and Cesare about to take the road north," Angela said. "I may be a fool, but even I am not so foolish as that. This is the wrong time."

"True, and besides that, I am not sure that the duke any longer wants a French marriage. Can you imagine King Louis parting with the kind of dowry that your father was willing to give?" Nicola uttered a bark of laughter. "Or imagine the duke returning your dowry?"

Even Lucrezia laughed, albeit rather shakily, at that idea. Duke Ercole d'Este was extraordinarily tight-fisted—except about the theater. He adored plays and was truly musical—the whole family was—and the duke had built a magnificent theater to display his love and his talents. Then she shook her head.

"It does not really matter why he said it. What matters is that if the murderer is not uncovered, everyone will remember Alfonso's accusation and I will never be rid of the mark of the serpent who poisons."

2

 "DO NOT be ridiculous! No one really believed it. No one!" Angela ran to Lucrezia and embraced her.

"No one who knew our lady believed it," Nicola said, but her voice was sad. "Unfortunately, those who did not know her loved to whisper one to the other and shiver and plan what they would do or say if they were invited to dine at the Borgias' table. It did not matter that there was about the same chance of their being invited as of their being able to fly, but the whispers spread." She too came to embrace Lucrezia. "I am sorry, madonna, but—"

"You were not at fault and have nothing to be sorry for, Nicola, but somehow I must discover who really killed that poor, silly woman and I must expose the criminal so that my name is cleared of any suspicion."

"Oh, if only you could," Angela cried. "Bianca was not much.

She was as silly as . . ." Angela's lips quivered. "As silly as me. But she did not deserve to have her life cut short. It is not *fair!* Whoever did it *should* be exposed."

Nicola's lips thinned. "I would like to see Don Alfonso's accusations flung back into his own teeth, but I cannot see any way that you could prove what the killer had done."

"At the moment, I must confess that I do not see any way either," Lucrezia admitted, "but we can start by finding out everything about poor Bianca's death—who found her, what that person saw, who visited her."

"Reasonable enough, but how do we find out?" Nicola asked.

"First let us pool what *we* know," Lucrezia said slowly. "And for me that is virtually nothing. I spoke to her only a few times before I left to spend Easter at Corpus Domini, and not at all after we returned. I thought her sweet-natured—she never made any sharp remarks like the others and she seemed truly interested and concerned when she asked after my health—but she seemed to have no interests except health, lotions and perfumes, and clothing."

"That is all true," Angela offered. "We were friendly. She was as good-natured as she was silly, but it didn't matter. She could afford both. She was a widow and her husband left her very rich."

"No children?" Lucrezia asked.

"No."

"Then who benefits? We must find out whether she left a will and who is named as her heir . . . or heirs." A tinge of excitement had come into Lucrezia's voice and she drew a deep breath. "I think perhaps Don Sigismundo could obtain that information for us."

Angela giggled. "If it is written down, doubtless Don Sigismundo can find it." Then she frowned. "If Don Celio Tedaldo was alive I could not help but suspect him. Donna Bianca was of two minds about her husband. She praised him for being gentle and loving, for being generous, and for caring for her, but sometimes when she talked about him she would look sad and sometimes angry. She never said in so many words, but I think it was not only money with which he was generous. I think he spread his favors around very generously, too."

"What man does not?" Nicola asked, with a rather hard laugh. "Frankly, I had no patience for the woman. She was not only empty-headed but had no common sense. I know she lent money to several of the other ladies-in-waiting because I overheard her speaking of it to Teodora Angelini."

"Did she want the money returned?" Lucrezia asked.

Nicola made a delicate snorting sound. "Not at all. She was assuring Donna Teodora that she would help them again if it was necessary." Her brows went up. "You know, madonna, that for many of them, as for me, the appointment to your service is a way to live with elegance and even to help their families. But you have refused to support them—even to invite them to your table, so they must find their own food—because of your quarrel with the duke about your appanage. And the duke has not paid their allowance either. Some are in a bad way."

Lucrezia's mouth set hard and her blue eyes took on the glint of steel. "Yes, of course I know. The duke says they are my ladies and I must support them. I told him I did not choose them, did not want them, and they could either go home or starve, for all I cared. If he will not pay me my full appanage, I have no money to spare for them."

"Then why do they stay?" Angela wondered.

"I assume because the duke ordered them to do so," Lucrezia said, her voice redolent with mulish determination. "And because he provides those who want it with free lodging . . . in a palace, no less, which no doubt suits their pride. Certainly they do not stay for love of me." And then her expression softened and she smiled at the ladies who *had* stayed for love of her, ignoring the duke's orders.

Angela tilted her head in a charming quizzical gesture and then shook it. "Not because of the duke's orders, at least not Bianca. She wanted to be at Court whether you paid her or not, and she had plenty of money. Also, she was silly, but not so silly as to throw away good money. She wanted to stay at Court, so she needed to be one of the ladies-in-waiting. If the others left because they could not support the expense, she would have had to leave also."

"But she had no family to advance," Nicola said. "No father or brother that news from the Court could help. And I cannot believe *she* had any interest in politics, so why did she want to stay so much that she would support several other ladies?"

Angela giggled. "For the only reason she did almost anything, as far as I know. Where else could she be surrounded by so many elegant gentlemen? I know too she was recently successful. She had just taken a new lover and did not wish to be parted from him."

"Alfonso?" Lucrezia gasped, her eyes full of doubt.

"Oh, no." Angela shook her head. "She could not have kept a coup like *that* to herself. Another thing, Bianca took wooing, a lot of wooing. I know she was more interested in the sweet words and love letters and poems than the actual . . . ah . . . loving. And Alfonso . . . bam, bam . . . gone."

Lucrezia colored slightly; Alfonso was not as bad as that, but she made a little sniffing sound. "Wooing is not Alfonso's way," she agreed, then mused, "A new lover, and one who is fixed at Court. She gave no hint of who it was?"

Now Angela looked stricken. "No. Oh, dear. I suppose I could have teased it out of her, but we were just about to leave for Corpus Domini and I was too busy to play her games. I am so sorry, madonna."

"How could you guess?" Lucrezia put out a hand to Angela. "How could anyone guess that Bianca would be killed?" Suddenly

Lucrezia's eyes widened. "And are we sure of that? All we know is that Alfonso said I had poisoned her. What if she just . . . died?"

"But she was young!" Angela protested.

Lucrezia shook her head. "It does happen, even to young people."

"There cannot be much chance of that," Nicola put in. "If she had simply died, Don Alfonso would not have been so upset. Someone with some authority must have told him she had been poisoned."

"I suppose so." Lucrezia sighed.

However Angela's eyes had grown rounder with concern. "It could have been the new lover," she said. "*He* must have told Bianca to keep their affair secret, I suppose because he had other obligations. Otherwise Bianca would have told everyone at once." Her eyes got even rounder. "Then maybe he learned that Bianca babbled everything, and . . . and . . ."

Lucrezia looked from Angela to Nicola. "Men gossip worse than women. Do you think Don Ferrante or Don Giulio would know?"

"If not," Nicola said immediately, "we can set them to finding out, eh, Angela?" She looked back at Lucrezia. "Do we tell them why we want to know?"

After a moment of nibbling on her lower lip, Lucrezia nodded. "Yes. I think so. They should know that I am seeking the real murderer in case Alfonso takes it ill and blames them for helping me."

Nicola laughed. "That would scarcely bother Ferrante. If he can do something that will annoy Don Alfonso, he will be delighted."

"Giulio also," Angela agreed. "Both Ferrante and Giulio like you very much, madonna. They will be outraged when they hear about Alfonso's accusation."

"Good enough," Lucrezia said, frowning as she gathered her thoughts. "I think we have done as much as we can on our own. I will write to Ercole Strozzi and tell him what has happened. He has good friends among the jurists, who might be able to help. You should summon your cavaliers here also. As soon as I have finished my note to Ercole, if you ladies will help me dress, since Lucia is busy elsewhere, I think it is time that I went out to greet my . . . guests."

"What will you wear?" Angela asked, brightly interested. "It is important to look just right."

Lucrezia smiled at her. Angela might be light-minded in that she never read a book or gave a thought to philosophy or any other serious subject; though she was often called silly she did know the nuances that could be communicated by mute witnesses, like clothing.

"It will be a delicate balancing act," Lucrezia agreed. "I must not look sad lest I seem to have taken Alfonso's accusation seriously, but I do not wish to appear indifferent to poor Bianca's fate either."

"Let me look," Angela offered, turning toward the door at the back of the room.

Lucrezia watched her open the door, which led to a narrow corridor that connected with a similar corridor in Alfonso's apartment. The arrangement permitted him to visit Lucrezia at any time without going through the public corridors or rooms—and without giving her any warning. To give him credit, he did not seem suspicious of her and had never come that way except to do his marital duty, or more than his marital duty. . . . Lucrezia's bottom lip crept between her teeth again as she thrust that thought away. She would be mad to allow herself to become fond of Alfonso. He had not come through the private door to accuse her and declare that Bianca was his mistress. He had come through the public rooms because he wanted that information spread.

There were three other doorways in the private corridor: one opened into a chamber with tiled floor and walls in which there was a tub large enough for two to share; the second chamber was a study, paneled in polished wood—it held a stove, a comfortable chair set on a Turkish rug, a table with a writing desk, two well-padded stools, and several shelves for books; last was a room in which the walls were lined with wardrobes and chests stood under each window. Angela entered that room.

Lucrezia followed, watched her opening the wardrobes, and then went into the study to use her writing desk. Lifting the lid, she withdrew a small sheet of heavy, scented paper and indited a note to Ercole Strozzi. She did not, after all, say anything in her note about what had happened in her private reception chamber—her lips tightened and tears rose into her eyes. Likely he would have heard about that, so she only asked that he wait upon her as soon as was convenient.

Nicola waited until the note was written, then took it to the private reception room, where the tinkling of a bell brought a page. She regarded Ascanio for a moment in silence. He was Ferrarese, one of Duke Ercole's appointees, but Lucrezia did pay him, and smile at him, and see that he had treats now and again also. She was very soft to young boys because of her own little son and the half-brother she had been raising and had been forced to leave in Rome.

The child might well be one of the duke's spies despite Lucrezia's kindness—Ercole d'Este was a man whose commands few adults would disobey, much less a child—but Nicola had no choice but to use him if she wanted to send messages to Ferrante and Giulio. Obviously it was impossible for her to seek the young men throughout the palace, and the accusations against Lucrezia might keep them away. She knew the duke was not pleased with Ferrante's interest in her and had tried to curb the frequency of his visits, but since the message included Giulio and was actually from Lucrezia, she hoped it would be safe enough.

To the page she said, "Please find Don Ferrante and Don Giulio and ask them to come as soon as convenient to Madonna Lucrezia's apartment. You may tell them it is because of Donna Bianca's death. Then deliver this note."

The boy's eyes widened at the mention of Bianca, but he nodded. "Yes, madonna," he whispered.

"And you need not stop to answer questions from those in the outer room," she said sharply.

"But they . . . How can I not?"

"If you must answer a question, say only that you have a message to carry . . . ah . . . about Donna Bianca's death. You are small. Do your best to squirm out of their way." He looked very doubtful and Nicola smiled at him. "I will help as I can. I will stand just outside the portiere and watch. Likely the ladies will hesitate to try to pry information out of you under my eyes."

The maneuver was more successful than she had expected. Not only did Ascanio get out of the public reception room without being stopped, but she had the satisfaction of dropping the portiere right in the face of Teodora Angelini, just as the chief of the ladies in waiting was about to speak to her.

When she returned to the bedchamber she found Lucrezia examining the gammura Angela had chosen. The overgown was of a bright azure blue velvet trimmed in pearl-studded black, but Angela had not brought out the usual black silk underdress, which in contrasting with the azure blue made it even brighter. Instead she had chosen a sleeveless underdress of delicate gray silk lavishly embroidered in silver around the bottom of the skirt. When the blue overgown was raised and pinned just above Lucrezia's hip, the embroidered underdress would show. The sleeves she had brought out were also gray and silver and, when attached at the shoulder with silver points, muted the blue.

"Perfect," Lucrezia said. "Not mourning at all, but gently saddened."

As she spoke she undid the belt of her loose morning gown. Nicola lifted it off her shoulders and carried it away, bringing back a fresh shift. This was a voluminous garment with a high neck that could be drawn into graceful gathers by a ribbon, and very full sleeves, buttoned at the wrist. Lucrezia pulled off her bedgown and Nicola dropped the shift over her head. She then tightened the neck ribbon, making sure that it was modestly high and that the gathers lay just so.

Angela then brought the undergown and laced it to fit Lucrezia's slender body, which at this early stage showed no sign of her pregnancy. The gammura was then slipped over her head and buttoned. Then the upper sleeves were drawn up over her arms. Nicola pulled the very full sleeve of the shift out into an elegant puff on the left arm while Angela did the right, fastening the points so that they complemented rather than crushed the puffs. Last, the lower sleeves were pulled on, equal care being taken with the shift-sleeve puffs over the elbows.

Finally, Angela brought over a tray of jewelry and Nicola carried out several headdresses. At those, Lucrezia shook her head.

"I don't want to look imposing. I think I will just wear that silver chain with the sapphire in it over my hair."

"And turn most of the ladies green with envy," Angela said. "You have beautiful hair, madonna, true gold, and hardly needing a touch of the sun to keep it bright."

"Hmmm." Lucrezia considered that. "Braid it, Nicola, and I will wear a blue net. I don't want to fix the attention of the ladies on me more than necessary. What I want is to set them to quarreling with each other."

When her hair was gathered into the net, Lucrezia examined herself carefully in the cheval mirror that stood not far from her bed, then bade Angela bring a large silver and sapphire brooch. She used the brooch to pin up the skirt of her gammura so that it exposed the gray underdress with its lavish embroidery and fell in elegant folds to either side. Satisfied, she looked at her ladies, who both smiled their approval. Drawing a deep breath and squaring her narrow shoulders, she made her way to the door and went out into the private reception room.

She did not pause when she came to her usual chair, but continued across the room toward the open doorway covered by the portiere, behind which she could hear a buzz of voices.

"Lucrezia."

The voice was soft, hesitant. Nonetheless, Lucrezia started and turned so quickly toward the sound that her heavy skirts nearly tripped her. A shadow detached itself from beside the massive chimneypiece and came forward. Lucrezia drew in her breath, but a few steps resolved the shadow into a short, slender gentleman wearing a soft black velvet cap adorned with two brilliant peacock feathers pinned to it with gold and emerald pins. To ward off chill, a green cape covered a sober black velvet jerkin with no more than a modest gold trim over a bright green doublet. It was Sigismundo, the youngest and, she thought, the best of her brothers-by-marriage, in one of his favorite sets of clothing.

"Sigismundo!" she exclaimed, nonetheless keeping her voice low. "Where in the world did you come from?"

"I have been here all along," he said, blushing painfully. "I came with Alfonso." He swallowed. "I was trying to calm him, to make him reconsider what he was about to say." He shrugged. "As you saw, I was as ineffective as usual."

Lucrezia held out her hand. "You are gentle, not ineffectual, as you well know. Mostly you have not the slightest trouble persuading people to do what they should. Alfonso—" She sighed. "Persuading Alfonso to anything without the application of a war hammer to his head is a feat beyond anyone's ability, even the duke's."

Sigismundo shook his head. "But to accuse you like that! It was insane!"

"No." Lucrezia smiled. "It was a very poor attempt to divert attention from something Alfonso wished to hide—and not that

Bianca or any other lady of my Court was his mistress. I suppose it is something that might be exposed by Bianca's death." She hesitated and then asked, "Was Alfonso short of money? Bianca, I understand, was quite rich. Had he borrowed from her to . . . oh, I don't know what he might have needed money for."

"I don't think he was short," Sigismundo replied without any hesitation. "He has only just finished a new cannon and is about to begin testing it, and it is the founding of the beast that is so expensive. Gunpowder is cheap enough, as are the stones to be used as shot. And I think he would have come to me before he borrowed from one of your ladies."

Lucrezia smiled again. "Do you often lend him money, Sigismundo?"

The young man shrugged and smiled back. "Books are expensive, but not so costly as cannon. I often have a bit extra, and he is very good about paying me back." Then he lost his smile and looked concerned again. "No one will believe him, Lucrezia."

"I am not so sure of that," she replied sharply. "It is the terrible truth that people love to believe the worst of others. Think of what was said of me in Rome! And it was not true, not any of it! No, Sigismundo, I will not again live with people whispering behind my back and making signs against evil when I enter a room."

"What do you mean? What can you do to stop them?"

"*Not* poison the whole lot!" Lucrezia said, giggling. "Although, to tell the truth, I have been sorely tempted. No, what I will do is discover who *really* killed Bianca and expose him so no one can have any doubt about my innocence."

For a moment Sigismundo stood staring at her in surprise and then nodded and said, "I think you will, Lucrezia. I think there is more in that golden head of yours than airy flights of fancy, although those are lovely."

"You may be sure of it." The mulish tone was back in her voice.

"I did not rule Spoleto for near a year by engaging in flights of fancy. There were two killings while I governed there and I sifted out the truth quickly enough, although I must admit the people involved were simple folk. Still . . . will you help me, Sigismundo?"

"Help? Of course. In any way I can, but I am not much of a swordsman or even a hunter."

Lucrezia wrinkled her nose. "We have those in plenty. Nicola and Angela will enlist Ferrante and Giulio as soon as we have some-one we want hunted or challenged. It is your brains I need, Sigis-mundo. I would like you to find out whether Bianca Tedaldo left a will, and if she did, who was named in it to inherit."

"Of course! What a fool I am. I could not understand why any-one should kill such an inoffensive creature as Bianca, but she was rich, you say? That might be reason enough. Yes, I am sure I can find out about her will and her heirs."

"She *was* inoffensive. She was more than that. She was a sweet-natured person, good and kind and always ready to be helpful. So tell me, Sigismundo, why is everyone so sure she was poisoned? There are fevers that kill in a few hours, and even without a fever, people have been known to fall dead without any cause that can be easily seen. I simply cannot believe that someone killed Bianca apurpose."

"It is hard for me to believe also," Sigismundo said, "but we were all with my father making our morning salutations when Ludovico dei Carri—"

"Your father's personal physician?" Lucrezia asked.

"Yes. He came into the room all of a sweat and said that he was sorry to report that Lady Bianca Tedaldo was dead of poisoning."

"What poison? How administered?"

Sigismundo shook his head. "I have no idea. My father exclaimed in horror, of course, and then turned on Giulio, who had burst into tears. Half the people in the room ran to Giulio, but I had been looking at Alfonso and I saw that he had turned green-white and I went to him in case he needed some wine or something. Amidst all of the excitement, no one thought to ask Carri any further questions. And then Alfonso began to mutter under his breath, and what he was saying . . . I went out with him, so I don't know whether Carri explained more."

"Can you find out for me what killed her and how it was given to her? Were there cups? Wine? Was the poison in the flagon or in her cup? Was someone drinking with her? Were the cups her best as for an honored guest or just her everyday ware as for a friend? Who found her? Was her room disordered?"

"Good God, Lucrezia, so many questions. How would it be if I brought Carri to you to question?"

"Oh, if you could, that would be wonderful."

"Perhaps after dinner tonight— No, there will be a play and he does not live in the castle. Tomorrow morning?"

Lucrezia's lips twitched. Sigismundo, of course, knew about her dilatory mornings, and had never tried to invade them. "I will be glad to receive you," she said. "I will tell the guard."

Sigismundo kissed her hand and turned to go, muttering to himself, "Will. A will. Now, who among the judges would be most likely to know . . ."

She watched him lift the portiere and slip out, moved closer to listen to the rising voices as those waiting in the outer chamber tried to stop him and pry something out of him. Amusement glinted in her eyes and she smiled at Angela and Nicola, who had followed close on her heels. Sigismundo was using his usual defense; she could not see him bowing but knew he was doing so while he mumbled irrelevant phrases that sounded shy and apologetic. In only a few moments the brief excitement had passed and the customary low buzz of talk took the place of the louder intermittent bursts.

"When should we go in?" Nicola murmured.

"As soon as I am sure Sigismundo is gone," Lucrezia replied equally softly.

Angela came forward, intending to peek around a corner of the portiere, but it lifted, almost striking her in the face. She staggered back, Nicola steadying her so she did not fall, and Lucia came through. The maid uttered a surprised squeak, which she suppressed with a hand over her lips. Lucrezia gestured for them all to retreat to the other end of the room.

"Did you hear anything about the murder?" Lucrezia asked.

Lucia nodded, her eyes bright with excitement. "They can talk about nothing else," she said.

"About what Alfonso said?" Lucrezia asked taughtly.

"No . . ." Lucia drew out the word uncertainly. "Not directly. Not . . ." She hesitated. "Not with their lips. Maybe with their eyes. . . . I am sorry, madonna."

Lucrezia sighed. "It could not be otherwise."

"But it brings them to go over and over what they know and dare to say," Lucia said brightly. "It seems that Donna Bianca's maid must have found her, because Beatrice Tisio, who has a room down the corridor from Donna Bianca, was awake early with a toothache, and heard the maid slam the door and run down the corridor crying. That surprised her so much—for you know that Donna Bianca was not the kind to make a maid cry—that she opened her door to look out."

"Did she go into Bianca's room?" Nicola asked eagerly.

"No, she wasn't dressed, but she thought something must have happened—she said she thought Donna Bianca had been robbed, so she decided to get dressed—but she left her door a little open to see what would happen. Well, Donna Beatrice's maid had barely tied on her sleeves when back came Donna Bianca's maid with the steward. He barely stepped in, then popped out again and sent the maid off."

"So Bianca must have been lying in her public reception room," Lucrezia said.

"Why do you say that?" Angela asked.

Lucrezia smiled. "Because apparently the steward saw her body when he was barely in the door. Go on, Lucia."

"This time Beatrice came out of her chamber—she has only the one room, not an apartment—and asked the steward what was wrong. He told her that Donna Bianca was dead. Of course, she said that was impossible, that Bianca had been perfectly well the evening before when they had walked together to the duke's play."

Angela frowned. "Beatrice and Bianca were not friends. . . . Well, Bianca was friendly to everyone, but Beatrice was very envious of her and sharp-tongued about her too. I wonder why Beatrice walked to the Palazzo del Cortile from Castel Vecchio with her."

"I think that Donna Beatrice wanted to ask Donna Bianca for money. Donna Beatrice did not tell the story as I have told it to you, madonna. It was all a few words here and a few words there, with the other ladies asking questions and saying this and that." Lucia's lips turned down in distaste. "They are not kind to each other, those ladies."

"They are not as comfortable as we are," Nicola said quietly. "We know our lady and do not need to strive with each other for her notice."

Lucia sniffed. "You have a good heart, Donna Nicola, and Donna Angela too."

Lucrezia smiled. "And you also, Lucia. But it is time for me to join those who wait so patiently." She sighed. "I had hoped they would give up and leave."

"No, madonna." Lucia's lips thinned. "They will wait until night, if necessary, so they can say you did not dare come out of your inner rooms after Don Alfonso spoke so harshly to you."

"And you have nothing more to tell me about what was said?"

"Only that when the maid came back it was with the duke's physician, Don Ludovico dei Carri. He told Donna Beatrice to go back to her room, but apparently she complained to him of her toothache and he said he would send her some oil of cloves. Elizabetta Dossi said that was only an excuse, that Donna Beatrice was waiting to get into Donna Bianca's chamber, but Master dei Carri bade her go and she had no more excuse to stay, so she did. Then she sent her maid to Donna Teodora Angelini to tell her what had happened. Donna Teodora then sent for the other ladies who were on duty today and they all came here to wait for news."

Lucrezia made a moue of distaste. "They got more than they expected, unfortunately for me. Well, it will do no good to wait any longer."

She walked back across the room with Lucia skittering ahead to raise the portiere for her, took one deep breath, and stepped into her public reception room. It had been so long since Don Alfonso had stormed out that no one was actually watching the doorway. Lucrezia took a few steps forward so that Nicola and Angela could follow her in. The motion caught a gentleman's attention.

Bernadino Zambotto's eyes glittered with interest. He bowed deeply and said, "Good day, Madonna Lucrezia."

The buzz of talk in the tapestry-hung chamber died away, leaving an expectant . . . a *hungry* . . . silence behind.

3

 "IT HAS SCARCELY been a good day for me, Don Bernadino," Lucrezia said quietly. "I have lost the most pleasant, kindly, and sweet-natured of my ladies-in-waiting, and my own husband, who—if I did not know that the men of the Este family were the most solid and sensible men in the world—I would need to think had run mad, has accused *me* of doing away with her."

Lucrezia paused and looked around at the women and a few men who were staring back at her with eyes and mouths open in shock. She was horribly tempted to laugh, but only allowed her lips to tremble a little, which could be taken for fear and grief instead of amusement. She knew her large blue eyes, opened very wide just now, gave her a look of childlike innocence. They had expected her either to hide from them—which they could have reported to the whole Court and all over town—or to try to brazen out a semblance of normality, pretending that no one had heard Alfonso's accusation.

"I can only believe," she continued, looking down for a moment at her hands, which were tightly clasped in front of her, "that Don Alfonso was temporarily bereft of his power to reason by shock and grief, and that he struck out at the nearest person"—she looked around at the women—"as husbands will do to wives when they are angered or otherwise troubled by matters those poor wives could not control."

"Then Bianca *was* his leman?" Teodora Angelini asked. Her lips were tight against a smile she dared not show.

Lucrezia shrugged. She had decided that if Alfonso was desperate enough to use an accusation against her to publish his connection with Bianca, she had better support him. She also had not forgotten how he had flinched when she said she did not care enough for him to resent his taking a mistress. She did not mind at all twisting that knife in the wound she had made while simultaneously protecting him.

Besides, she did not like Teodora Angelini, who had been named chief of her ladies by the duke. As she met the woman's eyes, she had a sudden memory of Donna Bianca's, soft brown and as innocent as a deer's. Teodora's eyes were brown also, but they had the hard, bright shine of polished chestnut shells and made a lie of the pale hair, which had been bleached so often that it looked like dead straw. Her mouth looked hard too; in fact, the whole woman was hard-looking, her tall, angular body not much softened by her clothing. Lucrezia had no compunction about misleading her.

"You all know how careful the duke is with money," she said. "You have all suffered, as have I, from that usually laudable trait. Don Alfonso is his father's true son. He is no more careless with gold than Duke Ercole, but his ceaseless efforts to ensure the safety of Ferrara have caused him heavy expenses in founding and testing cannon. Thus, he wastes no money on women and is known for taking the lowest and cheapest in the streets. Donna Bianca was rich and generous. She would have asked him for nothing. So . . . perhaps . . ."

Again the group stared at her with open eyes and mouths. Lucrezia swallowed hard. They might see that as embarrassment, but she was fighting laughter again.

"Have I said something wrong?" Her blue eyes were even wider with innocent appeal. "You all know how our marriage was arranged. Don Alfonso and I have not yet had time to come to know or care for one another. He has done his duty." Lucrezia patted her still-flat belly. "I have no complaint, and I could not expect him to change all his habits at once."

"But—but if you knew of his interest in Donna Bianca . . ." Marino Sanuto faltered to a stop, not knowing how to end the sentence he had begun.

"I would have a reason to have killed Bianca?" Lucrezia finished for him. "But why? I care as little for Don Alfonso as he cares for me. Leman or no leman, he has never failed a night in my bed or to do his duty in it. Why should I care what he does beyond that? For my pride? I am not so proud as to be a fool."

"In any case, madonna, no matter what you felt, you had no opportunity to do Donna Bianca any harm. None of us had." Nicola looked deliberately from Lucrezia to Angela and then out at the assembled group. "I am sure you all remember that we left for Corpus Domini before Easter and only returned two days ago. None of us spoke to or even saw Donna Bianca since our return. Can any of *you* say as much?"

"Are you accusing *us*?" Donna Teodora gasped.

"Of course not. How ridiculous," Nicola replied. "I am only pointing out that everyone in this room, and probably in the entire court, had a better chance to poison poor Bianca than my lady or Angela or I did. You were all here and free to come and go as you liked. We were among the nuns and would have been missed if we omitted even one prayer."

"Let it be, Nicola," Lucrezia said with a faint, sad smile. "This is not a Court of Inquiry, and those who wish to believe ill, will believe it no matter what proof there is to the contrary. What troubles me is that I simply cannot believe anyone, anywhere, could possibly wish Donna Bianca harm. She was so good and so sweet. I do not believe she was in attendance yesterday, was she?"

"No," Donna Teodora replied. As chief of the ladies, she was the one who set the days on which they were supposed to serve Lucrezia. "Donna Bianca was due to do her duty to you today."

Lucrezia lowered her head. "I am very sorry I will not see her. I do not believe I exchanged ten words with her since I came to Ferrara, but it pleased me to see her smiling face." She sighed. "Did anyone see her yesterday? Was she her usual self?"

"Her usual self!" Elizabetta Dossi cried. "Are you now trying to hint that Bianca was so distraught that she did away with herself?"

Elizabetta was also a tall woman, but not at all angular; she was, indeed, somewhat more than pleasingly plump. Her dark hair made no concession to the taste for blondes despite the fact that it was somewhat streaked with gray. Her lips were not naturally thin but were pulled tight against her large teeth, as if she needed to hold back inconsiderate words.

"No!" Lucrezia exclaimed. "How horrible! I do not believe Donna Bianca would ever have done such a thing, no matter how sad or oppressed she was. I thought she might have shown some sign that she was worried or frightened, that some enemy was threatening her."

"Bianca did not *have* any enemies," Donna Elizabetta said. "And she was not sad and oppressed yesterday. Wherever did you get that idea? She was in very good spirits. Diana and I spent the morning with her."

"Yes," Diana Altoviti agreed.

Aside from Bianca, Diana was the prettiest of the women, not as fair-haired as Lucrezia herself, but light-haired enough that sitting in the sun for a few hours made golden lights shine through the soft brown. Her short, slightly broad nose and full lips gave her a look of good humor, which was not always fulfilled by her speech, although Lucrezia could hear nothing beyond a faint tremor, perhaps of sadness, in her voice as she continued speaking.

"I was showing her and Elizabetta some new perfumes I had prepared. I thought Beatrice would be there too, but she only came in later. I suppose she did not wish to look at what she could not buy."

"Why should I buy from you?" Donna Beatrice snapped. "I have other sources. And why are we talking about perfumes and lotions when Bianca is lying dead? Do you all care as little about murder as they do in Rome? Not everyone is so hard-hearted. I heard that when the news was brought to the duke, Don Giulio cried out and began to weep."

Lucrezia did not respond, although she was surprised. Despite her wasplike appearance, large dark eyes, and pointed nose and chin, Beatrice was not usually so sharp-tongued. She was very thin, her wrists emerging sticklike from the full sleeves she wore to conceal her arms, and she was dark-skinned too, so that her lightened hair was incongruous. She cast a spiteful glance at Angela, whom she envied Don Giulio's attentions.

If Beatrice had been hoping Angela would show some jealousy, she was doomed to disappointment. Angela grinned at her, not a whit discomposed. She encouraged Giulio's attentions, but she encouraged the attentions of a number of other young men of the Court also. Angela might be called silly, but she was no more foolish about men than she was about clothes. She had Don Giulio's measure down to the smallest fingerwidth.

"He has a soft heart, Giulio," Angela said cheerfully. "And if he had been her lover, his shock goes a long way to proving his innocence. It shows he did not know Bianca was dead before Master dei Carri brought the news."

"I was not accusing Don Giulio of anything," Beatrice gasped, paling a trifle at the idea that she had pointed a finger at one of the duke's sons. "It was you who seemed to think he needs to prove his innocence."

"Until someone can expose the truly guilty party, everyone needs to be able to prove innocence," Nicola said.

"And who will try to do that?" Teodora asked bitterly, glancing at Lucrezia as if to say no one would dare try to prove her guilty.

"I will," Lucrezia said. "I could not have killed Bianca because I have not been near her for over a month, but I am eager to find the cruel person who cut short her life. And, of course, what I wish to kill, once and for all, is the rumor that I am a poisoner. After my husband's silly accusation, only the exposure of the real murderer can do that."

Lucrezia looked around at the men and women, who were again shocked by her frankness. "Will you not help me? Will you not tell me what could have driven anyone to hurt Bianca? I did not know her. Donna Elizabetta says Bianca had no enemies, but sweet as she was, I cannot believe that. Everyone has enemies. Who might have asked her for something that she could not or would not give? Who might have been her rival for a lover? Who might have gained from her death?"

There was a complete silence, the women who served with Bianca and knew her best casting sidelong glances at each other and at Lucrezia. Other women, who had come for the gossip, looked down at the floor or examined with great interest a seam or spot on their garments. They had nothing to offer, but did not wish to be excluded from any scandalous news or event. The men mostly looked at Lucrezia.

"Well," Bernadino Zambotto said, his narrow face vivid with curiosity, "I think Donna Lucrezia is right and very brave, and I hope that everyone will try to help her. To prove my words, I will begin. I know almost nothing about Donna Bianca, but I can say what I saw when we heard Don Alfonso through the portiere. At that time Don Guido del Palagio was standing beside me and he turned so pale I thought he would faint. I put my hand on his arm to support him, but he wrenched free of me and fled from the room."

"That signifies no ill of Don Guido," Diana Altoviti said quickly. "His shock likely bespeaks his innocence."

"Perhaps not," Beatrice remarked. "I think, if I had killed Bianca and suddenly heard the duke's heir accusing someone I knew could not be guilty, that I might grow pale."

"You have a tongue like a viper," Diana snapped back.

"Diana! Beatrice!" Donna Teodora's disapproval was plain in her voice. "We are trying to help Donna Lucrezia, not quarrel with each other."

"And I meant no ill of Don Guido," Don Bernadino put in, black eyes eyeing Diana speculatively, clearly wondering if her defense was significant. "I only thought his strong emotion must mean he knew the lady and deplored her fate."

"But is not Don Guido a Neapolitan?" Elizabetta Dossi asked, and then in a lower voice, with a glance at Lucrezia and then away, "I heard he was a spy for the Aragonese—or—or even for Spain."

Her voice had dropped almost to a whisper on the last few words and she again glanced flickeringly at Lucrezia. Ercole d'Este was a firm adherent of French interests. One of the reasons he had been very unwilling to accept the marriage of Lucrezia and his son was that he had been hoping that the French king would provide a noble relative of his own for Alfonso. Instead, Louis XII had urged him to accept Lucrezia because Louis wanted papal influence to smooth the path of his army across Italy to permit him to attack and swallow Naples, ruled by Frederico of Aragon. The Pope's influence was all the more necessary because Spain was also eyeing the weak city-state.

Lucrezia, on the other hand, was known to favor the Aragonese— no great secret, since her second husband, dearly beloved and the father of her son, had been of Aragon. In fact, Lucrezia was shocked by what Elizabetta had said. Guido del Palagio had been recommended to Lucrezia by Alfonso's sister, Isabella d'Este, who said the young poet wished to travel and enlarge his experience.

Palagio was a terrible poet, his verses derivative, sycophantic, and inane. Lucrezia had sourly assumed that Isabella had sent him as a veiled insult, implying that Lucrezia's taste was so bad she would not know good poetry from bad. Now she wondered whether Isabella had an even more insidious purpose: to infuriate Duke Ercole by making her seem to harbor an Aragonese spy.

Lucrezia had never suspected Palagio was supposed to be Aragonese because he was not. His accent was all wrong and he knew virtually nothing about Naples. Nor was he Spanish. The Borgias were Spanish, and although Lucrezia spoke Italian with the pure accent of Rome, having been born and raised in the city, she knew Spanish-tinged Italian very well indeed. The speech of most of the older Borgias, including the uncle who was caring for her son and, to a lesser extent, her father, was tinged with Spanish intonations. But Lucrezia was not about to divulge what she knew.

"A spy for Aragon?" Lucrezia repeated. "But what could he hope to learn here? The duke is firm in his alliance with France." Then she sighed. "And if Palagio wished to learn my sentiments—

though I cannot think what good that would do him, as I have not the slightest political influence on either the duke or my husband— whoever sent him should have sent a better poet. Really, I have not been able to listen to his effusions since two days after he arrived."

"Bianca listened, though," Donna Diana said, smiling.

"She was too *sweet* to hurt Don Palagio's feelings."

Beatrice made a softly derisive noise. "Too sweet or too stupid to know good poetry from bad . . . or just man-mad. For goodness' sake, just the other day . . . yes, it was the day you returned from the convent, madonna . . . I could have strangled her myself."

Lucrezia merely looked mildly inquiring, but there was a sub-dued gasp from among the other onlookers. Beatrice stared around at them challengingly

"I said strangle, not poison," she snapped. "Bianca was in here flirting outrageously with Niccolò da Correggio." She sighed osten-tatiously. "I could see he was bored and exasperated, but it took for-ever to pry her loose enough to get a word in. And even that did not help."

"Why did no one send a page to tell me that Don Niccolò was here?" Lucrezia asked, and her voice could have iced a flagon of wine.

Beatrice's breath caught and she took half a step back. Usually Lucrezia simply avoided her Ferrarese ladies, treating them with a distant courtesy. She had never yet actively reprimanded one of them.

"You had not yet arrived, madonna," Beatrice said, a trifle breathlessly. "We were waiting for you."

"And no message was left to say that Don Niccolò had come and likely wished to speak with me?" Lucrezia's gaze went past Beat-rice to fix on the chief lady-in-waiting.

"He—he did not ask . . ." Teodora Angelini's voice died away uncertainly. She was plainly aware of a real dereliction of duty, not a subtle snub or defiance of the bastard daughter of a pope that could be explained away. "I am very sorry, madonna. Bianca went out with him. All of us were so surprised. . . ."

Lucrezia was equally surprised. Don Niccolò da Correggio was no callow youth to be seduced by Bianca's blandishments. He was a man in his middle years, not romantically handsome, although he was by no means ugly. More important, he was one of the most intelligent men in Ercole d'Este's Court, a fine soldier, and a good philosopher. Lucrezia was flattered that he sometimes sought her out for conversation. She could not imagine what interest he could possibly have had in Bianca Tedaldo.

That puzzle woke a memory, and with a shock Lucrezia realized that she had been lying to everyone! She *had* seen Bianca and spoken to her quite recently. The very day before she had left for Corpus Domini, Bianca had carried to her a letter from Cesare passed along by Don Niccolò. That was not at all unusual—Cesare generally enclosed his letters to her in a packet sent either directly to the duke or to Correggio. To send a private messenger to his sister might have wakened suspicion, and Cesare had no desire to do that. He was coming north anyway, and could visit her personally to tell her anything he wished to keep secret from the Este. But usually Don Niccolò himself brought Cesare's letters.

Realizing that Donna Teodora's voice had faltered into silence and that the silence had lengthened, Lucrezia tucked away the puzzle about Bianca and Correggio to consider later. She was not sure she had extracted all the information she could from the ladies, but none of them was likely to say any more right now and her indignation would serve as a perfect excuse to retreat to her private reception room without allowing the openness of her conversation to imply she would now welcome their attendance.

"I will make no complaint over this matter," Lucrezia said softly, "but I hope you will not allow anything like this to happen again."

She turned on her heel, knowing she was leaving consternation behind her. All the women knew they were unwelcome to her and that the duke had ignored her distaste for them in the past and was not likely to replace them—just for his pride's sake—without a good reason; however, failing in one of the prime duties of ladies-in-waiting, which was carrying messages and reporting on important visitors to their lady's apartment, might give Duke Ercole the excuse he needed to dismiss them all. He might well do that to try to remove one of the weapons she was wielding to obtain her full appanage. He might believe he could find new ladies she would like well enough to sacrifice for, or even allow her to choose for herself Ferrarese ladies whom she would be willing to support.

In the safety of her private reception room well away from the portiere, she grinned at Angela and Nicola and said too softly to be heard through the curtain, "That put the fear of Lucrezia into them. Although if they didn't all have the brains of hens and no more knowledge of tactical maneuvers than hens, they would know I wouldn't dare put a weapon like that into Duke Ercole's hands. I mean, if he sent me one of Alfonso's young cousins or, oh, half a dozen ladies I could name, I would not have the heart to withhold their allowances no matter how thin my purse."

"I don't think you need to worry about it," Nicola said, also smiling. "*He* doesn't know enough about women to realize how easily he could defeat you on that score."

"But he was married," Angela protested. "And he had a mistress too."

Lucrezia laughed. "Yes, but you need to pay attention to a woman, to look behind what her voice speaks, to learn what she is thinking. I do not think women have ever been important enough to Ercole d'Este to make him bother. Not that he didn't love his wife; I believe he did and that he misses her sorely. He speaks of her to me often and with a kind of longing—"

"However, he did not know what Eleanora of Aragon was," Nicola interrupted. "I agree. Still, it doesn't matter. Unless you make a complaint, the duke will do nothing, even if one of those busybodies Zambotto or Sanuto carries the tale to him, and right now we do not want those women dismissed. We need them. I think they have more to tell."

"I think so too," Lucrezia agreed, "but I doubt I could get more from them right now and I think the page should have found Giulio and Ferrante by now. I expect them any moment."

"I will go out," Angela said. "No one is afraid of me. I will tell them that Nicola and I have managed to soothe you. Perhaps someone will seek to curry favor by confiding in me. And perhaps I can induce them to leave, since it will soon be time to dress for dinner. And if they do not go, as soon as Giulio or Ferrante arrive I can make sure they pass right into your private chamber and do not stand gossiping."

"Very good, Angela." Lucrezia chuckled. "Whoever compared you with Bianca was dead wrong, my dear. I have long suspected that you are only silly when you want to be."

"Oh, no." Angela's eyes widened with distress. "Oh, please do not say that. I beg you not to expect of me more than is in me. I love you, madonna. My greatest pleasure is in serving you, but do not ask more than I can give."

Lucrezia laughed again and gave her a brief hug, which she returned with enthusiasm and then went out. Lucrezia went to her chair, which she turned away from her writing desk so she could face Nicola, who had drawn up a stool.

"Did you hear that business about Bianca and Correggio?" she asked when Nicola had settled her skirts. "Whatever could it mean?"

"I suspect no more than that Don Niccolò is too kind a gentleman to be rude to the bird-witted little thing."

"That was my first thought, but then I remembered that I *had* seen Bianca—privately too—just the day before we left for Corpus Domini."

"You did?" Nicola stared.

"Yes. It was before you and Angela came in the morning. I was still in my bed, and she gained entrance by showing the door guard a letter from Cesare she was supposed to deliver to me. You know how she was always willing to run errands. She said the letter had arrived in a packet addressed to Correggio, which was likely enough. Cesare usually sent a packet either to the duke or to Correggio. But now that I think back on it, there was something odd about the seal on that letter. It was ... blurred ... rough ..."

"As if it had been lifted and replaced?"

Lucrezia sighed. "Very possibly. But that is ridiculous! Surely Don Niccolò would not bother lifting the seal of a letter from Cesare to me. First of all, he must know that Cesare would not confide any secrets to such a letter, and second, he knows he has only to ask and I would give him the letter to read."

Nicola thought that over in silence for a moment, then nodded. "True enough." She hesitated another moment and then said, "That means that someone else lifted the seal of that letter ... and that means you are going to have to ask Don Niccolò how Bianca got hold of the letter. Had he given it to someone else to bring to you? And if so, why did that person give it to Bianca? To hide the fact that he had lifted the seal? Was that fact important enough to make him want to silence Bianca?"

"Surely not," Lucrezia said. "I do not remember the letter very clearly, but I am sure there was nothing in it that anyone other than I could have found of interest. It was all family news—my son's health and that of little Giovanni and that the cardinal was going to write to me about clothing for them; children grow so fast at their age."

"Do you have the letter still? Perhaps you should take another look at it. The light cast on it will be quite different now."

"It must be here in my desk."

Lucrezia rose from her chair and began to lift the top of her desk when voices came clearly through the portiere. She closed the desk again and turned toward the doorway in time to see the portiere lifted and Angela, looking over her shoulder, step through. Don Giulio followed her with a hand on her shoulder, and finally Don Ferrante, who had been holding the door curtain open, came through, dropping it behind him.

Lucrezia had some difficulty in keeping her face suitably solemn. Both had the apprehensive look of boys who expected to be chastised. Don Giulio looked sulky too, which was too common an expression for him, but it only made him more beautiful. He had the smooth olive skin and large, liquid brown eyes of his Neapolitan mother. His soft, slightly pouting mouth was eminently kissable. Angela found it so and, according to her laughing assessment, so did at least half of the ladies of Ferrara.

Don Ferrante was also handsome, but less so than Giulio. There was no mistaking Ferrante for Alfonso's brother, although Alfonso could never be called handsome. Alfonso's features were brutally strong: large eyes, black and hard; a straight, thick, powerful nose; full lips firmly set; and a bush of rather unkempt black hair. Ferrante was physically more attractive. His features were like Alfonso's, but softer. It was the softness that made him handsome, Lucrezia thought, but it also made him look weak. Alfonso was . . . exciting.

Angela smiled at her. "Nearly everyone is gone," she said. "Only the ladies who are supposed to be in attendance are still there, and they are half asleep, having been waiting so long and being sure nothing more will happen now."

"Nothing *should* have happened," Don Ferrante said, his eyes shifting from Lucrezia's. "I never could have guessed, but even if I had . . . there was no stopping him. You know what he is like."

"You mean Alfonso accused me of murder at his father's morning salutation, before all the officers of the Court?" Lucrezia's voice was high with anxiety and disbelief.

"No! No! Of course not. He would not dare do that in the duke's presence. My father adores you. He would have eaten Alfonso alive. And I never suspected *that* was in his mind. But I could see he was terribly upset, frantic. And then he looked . . . looked . . . I do not know how to describe it except that he would get that look when we were boys and in trouble and he saw an easy way to escape."

Duke Ercole would have eaten Alfonso alive, Lucrezia repeated to herself. How interesting that those words should wake a spark in Ferrante's eyes. Then a cold finger traced its way down her spine. Inheritance of the dukedom was not strictly hereditary. If Alfonso offended his father sufficiently, Ercole could replace him with Ferrante—and Ferrante knew it. Lucrezia also knew that Alfonso was no favorite with his father, who thought him a crude brute because he was totally uninterested in art or literature or philosophy, in anything of a finer nature than blowing things to bits with cannon. Well, Alfonso *was* a coarse brute, but if he were disinherited, where would that leave her?

She swallowed, looking down at her clasped hands as if she were considering Ferrante's words, but she was thinking that Alfonso was not *totally* without appreciation of art. He did the most beautiful, most delicate paintings on majolica ware and he played the viol exquisitely. What he did not like was to *talk* about art or music. Surely that old miser Ercole knew that, and there were many things about Alfonso that his father did admire: his passion for the defense of Ferrara, his strength, his carefulness with money. She made a faint sound of outrage, and Giulio spoke quickly into the silence.

"And I, madonna, I saw nothing," Giulio said. "I could not

believe my ears when I heard dei Carri say that Bianca Tedaldo had been poisoned. I—I had been drinking a toast with her only yester-day afternoon in the grand salon below—" he glanced sidelong at Angela "—it was only a cup of wine. And then Correggio came in and she ran away to speak to him."

Giulio's lips pouted more. He was not accustomed to having any woman run from him to another man. Distracted from her disquiet-ing thoughts, Lucrezia swallowed a giggle and asked, "Were they old friends, Bianca and Don Niccolò?"

"Who knows?" Giulio said. "Bianca was 'old friends' with every-one." His glance slid to Angela again. "Which was how I happened to be drinking with her. I had come to wait for you, madonna—"

Lucrezia giggled aloud this time. "For Angela, you mean."

Giulio bowed. "For you also, always, madonna, because you are a light in all our lives and a pleasure to be with. We had heard you were on your way from Corpus Domini and so I and many others were waiting in the salon—and she came up to me with the cups of wine—"

"So you accepted her offer of a drink." Lucrezia nodded. "That was natural. It would have been rude to refuse."

"Yes, but how many knew that she had brought the wine to me rather than I to her? When I heard that she had been poisoned . . . And then she ran away from me. I feared that people would remember that we had been drinking together."

"I don't think you need to worry about that," Angela said, grin-ning. "When a girl runs away from you, Giulio, it is not from fear of being poisoned but of being stabbed."

"Angela!" he protested. "You know I desire only you."

"That is a subject you can discuss when you are alone together," Lucrezia said firmly. "Right now I asked you to come here—you and Ferrante—because I need your help in discovering who really did poison Bianca."

"Our help?" Ferrante looked astonished and faintly alarmed. "But we—I, at least—know nothing about Bianca Tedaldo. What help can I be to you?"

"For one thing," Nicola said, "you might try not to look as if Donna Lucrezia was about to accuse you of the crime."

"Nicola!" Lucrezia said. "Don Ferrante thought no such thing." *But he probably did,* she thought. *The way those brothers escape their father's wrath is to push blame off onto someone else.* "He is rightly concerned," she continued, "about how to go about helping when he has no personal knowledge of the lady."

Nicola came over and took Ferrante's arm. She squeezed it and looked up into his face. "It is really very simple," she urged. "All you need to do is listen to the men talking. And they will all be talking about Bianca, at least for the next few days. Probably no one will admit too close an association with Bianca . . . but they will tattle on each other, will they not?"

Giulio and Ferrante looked at each other. "A ha!" Nicola said. "They've been talking already, have they not? So, you listened, did you not? What did you hear?"

Now Giulio glanced slyly at Lucrezia. "But Donna Lucrezia has scolded us in the past for spreading harmful gossip."

"Well, I hope you will *not* be spreading it," Lucrezia said. "I hope you will gather it all carefully and bring it to me. What is harmful and useless, I will bury for all time and forget. Only what will show us who might be a murderer—a sin far worse than any petty misbehavior—will I examine carefully and use if I must to obtain justice."

"Just listen?" Ferrante asked. "Would it not help to ask a question here or there and do a little prodding?"

"So long as you do not drag Alfonso into the talk," Lucrezia warned. "He has been very foolish, but he is still my husband."

"And still deserves your loyalty? After what he said?" Giulio sounded disbelieving.

Lucrezia laughed. "Yes, because what he accused me of was totally impossible, so he knew I would be in no danger."

The words resonated in Lucrezia's mind. It was true, of course. She had known it all along; she remembered thinking that even if he had seen her dose Bianca with his own eyes, no charges would be made against her. Alfonso never cared what anyone said about him. Either he did not listen or he struck out with a hard fist if he was temporarily annoyed. It did not occur to him that whispers, particularly of something false, could hurt her. So to him it would seem perfectly safe to accuse her of murder to establish publicly his relationship with Bianca. Yes, but that brought her no closer to understanding *why* he wanted such a relationship to be known.

"Never mind Donna Lucrezia's bond with her husband," Nicola said. "Just be sure none of your questions or proddings revolves around Don Alfonso. You enjoy making mischief against him entirely too much, and in this case it might go too far and draw in my lady. So say what you like aside from that, and bring us the news. Now, you've already heard something, what was it?"

"She had a new lover—" Giulio began.

Angela laughed aloud. "We know all about that."

"No, no," Ferrante put in. "We think it was Don Niccolò da Correggio."

"That he was her lover?" Lucrezia breathed. "We knew she was pursuing him, but that does not mean that Don Niccolò was more than polite to a pretty, silly woman."

"It was whispered that she was seen leaving his apartment—"

"When?" Lucrezia asked.

"Well, it was in the morning," Ferrante admitted with a grimace, "and after breakfast, too late for her to have been with him all night."

He was still in gossip mode, Lucrezia realized, thinking more about sexual scandal than murder. Sex was always less likely at a morning meeting because, presumably, a man had been sated the night before. But Lucrezia, remembering the letter Bianca had carried to her, wondered if, perhaps, Bianca had served as messenger to others also.

"It was more than whispers," Giulio remarked, "because Correggio wasn't the kind of man who would be interested in her, and she didn't usually act so . . . ah . . . bold. Her way was to be welcoming rather than aggressive, but with Correggio . . ."

"Who noticed her behavior was different? Who started the whispers?" Lucrezia asked.

Giulio and Ferrante consulted each other in glances and then simultaneously shrugged and shook their heads.

"Then that will be your first attempt to help, to find out who watched Bianca so closely and to discover, if possible, why that person watched her. And, if Correggio was not her lover, who was? Who envied him that position?"

Again the exchange of glances and almost simultaneous nods. "We can do that," Ferrante said, "and perhaps also find out why anyone would want to kill her."

"That is an important point," Giulio remarked, looking surprised, as if he had not thought about that previously. "She was . . . sweet, inoffensive. I cannot think of anyone who had a harsh word to say about her—harsher, I mean, than that she was witless. Why should anyone kill her? Could it have been a mistake? The poison meant for someone else?"

4

 GIULIO'S IDEA that Bianca had been killed by accident was more riveting than most of his notions. All of them considered it with some seriousness because what stuck in everyone's craw was that Bianca should have been murdered at all. However, before anyone else could comment on the idea that it had been an accident, Lucia slipped in through the portiere. When she saw the gentlemen, she sidled along the wall until she was under the open-case clock. She touched it gently. The pulley lengthened a bit, and the clock struck.

The sound drew everyone's attention and Lucrezia looked at the clock with admiration. There were clocks in Rome, of course, but she had not had one herself, and none had been as pretty and engaging as this gift from the duke.

Another bond Alfonso had with his father was his love of mechanical things, although the duke's enthusiasm was for creations more elegant than cannon. He had one of the most beautiful clocks ever made enclosed in a special room in a tower of the Palazzo Cortile with its own servant who lived in that room with it and saw that its loud bell correctly marked the hours for the townsfolk.

Marked the hours! Lucia wanted her to notice the time, and for good reason. If she did not begin to dress at once for dinner, she would look unkempt . . . distraught. Lucrezia smiled at her guests, mentioned the time, reminded them that they too must dress if they were intending to attend their father's dinner. Both looked at the clock, then made hasty farewells and went out, with Angela and Nicola following to remind them about questioning and listening to the dinner guests and to hurry to their own apartments just down the corridor from Lucrezia's to do their own dressing.

By the time they returned, Lucrezia was already painted, a delicate blush on her cheeks, her translucent complexion barely dusted with powder so it would not shine, and her brows and lashes suitably darkened. She had donned a gown brought from Rome, a favorite, a gammura of black velvet with gold borders and black sleeves. The cuffs of the sleeves fastened tightly at the wrists—safer for navigating dishes with elaborate sauces than long, trailing sleeves—but the shoulders were slashed deeply to expose the dazzling white shift embroidered with gold. The deep décolletage of the gown was filled with a veil of gold thread, modestly hiding her breast, but its full swell was marked by the string of fine, large pearls around her neck.

Lucia had just loosened the braids in which Lucrezia's hair had been dressed and was combing it, preparatory to confining it in the green silk net. Her overskirt, also of black velvet but trimmed in lush fur, was lying ready spread across the bed.

"I cannot get Don Giulio's idea out of my head," Lucrezia said, meeting her ladies' eyes in the mirror she held. "*Can* it be possible that Bianca was killed in an unfortunate accident?"

Nicola frowned. "That *she* died may have been an accident, but murder was meant. Poison was given, no matter who should have drunk it."

Lucrezia shook her head. "But I cannot see how such an accident could come about. If several people were drinking together in Bianca's chambers and Bianca got the wrong cup . . ." She looked doubtful. "I suppose that is possible, but surely no poisoner would bring a witness?"

"An accomplice?" Nicola asked, then immediately corrected herself. "No, the person would have had to be an enemy if the intention was to poison that person and Bianca took the draught by mistake. But that is impossible. An enemy would have run to some official crying aloud the poisoner's name as soon as word of Bianca's death was spread abroad."

"It is equally impossible that only two were present, because then Bianca would have been trying to poison the guest with her." Angela shook her head. "No. Not Bianca."

Nicola wrinkled her nose. "Of course, it is not impossible that Bianca should have forgotten which cup was which and been killed by her own dose."

Angela's eyes widened. "No, Bianca would not deliberately harm another person, but if she were asked by a friend to invite a man for a drink—say, an old lover that the friend was now enamored of— and asked to give him . . . oh, say, a love potion . . ."

"She was certainly silly enough to believe in love potions," Nicola remarked dryly.

"And she was certainly obliging enough to do as she was asked," Lucrezia added thoughtfully.

"To bring together one of her old lovers and a new woman?" Angela frowned, then smiled. "Any other woman would have been outraged at such a suggestion, but not Bianca. She would have been delighted to think that someone who might be sad because of her would now have a new friend."

"Who? Who has she recently cast aside?" Lucrezia asked.

The pretty young woman's brows knitted. "The most recent was Nicolaus Marius, but I will swear he was not brokenhearted when she closed her door to him. Oh, a little annoyed, perhaps, because he would need to trouble himself to find a new source of free relief."

"You mean that idiot that read verses at me the day I arrived in Ferrara?" Lucrezia said. "I thought I had set my face so firmly in a smile that nothing could disturb it, but those verses nearly wiped it away. Well, I can easily imagine someone desiring to murder him—that poetry was worthy of death—but do you think you can discover who pretended to be enamored of him?"

"Most of the women do not gossip with us too freely," Angela said slowly, and then she smiled. "But I could ask Don Nicolaus himself. He might do a little subtle boasting."

Nicola nodded. "He does think he is wonderful. Oh, people like that . . . Perhaps he would not have taken Bianca's dismissal so lightly?"

"So, he might be a suspect as well as a possible victim?" Lucrezia said.

But before she finished the sentence, Nicola was shaking her head and with a gesture dismissed Don Nicolaus. She was reconsidering the original idea that someone had asked Bianca to use a love potion.

"No, I cannot believe it," she said. "No one could take such a chance. Surely Bianca would have named the person who gave her the poisonous 'love potion' as soon as she heard the victim was dead."

"Would she?" Lucrezia asked. "If you had just poisoned a man, would you run to confess it? Could you prove yourself unknowing of having given poison? Even Bianca must have had that much sense of self-preservation. No one wants to admit to using a love potion. Would it not be your word against that person's?"

"But would Bianca think of that?" A frown knitted Angela's brows. "No. She was so silly she might not have connected the 'love potion' with the person's death unless the poison acted so fast the person died there in her room. But even if she did not at once think of murder, that still would be knowledge worth killing to hide."

"But there have not been any unexplained deaths recently," Lucrezia protested.

Nicola shook her head. "Angela is both right and wrong. *I* think we are making up complicated stories about a simple fact. I think Bianca could well have come across some secret, even if it was not murder, that she did not even know was dangerous. Her death was no accident. She was killed to silence her."

Lucia had confined Lucrezia's hair in the green silk net, allowing a few short tendrils to curl over her forehead and around her cheeks before she fastened the whole with a chain of rubies from which a single stone, large as a thrush egg, depended down on her forehead. She signaled her mistress to rise from the stool on which she had been perched and fastened her overskirt securely to the points on her bodice. Lucrezia laid the mirror she had been holding down on the table and turned slowly so that her women could look over her finished appearance.

Lucia stood by near the dressing table, ready to make any adjustments the ladies thought necessary, but both were satisfied, and after agreeing that nothing was missing or awry, they made their way out the door to the private reception room. Lucrezia paused a moment to thank Lucia and turned to follow Angela and Nicola. Suddenly she stopped short and turned back to face the maid.

"Good heavens," she said, "we are guessing and groping blindly when we have a source of real information we have not yet tapped. Lucia, surely you know Donna Bianca's maid?"

"Yes, madonna. Her name is Maria."

"She is the one who would know all these things . . . who visited Donna Bianca and when, whether anyone had quarreled with Bianca, what Bianca was doing that night. I hope to heaven she has not left the palace. Will you find her for me, Lucia, and bring her to speak to me as soon as . . . No, there is every chance that the duke has devised some entertainment for after dinner, so I have no idea when I will be free. Bring her to me tomorrow morning. Let her share your chamber tonight if she has lost her place already or if she is afraid to sleep alone in Donna Bianca's apartment."

"Yes, madonna. She is a very nice girl, Maria." Then an expression of anxiety crossed Lucia's face. "No one will blame her for what happened, will they?"

"I hope not," Lucrezia said, frowning. "Make sure you bring her to me as soon as I am awake, or tell me if you cannot find her." She bit her lip as she turned away. If someone important was suspected, the maid might not be safe. It was not at all impossible that poor Maria would be made a scapegoat.

Lucia sighed with relief. "Yes, madonna. And—"

Lucrezia had turned away, but she looked back. "Yes?"

"Madonna, if Maria has no place to eat, can I . . ."

"Yes, yes, of course. Let her eat with our servants."

Although Lucia was the only one visible most of the time, Lucrezia had many other servants: laundry maids, maids to wash floors and sweep and dust, men to move carpets and furniture and to do small repairs; she even had a small kitchen staff who cooked and served meals when she wished to eat in private with her ladies or with some gentlemen guests, like Ercole Strozzi. Her lips thinned. Where was Strozzi? She had sent him a note hours ago.

The answer to that was in her private reception room talking anxiously to Nicola and Angela.

"I was not at home," he said breathlessly, his crutch beating a familiar tattoo on the floor as he hobbled over to her. "I had ridden out to my estate at Ostellato early this morning. I had no idea. . . . Well, how could such an idea occur to anyone?"

"You heard, I see, as soon as you stepped into the palace? Perhaps out in the plaza?"

"At home!" There was a tinge of bitterness in his voice. "There were three notes describing what had happened and Zambotto was waiting in my sala . . . drinking my wine, no less. He is as curious and tactless as a monkey. What do you want me to do? I can write an epigram that will make Don Alfonso the laughingstock of all Ferrara—"

"No!" Lucrezia exclaimed. "I do not want Alfonso brought into this matter any more than his own foolishness has made unavoidable. What I have determined to do is not to proclaim my innocence— which must be clear to all because I was away at the convent of Corpus Domini for all of Easter and did not speak a word to Donna Bianca since I returned home. Instead I intend to discover who killed the poor woman and expose the murderer to clear my name."

"And Don Alfonso's too?" Strozzi asked waspishly.

"Oh, Alfonso did not kill her," Lucrezia said, smiling. "If she had been strangled or her head bashed in, I might have been worried, but poison? No. What I want you to do, Ercole, dear, is to find out what you can from your friends around the countryside about her family, her husband, whether there is anyone who would profit by her death, and whether that person has any connections with anyone in this court."

Strozzi nodded. "I can do that. I even knew—or, rather, once or twice met—Don Celio Tedaldo, her husband. They were a perfect pair. He was not as stupid as she . . . not quite, anyway, but he was as generous and sweet-tempered. His only failing, as far as I know, was a decided weakness for women—anytime, any kind. He was always in rut."

"How long has he been dead? Of what did he die? Do you know?"

"Not certainly. I will discover that too, although I cannot see how it can have any effect. I think I also ought to—"

He stopped speaking abruptly as the clock on the wall chimed. Angela and Nicola, who had had the portiere raised and were watching the public reception room, hurried over to Lucrezia.

"He will not come tonight," Nicola said, lips stiff with anger. "We will have to walk to the Palazzo Cortile without escort."

Lucrezia drew in a deep breath and let it out in a long sigh. She had hoped that Alfonso would not compound the stupidity of his accusation with this kind of petty harrassment. It was no great distance from the Castel Vecchio to the Palazzo Cortile, the duke's residence. Nor was there any danger to be feared in walking from one to the other, especially in the company of Nicola and Angela and the other ladies-in-waiting, as the duke's guards stood at the entryways to both buildings and could see the path between. However, ever since she and Alfonso had moved from guest quarters in the Palazzo Cortile to their permanent apartments in Castel Vecchio, Alfonso had come whenever they dined at the duke's table to escort her. Probably he had come by his father's orders, but that he should not come today . . .

"I will come with you, of course," Strozzi said.

Lucrezia thanked him and they all moved toward the doorway, hesitating only slightly as a subdued hubbub broke out behind the portiere. Strozzi lifted it politely and allowed Angela, Nicola, and last Lucrezia to pass though. As he did so himself, awkwardly because of needing to hold the portiere open with one hand while he manipulated his crutch with the other, Lucrezia uttered a formal greeting.

"How kind of you to come, Don Niccolò," she was saying. "I do hope Alfonso is not—"

"Don Alfonso has been delayed by his father," the courtier interrupted hastily. "Knowing he usually escorted you to the Palazzo Cortile, the duke was concerned for you and sent me."

"Thank you, you are most welcome although not necessary. As you see, Don Ercole is here and has offered to escort us."

"But I will gladly relinquish you to the protection of Don Niccolò," Strozzi said with a smile. "As you can see, I am scarcely fittingly dressed to attend the duke's dinner. And to speak the truth, madonna, I am weary to the bone."

"I did not think," Lucrezia said, walking the few steps back to him. She took his hand and squeezed it gently.

She was so accustomed to Strozzi's halting gait that she often forgot what an effort it was for him to walk. Riding was less painful, but was not as easy as for a whole man. And now that she really looked at his clothing, she could see that although his garments had been brushed, he was still wearing his riding clothes.

"Go and rest, my dear," she added, releasing his hand. "I will see you tomorrow."

"Late, I fear, or even not until the next day if I am to find answers to the questions you asked me."

"Then as soon as you can manage," Lucrezia said, smiling and touching his arm gently.

Strozzi bowed and limped out. Correggio watched for a moment before he turned to Lucrezia, who had come back to his side, and held out his arm. She set the fingers of her left hand on it, lifted her skirt with her right, and then looked questioningly up at him when he did not start toward the door.

"What sort of questions did you ask Strozzi?"

Lucrezia blinked, then lifted her brows. "I asked him to discover for me what there is of Donna Bianca Tedaldo's family, what claim they have upon her, and whether they are in need of her wealth. I also asked him to find out when her husband died and of what, and whether there are those in his family who resented what he left to her."

"You mean that what I heard was true? That you intend to try to discover who killed Donna Bianca?"

"Yes, of course it is true. How else am I to clear my name from any suspicion?"

"There is no suspicion of you. There cannot be!" Correggio exclaimed.

"It is true enough that it was impossible for me to have poisoned Donna Bianca," Lucrezia said calmly, "quite aside from the fact that I had no cause—even if she was Alfonso's leman. But I have never found that truth and logic had the smallest effect on whispers and fingers pointed behind one's back. I have every intention of discovering who killed that poor woman and bringing that person to justice."

"The duke will not permit it."

Lucrezia's brows rose until they almost touched the ruby-set chain that bound her hair. She was aware of Teodora Angelini and the other three ladies listening avidly.

"How can he stop me?" she asked. "Why should he *want* to stop me?" Her big blue eyes shone as bright and hard as polished steel.

Correggio made a strangled sound, and started toward the outer door. "It would be best," he got out, "if the lady were quietly buried and the whole matter were quickly forgotten."

"This is not Rome." Lucrezia's voice was sharp. "You said that to me not long after I came here, and it is true. In Rome, a new scandal buries an old one every day. In Ferrara a murder will not be forgotten, quickly or slowly, until the killer is brought to justice."

The guard at the door opened it and Correggio led Lucrezia through, into the wide corridor that led to the broad marble stair descending from the piano nobile to the grand sala and the outer doors. Angela and Nicola followed just behind Lucrezia, Donna Teodora and the others trailing.

"What if the murderer cannot be brought to justice?" Correggio asked very softly.

"What can you mean? Surely no one is beyond the duke's justice, except himself and perhaps Alfonso. I do not believe the duke knew more than Bianca's name, for she was recommended to him for my service by Donna Teodora Angelini, and Alfonso did not kill her, so—"

Lucrezia stopped speaking and looked up at Correggio as he let out a long harsh breath. Then she laughed and continued, "Oh, my, did you think I was going to try to blame Alfonso out of spite because he accused me? My dear Don Niccolò, Alfonso did not kill the poor woman . . . unless I heard wrong? I heard that Master Ludovico dei Carri declared she was poisoned. Now, if she had been strangled . . ." She laughed again. "I could easily see Alfonso choking Bianca to death out of pure boredom."

Now Correggio smiled at her and patted the fingers that lay on his arm. "No, she was not strangled, nor beaten to death." They nodded at each other, acknowledging and dismissing in this case Alfonso's propensity for violence. "She was poisoned. Dei Carri was certain of it, although I admit I do not fully understand why he was so sure."

"How came he to announce it to the Court at large?"

"He was very shocked by what he had found." Correggio shook his head. "I do not think dei Carri was even aware of all the attendees at the morning salutation of the duke. He saw only His Highness and blurted out the news."

"I suppose if the duke had heard in private, he would have told Master dei Carri to forget what he had discovered." She hesitated while they walked around the corner of the great marble court that fronted the Palazzo Cortile and then looked up at Correggio again. "Perhaps that would have been easier for everyone, but it would not have been *right*. Donna Bianca was a good, sweet woman. It is not right that she should be slaughtered and forgotten."

To that Correggio made no reply beyond a deep sigh. He knew what was right. He also knew what was expedient, and the choice that Ercole d'Este would make. They went up the stairs, past the guards, who bowed in recognition, and entered through the open doors into the Sala Bianca. Once the great chamber must have been painted white, but now the walls were covered with scenes framed in dark wood, which Lucrezia knew celebrated the Este family in the guise of the legends of Charlemagne and other heroes. Below the painted walls, at about the height of the doorframe, was an elaborate molding from which hung handsome painted fabrics.

Lucrezia was too familiar with the chamber to feel more than a brief gratitude for the draperies of cloth, which deadened the sound of the many voices of Ercole d'Este's guests. But the effect was not strong enough to hide the sudden diminution of conversation when she and her party entered the room. Correggio moved steadily toward the far end, where a long table was set on a dais for the noble family. Standing off to one side were Duke Ercole and Alfonso.

The duke said something sharp to his son, but in too low a voice to carry, especially as the low roar of conversation had begun again. Lucrezia thought that Alfonso had slightly shaken his head, but her view was blocked by the shoulders of Don Ferrante, who was bowing before her. Don Giulio was just behind him, and Sigismundo to the side was nodding and smiling at her. Good, Lucrezia thought. He must either have already found out the provisions of Donna Bianca's will or made contact with someone who would provide that information.

The duke's sons stepped aside, allowing Lucrezia and Correggio to pass, and then fell in behind. It was like an honor guard, Lucrezia thought, but she suspected Ferrante and Giulio had merely taken the opportunity to close in on the ladies they desired. They were near the dais now, and the sour look on the duke's face rather confirmed that suspicion, as did the whispers behind her.

Then the duke himself had stepped forward to offer his hand to support her step up onto the dais. Correggio stopped and turned aside, and Lucrezia saw Ferrante and Guilio escorting Angela and Nicola to the first table, where the ladies and high officers of the household sat.

"This is a most unfortunate day," the duke said.

"For poor Bianca," Lucrezia agreed. "I am sorry now that I never even set eyes on her since before I left for Corpus Domini. I did not know her well, but Angela and Nicola tell me that she was a sweet, gentle lady and did not deserve her fate."

"I am very sorry that Master dei Carri was so overset that he completely forgot the discretion he usually employs. It will not happen again."

Lucrezia widened her eyes. "You mean you expect another poisoning? Why, Alfonso assured me that such a thing had never happened before in Ferrara . . . until I came. Do you believe the contamination of my presence will cause an epidemic of murder—"

"Lucrezia!" the duke protested. "I cannot think how I came to be the father of such an idiot! He will apologize! On his knees before the whole Court!"

"That will be useless," Lucrezia snapped. "Only the discovery of who truly killed Bianca and the exposure of that person to all Ferrara can prove me innocent."

The duke's eyes shifted. "No! I cannot permit it. It would be better to bury the woman and forget, despite the stain on my justice."

Lucrezia burst out laughing. "Oh, no! Whatever can have made you and Don Niccolò suspect Alfonso? I assure you, I do not. Why *should* he kill her, even if she was his leman? Really, Your Highness, can you imagine Alfonso taking the time to discover a poison, find someone to sell it to him, arrange for Bianca to take it? If she had been beaten to death . . ."

"You do not seek to revenge yourself on him?"

"No, indeed, Your Highness. I seek only the truth. What I wish is to avenge Bianca. Murder is *never* right. Never! I have been helpless in the past, but this time I will expose the killer. My name will be clean . . . and so will Alfonso's."

"You are a good, sweet girl, Lucrezia," the duke said, and gestured to his eldest son, who was still standing at the side of the table some distance from them.

Alfonso came forward and lifted Lucrezia's hand, which he kissed. She glanced at him and sighed in a long-suffering way. His skin darkened noticeably as color rose up his neck. Lucrezia sighed again, patience personified. Alfonso's free hand balled into a fist. Lucrezia smiled.

The duke had walked aside and raised a finger. A page bounded to the edge of the dais. The duke said something and the page hurried over to the first table, where Ferrante and Giulio were bending over their chosen ladies. The page spoke. Both young men straightened up and left the table. Sigismundo, who had been talking to two very young ladies at the end of the table, bent to kiss each on the cheek and then hurried after his brothers. When they were all on the dais, the duke nodded at his maestro di sala, who pounded his staff on the floor and called for all guests to take their places.

Alfonso led Lucrezia around the end of the table and seated her to the right of his father's chair. He then took a place beside her. Lucrezia's brows rose. That had to have been arranged earlier by the duke both to signal Alfonso's partial disgrace—usually when there were no important guests Alfonso was seated beside his father—and to show that Lucrezia had forgiven him. Tonight Gian Luca Castellini da Pontremoli came striding across the emptying sala floor and stepped up to sit beside Duke Ercole.

Lucrezia smiled at Don Gian Luca. She liked him and he liked her. He had been sent by the duke to Rome when the negotiations for her marriage to Alfonso became serious, to judge her appear-

ance, manners, and character. He was called sharp-eyed by the duke
and was much trusted. And sharp-eyed he had been, to Lucrezia's
relief, for he had written to Duke Ercole that there was no founda-
tion at all to the rumors about her, that—she remembered he had
said—at home her life was more than Christian, it was religious.
His answering smile and brusque nod assured her that Alfonso's
outburst had not changed his mind.

A fanfare of music heralded the arrival of the first course.
Lucrezia's mouth watered in anticipation. She had not been aware
of being hungry before and now realized that she had been frightened and nervous. Don Gian Luca's easy response had calmed her,
and she suddenly realized that Correggio's questions and manner
had not reassured her at all. Now, why had Correggio been so hostile to her examining the facts of Bianca's death? Was it only
because he had feared she wished to push the blame on Alfonso?
What about that talk of Bianca's pursuing him?

Before the duke, the chief carver was twirling a succulent
haunch of venison, his knife making incredibly thin, round slices
which almost floated onto one of the d'Este silver platters. As the
first layer filled the plate, a younger man, a saucier, stepped forward
and ladled a thin, steaming gravy onto the meat. A second layer of
slices began to fall onto the first.

Meanwhile, other cooks and helpers were carrying to the table
bowls of pork stew and oysters in a savory sauce, platters of sea-
soned roots and beans and whatever other vegetables were available
in the season, and deep bowls of rice flavored with raisins and nuts.
Lucrezia could barely refrain from scooping some of the fragrant
stuff onto her platter. She watched similar platters and bowls being
carried to the table at which her ladies sat and to another on the
other side of the room seating rich merchants from the town and
their families. Below those tables were places for the lesser folk,
wealthy farmers and owners of vineyards who had come to the city

and appealed for audience with the duke or made their bows at Court.

Finally the duke indicated which pieces of meat he wanted and the platter was presented to Lucrezia. She smiled at the cook and told him it all looked so wonderful she would leave the choice to him. It was safe enough. From the day she had first eaten at the duke's table, the carver had watched her selection. Now he knew better than she what would please her. With his long, two-tined fork, he lifted slices, three from the top layer and four or five from the bottom, and laid them on her plate. Other servers offered rice and vegetables. Lucrezia sighed and began to eat.

"I am sorry to have spoken so loudly of my relationship with Donna Bianca. I was more overset than I realized when I heard of her death." Alfonso's harsh voice broke into Lucrezia's almost mindless pleasure and recalled to her her consideration of Correggio's association with Bianca.

"You were, indeed, but I doubt it was because you were futtering her," Lucrezia said coarsely, although she kept her voice low. "I could not care less about your sleeping with her, if you ever did, but I would like to know why it was so important that the whole world know about it." She picked up another slice of meat, rolled it with her fork and knife, and popped it into her mouth.

Alfonso had already finished what was on his plate. "It was *not* important," he insisted. "I was overset, grief-stricken. I did not know what I was saying."

She looked at him and snorted gently, unable to reply immediately because her mouth was too full. When she had swallowed she said, "I think you knew perfectly well what you were saying. I think you felt your accusation could not do me any harm, since no one would dare accuse the pope's daughter or Cesare's sister of murder—not when Cesare was on his way north with an army—but it would be shocking enough to spread the word of Bianca being your leman far and fast."

"Well, you are right about my accusation not doing you any harm." Alfonso glanced at his father, his full lips turned down. "My father almost took off my head when he heard, and made a great point of Cesare's fondness for you."

"But you were not right!" Lucrezia had forborne to take another bite and her voice rose while color flooded her face. "Not about Cesare's love, but about doing me no harm. I have been happy here! People look straight into my eyes and smile when they greet me and their welcomes are sincere. Do you think I wish to see their eyes slide away from mine as they wonder why I killed a most inoffensive lady and against whom I will next take a spite?"

"Nonsense, Lucrezia," the duke said, turning toward her and laying down his eating utensils. "No one thinks ill of you. And you are quite safe here in Ferrara, no matter what anyone thinks."

Lucrezia stabbed another piece of meat with such vehemence that sauce splashed the tablecloth. "You have that wrong, Your Highness! Cesare is on the move, or will soon move. It is not that I am safe in Ferrara that you should remember, but that Ferrara is safe as long as I am married to Alfonso!" With which pronouncement, she bit the meat off her fork, chewing violently and swallowing fast.

The duke's face turned puce and his voice also rose. "You are uncivil, Lucrezia!"

"I am outraged, Your Highness!" Her voice, clear as a bell, rang through the suddenly silent chamber. "I will not be blamed for a crime I could not and would not have committed. I will find out who did commit the crime and clear my name by exposing that person! And it will do no good for you to try to forbid me."

"My dear," Ercole d'Este said, his voice also clear in the near silence, "I might not think such an investigation entirely proper for a lady of your station, but nonetheless I will not forbid you to engage in so noble an attempt. Rather, I will help you if I can."

Lucrezia took a last bite of stew and pushed the platter away slightly. A server hurried to collect it and other emptied plates. The musicians struck up a lilting air.

Under cover of the sound and the bustle of servers removing everything from the tables so the cloths could be changed for the second course, Lucrezia said, "I am delighted to hear it. Did you by any chance know Donna Bianca's husband, Celio Tedaldo?"

The duke looked taken aback by her acceptance of his offer to help as real and her clear intention of using it. "I never met the man, no," he said, "but I had heard about him from the French ambassador, who was very fond of Don Celio. In fact, it was at the ambassador's request that I gave Donna Bianca a position as your lady."

"At the French ambassador's request?" Lucrezia echoed. "I thought it was Teodora Angelini who arranged that Bianca be my lady."

"No, it was Don Philip della Rocca Berti." A deep crease formed between Duke Ercole's brows. "He was fond of them both. I think Don Celio's mother was some relation of his. In any case, when Don Celio died and he saw that Donna Bianca was totally forlorn, he decided that being at Court would be good for her."

"Oh, it was," Lucrezia said, then drew in her breath sharply. "Until . . ." She did not know how to finish that sentence, so she went on briskly, "As I said before, I did not know her at all, but when I saw her among the other ladies, she was always smiling and had the sweetest laugh."

The duke nodded. "An engaging if not terribly clever woman, Don Philip told me. I shudder to think what he will have to say about this matter. He has not yet heard, as he had gone to his country estate last week. If he takes offense . . ."

"Then he will be glad to hear that I am determined to discover who did such a dreadful thing and avenge her."

"He will be more glad to learn that I have put Don Niccolò da Correggio in charge of investigating the lady's death," the duke said dryly.

"You have put Don Niccolò in charge of the investigation of Donna Bianca's death?"

"Yes." The duke's eyebrows rose. "Do you have any objection to that?"

"No, none at all," Lucrezia said, feeling considerable relief.

It was a good reason, having no connection with any personal relationship between him and Bianca, for Don Niccolò to have objected to her announcement that she would try to solve the murder. Doubtless he thought their investigations would cross and perhaps impede each other. And Don Niccolò was very traditional in his attitude toward women. Although he enjoyed conversing with her, their talk was all about subjects Don Niccolò deemed suitable to a female—art and poetry and sometimes the less abstruse aspects of philosophy. He never talked to her about politics.

"Then will you give over this nonsense about pursuing the killer on your own?"

"No! Why should I?"

"Partly because if Don Philip hears of it, he might wonder whether you were trying to shield some Neapolitan friend. He was protesting to me before he left the city that he felt there might be some change in my political position. He had heard some talk about balancing between the French and Spanish influence—"

"Not in *my* apartments," Lucrezia interrupted.

But even as she spoke, Lucrezia realized guiltily that she knew virtually nothing about what her ladies said and did because she avoided them so assiduously. However, it did not matter; she could see that the duke's eyes had gone past her and were fixed on his son.

"No." Duke Ercole's voice was milder, almost absent when he replied. "You understand that it is important to put aside your past sympathies. Still, to have you meddling in the matter of Donna Bianca's death might be misunderstood."

"Send Don Philip to me," Lucrezia said, smiling. "I will explain why a woman needs to be involved."

5

LUCREZIA WOKE suddenly the next morning and lay for a moment repressing the impulse to leap out of bed and trying to remember why a feeling of such urgency possessed her. Everything had been as usual last night. Alfonso had come and made love . . . As the thought came, her eyes widened. She had been so surprised when Alfonso appeared just as usual that she had been struck mute. And, recalling her surprise, she recalled everything else—Bianca's death, Alfonso's accusation, her exchanges with the duke, the behavior of the guests when music and dancing had followed the dinner.

Yet last night, despite the knowledge of what had passed between them, despite the fact that she was already carrying his child, Alfonso had come and been more passionate than ever. Remembering, she could feel a warmth in her loins, feel the cloth that covered her tickle her suddenly upstanding nipples.

Momentarily pure lust distracted Lucrezia from something that had troubled her about Alfonso's behavior. Her memory leapt further back than last night to her wedding journey to Ferrara and the stop at Castel Bentivoglio, where Alfonso had appeared unscheduled and unexpected, perhaps looking for a reason to reject her before she arrived at Ferrara. He had been sullen, scowling, mouthing polite words he clearly did not mean nor intend for her to believe. Perhaps she hid what she felt better, but her determination to dislike him was no less. She had come to Ferrara prepared to endure a husband she knew she could not love, not after her first Alfonso, not after Cesare had murdered her heart with her second husband.

Even so, even thinking of her dead love, she had responded to Alfonso's sullen strength then as she had last night when she should have been nursing her indignation. He had always affected her that way, even at first when his passion had been mixed with an angry resentment. He was an exciting man, a man of brooding violence barely held in check, and when he came to her, naked under his bedrobe, her nether lips swelled and moistened without any need for tender words or touches. It was just as well, for she got none of those.

Lucrezia sighed, part regret, part satisfied memory. Her eyes started to close, the better to enjoy her body's sated languor—and then snapped open. She pushed herself higher on her pillows, separating her remembered pleasure from her husband's behavior. There had been something different, no, something wrong last night. There had been . . . she fumbled in her mind for a description of what had been almost totally obscured by her own violent pleasure . . . desperation.

Yes, that was the word. There had been desperation in Alfonso's lovemaking. He had lingered, holding back as if he could not bear to permit a release that would end their coupling. He almost never did that. Usually he drove forward to his own pleasure without much regard for hers. Last night she had come to climax twice before he had surrendered to his own need.

Why? Lucrezia could not believe that the sudden change was a coincidence. Was he trying to please her? Why now? Because of her investigation into Bianca's death? If that was true, then he had something to hide. Why did he behave as if she would no longer be available to him? Good God, *could* he have killed Bianca? By poison?

She had dismissed the notion but now realized she had no idea what substances were available to him in the brass foundry that made the cannon he loved so dearly or, for that matter, among the glazes he used on the majolica ware he decorated so beautifully. He would know if the substances were poisonous because he would have been warned to be careful with them. If something was freely available for the taking so that he would not need to get it from someone else and make himself vulnerable to that person, and if he knew he would need to be rid of Bianca, could he have poisoned her?

In the next moment Lucrezia was smiling and shaking her head. No, ridiculous. It was not murder Alfonso was trying to hide. If he had killed Bianca, he would not be making scenes to mark their association. Nor would he make scenes to mark their association if she had simply been one of his women.

Suddenly Lucrezia remembered the way Duke Ercole had looked at Alfonso when he said someone had been talking about balancing French and Spanish influence. If Bianca had had a relationship to the Spanish ambassador and Alfonso had been using her to meet with or transmit messages to the Spaniard, he might prefer his relationship with Bianca to be thought one of the bed. But Bianca's friendship was to the French ambassador, which made the whole argument nonsensical.

Impatient with thoughts that got nowhere, Lucrezia pulled back the bedcurtains and opened her mouth to call her maid. To her surprise, two girls jumped up from the long narrow chest that made the step to the bed.

"I have brought Maria as you asked, madonna," Lucia said, smiling and slightly pushing forward the girl with whom she had been sitting.

Maria made a deep curtsy. "Thank you for allowing Lucia to invite me to eat with your servants, madonna."

Lucrezia smiled at her. "I could not let you starve because a tragedy had overtaken your mistress. I am so sorry about Donna Bianca. I hardly knew her, but she had the sweetest smile. It quite lit up the sour faces of the other ladies."

Tears filled Maria's eyes. "She was the best mistress any maid could have. So sweet-tempered. So generous. I know I am spoiled for service with any other." She sobbed. "I will be miserable, always remembering how good my lady was."

"You found her too. How dreadful," Lucrezia said.

The girl's face was wet with tears. "It was so terrible, so terrible," she whispered. "I did not know at first that she was dead and I ran to her and tried to lift her up and . . . and she . . . Her face was all beslobbered with spit and vomit and she . . . she smelled! She had voided on herself! My lady! My sweet lady, who was always so clean, so neat." Sobs racked her, and before she covered her face with her hands, Lucrezia saw that her eyes were enormous with horror.

That was how dei Carri knew Bianca had been poisoned, Lucrezia thought. Many things could make a person vomit and void, but it was very rare to die of it in a few minutes. Had the poison been less powerful so that it took Bianca hours to die, her illness might have been thought natural, due to some tainted food or water. But to die so quickly that she had not had time or strength to crawl away from her excreta, that must be poison. The thought reminded Lucrezia that she needed to relieve herself, and she went to her close stool behind an elegant screen.

When she returned, she seated herself at her dressing table and repeated, "I am sorry, sorry for what happened to your kind mistress and sorry that you were the one to find her and need to remember such things. I am sorry for myself also, because in an excess of grief, my husband blamed me for poisoning your lady. It is not true—"

"No, madonna, it could not be, for my lady never ate at your table and never received any gift from you. But I do not understand why Don Alfonso should grieve . . . well, anyone might grieve for so good and sweet a lady, but an *excess* of grief?"

"Then he was not her lover?"

"Don Alfonso? The duke's eldest son?" Maria's eyes were wide again, but this time with simple astonishment.

"He was not a frequent visitor to Donna Bianca's rooms?"

"Frequent? He was never a visitor."

"He could not have come cloaked and masked? Or disguised in some other way? Or could Donna Bianca have sent you away to keep his visits secret?"

There was a silence while Maria looked down at her own toes and bit her lips uncertainly.

Lucrezia continued softly, "I will not blame Donna Bianca no matter what you tell me. I understand that her heart was so soft she might be led into some errors . . . and I am not jealous. Don Alfonso and I do our duty to each other, as is right and proper for his place and mine. If his heart was engaged elsewhere—"

"Not with my mistress," Maria said, looking puzzled. "She did not keep secrets from me. Oh, she did sometimes send me away so that her visitor should not be alarmed or embarrassed, but she always told me either before or later who it was." She sighed and smiled fondly. "She was not a very good keeper of secrets, Donna Bianca."

No, Lucrezia thought, and that may have cost her her life. "But clearly you were not with her when she . . . she was killed. And she was expecting a visitor. Do you know who was coming?"

"No," Maria said, retaining her smile, albeit tremulously. "He was a new lover and he had sworn her to secrecy. She told me only how gentle and loving he was, that he wrote poems just for her, that he had no buboes—"

"No buboes?"

Maria blushed and she uttered a self-conscious laugh. "I told you how clean my lady was. She would not lie with a man who had those sores. Her husband . . . she loved him dearly, but he was one for the women and . . . he had sores."

"So it was her new lover who was coming the night before last? Did you make ready some refreshment, some wine, some cakes?"

Maria was frowning again. "I am not sure it *was* her lover who was coming. Usually when he was expected she . . . she received him in dishabille. That night she changed to a more elegant gown. It might have been someone who wished to . . . to borrow money. She was so generous. But she was not stupid about money. She never outspent her income. I have heard her say no, sometimes with tears, explaining that she would have no more money until the next quarter."

"But she would give when she had more?"

"Sometimes the need had passed." A look of resentment tightened Maria's lips. "Some of those who borrowed gambled and did not wish to give up their jewelry or ornaments to pay their debts."

"So Lady Bianca would not have ordered refreshments if it were someone who was begging a loan of her?"

"Oh, yes, but she did not like cakes to stand in the open because of the flies and she never served an open bottle of wine. Sometimes she would herself finish a bottle she had opened earlier, but she would not present an open bottle to a guest. When she was dressed and ready to receive her guest, I went down to the kitchen to tell the cooks to make ready small savories and cakes and a bottle of the soft red wine she favored. Then I went into the closet behind her bed-chamber where my cot is."

"You heard nothing?"

"Nothing at all, not even . . . Sometimes I would hear . . . sounds of love, but it was so quiet I supposed he had not yet come. I . . . I was bored. I fell asleep. I knew I would hear if she rang her bell. Then I would have run to fetch the cakes and wine. I would have set them and her fine goblets on the chest in her bedchamber, and she would have carried the tray into her reception room herself."

Lucrezia stared past the maid for a moment, nibbling gently on her lower lip. "But she never rang the bell and there was nothing in her reception room or bedchamber to eat or drink—not even empty cups or goblets."

"That is so, madonna."

"Could she have been dead already?" Lucrezia murmured. "How long did it take you to order the cakes and savories?"

Maria began to sob again. "Perhaps half a candlemark? I did not hurry, madonna. I gossiped in the kitchen. I did not think my lady expected anyone very soon."

Her weeping intensified and Lucia rose from the chest on which she had been sitting and put her arm around Maria's shaking shoulders.

"I cannot believe it," Maria cried. "I cannot believe that she cried out for help from me and I was gossiping in the kitchen."

"You could have done nothing for her, Maria," Lucia said, trying to console her. "What killed her was too fast."

"I could have been with her," the maid wept. "I could have wiped her face, brought the chamber pot, offered some comfort."

"I only made a wild guess, Maria," Lucrezia soothed. "More likely it happened later, and whoever killed her made sure she did not cry out and summon you."

"I should have been awake. I should have listened. Oh, my poor lady. My poor lady."

"Maria, think," Lucrezia said. "If he had poisoned Donna Bianca and you came in . . . what do you think would have happened to *you*?"

The girl stopped sobbing and her eyes widened.

"Yes," Lucrezia continued. "Like as not you would be lying beside your mistress. Let us hope that whoever did this is not wondering if you did hear something and know too much. You could not have saved your mistress, but you can help avenge her and protect yourself. Are you sure there was nothing to drink in the chamber? A pitcher of water?"

"No, there was nothing. The table was bare. You are wondering how she came to take poison if there was nothing to eat or drink. I have wondered myself. I can only think that whoever came brought cups and wine with him."

Lucrezia sighed. "Not impossible. Likely, even, if he had prepared a cup with poison in it so he could pour from a closed bottle into both cups and drink without fear. That would look most innocent. And it could be he knew her well, knew that she had food and wine brought fresh." She sighed again. "Now, I am sorry to cause you pain, Maria, but I must know everything you saw when you first found your mistress. Others must have been in that chamber before you, and I will ask what they saw. Perhaps any difference will reveal who killed her."

Maria bit her lip. "I will try," she whispered. "The reception room is nearly square and has chests for seating and storage around the walls. Between the windows is a daybed and in front, near the head, a table." She paused and shivered.

"Go on," Lucrezia urged gently.

"My lady lay on her back between the table and the daybed. Her legs were a little bent and—" the girl's lips quivered and it took a moment for her to steady them "—and her dress was all . . ."

Lucrezia leaned forward and patted her hand. Maria swallowed and forced her voice on.

"Her dress was all soiled. One hand was outstretched toward the table, as if she had been holding to it, and the other . . ." Maria frowned and her eyes slid away from Lucrezia's.

"What is it?" Lucrezia asked. "You know I am most eager to discover who harmed your mistress for many reasons: to clear my name of any suspicion that I did, to be sure the killer does not become suspicious of you, and because Donna Bianca was a sweet, good lady and I cannot bear that her killer should escape. I promise you I will keep anything that does not point to the murderer secret."

"I don't know," Maria said uncertainly, still looking away. And then, as if she had decided the secret could have nothing to do with the murder, she said, "I don't remember."

Lucrezia was annoyed. Likely enough the maid was right and what she was hiding had nothing to do with her mistress's death, but who could tell? However, it was pointless to press her now. It would frighten her and make her stubborn. Certainly it was not guilty knowledge. Doubtless, the girl was keeping a secret her late mistress did not want revealed.

"Very well," Lucrezia said with a sigh, "but if you do remember, I hope you will come and tell me. I will not judge or betray poor Donna Bianca." When no response was forthcoming, she continued, "There was no other disturbance in the room? The table was not pushed awry, the chairs and stools were in place? Nothing was spilled anywhere?"

"The table . . . perhaps it was turned a little, as if my lady's hand held to it and then slipped, and . . . and a stool that had been near the table was overturned."

Maria fell silent and Lucrezia could see that she was going over the room in her mind's eye. Once the girl winced, as if she saw something that troubled her, but it might be that she was trying to close her mind to the image of her mistress's body. Finally she shook her head.

"I am sorry, madonna. I think everything else looked just as usual."

"Thank you, Maria," Lucrezia said. "Unless some other arrangements you prefer have been made, you can continue to eat and lodge with Lucia. I would prefer that until we have an answer about your mistress's fate you remain where you can easily be reached."

"Yes, madonna." She turned to go, then said softly to Lucia, "I will be in my mistress's apartment."

Lucia patted Maria's arm and then went to get warmed washing water for Lucrezia, which she set on the dressing table, and soft drying cloths. While Lucrezia washed and patted herself dry, Lucia brought clean undergarments and then a dressing robe. A brief colloquy decided on a morning gown and headdress. While Lucia went to fetch the garments, Nicola's voice from behind the portiere asked softly for admittance. Lucrezia called her in and Angela came with her.

"Did Maria tell you anything of importance?" Nicola asked. "The page Ascanio told us that Lucia had brought Maria, but we heard no voices for the longest time."

"I was asleep." Lucrezia smiled involuntarily. "Alfonso was even more lively than usual last night."

"Don Alfonso was here last night?" Angela's face showed the astonishment Lucrezia had felt when her husband arrived.

"After what he did?" Nicola added, more disgusted than surprised. "I know he does not waste money on women, but to use you after calling you a poisoner is beyond discourteous."

Lucrezia almost snapped at Nicola that Alfonso had come

because he wanted . . . needed . . . *her*. She swallowed back the words because . . . because she did not want to expose her husband's vulnerability or her awareness of it, her pleasure in his seeking her. What was wrong with her? Alfonso *had* accused her of poisoning Bianca. She should not care what he felt or thought. But all that seemed to matter was the way he had clung to her, fighting against his own pleasure to linger longer in her arms.

Instead of replying to her ladies, Lucrezia returned to the stool before her dressing table. By the time she settled herself, she had suppressed her feeling about Alfonso.

"I think he feels he has accomplished his purpose—" she laughed at the gasps Angela and Nicola uttered "—not to blacken my name, but to establish the notion that he was Bianca's lover. That done, and being Alfonso, he simply decided to forget everything else that happened, so he acted just as he usually would. Certainly he gave no reasons for his behavior to me."

Nicola sighed. "I suppose you could not expect anything else. I am sure he would choke to death on an apology."

Lucrezia laughed again. "Yes, I think he would. But it is not only I who suffers. He is just as bad with his father. In any case, I am now reasonably sure that he was *not* one of Bianca's lovers. Maria was astonished when I mentioned his name. Apparently she never saw him in Bianca's apartment and she was very certain that even if she had been sent away Bianca would have mentioned him."

"Did she know who Bianca's new lover was?" Angela asked.

"Unfortunately, she did not. He had apparently asked Bianca to keep their affair a secret and she was trying to obey him. She did send Maria away when he came and had not yet mentioned his name, but Maria was sure she soon would."

"Even if the man was Don Alfonso?" Nicola asked. "Bianca was not clever, but even she must have realized that to betray the duke's son might lead to very serious trouble."

"Oh, my, I never thought of that," Lucrezia admitted, frowning, but after a moment she shook her head. "But why should he tell Bianca to keep it a secret? Surely not for fear of offending me. And his father would not have cared. He took one of his own wife's ladies-in-waiting to bed with him. In fact, Duke Ercole would have been pleased. You know how much he deplores the kind of women Alfonso uses. He would be glad to see his son with a woman of decent family."

"That is a puzzle," Nicola admitted. "Unless he killed her and planned to use his dramatic announcement of their affair as a screen for what he had done."

"But why?" Lucrezia cried. "Why should he kill her?"

Even as she spoke the knowledge that he might well have poisons readily available and might have had a political reason to silence Bianca flashed through her mind. She lowered her mirror a trifle and looked down into it so that her women should not see her eyes.

"Why should *anyone* kill her?" Angela said in a disgusted voice. "I wish she had been a mean, cruel person so we could find *someone* with a reason to hate her. When I last spoke to Giulio, he had not heard a single harsh word spoken against her."

"Ferrante too." Nicola nodded.

"But that was before dinner, was it not?" The women murmured agreement, and Lucrezia continued, "Let us see what they have to say this morning."

However, it was not Giulio or Ferrante who first craved admittance to Lucrezia's private reception room as she, Nicola, and Angela were breaking their fast, but Sigismundo. He was welcomed immediately and, despite his protests, another chair was set for him.

"Have some wine if you do not want more than that," Lucrezia urged as Lucia hurried to bring a plate—actually one of Alfonso's lovely majolica pieces—a fork, and a cup of wine for him.

"I have learned something very interesting," Sigismundo said, after polite greetings to the ladies.

"About Donna Bianca's will?" Lucrezia asked.

Sigismundo nodded. "Her husband's fortune mostly goes back to his family in various ways. I have not all the details. I will know more in a few days, but I doubt any of them are involved in Donna Bianca's death. And there are the usual small bequests, mostly to servants on her estates."

"Have any of them visited her here?"

"I knew you would ask that." Sigismundo smiled. "So far I have only heard of one man who came regularly from the country. He brought what was available—cured ham the last time he was here, but in season produce and fruits."

"Wine?" Lucrezia asked.

"Hmmm. I don't know. Wine was not mentioned. But yes, I see. If he brought a bottle of wine with poison in it, it might be weeks, even months before that bottle was opened. Still, is that likely? Such a bottle could poison a whole roomful of people."

"What better way to keep the particular object of the poisoning secret?" Nicola remarked. "It is much harder to discover a murderer when his victim cannot be identified."

Sigismundo frowned. "Very well, I will ask more particularly about this man. I did not think of it because I was concentrating on the matter of the will, and that, as I said, was interesting enough to hold my attention."

"Yes?" Lucrezia leaned forward.

"Your ladies-in-waiting will profit by Donna Bianca's death." Sigismundo nodded. "Profit substantially."

"All of them, under a general benefaction?" Lucrezia asked.

"No." Sigismundo smiled. "Very specifically. First, Teodora Angelini is forgiven all her debts to Donna Bianca, which must be substantial, as they are noted as being recorded elsewhere. I have already set one of the clerks to finding those records. I am sure all the other ladies' debts will also be recorded there."

"But Angelini's must be the greatest if they were actually mentioned," Nicola said.

Sigismundo nodded. "But that is less important than the next provision, in which the proceeds of one of Donna Bianca's estates, which came to her from her mother, is to be divided in quarters and paid to, again, Teodora Angelini, as well as Diana Altoviti, Beatrice Tisio, and Elizabetta Dossi."

"Oh, my," Lucrezia breathed.

"And one last thing," Sigismundo said most deliberately. "The will is recent, less than a month old."

"Now that *is* interesting," Lucrezia said. "I must find out whether Bianca knew those women before she was assigned to my service. If not, she cannot have known them long. Did she leave them the money because she knew they needed it?"

"Well, of course she knew they needed it, if they were borrowing from her," Nicola said. "Didn't Lucia tell us that Donna Beatrice wanted to borrow money from Bianca the day before she died?"

"I wonder if she got what she asked for," Lucrezia said thoughtfully. "Maria—she was Donna Bianca's maid—told me that Bianca would lend, but not ever overspend her income. I am not sure what Bianca's quarter-day was, but if she was short, she would have told Beatrice to wait—"

"And it might have occurred to Donna Beatrice," Sigismundo remarked, "that it would be better to have her own income instead of having to beg Donna Bianca for money all the time."

"Yes, but did the ladies know Bianca had left them anything?" Lucrezia cautioned.

"I have no idea," Nicola admitted, "and that group is not on duty today, so you cannot call them in and ask. You could send to those who have chambers here. . . ."

"No, I do not want to mark them out in any special way unless I must."

"I could go to each one and ask," Angela offered. "You know they think me so empty-headed they are never surprised by what I say."

Sigismundo made an abrupt gesture to draw their attention and got it promptly. "You have not heard the last and the best," he said. "Don Niccolò da Correggio is named to administer the estate and the payments—at a very nice stipend out of the revenues."

He seemed disappointed when Lucrezia was not surprised, and she told him that the same group of ladies had informed her that Donna Bianca had been pursuing Don Niccolò. "I suppose that was the reason," she said. "Don Niccolò could not have been best pleased about being burdened with more work, even at a good price. You know, Sigismundo, that his duties would never be simply to hand over the ducats. He would be the target of pleas and complaints and demands for help and advice—and he has his own property and enough to do for the duke."

"You are right about that," Sigismundo agreed. "So he would certainly not want Donna Bianca dead."

Lucrezia nodded with a sense of relief. The idea of the elegant and intellectual Don Niccolò succumbing to the lovely but brainless Bianca had troubled her. Don Niccolò was traditional in his view of women; he did not discuss war or politics or the deeper aspects of philosophy or religion with them. However, when he spoke of literature or art or some other topic he deemed suitable for a female, he enjoyed thoughtful, intelligent responses.

"So why did Bianca choose Don Niccolò?" Sigismundo continued. "How did she come to know him well enough?"

"Bianca did not need to know someone well enough," Angela said. "If one of the women mentioned him as honest and clever and a favorite of the duke, it would have been enough. Bianca was very impulsive."

"You are sure of that, Angela?" Lucrezia asked.

"Oh, yes. A thing was beautiful one day and hateful the next, according to the last opinion she heard."

"Then that eliminates persons in a previous will who might have been angered by her leaving to my ladies an estate they expected. Revenge would be stupid when there was a good chance that a living Bianca could have been convinced to return the estate to the original heir."

"Oh, good," Sigismundo said, grinning. "Then I will not need to chase down the older versions of her will." He picked up the cup of wine Lucia had placed before him and sipped from it. "Do you have any more questions, Lucrezia? If not, I will fetch Master dei Carri to you. I warned him that you wished to speak to him."

"Yes, I would like to see him," Lucrezia agreed, and smiled when Sigismundo rose, took her hand to kiss, and then went out.

All three women listened, but no murmur of greetings came through the portiere from the public reception room and they nodded at each other. No one had come early today, which was a good indication that neither her attendant ladies nor the gentlemen who kept diaries and wrote memoirs or, for that matter, letters of news, expected any more scandal. So much the better, they would not see Master dei Carri arrive.

Lucrezia and her ladies hurriedly finished breaking their fast and Lucia cleared away the plates. However the wine and several handsome glass goblets inscribed with the Borgia seal remained on the large credenza that stood opposite the windows which opened on the hanging garden. Most of the silver platters also bore the bull of the Borgias, but two exquisite candlesticks carried the crest of Aragon, and there were cups and dishes of majolica ware; a few were early gifts but most were from Alfonso's studio.

Nicola and Angela withdrew somewhat to a chest, well padded with a beautiful Turkish carpet, directly under one window.

Lucrezia remained in her chair, watching the doorway. Her patience was not much tried. Before she could grow restless, the page ran in to announce Sigismundo and Master dei Carri, and the two men followed virtually on his heels. Sigismundo bowed and went to join Angela and Nicola.

The physician looked carefully at Lucrezia's face while he offered formal greetings, then smiled and said, "I can see from your blooming appearance, Donna Lucrezia, that I have not been summoned to amend any complaint."

"No, indeed, Master dei Carri," Lucrezia assured him, laughing. "I am feeling very well. As you know I was suffering from some nausea before I left for Corpus Domini, but my stay there seems to have put that right as well as my irritable temper. That was a rest I needed and enjoyed. To pray, to sleep, to speak of the love of our Lord and His Mother, to read sermons, all without contention or interruption restored me. In fact"—she laughed softly again—"the calm of the convent has survived the very unpleasant experience I had yesterday. I am sure you, like everyone else, have heard how my husband stormed into my apartment and accused me of poisoning Donna Bianca."

"Oh, heavens, madonna, I pray you will forgive me. The duke was *furious* that I had blurted out the facts of the poor lady's death. But how could I know? How could I guess what His Highness Don Alfonso would do? And it was impossible that you should be at fault! Impossible!"

6

5 April,

Lucrezia's private reception room

"I AM MOST relieved to hear you say so, Master dei Carri, and I will readily forgive you because, as you said, you could have no idea that Don Alfonso even knew the lady, but I would like to know why you are so sure I could not have harmed Donna Bianca." Lucrezia smiled at him. "I hope you will not say it is because you know I have a fine character and would not poison anyone."

The physician, who had been tense and anxious, relaxed at her easy tone and pleasant smile. He too smiled. "Well, that is true too, madonna, I mean that you are a good, Christian lady and would not poison anyone, but it was not my reason. Donna Bianca was killed by a dose of aconite—the Mother of Poisons, which is commonly called monkshood or wolfbane. It is a terrible poison because there is no antidote, and it works so quickly that one cannot even save the victim by making him or her void the substance. If you were not there with her when she died or less than a half candlemark before she died, then you did not kill her."

"I see," Lucrezia breathed, then looked startled. "Who called it Mother of Poisons? I know of monkshood, but I have never heard of it being used as a poison recently. Is it not very dangerous to handle? Do I not remember that monkshood was deadly even to the touch? And where could one obtain such a thing?"

"The ancients called it Mother of Poisons, and as to obtaining it, it grows wild in the mountains. Many apothecaries keep the roots. It can be handled with reasonable care and is used by some—but not by me—in small doses to relieve pain and induce sleep. More often it is used in ointments to ease the pain of bruises or aching joints, but I believe it to be too dangerous."

"Still, you recognized its effects. How clever," Lucrezia said with a look of admiration.

Master dei Carri's mouth tightened. "It was not cleverness, but a horrible memory that will forever haunt me. Years ago when I was coming home before the snow closed the passes from a time of studying in Paris, the party I was riding with passed a small house used by those who bring their goats to graze in the mountain valleys during the summer. One of the party dismounted to get a drink. He went to the door to ask for a cup to dip from the bucket and screamed for me to come at once. There were five in the family, the parents, two sons, and a daughter. Three were already dead and the other two dying. I will never forget. So when I saw Donna Bianca looking exactly the same . . . I beg you again, madonna, to forgive me for my thoughtless outburst, but I was so overset—"

"I understand." Lucrezia's eyes were round with horror. "But who had poisoned a whole family? Did you ever discover who committed so horrible a crime?"

"It was no crime, merely a terrible accident. They were eating roast kid and using what they believed was horseradish for a condiment . . . only it was the root of monkshood that the women had ground up. One plant can easily be mistaken for the other if the monkshood is not in flower."

"I see. How terrible. And you could do nothing?" Lucrezia shuddered and pressed a hand to her lips.

"No, madonna. I tried. One son had eaten less—he was the one who told us about the horseradish, and I tried to give him a draft of ground chalk, hoping it would soak up the poison . . . but it was too late. And, truthfully, I do not believe it could have saved him even if he could have taken it. His retching was so continuous he could not swallow, and he died in less than half a candlemark. He said his mother, who loved the hot condiment and used it liberally, had died before she could finish what was on her plate. They all stopped eating, of course, when she collapsed, but . . ."

"And you are sure it was the same poison?"

"Yes. The vomiting, the voiding, were the same, and the look of the skin and the eyes. The only thing . . ."

"Yes?"

"Donna Bianca's mouth was not as marked as those of the folk in the mountains. But I suppose that was because she did not eat the rough, ground-up root. I suppose the poison was given to her . . . I am not sure how. There was nothing in the room from which she could have eaten or drunk, and her vomit had no . . . recently eaten . . . ah . . . undigested matter in it."

Lucrezia made a muffled sound and he glanced at her, his expression suddenly mortified. "Oh, I beg your pardon, madonna. I should not have described such disgusting symptoms to you. I get interested and I forget my audience."

"There is no need to apologize," Lucrezia said. "I asked, and it is important for me to know how quick-acting the poison was and that poor Donna Bianca had not taken it in food. Could you tell if she had recently drunk wine, from the look of the"—she swallowed hard—"the vomit?"

"I can tell you she had drunk no red wine—the color, you know. But if she had drunk white wine or that golden wine that ladies favor . . . no, I doubt I could have noticed that." Master dei Carri cocked his head at her. "But why should it be important to you to know such things?"

"Because I intend to find out who killed that sweet, harmless woman, to clear my name and Alfonso's too."

Master dei Carri studied Lucrezia's face for a moment. He seemed to read something beyond the innocent look of her large blue eyes, and he nodded. "I see. I will help you in any way I can, madonna. If you can uncover and expose the killer, it will reduce the duke's anger against me."

"Thank you," Lucrezia said, pleased at the acceptance and the offer of help. "Everyone is puzzled about how Donna Bianca took the poison. Her maid assured me there was not even a pitcher of water in her chamber. Bianca had arranged for wine and cakes to be brought up later, but, of course, she had never rung for the maid. Can you hazard a guess as to how she was poisoned?"

"Ah, you questioned the maid."

"Well, of course. Who would know better what poor Bianca ate or drank and who was coming to visit her?"

It was apparent from his expression that Master dei Carri had never thought of asking a maid for the information needed to discover Bianca's killer. Lucrezia suppressed her desire to shake her head, and instead continued, "Unfortunately, Maria knows very little. As soon as her mistress was dressed, Maria went down to the kitchen to give the order about the refreshment. When she came back up, she came in the back way and lay down on her bed to wait for Donna Bianca's summons."

"Why did she not notice how long the summons was in coming?" Master dei Carri asked suspiciously.

Lucrezia was annoyed. Just mention a commoner in connection with a crime among the nobility and somehow that commoner would be blamed. "She says she fell asleep, and I have no reason to doubt her. Her mistress was extraordinarily kind and poor Maria is in despair, knowing she will never find another lady so gentle and generous. Also her room is behind Bianca's bedchamber and Bianca was in her reception room with the door closed, waiting for her guest . . . whoever that was. When the poison struck, would she have been able to call out?"

"Probably not," Master dei Carri admitted reluctantly. "At least not loud enough for the maid to hear her through a closed door and another chamber. It affects the mouth and throat first, then the stomach . . . but by then it is too late. The vomiting precedes death by only a few minutes."

"You studied the poison?" Lucrezia asked, but now, recalling dei Carri's distress over the dying peasant family, her voice was sympathetic.

Dei Carri nodded. "You understand, I see. That dead family stuck in my mind. I had to discover whether by my ignorance I had failed the two who were still alive. I suppose it was some relief when I learned that nothing I could have done would have saved them. If the boy had eaten less, he might have recovered on his own, but there is no antidote or treatment that will help."

Lucrezia came back to her original question. "But how could Bianca have taken it?"

The physician shook his head. "I have heard that the ointment for joints can be deadly if rubbed into an open wound, but Donna Bianca had no cuts on her face, hands, or arms, nor on her legs, which were exposed by the disarrangement of her skirts. And surely she was too young to need an ointment for painful joints."

"And never complained of them that I know of." Lucrezia turned in her chair to face her women, who were talking very quietly with Sigismundo. "Angela, did you ever hear that Donna Bianca complained of aching joints? Or other pain? Or being unable to sleep?"

"No, madonna." Angela rose and came to stand beside her mistress. "I never heard her complain of anything, and from the way she danced, I would swear her joints gave her no trouble."

The physician nodded. "I would agree from looking at her fingers, elbows, and knees that she had no stiffening of the joints. And there was no ointment in the reception chamber. Hmmm. Perhaps I had better go and examine her bedchamber. It is possible that such an ointment could be made too strong and that taken in through the skin the poison would act more slowly. Yes. I will look."

"And you will tell me if you find the ointment?" Lucrezia urged.

"Yes, indeed, madonna—or if I discover anything else."

Master dei Carri bowed, and Sigismundo, catching the movement, bade farewell to Nicola and followed him out of the room. This time voices greeted the two men. Nicola left her seat and moved silently to stand behind the portiere and listen. The clock on the wall chimed for the hour. Lucrezia looked up at it. To her surprise, it showed the eighteenth hour, noon hour of the day. It did not seem that she had been talking for so long, but ordinarily her mornings were very lazy—a long time for breaking fast, a little desultory conversation with Nicola and Angela, perhaps a little reading or needlework. Time usually moved slowly; today it had sped.

She sat silently for a little while, staring out of the windows at the hanging plants. They were not yet lush, for the climate of Ferrara was somewhat cooler than that of Rome, but she could see that they would be beautiful within the next month. She wondered whether they would be another drain on her purse. Would the miserly duke pay gardeners to care for the plants or would she be expected to do so? As she was expected to pay the keep of ladies she did not like or want.

That thought together with the memory of shrill voices greeting Sigismundo brought Teodora Angelini to her mind. She was the chief of the ladies. She owed Bianca money. Lucrezia smiled wickedly to herself. She did not like Teodora Angelini. It would cause her no pain to squeeze Donna Teodora for information. She looked up at Angela, who was still standing beside her.

"Find a page and bid him tell Donna Teodora that I would like to speak with her at, say, the twentieth hour. That will give us time to have a midday trifle and for me to write to my father and tell him . . . No, I will tell him nothing until this matter is resolved. The last thing I want is to have Cesare up here roaring with rage because I have been insulted by my husband." She shuddered. "I do not wish to be a widow again."

"No fear of that here," Nicola said, nodding to Angela, who went out to speak to the page. Nicola turned away from the portiere and came close to put an arm around Lucrezia. "Not in Alfonso's own land."

"No, of course not," Lucrezia sighed. "Cesare has a quick temper, but he understands that the duke could not allow him to escape retribution. But he could embarrass the whole court by demanding apologies or making threats." She looked away from Nicola toward Angela, who had reentered the room as she spoke, and then quickly and brightly asked, "What would you like to eat and drink?"

Angela began to suggest a variety of breads and cheeses and perhaps some thin slices of cured ham with a light golden wine. Nicola said nothing but looked at Lucrezia with a faint expression of puzzlement, as if she knew Lucrezia did not care a fig for the embarrassment of the Court or the duke but wished to spare Alfonso.

The tinkle of a small bell on Lucrezia's standing desk brought Lucia from the bedchamber. Angela made her suggestions.

Lucrezia nodded approval, although the truth of the matter was that she scarcely heard what was said. She too wondered why she wanted to spare Alfonso. No, that was silly. She knew the answer. If Alfonso was frightened or beaten by Cesare, he would surely blame her and find ways to revenge himself on her as soon as Cesare was gone. It was her own safety she was ensuring in protecting Alfonso.

A moment later, however, it was clear that Nicola had not been thinking about Alfonso at all. She said, "If you do not intend to write about this matter to your father, you had better find a solution to Bianca's death quickly because someone else will surely tell him . . . and likely make the matter sound much worse than it is."

"Oh, blessed Mary," Lucrezia sighed, "you are right about that. I will have to write, but I can tell him that Master dei Carri said I must be blameless, and about the duke's strong support, and that despite his silly accusation, Alfonso came to me that very night and did his duty as a husband. Surely that will imply he does not think ill of me."

"Or even that he approves of what you did," Nicola said with a chuckle. "Likely that will make Cesare think better of Alfonso. You know Cesare could never understand why you were so grieved and angry about the death of your second husband. He said to me that husbands for you were like ripe figs in August."

Lucrezia shuddered and turned away from Nicola to open her writing desk and look for materials for her letter. Even as she drew out a sharpened quill, which she laid on the ledge of the desk that did not open, where the inkwells were inset, she realized that the pain of being reminded of her dear duke of Biscegli's death was less sharp, more distant. That caused her pain in itself. She chose a heavy sheet of paper, pulled it out, lowered the lid of the desk, and laid the paper down on it. Was she forgetting her love?

"Sorry," Nicola said, coming closer and touching her shoulder gently. "I should not have said that. I thought you were recovering from your grief."

Am I? Lucrezia wondered. She found a smile for Nicola but did not answer her, bending forward to dip her pen and begin her letter. She wrote the familiar salutation, but when she had to think what to write, her pen was soon idle. She stared ahead as if she were seeking words, but she was thinking of the first Alfonso. Her heart lightened as she realized she loved him still, a warmth of memory almost caressing her—but it no longer left an endless echoing emptiness because of knowing he was gone. Resolutely she bent her head over her letter. She would not think about what was filling that emptiness just yet.

By the time she was finished writing and had folded and sealed her letter, Lucia was back at the head of a short parade of kitchen staff. The maestro di sala ceremoniously carried a small table from against the wall; his assistant laid a fine white cloth upon it. Carefully folded napkins were laid alongside the three majolica plates that had been carried from the credenza. Lucrezia left her letter lying on the desk and allowed the maestro de sala to move her chair to the table. Stools to either side of the chair accommodated Nicola and Angela, and dishes were set, covers lifted off. Lucrezia smiled and shook a reproachful finger.

"Adriano, this was supposed to be a trifle, just a bite to tide us over until dinnertime. Now how will I eat my dinner if I must taste all this? And it all looks and smells delicious!"

The cook bowed, smiling. "This *is* only a trifle. Look, there are only four dishes, really. The little sides are condiments sweet and savory. No, no. I have no intention of spoiling your appetite for tonight's dinner. I have not forgotten that you will be eating here. I have some fowl that will be a delight and some forcemeat to be molded around a savory center. Ah"—he kissed his fingers—"you will eat and eat well, not only for yourself but for the little one also."

"Very well, Adriano, I will try," Lucrezia said, smiling as the cook served small, delicate portions from each of the dishes, "but I do not want to get so fat I can hardly waddle about."

She tasted a bite-sized morsel of glazed pork and followed it with some shredded cabbage in a sweet-tart sauce that perfectly complemented the meat. Then she reached eagerly for the next portion on her plate, which looked like finely minced fowl breast. She was surprised at her appetite. She had expected that the moment she started to eat Master dei Carri's description of Bianca would rise to her mind. And it had. But it hadn't curbed her hunger at all. The baby was demanding its share, she supposed, and then patted her still-flat belly, thinking, *I hope you closed your ears, little one; you are too young to learn about the horrors the good doctor was describing to me.*

While they ate, all three having second and even third helpings of this or that, Angela had been telling a long, pointless story into which Nicola interjected caustic comments now and again. Lucrezia silently blessed them both, pleased with being able to think her own thoughts. Those had been circling around her conversation with dei Carri, not about how he knew what had killed Bianca, but about the Mother of Poisons itself. There was something dei Carri had said, something about which she should have asked questions, but she could not pin down what sparked that thought or even the kind of questions she should have asked.

Eventually they were all replete and sat toying with their wine. The cook's staff asked whether they should clear the table, but Lucrezia shook her head.

"At the twentieth hour I am expecting one of the Ferrarese ladies, and I want *not* to offer her any food."

Adriano's dark eyes sparkled with rage. "Do they say that *my* food caused the lady's death?"

"No, no. Not your food. They have all, before I lost patience with them, eaten your food. They blame the poison that *I* put in the food."

"Ridiculous!" the cook exclaimed. "I know who comes to your table. We"—he gestured at the maestro di sala and his assistant, his own assistant, backed up near the credenza where they could step forward to remove and replace dishes or serve additional help- ings—"can assure the world that none of the ladies, except for Donna Angela and Donna Nicola, have eaten at your table in over six weeks. And Donna Angela and Donna Nicola are in the best of health. My food is good, and nothing in it caused any harm."

"Of course, Adriano. But I want to remind the lady I have invited to speak with me of that fact. When she sees all of you, she will remember that you were here when she was a guest also. She will remember that I have witnesses as to who eats at my table."

The cook bowed and stepped back against the wall. Angela looked at Lucrezia, who glanced at the clock, and then nodded to her. It was amost a quarter of an hour early, but it would seem gra- cious not to make Donna Teodora wait longer, or, if she was not there, put her in the wrong for not being there, waiting.

However, the page had delivered his message, Teodora was there, waiting, and Angela held back the portiere for her to enter. Angela then went back to the chest on which she and Nicola had been sit- ting earlier; Nicola followed her. Lucrezia nodded at Donna Teodora, but didn't invite the angular woman to sit.

"I will not offer you anything from my table, Donna Teodora," she said, "nor even offer you a stool . . . in case there should be some noxious substance in the food or on the seat."

"It was not we who made accusations," Teodora said.

Lucrezia grinned. "No, but the accuser has already been much closer to me than sitting on a stool . . . and without the protection of any clothing, so I must believe he does not really suspect me of using lethal substances. However, if you feel assured of my inno- cence, you may, of course, sit and, if you wish, eat."

"I have eaten already," Donna Teodora said. "However, I will be glad to accept your invitation to sit, madonna."

"Do take the stool from which Nicola rose in your presence. I could have had no time to contaminate that."

Donna Teodora seated herself and said, with scarcely veiled hostility, "To what do I owe the honor of this summons, madonna?"

"To the desire to give you news, some of it very good," Lucrezia said, smiling. "As part of my investigation into how Donna Bianca died and who could have desired the death of such a sweet and innocent person, I asked Master dei Carri, who examined the body and reported her death to Duke Ercole, how she died. He told me she was killed by aconite, known as monkshood or wolfbane, and called Mother of Poisons by the ancients. The poison works *very* swiftly. Thus the murderer would have had to be with her at the time she died or no longer than half a candlemark before."

"Then, of course, you are innocent," Donna Theodora said, "for we all know you were at the duke's play that evening and walked home with your ladies, Don Ferrante, Don Giulio, Don Sigismundo, and Ercole Strossi. In fact, we were with you for some time after we reached your apartment."

"Until, in fact, Don Alfonso summoned me to my bedchamber," Lucrezia said. "It is, of course, my hope that you will pass this information to all the ladies, as I would not want them to be anxious about their safety."

"I will be sure to do so," Donna Teodora said, seeming to make ready to rise.

"Do not go yet," Lucrezia urged. "I have only given you news, not the good news."

"I am sure Master dei Carri's news is very good news for all of us," Donna Teodora said, her voice flat.

"But mostly for me," Lucrezia nodded. "However, the news Don Sigismundo brought this morning will be specially good for you and Donna Bianca's fellow ladies-in-waiting. In a new will, Donna Bianca excused all debts owed to her and bequeathed to her fellow attendants equal shares in an estate. You, Elizabetta Dossi, Beatrice Tisio, and Diana Altoviti will share the income from that property."

To Lucrezia's intense interest, more relief than surprise showed on Teodora Angelini's face. "She did it!" she breathed. "I did not think she would."

"Whatever do you mean?" Lucrezia asked.

Donna Teodora blushed slightly but then looked accusingly at Lucrezia. "Some time ago we were talking, Elizabetta and I, about the difficulty of keeping up our appearance at Court. Bianca overheard us and told us that we must learn to manage better. I am afraid I lost patience with her and I answered that one must have something to manage before one learns to manage it. It seems that she had never understood that we had no income at all, that we had expected to be paid an allowance as your ladies—"

"Yes, indeed," Lucrezia interrupted with wide-eyed false sympathy. "I was sure that since Duke Ercole had appointed you, he would furnish that allowance. I understood, of course, that those people I brought with me would be my responsibility. Naturally, if the duke had provided an appanage suitable to the dowry I brought, I could have been more generous. But you know all this. What did Donna Bianca say when you told her of your sad state?"

"She said she would help us with loans while she was with us and . . . and leave us an income if she should happen to need to leave Court. We—we did not really believe her, although she gave us some money later that very day, because she was so . . . so scatterwitted. But it appears she was as good as her word."

Donna Teodora's voice trembled and her eyes filled with tears. Lucrezia was a touch regretful at wakening grief, but she also wondered whether the tears could be owing to fear or guilt. "You did not believe her, but you hoped?"

"Not enough to murder her," Teodora spat.

"Good gracious, no. I am not accusing you, but since I have accounted for where I was that night after the play, I hope you will forgive me if I ask the same of you?"

The woman's eyes glared hate, then she lowered them. "Unfortunately, I went alone to my apartment after I left yours and I remained quite alone. But then, I have no pages or messengers or devoted servants who can deliver 'gifts,' and I had no idea Bianca was going to die that night."

Lucrezia's breath caught. Stupid! How stupid she was not to realize that those determined to spread disgusting rumors about her would claim that if she did not administer the fatal dose to Bianca herself, she could afford to find someone else to do it for her. She forced herself into a slow curving of her lips—perhaps not a smile but apparently an expression that Donna Teodora took as a threat, because she bit her lip nervously.

"How fortunate it is that my sending a gift to any of the Ferrarese ladies would be so exceptional an act as to be remembered clearly by any messenger," Lucrezia said. "You have my leave to ask. Indeed, I would urge you to do so. And the other ladies? Donna Beatrice's room is very near Donna Bianca's apartment, is it not?"

"I suppose so, but she did not walk there with Donna Bianca. Bianca left us immediately after the play. She did not accompany us to your apartment. I assume she went back to her rooms, since she had told Elizabetta that she was expecting a visitor."

"I wonder if she told Elizabetta whom she expected to meet," Lucrezia mused, and then said more directly to Teodora, "Those ladies are not on duty today, are they?"

"No, madonna."

"Then I wonder if I could prevail upon you to find Donna Elizabetta and send her to speak to me . . . anytime this afternoon will do."

"Are not Ferrante and Giulio coming this afternoon?" Angela asked, sounding aggrieved.

"Oh, yes. I had forgotten. Oh, well, they may be gone by the time Donna Teodora finds Donna Elizabetta or . . . We will arrange something."

"I am sure you will," Donna Teodora said through tight lips as she rose.

She bowed only very slightly and, when Lucrezia had offered a nod and a bland smile in return, she stalked out, all stiff resentment.

"I think she does not like you," Nicola remarked, chuckling throatily.

"It is mutual," Lucrezia said. Then she rose and smiled at her cook and maestro di sala. "I thank you both, and your assistants also, for being so patient and standing witness for me. Now you may clear away. I hope I did not keep you so long that I will have made your preparations for dinner more difficult."

"I hope so too," Adriano said with a grim smile. "I left directions for Innocenzio to begin several dishes, those that take the longest to prepare. If they are not well under way, pity Innocenzio."

"Oh, if he was neglectful, I do," Lucrezia said, returning the smile, "but I cannot believe he was. I am sure you will find everything proceeding as it should."

She gestured for Nicola and Angela to join her in her bedchamber and left the cook and maestro di sala to clear away the remains of the meal and restore her reception room.

"Now, what shall I wear that will make me look fragile and helpless?" Lucrezia asked.

"For Ferrante and Giulio?" Angela sounded very surprised. "You know they are both very fond of you already and eager to help in any way they can."

Nicola laughed. "Yes, Angela, but you know how men are. They are all too likely to hold back this or that which they feel are peccadillos of male privilege and no business of a woman who might cavil or criticize. If Lucrezia looks weak and helpless, they will not bristle up their neck ruffs."

Angela sniffed and shook her head at both the other women, who were laughing. "You want to wear that dark blue gammura, then," she said. "We all agreed that it made you look too pale, and silver sleeves or a very pale blue to make your arms look limp. And not too much jewelry . . . silver, not gold, I think."

Lucia went to get the articles called for and laid several pairs of sleeves out on the bed while she sought for the silver ones. Both Angela and Nicola exclaimed over two sets they had forgotten. By coincidence the sleeves were just the right colors for what they were wearing and Lucrezia bade them try the sleeves on. The effect was so pleasing that they decided to wear them and save themselves the trouble of changing for dinner, which they would be eating privately in Lucrezia's apartment.

All three were admiring themselves and each other when Ascanio scratched on the door and called through a crack he opened that Donna Elizabetta had arrived and said Madonna Lucrezia wished to see her. Lucrezia looked from Angela to Nicola and whispered that they should go out into the public reception room and, if Giulio or Ferrante or both should arrive while she was with Elizabetta, they should keep the men there. Then she led her ladies into the private reception room and told Ascanio to show in Donna Elizabetta.

Angela and Nicola followed the page out into the public reception room and a few moments later the portiere lifted again to show Elizabetta, plump and uncertain, hovering in the doorway until Lucrezia gestured for her to enter.

"If you are not afraid I have poisoned the seat, please take a stool," she said, but she smiled because Elizabetta was the quietest of the women.

"I am not afraid of you, madonna," Elizabetta replied, bringing one of the stools near to Lucrezia's chair. "All that shouting, that was only Don Alfonso being Don Alfonso. Something had angered him and it got all mixed up with poor Bianca's death and you are his wife and thus to blame."

Tears filled her eyes and she raised a kerchief to her face. Lucrezia made no reply for a moment, stunned by Elizabetta's keen perception. Could she—and common rumor—have been wrong about Alfonso? Could he have had noble-born mistresses and been so secretive about it that no one had ever discovered? Could Elizabetta have been one of his women, Bianca another?

"You know Don Alfonso very well," she finally managed to say.

Elizabetta smiled. "I do not know Don Alfonso at all, but I did know his late wife well, and we who waited upon her heard Don Alfonso often enough, even if we seldom saw him." She sighed. "Donna Anna was not as sensible a woman as you, madonna. She was virtuous herself and found herself happy, except for Don Alfonso's behavior. She was sure that Don Alfonso would be equally happy were he equally virtuous—"

Lucrezia choked on a giggle. She had a sudden vision of her husband mounted above her, his face rigid with passion, totally enwrapped in his quest for sexual pleasure. A strangled sound forced its way past her lips as she imagined Alfonso's reaction to any woman urging virtue on him.

"Yes," Elizabetta said. "But Donna Anna could not laugh and he . . . ah, expressed himself freely about her opinion. True, he did not accuse her of poisoning anyone—"

"Indeed, it is the poisoning about which I wished to speak to you," Lucrezia said hastily. It was pointless to pursue any question of Alfonso's involvement. "Did Donna Teodora explain to you what we discussed when she was with me this morning?"

"No, madonna. She said only that you wished to question me about my whereabouts the night that Bianca died. We were all— well, all except Bianca—in your reception room until Don Alfonso called to you from your bedchamber. Then we all left. Donna Diana and I walked together to the outer door, for we were engaged in a discussion of whether sweet floral or sharp citrus scents were more refreshing."

"How interesting," Lucrezia said.

"Perfumes are one of my weaknesses," Elizabetta admitted, "and I have collected sets of scents and lotions, some of which I use to lighten my mood. Diana has been angry about something for weeks and I wondered whether my perfumes could calm her. We walked to my lodging together, but I cannot say exactly how long she stayed before I summoned a manservant to see her home."

"You did not hear the church bells?"

Elizabetta frowned. "Yes, I did. That was just before Diana left. She heard the bells too, and said it was late. So that must have been Matins? Lauds? I cannot be sure."

"It is not idle curiosity on my part," Lucrezia assured her, and repeated what dei Carri had said about how quickly aconite worked.

"I see," Elizabetta breathed. "Then if we were together when Bianca died, neither I nor Diana could be guilty."

"That is true."

"But . . . but why in the world should any of us want to hurt Bianca? Even if Diana resented Bianca's flirting, Bianca was the kindest, most harmless person in the world."

"She also left you a very nice income in her will."

"Left me an income?" Elizabetta's eyes grew round as florins.

"You did not expect it? Donna Teodora told me that you and she were discussing how short of money you were, that Bianca overheard you and gave you a little lecture on managing your income better, and that she said, when it was made clear to her that you had no income, that she would lend you money for the present and leave you an income in the future. Had you forgotten that?"

"Forgotten? How could I, when I had to go to her for help more than once? She wanted me to pawn my jewels, but I could not. They are all that is left to us. If I pawn them and cannot redeem them, my daughter will have nothing."

There was bitterness in Elizabetta's voice, but then she shook her head and her eyes widened with wonder again. "I never believed she would leave us anything. Why should she? I cannot believe it now."

"Then you had better ask Don Niccolò da Correggio. I understand that he has been made the executor of that estate and, for all I know, of Donna Bianca's entire estate."

"Thank you for telling me, madonna. Thank you."

Lucrezia nodded acceptance of the thanks and said that Elizabetta could go. She watched the woman walk out, wondering whether she realized how desperate she had sounded when she talked about saving her jewels for her daughter. She said she never believed Bianca would leave her anything, but she also called Bianca the kindest of women—even though Bianca had urged her to give up her precious jewels. During one of those discussions, had Bianca assured her she would not need to worry about pawning the jewels in the future? Had Elizabetta believed her at the moment and decided to act before Bianca could change her wavering mind?

Elizabetta had been quick enough to see that she could not be accused if Diana had been with her when Bianca died. Lucrezia bit her lip in frustration. But no one knew just when Bianca had died. How was she to discover that?

7

LUCREZIA WINCED slightly as Don Giulio's and Don Ferrante's loud voices preceded them through the portiere. She could have used a few more moments of quiet to think, but she smiled at the two men, realizing that they were excited and flushed with pride.

"We may have found what you want," Giulio said with a laugh. "There is a young man who Donna Bianca refused, and he was seen by, believe it or not, Alfonso's manservant, hanging around the corner of the corridor in which Donna Bianca's apartment is."

"It was not he who killed her," Don Ferrante said. "I do not believe that. Alessandro Guadaruzzi *likes* to be scorned. It gives him an excuse to linger at a distance and moan of his blighted life . . . which encourages other women to try to soothe him. Guadaruzzi is the kind that likes being petted by older women. I am not certain he would know what to do with a passionate young woman who responded to his advances."

"Ferrante! What a dreadful thing to say." But Nicola was laughing as she spoke.

"Do you know Guadaruzzi?" Lucrezia asked.

"Yes, and so do you," Nicola replied. "Do you remember that Moresche dance when the men were naked above the waist and below wore *very* short kilts? The women were all laughing and pointing when they leapt and their private parts peeped out, but Guadaruzzi was standing as close to the stage as he could get with his eyes and his mouth both wide open. . . ."

"I remember," Lucrezia said. "But a catamite can be vicious." She glanced sidelong at Ferrante, who was not, according to rumor, totally immune to a pretty boy.

"Oh, certainly," Ferrante agreed, impervious to her look, "but his situation with Donna Bianca would not arouse any *real* jealousy"— he shrugged—"any jealousy at all in him. He only chose her so that he *could* moan about her taking other lovers. He would not have killed her because she rejected him. I think he moans about poverty too and the older ladies 'help' him. Anyway, I discovered something more interesting than Guadaruzzi. I was talking to Marino Sanuto and he told me that when Alfonso was heard accusing you of poisoning Bianca, Guido del Palagio turned pale and wavered on his feet."

Lucrezia frowned. "I remember someone saying that, but I thought nothing of it. Palagio is a poet . . . or thinks he is a poet. Very likely he believed turning pale and growing faint was the romantic thing to do."

"That is possible, but Palagio was there, in Donna Bianca's apartment the night she died." Giulio cast a triumphant glance of mingled dislike and irritation at his half-brother. "Which is why I mentioned Guadaruzzi first. I am not a fool and know what Guadaruzzi is as well as anyone. But when I taxed him with being jealous of Donna Bianca and killing her because she rejected him, he wept with terror and swore he had never entered her rooms but that others had. He then told me that Palagio had been in and that there was another visitor to Bianca's apartment while he was watching."

"When?" Lucrezia asked eagerly. "If I know when Bianca died, I will be able to mark some people as innocent and cross them off the list of those who might have committed the crime."

"Hmmm," Giulio said, looking a trifle shamefaced at not realizing something so obvious. "I didn't ask him the time, but he told me he followed Bianca back to her apartment after the play."

"Then we can make a good guess at the time," Nicola said. "The play ended near midnight—seventh hour, that would be—and I doubt Guadaruzzi would have waited more than an hour if no one came. That would be long enough and yet short enough for him to get himself to one of his ladies before she actually went to bed."

"Yes." Lucrezia nodded. "That is about how long we were in my rooms that night. I did not expect anyone would stay, but the play was really good and we were all talking about it. I remember I was thinking that perhaps I should send Lucia for cakes and wine and then I heard Alfonso asking where I was. So the men Guadaruzzi saw must have arrived between half or a quarter after the seventh hour and the beginning of the eighth."

"I agree," Nicola said.

"Yes, but that doesn't say whether Bianca was alive or dead." Lucrezia sighed.

"I think she must have been dead before the second visitor arrived," Giulio said slowly, his brows knitted in thought. "Guadaruzzi saw Palagio enter, but he did not leave immediately, I am not sure why."

"How could you be?" Angela said, encouraging him.

Giulio smiled at her. "Anyway, Palagio stayed for a half candlemark . . . perhaps a little longer or a little less. He was going down the corridor in the direction that Guadaruzzi would have to go, so Guadaruzzi waited and, to his surprise, another man went into Bianca's room. He, however, scarcely went in before he came out again and ran back the way he had come."

"You are right, Giulio," Angela said. "Bianca must have been dead, so the second visitor was frightened away. Who was he?" She was proud as a hen with one precocious chick because Giulio did have a brain he could use when he wanted to do so.

"I asked that. Cloaked and with a brimmed hat pulled far down over his face," Giulio said, shaking his head. "Guadaruzzi could not see who the second visitor was."

"Could it have been a woman?" Lucrezia asked.

Giulio shrugged. "I have no idea, but I cannot see how that matters if Bianca was already dead. If she was, then Palagio is the killer."

"He might have been," Lucrezia agreed slowly. "He was there long enough, according to what Master dei Carri told me about how long it would take for the poison to work, but how did he give it to her? There was nothing to eat or drink in the apartment. Did he bring it with him? Did Guadaruzzi say he was carrying anything?"

"He didn't say anything about that," Giulio admitted. "I think the best thing you could do is talk to them yourself."

"Which? Guadaruzzi? Palagio?"

"What's this about Palagio?"

Everyone started and turned toward the doorway, where Alfonso was holding the portiere aside. He had obviously come in the front door of Lucrezia's apartment and walked through the public reception room. However, the silence in there was palpable; only because she had previously heard voices did Lucrezia know of the avid listeners. Lucrezia closed her mouth, which had been, like everyone else's, open with shock.

"Come in, my lord," she said, rising and extending her hand.

Alfonso looked doubtful of the welcome, but he let go of the portiere and walked forward into the room. "Why are you discussing Guido del Palagio?" he asked.

His harsh voice was by no means hushed, but it was also not pitched to carry through the door curtain. Lucrezia was tempted to smile at the confirmation of her assumption that his bellowing about Bianca's death was designed to reach the listeners outside. It was interesting that for a man seemingly so indifferent to those around him, Alfonso understood just how to use his voice. Clever, she thought, he was much cleverer than he allowed to be seen . . . which made him cleverer still.

"Palagio," Alfonso repeated, still not raising his voice. "Why are you talking about that Neapolitan at all? I hope you are not trying to turn my brothers toward Spain. You cannot tell me that his poetry enthralls you!"

"Good God, no!" Lucrezia exclaimed. "I have many faults in your eyes, I know, but please do not add a complete lack of taste to them."

She was thinking that it was not Giulio or Ferrante that Duke Ercole suspected of leaning toward Spain; however, she decided it was safer to ignore the political taunt, and seeing the spark of impatience in her husband's eyes decided to answer his real question.

"We were talking about Palagio because he might have been Donna Bianca's lover and was seen entering her apartment on the night she died." Then, to be totally safe, she added, "But he is no Neapolitan."

Alfonso looked startled. "Not a Neapolitan? How can you say that?"

Lucrezia laughed. "Because he has not the accent and he is totally ignorant of Naples."

After a brief silence while he seemed to digest her answer, Alfonso said, "But I thought it was because he was Aragonese that you accepted him into your court and allowed him to wait upon you."

"I accepted him because he came with a letter from your sister, Madonna Isabella, saying he had been at her court and wished to enlarge his experience by travel." Lucrezia smiled wickedly. "To her credit, Isabella said nothing about his poetry, and once I heard it, I thought she was simply trying to be rid of him—or that by sending him to me she was commenting on what she thought of my literary taste. Still, Isabella *had* sent him, so all I could do was refuse to listen to his dreadful verses or accept his written poems. I could not turn him away."

Alfonso drew closer. Politely the other four drew back toward the windows. "Did he not say to you that he was Neapolitan or . . . or Spanish?" Alfonso asked softly.

"Yes, he did, which was how I came to discover he was no such thing. Naturally, when he claimed connection with Aragon, I asked about Naples. Palagio knew nothing, nothing at all, not so much as a common traveler through Naples and the surrounding area would know. And then I realized that his accent was not at all like my uncle's or my father's when he grows excited and forgets to watch his speech. And he did not know one single word of Spanish, not even a common exclamation."

"His speech is not of Ferrara either," Alfonso said, "nor of Mantua or elsewhere in the north."

Lucrezia nodded agreement. "Even though he used many little phrases that I have heard Isabella use, it was as if that was apurpose to hide other forms of speech. Of course, I only spoke to him at length that once. His poetry was awful, and I had no interest in the man. If he wanted to hide from where he came and imply it was from Aragon, I did not care."

"A spy, perhaps?"

"If he was," Lucrezia said, laughing, "there was little enough to be discovered from spending time in my reception room."

"Unless he thought I would be there more often than I was," Alfonso said thoughtfully. "That was what I believed when I thought he might be a spy for the Spanish. Which brings me back to what I asked in the beginning. Even if he was Donna Bianca's lover and was in her apartment that night, why should you want to talk to him?"

Lucrezia stared at him for a moment with wide eyes and thinned lips. "Did you not listen to me at dinner last night? Do you not listen to *anything* I say? I told you then that I intend to discover who killed that poor woman, both to avenge her and to clear my name, *which you smirched.*"

"Nonsense. That was a mistake." Now Alfonso's voice was loud enough to make Lucrezia back up a step. "I was overset by shock and feared that you had taken a dislike to my latest mistress. But I have spoken to Master dei Carri about Bianca's death and he tells me whoever killed her would have had to be with her when she died or only a short time before her death." He laughed obscenely. "I know where you were at that time—under me, not killing Bianca."

Lucrezia was sorely tempted to slap his face, but she repressed the impulse. Knowing Alfonso, he might slap her back—although she had to admit that he had never struck her, nor tried to hurt her, even when his hands worked with fury because she had deliberately provoked him. She repressed a sigh also. He was not angry despite the loud voice. He was being subtle and trying to make up for accusing her by raising his voice enough that another set of listeners would hear him say she could not have committed the crime.

"Unfortunately," she said, coming closer again and speaking too softly to be heard in the next room because there was no sense wasting Alfonso's effort, "one of the Ferrarese ladies your father appointed to be in waiting has already told me—and I suppose others too—that a lady in my position had no need to go to Bianca herself. I could have sent someone to her with a gift of poison."

"Who said that? Who dared say such a thing?"

"You did first," she remarked, but her voice was calm and amused. "It is not so easy to clean a stain from a reputation when there are those who wish the smirch to remain. I told you that to clear my name—and yours, because by tying yourself to Donna Bianca you have given a reason for wishing to be rid of her—the true killer must be exposed to the world."

"But your women can and will be silenced!"

"Alfonso . . ." She stepped still closer and took one of his hands, which were now closed into fists. "To threaten or dismiss the women would make matters worse. Instead help me, or at least do not hinder me, in trying to find the killer."

"How can I help? I know nothing about Bianca's death. She was—" He stopped speaking abruptly and looked fleetingly at his brothers and her women. "She was just another woman," he went on, "and she cost me nothing to use. There was no reason at all for me to wish her ill."

"Just now the help I need is in speaking to Don Niccolò da Carreggio in private," Lucrezia said promptly. "You could bring him to me through your apartment. I am reluctant to send for him myself because—"

She stopped speaking when the portiere was lifted and her maestro di sala, Roberto Malaleone, stepped into the room. He moved a few steps sideways and stopped, his back to the wall, waiting until she had time to attend to him. Lucrezia silently blessed his arrival. She had reconsidered her first impulse to tell Alfonso about Bianca's pursuit of Correggio and needed a moment to decide on the best reason for needing to speak to him privately. Thus she gladly gestured for Roberto to approach.

"May I set up the table for dinner, madonna?" he asked.

"Yes. No, wait. Alfonso, will you join Angela, Nicola, and myself for dinner?"

"Are you going to invite Ferrante and Giulio?" he asked, glancing sidelong at his brothers.

"Of course, since they are here," Lucrezia replied blandly, suppressing a smile.

It was impossible to tell what Alfonso thought, from the lack of expression on his face. All he said was, "My father is not thrilled with their devotion to your ladies."

"I am not thrilled with your father," Lucrezia snapped in response. "When he chooses to please me, I will try harder to please him."

Alfonso stared at her for a moment, his full lips twitching. "Are you going to speak about nothing but the murder the entire time we eat?" he asked.

"No." Lucrezia sighed. "I have had enough talk about that today, but I really must speak to Don Niccolò." She had found an excellent reason for wanting to see Correggio and for keeping it secret—and it was true too. "Your father told me last night that he had put Don Niccolò in charge of investigating Bianca's death. I want to know whether he has discovered anything I have not and to share with him what I have learned."

Alfonso rolled his eyes heavenward. "If this is absolutely the last word on this subject . . . yes, I will bring him and I will stay to dine."

Lucrezia laughed and called out to Nicola to ask Ferrante and Giulio if they would stay and eat and, when her question had been answered in the affirmative, told Roberto to set up a table for six and send a message to Adriano in the kitchen that six rather than three would dine. Roberto drew himself up and replied that Adriano was already waiting and that there would be food enough. Of course there was. Nor was there any awkwardness about finding a subject for conversation.

No sooner were they seated than Angela said, "We have been talking about the masked ball that the duke plans to hold on Saturday. What costume will you wear, Don Alfonso?"

"Now, if I told you," he responded, smiling slightly—most men smiled at Angela even when she was being particularly bird-witted—"would that not betray who I was?"

Angela pouted. "Yes, of course. That is why I am asking. I am no good at guessing. I know everyone's clothes, and when they are dressed differently I do not recognize them at all. Giulio has told me that he will come as one of the Pope's Swiss guards."

"Ah, but Giulio wishes you to recognize him."

"And you do not?"

Alfonso laughed. "Of course not. What if I wished to do something at the ball that might not be approved? Would that not be a wonderful time to misbehave? When no one could recognize me?"

Lucrezia glanced quickly at her husband and then away, considerably surprised by his playfulness. Then she lowered her eyes to the plate that a servant was filling and gestured for him to stop, that she had enough. She was also surprised by the irritation she felt over Angela's ability to induce a lightness in Alfonso that he had never shown with her. That was ridiculous. She had never envied Angela's light touch with men. Only with Alfonso? That too was ridiculous. With some concentration Lucrezia began to eat.

"And you, Lucrezia, what will you wear?" Alfonso asked, turning his dark eyes on her.

"I will be dressed as Hebe." She saw from the blankness in Alfonso's expression that he had no idea what she was talking about and went on to explain, "Hebe was the cupbearer of the gods." And then, before she knew what she was going to say, she added, "I have no intention of doing anything I would wish to conceal, so I don't mind anyone knowing my costume."

To her intense chagrin, Alfonso's lips twitched again and a fleeting expression of gratification touched his face before he turned away. He was as expressionless as usual, however, when he looked at Ferrante and repeated his question. Ferrante replied that he too had nothing to hide and said he was coming as Ares, the Greek god of war. Lucrezia knew Ferrante had very shapely legs, and she suspected their exposure by a costume of little besides a lion skin had been a determining factor.

After that the talk became more general as everyone first tried to guess what costumes their acquaintances would wear and then went on to suggest appropriate costumes for those they liked least in the Court. Alfonso had withdrawn into his usual taciturnity, although he laughed once or twice at Nicola's sharp-witted costume choices and shook his head over some of Giulio's and Ferrante's implied descriptions of his father's favorites. He made no suggestions himself, nor did Lucrezia, who claimed that as Alfonso's wife she wanted to be sure she offended no one.

They all had seconds of favored dishes, and Roberto twice sent down for more wine, but eventually the sweets and savories were finished. Then, while the servants cleared the dishes and replaced the table against the wall, Nicola took her lute from one of the chests and played while Angela sang. Giulio and Ferrante entreated Lucrezia to dance, but she shook her head at them, whereupon Alfonso took his leave. Not long after, the other men also departed. Nicola put away her instrument, Angela pushed together some large cushions and dropped down on them, supporting her back against the daybed that Lucrezia first sat and then lay down upon.

After a few minutes of comfortable silence, Angela giggled. "I think we are going to civilize Don Alfonso," she said. "Did you hear him jest with me about his costume for the ball? I don't believe he ever did so before."

Nicola did not smile or laugh. She looked uneasy. "What did he want, madonna?" she asked.

Lucrezia slowly shook her head. "I don't know, unless someone brought home to him how stupid he was to accuse me and he is trying to prove that he never really thought me guilty. Certainly to eat a meal with a person implies you do not suspect that person of using poison. I know the duke was very angry with him. It is possible that he spoke to Alfonso again after last night's dinner." She laughed softly. "I was rather pointed in my objections to what Alfonso had done when I spoke to Duke Ercole."

Nicola chuckled. "Yes, we all heard that remark about Ferrara being safe while you were living in it. I think—"

"Madonna?" the voice of the page stopped whatever Nicola was about to say.

Lucrezia turned toward the boy. "Yes, Ascanio?"

"Donna Diana Altoviti is here. She said that Donna Teodora Angelini told her you wished to speak with her."

Lucrezia frowned. She remembered asking Donna Teodora to send Elizabetta Dossi to her, but she was sure she had not asked for anyone else. Not that it mattered, since she did want to speak to all the women, but she did not trust Donna Teodora and wondered why she had done more than she was asked. Possibly talking to Diana would make that clear. She nodded to the page and he stepped out. At another nod, Nicola and Angela again withdrew to the chest by the window.

"You wished to see me, madonna?" Diana asked as soon as she had come close enough not to need to shout.

For one moment Lucrezia did not respond. Something about the way Diana spoke—not what she said, but her accent—seemed important. Then she pushed that notion to the back of her mind, resolving to try to remember and consider it later. To Diana she smiled and nodded, gestured toward the stool on which Nicola had been sitting and equally to the cushions Angela had used.

"Yes, I did, but the matter is not important." Lucrezia made a deprecating sound and shook her head as Diana sat down on the stool. "Now, that is a stupid thing for me to say. It was not important that I speak to you at once, but the matter may indeed be important to you. I have learned that Donna Bianca left you a share in one of her estates so that you would have an income."

Donna Diana did not look at all surprised and only very mildly pleased. "That was very kind of her, because when she told me I thanked her but said I did not need it. I have sufficient income from the perfumes and lotions I mix. Then poor Bianca said it would be wrong for her to leave me out when she was naming the other ladies who shared her duty." Diana smiled. "I did not argue very hard. An extra and assured income is never to be despised, and, of course, there was a very good chance that she would change her mind. Poor Bianca was not known for her steadiness of purpose."

"Could that have been a reason for doing away with her?" Lucrezia asked innocently. "I mean, if someone was in desperate need of the money, could that person have decided to assure him-self—no, herself—of obtaining it by making sure Bianca died too soon to change the provisions of her will?"

"No. Impossible." Diana shuddered. "Only Donna Beatrice is hard-pressed for money, and I cannot imagine . . . I cannot believe . . . No. Besides, no one was really sure that Bianca had even added that provision to her will. She spoke to us about it only a few weeks after we were assigned to your service and never mentioned it again . . . at least she never mentioned it again to me."

"That seems to have been the case. Donna Teodora—I believe it was she who told you to come and speak to me?" Diana nodded. Lucrezia continued, "She seemed surprised that Donna Bianca had not changed her mind or, more likely, forgotten about the promise she had made."

"Yes. Donna Bianca was very good-natured, very desirous of being helpful, but . . . light of purpose. And she did not seem to see that her lightness could do harm, never realized how much suffering—" Diana stopped speaking and shrugged.

"Surely you do not mean that she aroused hope about financial relief and then one of the ladies was bitterly disappointed?"

"Oh, no. I should not think so. We all knew her well by then. I was thinking of the men she encouraged and then dropped. Some of them . . . ah . . . looked to Bianca for help. She might not have been aware of how much of a disappointment they felt when she no longer accepted their attentions."

"Was Guido del Palagio one of those?"

"Guido del Palagio?" Diana repeated, her expression gone blank. "I do not know . . . Oh, yes, the young poet who was so overset when he heard Don Alfonso shouting that you had poisoned Bianca. I cannot see why he should have been. He knew her, of course, from waiting to see you in your public reception room, but they gave no signs of being . . . attached. Why do you ask?"

"Because Palagio was seen entering and leaving Bianca's chamber after she had returned from the play. She had told Donna Teodora that she was expecting a visitor—I suppose to ask her to make her excuses to me for not finishing her duty with the rest of you. Palagio could have killed her."

Diana's lips parted as if to speak, but she closed her mouth again and shook her head. "I had no idea," she said finally. "I knew she did not appear in your chamber with the rest of us, of course, but I did not know she had gone off by herself or that Palagio intended to see her that night."

"I know you were discussing the play with Don Guilio and Angela, but where did you go after my husband called me away?"

"I did not go to Donna Bianca's room and murder her," Diana said angrily.

Lucrezia laughed. "Well, even if you did, I do not expect you to tell me that. Still, I would like to know."

Diana looked at her, then shrugged. "I went off with Elizabetta Dossi. She wanted me to smell some perfumes she had. I suppose she wanted me to duplicate them, although she did not say so. There were several she had bought from Madonna Isabella when she was here for your wedding. Elizabetta pretends to have money enough and flaunts those diamonds of hers, but she cannot really afford Donna Isabella's prices. Likely she will ask me to make up a perfume and put it in Isabella's flask when she has used up what she has."

"You were in a good mood?"

Diana looked at Lucrezia in apparent surprise, then shrugged. "Not particularly, but not in a *bad* mood either. I suppose I felt dull after the play and the talk." Then her expression became shadowed and she shivered. "After we knew what had happened, it was terrible . . . terrible. I kept thinking about poor Bianca. Not all the time. I remember laughing at some things Marino Sanuto said about Bernadino Zambotto who had rushed off after you left us, but . . ."

Lucrezia nodded. "But the thought of her death returns. Yes. And the question of who would have done such a thing. I do not wish her murder to haunt me forever because she is unavenged."

"Madonna, it is not my place to advise you, of course, but you should put it aside. No one ever seriously believed that you had anything to do with Bianca's death. We were all shocked by what Don Alfonso said, but within five minutes we knew it was a mistake that he was making. And as for vengeance, I don't believe Donna Bianca would have wanted that. She was a sweet, forgiving creature."

Lucrezia laughed, but then her eyes and mouth grew hard. "Perhaps she was, but I am not. I will see her killer caught and punished."

Diana sighed. "You are a most suitable bride for the Este family. The duke is so . . . determined."

"Not as determined as I," Lucrezia said, thinking more of her appanage than of the murder. "And if I win this battle, you and my other ladies may profit from my victory."

"Then I must wish you good fortune," Diana said.

"Thank you." Lucrezia smiled too. "And I will not keep you any longer. Thank you for coming and giving so much of your free time to me."

"I was glad to come. We would all be glad truly to serve you, madonna."

"Perhaps someday . . . if the duke is less determined than I."

Nicola and Angela did not remain long with Lucrezia after Diana Altoviti was gone. It had been a day full of tensions, and even though it was not as late as an evening in which the duke had a play presented, they all found themselves tired and longing for their beds.

Even so, Lucrezia had no intention of falling asleep before Alfonso made his nightly visit, and she had Lucia brush her golden hair into a shining waterfall. But he did not come at his usual time. To her surprise, she felt bitterly disappointed and then furious with herself for that disappointment. She remembered what Nicola had asked her after Angela remarked that they were going to civilize Alfonso. Nothing was going to civilize Alfonso; he did not wish to be civilized. But Nicola had asked, "What did he want?" And now that Lucrezia thought back on what he had said and done, she sensed all his talk had been a cover for something.

It had nothing to do with his reason for coming and for coming through her public reception room. That, she was sure, was to show everyone that he no longer thought, or had never thought, her guilty of Bianca's death. And that was likely why he had stayed to eat at her table, but the conversation about Palagio . . . Apparently Alfonso had believed Palagio to be a Spanish spy or to have Spanish connections, and something about learning he was not Neapolitan or a spy for Spain had . . . had lightened his spirit.

Lucrezia sighed and turned to her side. If he had come last night as if he were desperate to be with her, why not tonight? What had changed? Dimly Lucrezia knew she knew but did not want to know, and she let sleep take her.

Not for long, however. She had barely closed her eyes when a weight on the edge of the bed that was Alfonso's brought her awake. His body was warm and hard when it slid in beside her, but instead of pushing her onto her back and mounting her, he pulled her into his arms.

"Are you awake, Lucrezia?"

"Yes," she replied sleepily, and then laughed. "Would it matter to you?"

"Not for my ordinary purpose, but I need to talk to you. I gather it was my brothers who squeezed Guadaruzzi, so that he spilled the story of Palagio. How did they discover that Guadaruzzi was watching Bianca's apartment?"

Lucrezia searched her memory. She knew Ferrante . . . no, Ferrante had told her what Guadaruzzi had said, but it was Giulio who had told her how he found Guadaruzzi.

"Giulio said your manservant had seen . . ." Her voice trailed off as the significance of that became apparent.

"Yes, my manservant." Alfonso's words grated like a saw tearing at a hard log. "When I saw Giulio and Ferrante and heard Palagio's name, I guessed you were hearing too much. And now you are asking yourself what my manservant was doing near Bianca's apartment."

Lucrezia shuddered once but did not raise her head from her husband's shoulder. Had his manservant been keeping watch for him? Had he already been in the apartment waiting for Bianca? Had he killed her and left by the back door so that Guadaruzzi never saw him?

"Perhaps she *was* your leman and he was waiting to let you know when she returned and whether she was alone."

Lucrezia kept her voice low and even. Had she not had years of practice at hiding terror and revulsion, she would have torn free and screamed for help. But she knew there was no help for her. Not if Alfonso was Bianca's killer. Her only safety was to deny what she knew—but she had been so sure murder by poison was not Alfonso's way. She tried not to let her body stiffen, and must have been successful, because Alfonso showed no sign of noticing her tension.

"He was waiting for just that purpose," he admitted, "and fortunately he saw Guadaruzzi and warned me he was there, which was why I was cloaked and hatted."

Cloaked and hatted! Lucrezia barely restrained herself from hugging and kissing her husband. If he was the cloaked and hatted man that Guadaruzzi saw enter and leave Bianca's apartment, Alfonso had not killed her. He had not been inside long enough even to force a drink down her throat.

Through her thoughts, Lucrezia heard Alfonso continue, "But as soon as I opened the door, I saw . . ." He lay silent for some moments, his arm tightening around Lucrezia as if he sought comfort from her warm, living body. "I stepped out faster than I had walked in. I did not go near her or touch her. I had no idea that Palagio had been there before me. But why? Why should he kill her?"

"Tomorrow I will ask him," Lucrezia said, her body soft now against her husband's.

8

LUCREZIA WOKE from a restless sleep far earlier than usual on Friday morning and rang her bell for Lucia. She remembered clearly that she had as much as promised Alfonso that she would find out whether Palagio had killed Bianca, but the truth was that she had no idea how to lay hands on him, and she was also afraid to confront him. Unlike Duke Ercole or Alfonso, Palagio—who had probably killed one woman already—had more to fear from exposure of his crime than from Cesare or the Pope. Palagio had no realm on which the wrath of those might fall, no great inheritance to preserve.

Aside from that, she did not even know where he lodged, except that it was not in either palace. Possibly one of her women knew where to find him, but she hated to ask them and open the door to more gossip, or, worse yet, have word of her seeking him come to his ears and warn him. She had fallen asleep with those doubts in her mind, which accounted for her uneasy slumber, but she had somehow solved the problem, perhaps in her dreams.

Before she and Alfonso had parted the previous night, she had reminded him of his promise to bring Correggio to her, and he agreed to do so before breakfast. Correggio, of course, was the answer to seizing Palagio for questioning. That was rightly his duty, if Duke Ercole had assigned the investigation into Bianca's death to him. Moreover, Don Niccolò was far more likely to be able to extract the truth from Palagio—especially if some force were required to extract that truth—than she.

Smiling, Lucrezia instructed Lucia to help her wash and comb her hair. Then she donned her loveliest bedgown, having decided to receive Correggio in her bedchamber. With Alfonso there, no doubts could be raised in his mind or anyone else's as to the propriety of the meeting. No one might ever know at all. If Correggio came and went through Alfonso's apartment, not even the pages would know he had come, nor could the sound of his voice carry to any curious ears in her public reception room.

Elegantly arrayed, propped on pillows, and with the bedclothes straightened, Lucrezia bade Lucia bring her small writing desk and prepared to explain to her father and her brother what had happened the previous day. She had already written short notes describing Bianca's death and mentioning very lightly and in passing Alfonso's behavior. Now she was prepared to write at length about his efforts to exonerate her, about how he had come to her bed the very night he had been so hysterical, had said for all to hear that she could not have harmed Bianca, and had capped that by dining at her table together with his brother and half-brother.

She had completed the shorter, more direct letter to Cesare and begun on the more detailed explanation to the Pope when a brief scratch on the door heralded Alfonso's arrival. He stopped short when he saw Lucrezia in the bed; plainly he had not expected to find her in her bedchamber.

"Come in," Lucrezia urged, signing for Lucia to remove the writing desk. "I thought we would be more private here. There are often keen ears listening in my public reception room, and there is something I must ask Don Niccolò that it is important none should hear."

Alfonso began to look wary, but he advanced into the room. Don Niccolò followed. Lucrezia smiled at them both and invited them to sit on the low chests that were fitted around the sides and foot of the bed. Covered with Turkey carpets, the chests served for storage, as a step up into the high bed, and for seats for anyone who wished to talk to the person in the bed. Alfonso sat close beside her, where he could put a hand on her arm if he needed to signal her to abandon a line of questioning or disclosure.

Correggio bowed slightly and sat near the foot of the bed, where he would have the best view of Lucrezia's face. "I am honored," he said. "In what way may I serve you?"

"First and foremost by laying your hands on Guido del Palagio and asking him what he was doing in Donna Bianca's chambers the night she died. In fact, I have information that the lady was dead within minutes of his leaving her apartment."

"What?" Don Niccolò got out the word and sat staring.

"I would say to arrest him for her murder, except that I know there is a back way into her apartment. It is possible that someone was waiting, hidden, in her room and poisoned her before Palagio entered."

Correggio continued to stare, squeezing, "How? How?" out of a constricted throat.

"How?" Lucrezia repeated. "Do you mean how did he poison her? As to that, I have not the faintest idea. If I were you, I would ask Master dei Carri. If you mean how do I know Palagio was there, the answer is by asking questions."

Profound surprise had stripped Correggio's expression of its normal diplomatic neutrality. Lucrezia was amused by the mixture of emotions that showed—predominantly surprise, as if a lovely, pampered pet cat had answered him—but there was also a betraying mingling of distaste and admiration.

"It appears that you have got further with this investigation than I have," he said stiffly. "So far all I have to tell you in exchange is that no one in the duke's Court seems to have been involved."

Lucrezia smiled sweetly. "Thank you. That information will save my helpers a great deal of trouble. And for why I have learned so much, likely that is because you have many other duties and responsibilities, while my desire to clear my name is paramount."

"Nonsense," Correggio insisted. "I told you yesterday that no one could truly believe you were guilty."

"Believe it? No, likely they could not. But enjoy telling the suspicion to everyone they knew and speculating about why I would have done such a thing? Who in the Court could resist? No, Don Niccolò, I will not endure that again. I will find the guilty party. My mind is not as shallow as the decorative stream that runs through the garden, nor are my words like those of a parrot, an echo of what has been said to me. And not even you are above my suspicion, Don Niccolò. Indeed, I would like to know what your relations with Donna Bianca were."

"My relations? What the devil do you mean?"

Lucrezia sighed ostentatiously. "Did you think you were immune to gossip, Don Niccolò? My ladies tell me that Bianca was obviously pursuing you and that you allowed her attentions. Other informants report that Donna Bianca was in your apartment early one morning—"

"That flitter-witted idiot was never in my bed," Correggio roared.

Alfonso uttered a strangled choke and bowed his head.

Lucrezia raised her brows. "Of course not! Which is why I am *asking* what your relations with her were."

Recovering himself, Correggio uttered a brief laugh and shook his head. "My devotion to duty is like to ruin my reputation. As you show you realize, madonna, my taste was never for women like Donna Bianca, and I am not so vain as to believe so young, so pretty, so popular, and so *witless* a lady had any taste for me. Thus when she approached me I assumed it was for some purpose of della Rocca Berti." He glanced at Lucrezia and added, "The French ambassador."

"I know who the French ambassador is," Lucrezia said dryly.

Correggio did not look as if that were particularly pleasing to him, but, his diplomatic aplomb recovered, he continued smoothly, "Although I had no idea why the man could not simply tell me anything he had to say himself—"

Lucrezia's brows went up again. "Try to remember, Don Niccolò, that there are thoughts behind my big blue eyes. I can think of several things the French ambassador might not wish to say to you directly or, more likely, questions he wanted answered that would come better from an innocent like Bianca."

Alfonso choked again at the expression of affront that came into Correggio's face.

Lucrezia shook her head. "I am not impugning your taste or discretion, Don Niccolò, but the French ambassador is not the most perceptive of men with regard to women."

"But it was not della Rocca Berti to whom Bianca took the letter—"

"What letter?" Alfonso asked.

"Let me begin at the beginning," Correggio said, glancing sidelong at Alfonso, who was frowning blackly.

Correggio proceeded to tell them how Bianca had pursued him

and had insisted on making herself useful, mostly in running errands and in carrying letters that came in the diplomatic pouches from other courts to their recipients, particularly among the ladies. He had allowed it for several reasons. Most important because he was curious about why della Rocca Berti should want to know about letters to women. He had had Bianca watched to see what she did with the letters and messages she carried. Mostly, to his surprise, she did nothing except deliver what she had to the proper person. That being so, he had found her very useful because Bianca was welcome where and at times that pages or other messengers might cause embarrassment. Nor had anyone complained.

"Ah!" Lucrezia sounded satisfied. "That is how she came to bring Cesare's letter to me. And you say it was not to della Rocca Berti that she carried his letter?"

"How do you know she carried your letter from Cesare to anyone?" Correggio snapped.

Lucrezia laughed aloud. "Because you just said it was not to the French ambassador that she carried letters. And because I saw that the seal on Cesare's letter had been tampered with."

"Why did you not tell me?" Correggio asked sharply.

"I did not notice it at first. The letter arrived on the very day that I was leaving for Corpus Domini and I just cast a quick eye over the contents to be sure there was nothing important in it. It was only after Donna Bianca was killed that I looked at the letter more carefully. You see, I had told everyone that I had not seen the lady— except as one of a crowd in my public reception room—for weeks before I left for the convent. Then, I think it was Nicola who said something that reminded me I had lied to everyone by forgetting that Bianca had carried Cesare's letter into my bedchamber that morning. So I looked for the letter and I saw that the seal had been damaged beyond my breaking it."

"Did you think that *I* had opened your letter?" Correggio asked, his voice strained.

Lucrezia smiled at him, this time warmly. "For a moment, and then I realized how ridiculous that was. You had only to ask me and I would have shown you the letter." She laughed. "You know and I know that Cesare would never send anything to me in the diplomatic bag that he wished to hide from you or from the duke. Cesare is wild, but not stupid."

Correggio looked affronted again, but it was Alfonso who spoke. "But it was not della Rocca Berti to whom Donna Bianca brought the letter," he said, directing the conversation back to what seemed to be most important to him.

"No. It was Palagio."

"Palagio?" Lucrezia's and Alfonso's voices blended.

"Then he *was* a spy for Spain?" Lucrezia asked rather faintly; she was shocked and a little frightened, recalling that it was Isabella who had sent Palagio to her.

"No," Correggio said, carefully not looking at Alfonso. "I think he was seeking information for Florence, but I do not believe he was in the pay of the Florentines."

"You relieve my mind," Lucrezia said, realizing that Correggio had noticed her tension. "I should hate to believe the government of a city like Florence would hire a fool like Palagio to gather information. But if Bianca knew what he was doing, could he have killed her to silence her? Bianca twittered like a bird, and with as little consciousness of what the sounds meant."

"It is certainly another question I can put to him," Correggio said, "but if he asked her to bring the letters to him, he must have had some trust in her."

Lucrezia sighed. "Possibly he had asked before he really knew what she was or he may have told her something he himself did not

realize was important until later. I can tell you that it was not anything in the letter Cesare sent me that caused her death. I will get—"
She laughed as she arrested her motion to get out of bed, naked
except for the bedgown. "I am afraid I am not dressed for fetching
things. Alfonso, would you be so good as to look through my writing desk and bring Cesare's letter for Don Niccolò to read?"

"Not locked?" Alfonso asked, his black brows contracted.

"Against whom or what? There is nothing in my writing desk
that is secret. I would only lose the key and need to have the desk
broken open. I am forever losing keys."

Without replying, Alfonso went to get the letter. While he was
away, Correggio explained why he was almost certain the members
of the duke's Court and also any casual visitors to the palace were
innocent. Lucrezia agreed with him. Had there been any gossip
about Bianca, she was sure that Giulio or Ferrante would have heard
about it and passed the word to her. Maria would have reported an
intruder into Bianca's apartment. . . . Lucrezia reviewed that idea for
a moment, uncertain as she recalled that Maria had been hiding
something. But not that, she told herself. Surely the girl would not be
such a fool as to hide the presence of a stranger in Bianca's apartment.

When Alfonso returned with Cesare's letter—and Lucrezia
noted that he had not been away long enough to read anything
beyond the names on the other letters in her desk—Correggio read
it through quickly, shrugged, and returned it to her.

"I agree. There is nothing here that could interest anyone except
you, madonna." He showed his teeth in what was not quite a smile.
"Unless, of course, the names of all those relatives who are well, have
had babies, or have gone into the country early are a code for troop
movements—which would not matter, since the code is doubtless in
your head and I am sure you did not transmit it to Bianca or Palagio."

"What a clever idea," Lucrezia said. "But I am afraid the letter
was truly one of family news. You may write to your own agents in

Rome and easily discover whether it was true news or not. And I
hope you really believe that Cesare never tells me anything. He is
aware that I am not usually in sympathy with his desire for con-
quest . . . although I must admit that he is often a better ruler than
those he drives out. The people of Romagna adore him."

"I am aware," Correggio said coldly, and rose. "If there is nothing
else, madonna, I will see about finding Palagio and questioning him."

"And you will let me know the result of your questions?"
Lucrezia asked.

Correggio drew in a breath as if to speak sharply, but let it out
again in a sigh when he remembered that he would not have known
about Palagio's involvement if Lucrezia had not told him.

"Yes, madonna. I will let you know."

Alfonso went out with him and Lucrezia tinkled her bell, which
brought Lucia. They discussed briefly what Lucrezia would wear.
It was not a matter of importance because she did not expect to
receive anyone, except Angela and Nicola, of course. They would
spend the day happily making ready for the masked ball on Saturday and tonight Angela and Nicola would dine in one of their
rooms on a few dishes provided by Adriano. Lucrezia would have
dinner in the duke's apartment, but it would be a private affair with
only members of the family attending.

When Lucrezia came out into the private reception room,
Angela and Nicola had already seated themselves at the small table
made ready for breakfast. The three women ate quickly, talking
about their costumes. Angela was going as a shepherdess—at least
as a noblewoman's version of what a shepherdess would wear,
which was a pretty far cry from a true shepherdess's dirty rags.
Nicola made a point of that and suggested, laughing, that Angela
actually clothe herself in rags, although, of course, not dirty ones,
which could be arranged artfully to expose more of her body than
the kilted-up skirts of the shepherdess's gown.

Angela laughingly protested that rags better befit the slave girl Nicola had chosen to portray, but Nicola argued that a slave in a sultan's harem would not be clothed in rags, nor even in a very revealing costume, lest the sultan be attracted to the slave instead of the wife.

"Not that there is much difference between their states as far as I can tell—" she was concluding wryly, when Ascanio slipped past the portiere.

"Yes?" Lucrezia asked, frowning.

She had been enjoying the complete freedom and relaxation of talking about something of monumental unimportance that did not require any thought. She really did not want the kind of company that needed to be announced.

"Donna Beatrice Tisio says she is sorry she could not come sooner, but she did not get Donna Teodora Angelini's message that you wished to speak to her until this morning. She was away in the country, visiting her sister, and did not return until late last night."

Lucrezia's lips parted to say she was engaged and would see Beatrice the next day, but she remembered that they would all be dressing for the masked ball and she would be in even a less receptive mood to think about Bianca's death. For a moment she regretted that she had undertaken the task of discovering Bianca's murderer, then she felt ashamed. The poor young woman was dead and her killer had to pay for what he had done. That was more important than her own desire for peace and comfort.

"Bring her in," she said to the page, and when Donna Beatrice entered and approached the table, she said, "I would invite you to bring up a stool and join us if I were sure you would not suspect me of trying to poison you."

The woman's slightly bulging eyes swept the table and she swallowed. "I never thought you harmed Bianca. I would be glad to join you for breakfast if you were willing to invite me."

"This once, since I have summoned you," Lucrezia said. "As I told one of the other ladies, the duke has not seen fit to grant me an appanage equal to my needs. Since I am satisfied with Angela and Nicola to attend me, I cannot afford to support ladies I do not need and did not want. If Duke Ercole feels the attendance is necessary to my state . . . let him pay for it."

"Perhaps it is your right, madonna," Beatrice said through tight lips, "but it is hard for us who have no other means to live."

Despite her determination not to be forced to accept Duke Ercole's terms, Lucrezia felt guilty, especially when she saw the way Donna Beatrice's eyes skipped from dish to dish. The woman was actually hungry, Lucrezia thought, as Beatrice fetched a stool and seated herself. Nothing in the way she heaped her plate contradicted that supposition. Lucrezia fought down her guilt and then realized that she had no need to feel guilty. Donna Bianca's will would provide Beatrice with the means to avoid hunger.

"Did Donna Teodora tell you about what I wished to speak with you?" she asked.

"I did not see her," Beatrice said, hastily swallowing a mouthful. "She left a message for me saying I should come to you as soon as possible. I did not think that meant at nearly midnight when I returned, so I came as soon as I wakened this morning."

"And I thank you for that," Lucrezia said. "In fact, I do not remember asking Donna Teodora to tell those who served with Donna Bianca to come to speak with me. I gave Donna Teodora some news and I rather expected that she would pass that among you. However, I am not at all sorry to give you the news myself, since one piece at least is good news."

Lucrezia then explained to Beatrice how Master dei Carri's discovery of what poison was used and how quickly it acted cleared her of any possibility of having killed Bianca. Beatrice nodded at suitable intervals, but was clearly more interested in filling her stomach than in Lucrezia's claims of innocence. Not that Beatrice disbelieved her, Lucrezia thought; she simply wasn't interested.

"In addition," Lucrezia continued, "I wished to give you a piece of very good news that affects you directly. In her will, Donna Bianca left the income of an estate to be divided equally among you, Donna Teodora, Donna Elizabetta, and Donna Diana—"

Beatrice dropped the spoon with which she had assiduously been shoveling into her mouth polenta flavored with raisins and spices. "She what?" she gasped.

"You mean you did not know what she intended to do?"

Beatrice shook her head.

"But she told all the other ladies," Nicola said softly. "Can you guess why she did not include you?"

"Told the other ladies," Beatrice repeated. Her eyes looked slightly glazed. "Oh, yes. I suppose she did say something like that, but I never believed her. I never gave the matter a second thought. Bianca was always making promises that she didn't fulfill. Not long before she . . . she died, she offered to help me with a loan, but when I came to her for the money, she said she didn't have it, that her quarterly payment was due in . . . oh, I forget how long . . . perhaps a week or two. But I needed the money *then*. She could have got it. She could have drawn against her income a little in advance, but she would not!"

"I had heard that," Lucrezia said. "I know she was said never to borrow and never to spend above her income. But surely if you were . . ." She hesitated, hardly knowing how to mention to a lady of an old and honorable family a depth of poverty that caused hunger. "If you needed to eat at her table or . . ."

Lucrezia looked at the lace dripping from Beatrice's bodice and sleeves, at a necklace of gold and deep red stones.

"I did not need the money for myself," Beatrice hissed. "And you need not look at the lace on my gown or my necklace. That is only gold-washed brass and garnets and the lace could not bring enough.... It was for my brother. He ... he incurred a debt of ... honor—"

"He gambles, and he lost more than he could pay," Lucrezia said flatly, wishing to spare Beatrice the need to describe her brother's folly in words.

"Because Bianca would not lend me the money, my brother was beaten so badly he cannot walk. He was left like a package of offal by my father's back door." Beatrice uttered a sob. "That is where I was yesterday. I went home to see how he was recovering."

Lucrezia shook her head. "I am sorry to need to say it, but Bianca was right to refuse you the loan. If you give him money to pay his debt, he will only gamble again for even higher stakes and you will soon be worse off than before Bianca left you an income."

Beatrice's eyes, already large and protuberant, looked as if they would pop out of her head. "They will kill him," she breathed.

"I do not believe it," Lucrezia said. "Dead men pay no debts. They will beat him him and threaten worse, but they will not kill him." She looked at Beatrice's expression and laughed. "I am not a monster, only a woman with much experience with brothers. I have three ... had three, one is dead. Their promises for their own good mean nothing. You will see. Likely as soon as he is out of bed, he will be throwing the bones again." The expression on Beatrice's face made her laugh again. "Ah, you have seen this already."

"He is my brother," Beatrice protested. "I love him."

Lucrezia shrugged again. "You love him, but does he love you? Would he see you go hungry to pay gambling debts if he loved you?"

Beatrice made no reply. After a single angry glance she returned her attention to the food on her plate. Lucrezia said no more either. It was a bitter subject to her too. Cesare always said he loved her, but he had murdered the husband she adored without a thought for her grief.

She drew a deep breath and swallowed. It was done, over. Nothing would bring back her darling. At least Cesare could not hurt this Alfonso. Her spirits lightened at the thought and she gestured to Angela, who leaned toward her. She instructed her to have the remains of the breakfast wrapped up somehow and delivered to Beatrice's room. Angela kissed her cheek, implying that she had also noticed Beatrice's hunger and been distressed by it. She slipped off her stool and went into Lucrezia's bedchamber, where Lucia waited to be called, and sent the maid down to tell Adriano.

While Angela went out and returned, Lucrezia advised Beatrice to seek out Correggio, who had been appointed executor of Bianca's will and would be able to answer any further questions. And when the woman had cleaned her plate, thanked Lucrezia for the meal, and left, she sighed.

"She pretended not to know that Bianca left her money," Nicola said. "And she hated Bianca because of the brother. Could she be the one? She would know about the back entrance to Bianca's rooms, and Maria might not have thought to mention Beatrice being there."

"How could she have killed Bianca when she was in my apartment talking with the others about the play? Remember that the cloaked and hatted man barely stepped into Bianca's reception room, came out, and rushed away. That means Bianca was dead before he entered the room."

"Except that we don't know when he stepped in and left," Nicola pointed out.

"But I do know," Lucrezia said with a smile, "although I don't wish to tell you how I know. Just trust me that Bianca was dead before Alfonso called me to bed."

Both women looked at her reproachfully. They were accustomed to being full confidantes. Angela began to ask why they were to be excluded, but a deeper and deeper frown had been creasing Nicola's brow.

"But if that is true," she said, waving a hand at Angela to silence her, "then *only* Palagio could be the killer."

"Well, no," Lucrezia said, "there is that back entrance and it is possible that someone got in and hid from Maria, but I am afraid Palagio is the most likely. We will soon know for sure. Alfonso brought Correggio to my apartment before you arrived this morning and I told him what we had learned yesterday. He offered to lay hands on Palagio and question him. I felt that would be both safer for us and likely more effective too."

"I cannot believe it," Angela murmured. "I know I am not as clever as you two, but Palagio is not the kind to murder anyone. Milk and water, he is—"

"I rather thought so myself," Nicola said in a dissatisfied voice, "and yet there was something . . . I don't know . . . something sly? slippery? about him. I do not think he was an honest person."

"No one who steals *all* his lines from other poets is honest," Lucrezia remarked, laughing, then shrugged elaborately. "I want this to be over with. I want Palagio to be the killer, but to speak my heart . . . I feel uneasy and discontented about his guilt. Oh, well, if he confesses and explains his reasons for what he did, I am sure we will all look at each other with open eyes and mouths and say, 'Oh, of course, that was why. However did we not see it?' And we will be able to lay it aside."

"Satisfied or not," Angela said, "we had better lay the question of the murderer aside and think about our costumes. If there is anything missing, we will need to send out for it or go out for it today. Tomorrow will be too late."

9

6 *April,*

San Stefano market

LUCREZIA FROWNED at Angela's urging to abandon the murder to concentrate on the costumes for the masked ball on the next day. She felt compelled to do more, to call someone else to question—although in her heart she admitted she did not know what more to do or whom to call. It did look as though Palagio were the guilty man, and yet... Suddenly Lucrezia threw up her hands.

"Yes! Let us go out and look at the market. I could always use one or two more veils and I need a band to hold my headdress and hair—"

"You do not have a few of those already?" Nicola asked, laughing as she rose to summon the page and send him to order one of Lucrezia's carriages to be made ready.

Lucrezia laughed also. "But everyone knows those are mine," she said. "I need something that will not be recognized at the first glance."

"What you really need," Angela said quite seriously, staring at her lady and now speaking in a voice that would not carry, "is a wig. You know you could wear a black veil over your whole face, but so long as your hair shows, you will be known."

"A wig?" Lucrezia echoed.

Angela began to giggle. "With black hair . . . Yes, if you want to surprise people, throw a cloak over your Hebe costume and wear an elaborate headdress. Then when we come to the grand sala, you can go behind a screen or step out into the garden for a moment. Take off the headdress and the cloak and put on the wig with just a band to hold the loose hair. I swear no one will know you."

Nicola sent Ascanio on his way and came back toward them cocking her head to hear. Obligingly, Angela repeated what she had suggested. Nicola's brows went up, and her eyes lit with mischief.

"You know, madonna, we are much of a size. What if I buy a blond wig—"

"That will not go very well with the costume of a harem slave," Lucrezia said.

"No, it will not," Nicola admitted, "but you are known to be just a tiny bit vain about your hair? No?"

Lucrezia sighed. "It is one of my failings, yes."

"So you would not wish to cover that, no matter what the costume you wore. . . ."

"Then everyone will think you are the madonna," Angela said.

"Those who are not very wise or observant probably will think that." Nicola guffawed softly. "The cleverer ones will notice that the wig has not the luster of life that Madonna Lucrezia's hair has, but they will not be sure. Oh, this will be a pretty game."

"It will, indeed," Lucrezia said, giggling also. "Thank you very much, Angela."

But Angela did not look completely happy. "But if no one knows you, madonna," she protested, "you might be—be insulted. If Don

Ferrante thinks you are Nicola, he might drag you off and—and kiss you . . . or worse."

Lucrezia laughed aloud at that. "Do you let 'worse' happen, Nicola?"

"No, I do not. I rap him firmly—usually on the nose, which reduces his ardor. . . ." But her voice drifted away uncertainly and she looked sidelong at Lucrezia. "But I do not think it would be wise to allow Ferrante to draw you aside too publicly. Don Alfonso is not suspicious of you, madonna. I believe he trusts your virtue. If you went aside with any other man, likely he would not care, but with Don Ferrante or Don Giulio . . ."

"That is a good point, Nicola. I will be very careful to avoid both Don Ferrante and Don Giulio. In fact, I will make sure that I am clearly visible at all times." She hesitated, plainly considering giving up the scheme, but her grin returned and she shook her head. "I will be careful. If I must go to the necessary or out for some other private purpose, I will make myself known to Alfonso so he can take me. I certainly do not want to awaken Alfonso's jealousy over a joke . . . But it is such a good joke!"

They continued to refine their mischief until Ascanio ran in to say the coach and guardsmen to attend her were waiting. Then they donned the cloaks that Lucia had fetched for them and hurried down the broad marble stair from the piano nobile to the main floor. Lucrezia's balance was very good and she went quickly down the center of the stair. Nicola came more slowly, not touching the beautiful curved balustrade but near enough to seize it if she felt dizzy, and Angela descended most slowly of all, with one hand sliding over the polished marble for security.

The carriage waited in the outer court, one of the five that had been a gift from Duke Ercole when Lucrezia arrived. She suspected the carriages had originally belonged to his wife and had been refurbished rather than new-built, and at first she had been annoyed. Later she felt she had come out ahead, because the late duchess's carriages were strong, carefully constructed vehicles; if the duke had tried to economize on new-built carriages, they might have fallen to pieces on the rough roads. The guardsmen waited, four before and four behind the carriage. When they saw her, the captain and his sergeant dismounted and came forward to help her and her ladies into the carriage.

Lucrezia's favorite was done in red velvet and the roan horses that drew it were strong and placid. Lucia and the other two maids had come down a back stair and were already in a small cart drawn by a strong mule that would follow them to the market.

"Sebastiano the Mercer on Via di Santo Stefano," Lucrezia said to the guard captain.

He bowed agreement, which told Lucrezia that the city was quiet with no threat of riot. Not that riots were as frequent in Ferrara as they had been in Rome, but they did occur.

"You cannot try on the black wig," Angela said suddenly, speaking softly. "The tale will be all over the city by afternoon. I will try it on for you."

"And what of Nicola?" Lucrezia asked.

She shrugged. "I do not see that it matters whether I am known to be wearing a blond wig or not."

They talked it over for a while and agreed that Angela should try on the black wig and Nicola the blond one openly. Nor should either lady request silence from the wigmaker. They would act as if it did not matter whether he spoke of the matter or not, thus reducing the temptation to show that he was privy to a secret. Probably he wouldn't tell anyone besides his own family, and that was unlikely to get back to anyone in the Court. And a wigmaker was probably accustomed to keeping the purchase of extra hair quiet. Those ladies who needed to augment their own scanty tresses would not thank him, nor continue to patronize anyone who exposed their secret need. Nonetheless, the wigmaker would not be the first shop, nor the only one they would visit.

Although the distance from the palazzo to the market was not great, it took near half a candlemark to reach their goal. The carriage needed to move slowly through the narrow, crowded streets. Lucrezia had been greeted with great enthusiasm when she arrived as Alfonso's bride, and she did all she could to keep the goodwill of the people of Ferrara. Running someone down just to arrive at a shop more quickly would not enhance her popularity and her driver knew he must be careful.

In addition, the slow pace provided time for the news to spread that she was out in the city, and even more people came out to see her carriage pass, to cheer and wave. Lucrezia had to respond with smiles and waves of her own, but still the matter of the wigs was decided by the time the carriage had come to a stop in front of the mercery.

Recognizing the carriage and seeing it was coming to a halt, the people in the market shopping at the stalls under the arcades began to gather around it. The guards hastily dismounted, but there was no rush to overwhelm the carriage. A murmur of Lucrezia's name ran through the crowd and cheers welcomed her. After the frequently hostile Roman crowds, the pleasure with which she was greeted delighted her.

It took no more than a few gestures to clear a space around the carriage and Lucrezia was able to get out and smile and wave to the right and the left. Angela and Nicola stepped down and the guards began to close in.

"Madonna, wait. Please wait!"

It was a cracked old voice and Lucrezia's head turned in that direction. Her smile froze a little when she saw an ancient, wizened woman, clutching a roll of coarse paper, step forward from the respectful half circle of watchers. The nearest guard raised his hand to strike the paper into the muddy street.

"Stop," Lucrezia ordered. "Let her come to me."

To speak the truth, she was a little annoyed. She hated to have people present petitions to her because she knew she had little influence over her father-by-law. Oh, the duke was fond of her—he thought her pretty and graceful and found the huge dowry she had brought useful—but his fondness never extended as far as political favors or remitting someone's taxes or finding a place for the scion of a family not in his regard. Still, she did not want the crowd to see her refuse even to look at a petition.

"She could have a knife in that roll of paper," the guardsman warned as Lucrezia took a step in the old woman's direction.

"No!" the old woman cried. "It is a drawing by my grandson. Please take it."

"If you are worried," Lucrezia said to the guard, "bid her unroll it so I can see what she has."

The roll was pulled out flat before the guard could even speak, and the old woman held it inside out for Lucrezia to see. Both Angela and Nicola made soft murmurs of approval, and Lucrezia moved forward again to take the paper into her own hands so she could see it better. Two guards paced her, their hands on their weapons, but no one else in the crowd pushed forward and the old woman stood quietly, her hands now clasped before her.

"Delightful!" Lucrezia exclaimed. "Who did this?"

It was a sketch, done in what was clearly homemade charcoal, of a street fountain. On the edge of the fountain two children played, one splashing water on the other. At one side a woman with one hand on her hip and a fat-bellied water jar balanced on her head had paused to speak to a second woman, who had just removed her jar from the fountain and was resting it on the ledge. On the other side a man was leading a laden donkey. The figures were so lifelike that one expected to hear the children crying out, the donkey bray, and the voices of the women.

"My grandson," the old woman said, her voice trembling with eagerness. "From before he could walk well, he drew pictures. I beg you, madonna, can you not help to find an artist who will take him as an apprentice? I . . . I could pay a little . . . only a little . . . but . . ."

"Truly, such skill should not be wasted," Lucrezia said, her eyes still on the drawing.

"Perhaps Master Angelo da Siena would take him," Nicola said. The man was from her city and she had some influence with him.

Lucrezia frowned. "No. His work is good, but stiff, in the old style. He would try to train the boy in a more formal way. I think . . . yes, I could do the boy and the artist both a favor." She turned to the old woman and said, "I will need more drawings, as many as you can gather. Bring them here to Master Sebastiano and I will collect them or send someone to get them. I will leave a message for you with Master Sebastiano as to when and where to bring your grandson so that Master Giovanni Lateri can examine him."

"Thank you, madonna," the old woman whispered. "Thank you. May every blessing from every saint protect you from any harm and bring you every good."

Lucrezia smiled at her and beckoned her forward. The mercer, who had come to stand in front of his stall, looked carefully at the old woman, asked her name, and finally nodded to Lucrezia. "I will know her when she comes, madonna."

"Go now and fetch the other drawings," Lucrezia said, and the old woman bowed and hurried away.

Lucrezia then handed the drawing she was still holding to the mercer. "Put it with the others when she brings them," she said. "And let us see some veils. I need one, very fine, and two that are thicker and large."

He bowed, backing away so there was space for them to come behind the counter and then through the open door of his shop. He laid the drawing carefully on the counter and secured it with a silk-covered weight. Finally, he lifted some piles of cloth down from a high shelf.

"These are fine," he said. "If you whisper, the cloth stirs."

Angela and Nicola exclaimed and came forward to examine the veils. Several were tried against Lucrezia's complexion and two were chosen. Angela chose a third and Lucrezia urged Nicola to choose also, promising to pay. Then the heavier scarfs were examined. Again Lucrezia took two, and while Angela was selecting one to tie around her waist, Lucrezia asked the mercer if there was a wigmaker nearby. Not only did she receive directions and encomiums about the wigmaker's abilities, but it appeared there was a passageway behind the buildings that would take the ladies most privately to his shop.

Lucrezia lifted her brows, but forbore to comment. Apparently she was not the only woman in the court who bought wigs. Angela's choice made, the scarfs were wrapped in pieces of coarse cloth and handed to the appropriate maid to carry.

The captain of the guard paid. When she had outrun her allowance, Lucrezia told merchants to send to her clerk at some future time, but when she had coins to spend, she paid at once, which made merchants more eager for her custom. She always insisted on a lowered price, however; she knew that being seen to buy from a merchant increased his business and made up for any loss he suffered in what he charged her.

Taking only two guards and giggling, the three women and their maids followed Sebastiano through the back alley. A discreet knock brought the wigmaker's apprentice to the door. He ran to fetch his master Domenico, whose eyes widened when he saw who was waiting. Sebastiano said he would leave them in the wigmaker's hands until their business was complete, when Master Domenico would bring them back to his shop, from which they could leave as if they had never visited the wigmaker. The guards stepped to either side of the door to wait.

Master Domenico ushered them in hastily, bowing and glancing sidelong at their headdresses. Lucrezia laughed heartily and assured him her hair was her own, as was Nicola's and Angela's. Then she told him about the masked ball that would be held on the next day and confessed that Angela and Nicola wished to play a trick on their lovers. Thus Angela needed a black or dark brown wig and Nicola needed a blond one.

Bowing all the way, the wigmaker showed his customers into a surprisingly open and airy chamber that had several mirrors above narrow tables. Each of the tables held rather repellent-looking bald heads on which Master Domenico set wigs, black and brown on one and blond on the other. Some were already dressed, curled, and plaited in the height of fashion; some were simply loose falls of hair that could be combed into in the purchaser's own favorite style. Of the latter, most had slits in the cap through which the hair of the wearer could be pulled to blend in with the false hair.

Lucrezia then explained that the wigs they bought would need to be put on and then taken off again quickly so there was no question of blending real hair with false. Master Domenico quickly removed the falls of hair and produced additional styled wigs. Nicola then chose a blond one done in simple looping braids, a style that Lucrezia sometimes wore, but when she put it on, she wrinkled her nose, and Lucrezia, bending over her to see better, stepped back exclaiming that the hair stank.

Master Domenico clicked his tongue. "It happens sometimes when we store many wigs close together," he admitted.

He reached around Nicola to the back of the narrow table, from which he lifted a small, handsome vial, which looked familiar to

Lucrezia. She was distracted from the idea when Master Domenico removed the stopper, which released a powerful but pleasant scent, completely new to her.

He dabbed some of the perfume onto the wig. "If you like it," he continued, "we can scent it more thoroughly."

Now Lucrezia wrinkled her nose. "It needs washing, not scenting." She sniffed again and shrugged. Most of the peculiar odor was already covered by the perfume. "That is a powerful perfume. Still, is it not more expensive to perfume the hair than to wash it?"

"Only a little," the wigmaker said. "It takes great care to wash and comb a wig lest the hair be pulled out of the cap and the shape of the cap be distorted. If the customer is in a hurry or likes scent, it is quicker and easier to perfume the wig. And I have a most excellent and inexpensive perfumer. If you would like, madonna, I can tell you where to find her shop."

"Oh, yes, madonna," Angela cried. "Please, can we go to the perfumer's shop?"

Behind Angela, Lucia and one of the other maids had folded their hands as if they were praying in a silent plea. Lucrezia smiled and nodded agreement. She could not buy anything because she got all her scents from her sister-by-marriage, Isabella. Even if Lucia did not tell the tale—and she might because she was aware of the competition between Isabella and her mistress and enjoyed taunting Isabella—it might get out. Lucrezia did not want to annoy Isabella; she had no taste for competition and wanted the woman's goodwill. However, Isabella's prices were too high for Angela's purse and far above the maids'.

"Why not?" Lucrezia said. "We are here already. Let us buy whatever we need."

"The perfume shop is Anna Peruzzi's and it is at the far end of the Via di Santo Stefano." Master Domenico waved vaguely in the direction of the street, then frowned. "It is not really in the street.

You must go to the end and then turn into the alley behind. It is the second door . . . a poor place, but that is why her prices are low. Will you tell her I sent you?"

Sensing her ladies' eagerness, Lucrezia pointed out to Angela a black wig with an elaborate crown of braids over the top of the head and a long straight fall behind, saying she thought that would look best on her. It was a handsome enough style, but what recommended it most to Lucrezia was that the hair did not smell. Nicola had found another blond wig in a style of looped braids similar to the first one she had tried that also needed no scent. After some haggling, during which Lucrezia could not use her favorite weapon of bringing custom to the merchant because of the need for secrecy, a price was settled.

The wigs were wrapped and handed to Lucia, and Master Domenico led the way out. The two guards fell in behind, and Lucrezia said, "I have my guardsmen. You do not need to accompany us. Bring your bill to Master Sebastiano. He will have money for you."

At Master Sebastiano's shop, Lucrezia examined the pile of drawings that the old woman had brought while she sent two guards out to find the perfumer's shop. She was relieved to see that all the drawings were very good indeed. Master Lateri was a fine painter but very young and not yet rich in commissions. She thought he would be delighted to have an apprentice for whom she would furnish the fee. She was just telling the mercer that she would send a messenger when she had arranged the place for the boy when one of the guards returned to say they had found the perfumer's shop.

The carriage was too large to go into the alley and Lucrezia was glad of her high-platformed zoccolos, which kept her shoes out of the slimy mud. The ground had little chance to dry because the houses overhung the lane, which grew darker and darker. Even with three guards preceding her into the place and the five women clustered around her, Lucrezia was glad the shop was near enough the entrance to the alley that there was plenty of light.

The guard waiting at the door of Peruzzi's Perfumes opened it. "They know within that you are coming," he said.

Lucrezia smiled her thanks and entered a small room insufficiently lit by two small windows and two lamps hanging from the walls. She smiled again at the two women standing by the counter that stretched across the room because the old woman to the fore was so nervous that her hands were shaking.

"We have come because Master Domenico showed us a sample of your perfume and my ladies and my maids would like to look at your wares."

The mention of Master Domenico seemed to calm the woman and she bowed her head in acknowledgment and asked what kind of scent the ladies would like. Flowers? Something more exotic? And Her Highness? What would she like to see?

Lucrezia explained that she had perfumes enough and would not buy. Mistress Peruzzi should not waste time on her but attend to Angela, Nicola, and the maids. A sharp order from the old woman set the younger one to lifting boxes down from the shelves that lined the walls behind the counter. Mistress Peruzzi began to lift out small bottles, each carefully stoppered but none as elegant as the flask in Master Domenico's shop. Nor was the scent, when she opened a bottle, as penetrating as that in the wigmaker's shop. Perhaps the perfume had been diluted. Lucrezia wondered idly whether the wigmaker had an arrangement about recommending Peruzzi's Perfumes but actually bought his scents from someone else.

With nothing better to do, Lucrezia watched the younger woman fetch and carry. She was a handsome creature with dark hair, a short broad nose, and full, sensuous lips, somewhat better dressed than the shopkeeper herself. A moment later the girl almost dropped the box she was sliding off the shelf. Mistress Peruzzi spoke sharply, and Lucrezia turned away, realizing it was her scrutiny that was making the young woman uneasy.

Before Lucrezia could begin to wonder why her idle glance should be so disturbing, Nicola brought over a more elaborate bottle than Mistress Peruzzi had set out for the maids for her to smell. It was a richer scent than Lucrezia cared to use herself, dark with sandalwood and a spice she did not recognize.

"Do you dislike it, madonna?" Nicola asked.

"No, not at all," Lucrezia replied, "but I could never wear a perfume like that. It does not suit my spirit at all."

Nicola smiled. "No, it does not. You are full of light, quick of movement, quick to laugh. This is for a more indolent person . . . like myself."

"I would not call you indolent," Lucrezia protested.

"Whatever I am, if it does not repel you, this scent suits me."

"By all means, my love. If you like it, take it."

Nicola found two more little bottles whose contents attracted her and Angela also chose several, hers more sweetly floral than those Lucrezia normally wore, which always had a hint of citrus sharpness. The maids at the far end of the counter clucked and chattered with the younger woman, almost as if they knew her, and she seemed more assured and at ease with them.

While she waited, Lucrezia sniffed this and that. Several of the scents were attractive enough that she regretted being bound to buy from Isabella. One was very familiar and she remembered having the same regret when she was offered something very like it by Diana Altoviti. She thought about asking Mistress Peruzzi whether she bought her scents from Diana, but thought better of it. It would only embarrass the woman, who would want to keep her supplier a secret so customers would buy from her rather than going directly to the supplier. Eventually the clock in the bell tower rang out and Lucrezia reminded Nicola and Angela that they were due to dine at the duke's table again that night.

Transactions were then concluded quickly. Purchases were stowed away, and the carriage brought them back to Castel Vecchio. With much laughter, the wigs were concealed in the clothing chests near Lucrezia's bed. She did not really suspect that Alfonso would look through her things, but the box that held her combs and brushes and other hairdressing tools was frequently left open and she did not want an idle glance to betray her jest.

The rest of the afternoon was given over to the serious business of dressing. Since she hoped to hear from Correggio that he had seized Palagio, questioned him, and found him guilty of Bianca's murder, she no longer felt she needed to keep a hint of sobriety in her dress. A subtle appearance of triumph was in order, and she donned a gammura of gold cloth with purple satin stripes. The long, flowing sleeves were lined with ermine, and an ermine-lined cloak of gold-embroidered cloth lay ready on the bed.

When Alfonso arrived, in good time to escort her to the Palazzo del Cortile, Lucia put the cloak over her shoulders and Lucrezia nodded at Angela and Nicola, who went ahead through the private reception room to the public one. There Lucrezia hesitated, looking around at an unusually large group of ladies. Teodora Angelini came forward to murmur that a general invitation had been issued by the duke to all Lucrezia's ladies-in-waiting.

"Then you are all very welcome," Lucrezia said. "Any help the duke wishes to offer those he appointed is agreeable to me and accepted gladly." She smiled around at them generally, murmuring the names of those she knew best, "Donna Beatrice, Donna Diana, Donna Elizabetta."

Alfonso bent closer and said into her ear, "You never miss a chance to make the point that you are not responsible for them, do you?" As he spoke, Alfonso led her out into the corridor toward the broad marble stair.

Lucrezia laid the fingertips of her left hand on his arm and whispered back, "I want no doubt as to who placed them in their unfortunate situation."

She bent her head a trifle and lifted her skirt with her right hand as they started down the staircase. Angela sidled to the left, where she could clutch the banister as she descended. Nicola, balancing her movement, moved right. Behind her, Lucrezia heard the other ladies, with Teodora Angelini cautioning them to take care, also begin to start down.

Lucrezia had just turned toward Alfonso to ask whether he could arrange for her to speak privately to Correggio before dinner when she heard a startled exclamation behind her. Her right foot hesitated above the next step, and before she could put it down and turn her head, a violent blow struck her back.

Her right foot went down but missed the step. Her left heel slipped on the edge of the step above. She dropped her skirt and flailed wildly for support with her right hand, but there was nothing to seize on to, and with a gasping cry, she began to fall.

10

 BURNT AND CALLUSED and hard as steel, Alfonso's left hand whipped across his body and closed over Lucrezia's upper arm. He wrenched her upright and sideways, catching her about the waist with his right arm and lifting her so that neither of her feet touched the stairs. When his grip and balance were firm, he clutched her hard against his body. In the next moment, he let her down, still holding her tight so she could find footing and find her balance.

"Someone pushed me," Lucrezia breathed.

"No!" Donna Teodora cried. "I fell against you, madonna. Someone pushed *me*."

"Go down the stair!" Alfonso's voice grated. "All of you, get out from behind us and wait for us below." He turned to Lucrezia, his eyes black and angry. "Are you all right now?"

"Yes," she said, but her voice quavered, and when his arm

relaxed its grip on her, Lucrezia grabbed hold of it before he could release her. "I think I would like to hold the banister the rest of the way down."

He held her until she could lay her hand upon it, then took her other hand and began to walk down slowly. Lucrezia's eyes filled with tears.

"Someone hates me," she whispered. "Because your father will not pay me a fair appanage and I refuse to support women he appointed without my approval, one tried to kill me."

"I doubt it," Alfonso said with a grimace.

"You think I slipped? Or it was an accident?"

Alfonso looked at her, his expression unreadable. "Your refusal to pay is too slight a reason for murder. Besides, the result would undo the purpose. Dead, you would pay no one anything, all the ladies would be dismissed, and who knows who would be my next wife and who would be appointed to attend her. No, if harm was meant, it was for a larger reason than withheld stipends."

"Larger purpose? Bianca's death? But—"

"Are you so sure—" he began, but they had reached the huddle of women at the bottom of the stair and instead of finishing his question to Lucrezia he asked them, "Well? What happened?"

His eyes fixed on Donna Teodora, and she drew herself up, but her voice trembled as she said, "I am not sure. I certainly did not intend to push Madonna Lucrezia. I swear that on the health of my soul. I was coming down behind Madonna Lucrezia and I was watching my skirt and the distance between us so I would not tread on her heels. Suddenly my skirt was drawn tight around my ankles . . . as if someone had stepped on the back of it . . . and I was falling forward. I beg pardon most sincerely. My hands went out as they do when one begins to fall and I struck Madonna Lucrezia's back. But I did not intend to push her!"

"Did you not say that *you* were pushed?" Alfonso asked.

"I don't know," the woman cried, looking genuinely distressed. "I did feel a hand on my back, but I cannot say it pushed me—"

"That was me," Diana Altoviti whispered, stepping forward. Her eyes were wide, her face white with fear. "But I didn't mean to push Donna Teodora. I swear it. I was trying to pull her back. I thought she was about to fall and I grabbed for the back of her gown—"

"It is true," Elizabetta Dossi remarked calmly. "Donna Teodora was tilting forward as if she might fall before Diana reached for her. I reached out too, but I was too far away."

"And I saw her hand closed around Donna Teodora's dress," Beatrice Tisio added. "One does not clutch at a garment when trying to push."

"Then it was an accident," Lucrezia said eagerly. "Donna Teodora's feet got tangled in her skirt—it happens; it has happened to me—and when Donna Diana tried to catch her, Donna Teodora's hand struck my back. It was pure misfortune that I was just about to take another step down and was off balance. But my husband saved me, so no harm is done."

"It was pure good fortune that both my feet were set solidly," he said, his face totally without expression. "If I had been off balance too, we could both have tumbled down. But such an accident happens only once."

"Yes, indeed," Lucrezia agreed, taking one of his hands in both of hers. "And in a way it was my own fault for being so proud of my balance and grace and always going down the center of the stair. In the future I will be more careful and hold the banister."

"Very wise," Alfonso said, suddenly smiling at her. But when they had all formed up to walk to the Palazzo del Cortile—this time with Angela and Nicola protectively behind Lucrezia—he said, "I know that Giulio is pursuing Angela, and Ferrante, Nicola, but do you know if either of them has shown any particular interest in any other of your ladies?"

Lucrezia glanced sidelong at him, recalling suddenly the blankness on his face when he remarked about the good fortune of his feet being solidly set and the chance that they would both fall. She swallowed hard. Giulio and Ferrante both seemed quite fond of her; neither seemed overtly ambitious, but it still was not impossible that one of them might have thought of such a way to be rid of the heir to Ferrara. The hand holding her skirt suddenly pressed more firmly against her belly where the heir of the heir might lie. Two birds with one stone. She tightened her grip on Alfonso's wrist.

"I suspect that Beatrice Tisio has a tendre for Giulio," Lucrezia said, too softly to be overheard, "because she has sharp words about his variability whenever she speaks to Angela."

Even as she said the words Lucrezia began to rethink the fears Alfonso had awakened. No, even in Rome such a devious and convoluted plot—so unlikely to succeed and so very likely to be betrayed—would be considered ridiculous. Not that Alfonso did not need to be wary of his brothers; they were both foolish enough to believe that being duke was no more than a matter of being free of supervision and able to give orders. Alfonso . . . he hid everything, but she suspected he knew better. She frowned in thought, shook her head.

"I do not remember any preference from Donna Teodora or Donna Diana," she finished.

She hesitated a bit over that last name, a new memory being awakened. Diana had flown to the defense of Palagio when his name came up in connection with Bianca's death, but she could not have known what Lucrezia had told Correggio. And Correggio would not have mentioned Lucrezia in his questioning of Palagio.

"Tomorrow see if you can find out where each woman was while they were coming down," Alfonso suggested.

"You do not want me to call them to me in private and question them, do you? If so, the questions will have to wait until at least the day after tomorrow. There is the ball, you know, and tomorrow everyone will be making ready."

"Whenever it is convenient," he said, "but the sooner you ask, the less likely everyone will have forgotten where they were."

Lucrezia nodded, but perfunctorily. She did not really believe that the women were involved in any plot to get rid of Alfonso, and her thoughts about Palagio and Correggio had reminded her that she had just been about to enlist Alfonso's help to speak privately with Correggio when she had almost fallen. She promptly raised the new subject and found to her relief that Alfonso was easily diverted. He readily agreed to try to find a few private moments with Correggio, since, he admitted, he himself was curious about what Palagio had said, particularly about his reasons for killing Bianca.

They were fortunate in seeing the courtier dismounting and throwing his reins to a groom near the entry to the Palazzo Cortile as they were themselves nearing the external stair. Alfonso dropped Lucrezia's arm and hurried away to intercept Don Niccolò, and when he succeeded and they were both approaching Lucrezia and her women, she bade Angela and Nicola to continue on into the sala, and slipped away from them to join the two men.

"Do you have him safe?" she asked Correggio as soon as Alfonso had shepherded them into a sheltered nook.

"Have who safe?" Correggio asked.

Both Lucrezia and Alfonso looked at him with such blank amazement that his eyes shifted. "Palagio," Lucrezia said, with ostentatious patience. "You agreed yesterday morning to question him about Donna Bianca's death."

"Oh. Oh, yes. Well, yes, and so I did, but he swears that the lady was already dead when he entered the room."

"And you believed him?" Alfonso growled.

"Well, yes. Actually, I did. He had no reason to want her dead and a most compelling one for wanting her alive. He was poor, she was rich, and she had agreed to marry him."

"I do not believe it!" Lucrezia exclaimed. "I cannot believe Bianca agreed to marry and did not tell a soul, not even a hint to her maid. She would have been bubbling with joy and excitement. Why should she keep it a secret?"

"Because, presumably, her guardians would have objected to so foolish a marriage," Correggio said dryly.

"She had no guardians! Sigismundo saw her will—" Lucrezia stared at Correggio, who had also seen Bianca's will, who was, in fact, named as executor.

He cleared his throat, looking annoyed, but it was Alfonso who spoke. "Perhaps she refused him and he was angry, so he killed her."

Correggio shook his head, but he answered benignly, grateful, Lucrezia thought, for the interruption. "An angry man beats a woman or in an extremity of rage might stab her. Do you think it likely that Palagio walked around with poison in his purse in case some woman should refuse him?"

"For all I know he did," Alfonso snarled.

Correggio shook his head again. "I . . . was given reason to believe it better to take his word. I would like to find him guilty"— Correggio's jaw jutted for a moment—"but he is not . . . at least, not guilty of Donna Bianca's murder."

Lucrezia was less amazed by this statement than she was by the long look Correggio gave Alfonso, but Correggio sounded as if he believed what he had said.

"But he was in there with her for near half a candlemark," Lucrezia protested. "What was he doing with a corpse for so long? Do you believe he was grieving?"

"No, nor did he claim he was grieving. He admitted he was looking for his letters to Donna Bianca." Correggio's glance at Alfonso was again significant.

That look had to mean that Palagio had found other letters among Bianca's correspondence and had used what he had found to force Correggio to free him. Lucrezia struggled to keep her expression blank. *Could* Alfonso have been Bianca's lover? Could he have written her love letters? A single stab of jealousy pierced Lucrezia as she remembered the few stilted words with which he had replied to her letters during the negotiations for their betrothal. Alfonso writing the flowery effusions that Bianca favored? A single glance at Alfonso's face cured that notion. His thick brows were drawn together, but in puzzlement, not embarrassment.

"Are you implying that Palagio found and stole other letters too? But I never wrote to her—"

"He says you did and that he has the letter."

"But—" And then Alfonso's eyes widened in remembrance and he snarled, "Oh, the little bitch! She said she would need the note to convince him that I desired a meeting and swore to destroy it."

Now he looked at Correggio, lips thinned. "I gather that Palagio will be leaving the duchy or has already left."

"Not yet, although I am sure he recognizes the danger to his health if he remains in Ferrara. He said he had some business to complete here. I warned him that doing business with you might be dangerous, and he laughed and said he knew that and all he craved from you was a few days to mend the sad condition of his purse."

"So long as he does not expect me to mend it," Alfonso said, and then suddenly he laughed. "If he thinks any man in the court will pay to keep secret a laison with Donna Bianca he is doomed to disappointment. Apparently it was an amusement common to all."

With the words, he extended his arm to Lucrezia, who automatically put her hand on it and allowed him to lead her out of their private nook and around to the foot of the stair. This time he guided her to the right so she could touch the marble banister as they went up, but there was no need. They arrived in the great sala without any further alarms.

There, within feet of the door, Ercole Strozzi was waiting. Alfonso would have walked by without even vouchsafing him a greeting, but Lucrezia stopped, released her husband's arm, and turned to her friend. She was aware that Alfonso scowled horribly, but he merely walked on, and she put out her hand to Strozzi, who took it, and kissed it.

"You look very beautiful," he said.

Lucrezia laughed. "I am not beautiful. I merely have a lively expression. I have that on the best authority."

"Whose?"

"Isabella's."

Strozzi snorted. "She is a little blinded by envy."

"Hush. We must not say that. And where have you been all day yesterday and today? I have felt abandoned."

"I have been about the business you set me," he said, cocking his head and looking puzzled. "You wanted to know of what Donna Bianca's husband died and whether his family had any animosity to her. Have you decided not to seek her killer after all?"

"No, but I thought we had found him." She explained about Palagio being seen entering Bianca's apartment and his extended stay there, and then, murmuring in his ear so that no one else could hear, about Correggio insisting the man was innocent.

"That is not like Correggio," Strozzi protested equally softly. "It is not himself he is trying to shield. I suspect it is Don Alfonso."

"Alfonso admitted that he had written her a note. He said she asked for it to convince . . . him . . . he did not say who the 'him' was . . . to meet with him . . . Alfonso, I mean."

Strozzi turned, drew her arm to his, and began to move slowly toward the top of the room, swinging his crutch a little wide so that no one could approach too closely. "I fear the 'him' was Palagio himself and that Alfonso believed Palagio could pass messages to the Spanish."

"Could he? He was not Spanish or Neapolitan. I know that. He could have had no personal loyalty to Spain."

Strozzi shrugged as best he could while leaning on his crutch. "I doubt he had personal loyalties to anyone. He was the kind who might well look for a few coins by passing information to the Spanish, but I cannot say whether it was true in fact or not. What is true is that the duke, as he grows older, grows more cautious and also more absolute."

"Surely you cannot think he will disinherit Alfonso!"

"No. I think he is still clear-headed enough to remember that Alfonso is the best of his sons—at least best to inherit the dukedom; Sigismundo is the better man, but he is not strong enough to be duke—but you know how fixed Duke Ercole is on his French alliance and how fearful the French king will find some fault in him. If he heard that Alfonso was making gestures toward the Spanish . . ."

Ice ran up Lucrezia's spine. She knew that few heirs survived to be disinherited. And where would that leave her? A widow again? To be sold again? Lucrezia barely prevented herself from bursting into tears, but Strozzi seemed to understand. He shook his head, relieving her fears somewhat.

"I don't think a single meeting would tip the duke's balance toward Ferrante, but Correggio is also a cautious man and he would not want such information to be exposed because the duke might well confront Alfonso and they do not need any new causes of conflict."

Even at the slow pace they were moving, they were approaching the top of the room where the duke was talking to Correggio and Don Gian Luca Castellini da Pontremoli. Lucrezia cast a glance at the duke and abandoned the dangerous topic of Alfonso. To turn the subject, she asked, "So of what did Celio Tedaldo die? Was there any suspicion of foul doings?"

"None at all. Tedaldo died of the French sickness. He was covered with sores nearly from head to foot and they became inflamed and then his limbs rotted. It was a horrible death."

"Ah, no wonder that Donna Bianca would not take a lover who had buboes. Poor woman. It must have been terrible to watch him die . . . or did she flee him?"

"No, she tended him, often herself, with the utmost patience and the greatest resolve. And it must have taken resolve, for he was all gangrenous and stank . . . That, I suspect, was one reason why his family so easily accepted that she inherited everything. Besides, they are only cousins—he had no siblings—and they are rich enough. More is always welcome, but not to the point that murder becomes acceptable when there is no real need."

"I did not really think that they could be guilty, but I did not wish to dismiss anyone who benefited by her death."

"I think you can dismiss the Tedaldos. Also they are simpler people than Celio Tedaldo was, and have, as far as I could determine, no connection at all with the Court."

They had almost reached the duke and Strozzi hesitated, cautious about breaking into what seemed like a family group. However, it was Sigismundo who broke away and came toward them, smiling. He was wearing his favorite clothing, a black velvet jerkin over a green doublet that matched the short green cape he seldom removed. *Poor Sigismundo,* Lucrezia thought, *he is always cold.* Then he doffed his soft black velvet cap, sweeping the floor as he bowed with the bright peacock feathers that adorned it.

Ercole Strozzi slid his arm out from under Lucrezia's hand and Sigismundo offered his. Lucrezia drew her breath in a short, disdainful sniff, but she accepted Sigismundo's arm. There was no sense in starting an argument with Alfonso that would embroil the entire d'Este family just before the whole Court sat down to dinner.

Alfonso disliked Ercole Strozzi, whom he called a puling pedant, and particularly disliked the fact that Lucrezia made much of Strozzi and agreed with the judgment of many scholars that Ercole was one of the best Latinists in Italy. Alfonso considered Latin an effete and unnecessary language that should be allowed to die and molder away.

Fortunately for Strozzi, the duke was of Lucrezia's opinion, which made him safe from all but Alfonso's bitter remarks. As long as their exchanges—for Strozzi, although far more subtle, was not at all reluctant to give as good as he got from Alfonso—took place out of Duke Ercole's hearing, no one cared much. However, the duke could become very irritated with Alfonso, whom he considered an uneducated idiot and a boor, if Alfonso made an unpleasant remark to Strozzi for escorting Lucrezia, and no one wanted him roaring and upsetting all his guests.

The exchange of escort removed most chance of that. Alfonso was unlikely to speak unpleasantly about Strozzi to Lucrezia when she arrived on Sigismundo's arm and, in fact, he greeted her with no worse than a curt nod. The duke shook his head and sighed, welcoming her more pleasantly, as did Giulio and Ferrante. She was surprised when no one mentioned Palagio and then realized that Correggio probably had not spoken of him, wishing to make that report to the duke in private.

Then Duke Ercole came forward to hand Lucrezia up to the dais himself, making a remark about the masked ball the next day and asking, as he seated her, about her costume. When she would not reveal what she would wear, he teased her gently about what mischief she planned to get into while her face was masked. She giggled and challenged him to recognize her and he shook his head

and said that she was sure to make a May game of a dull old man.
Both forbore to touch on any sensitive topic, like all twelve ladies-
in-waiting taking their places at the second table down or Ercole
Strozzi being solicitously helped to his seat between Angela and
Nicola.

The entire meal passed in pleasant, idle talk, most of it, after discussion of the masked ball was worn out, about future entertainments when the weather grew warmer in the great country estate of
Belriguardo. And when the sweet and savory were cleared away, the
duke called on the musicians to play music for dancing. The tables
were removed; Duke Ercole asked Lucrezia to dance, after which
he handed her to Alfonso. Much as Alfonso irritated her by his
sullen refusal to credit the value of art or literature, he was remarkably graceful—as he was a remarkable performer on the violin—
and Lucrezia enjoyed dancing with him.

It was well after the sixth hour of the night when Alfonso
escorted her to her apartment, and near the ninth hour before he left
her bed. She slept as if stunned and woke only when Lucia opened
her bedcurtains and let in the light of a late morning. For a little
while she lay still, blinking, recalling the two significant things said
last night, the first before dinner—that Correggio believed Palagio
was innocent of Bianca's murder—and the second while dancing
with Ferrante, who told her that Guadaruzzi swore that Palagio
had carried nothing out of Donna Bianca's chamber too large to be
slipped into his doublet.

She rose frowning, telling herself that what Correggio had said
were only words extorted by Palagio's threat to expose something
about Alfonso that Correggio did not want exposed. No one but
Palagio could have killed Bianca. He was in her chamber long
enough to have done it. But how? She remembered Correggio's
caustic remark about Palagio carrying poison in his purse.

One could carry a vial of poison in one's purse rather than a whole bottle of poisoned wine. But there had been no wine, no bottle, no cups, nothing to eat or drink in Bianca's room. Had Palagio seized Bianca and forced her to drink the poison? Impossible. He could have muffled her cry when he seized her, but he had to leave her mouth free to pour the poison in and she would have screamed and wakened Maria.

Was that why Correggio said he believed Palagio? He had sounded sincere, not cynical, as he often sounded when he said what was expedient rather than what was true. But if it was true that Palagio had not poisoned Bianca, they were back to someone who had hidden in her chambers, killed her as soon as Maria went down to order the refreshments, and fled before Maria returned. Had Maria locked the back door? Lucrezia could not remember asking that question.

She got out of bed and said to Lucia, "I must speak to Maria again. Can you fetch her to me?"

"Today, madonna?" Lucia looked very distressed.

"Why not today?" Lucrezia asked. "She has nothing much to do, does she?"

"Usually no, madonna, but because of the masked ball, Madonna Adriana Castelli asked for a second maid and we recommended Maria to her. If she does well, possibly Madonna Adriana will employ her. . . ."

It would be very important for the girl to find a new place, and to find one with a woman who no doubt knew Maria's previous mistress had been murdered was a double benefit. Lucrezia thought about whether her question was really important enough to interfere with Maria's chance of new employment and decided she could wait until the next day to ask. Besides, she had better start thinking about her own costume and summon Angela and Nicola so they could dress together.

"Very well, Lucia. I will not pull Maria away from Donna Adriana now, but I want to speak to her first thing tomorrow morning. Will you see that she is here when I wake?" Lucia nodded and dropped a curtsy and Lucrezia went on, "And send Ascanio—or whatever page is on duty—to tell Angela and Nicola that I am ready to break my fast and then start trying on our costumes."

The ladies, wide awake and eager, arrived with their maids carrying well-covered bundles before Lucrezia was enveloped in a soft robe. The maids carried their burdens into the bedchamber to join Lucia, and Lucrezia came out to join Angela and Nicola at the table set up in her private reception room. As soon as breakfast had been carried in, she told Angela to softly close the door behind the portiere to the public reception room. She did not want anyone peeping around the curtain if their voices should rise in excitement and awake curiosity.

Angela peeped out before she did so and told Lucrezia there was little chance of being spied upon, that the only persons in her public reception room, aside from the page and the guards, were the ladies assigned to wait on her that day. That made Lucrezia hold up her hand to stop Angela from closing the door. Then she herself stepped out into the public reception room and told the ladies that she gave them permission not to wait upon her that day but to spend the day as she intended to do, trying on and embellishing their costumes for the ball that evening.

They seemed actually grateful, and thanked her, and she waited until they left the room. Then she returned to her own private room . . . and closed the door anyway. After that she sat down to eat. All of them had excellent appetites and the talk was all about their costumes. When the dishes were pushed aside, they rose as one and trotted into Lucrezia's bedchamber. There the maids had laid out the garments on Lucrezia's bed.

For one moment Lucrezia considered locking the door that led to Alfonso's apartment, but then she laughed silently at herself. The last thing she wanted was to wake any jealousy in her husband. At the present time, despite his obvious displeasure over some of the men she favored, like Ercole Strozzi, he did not seem to distrust her at all, and it was the dearest wish of her heart to keep his trust. She reminded herself that she had intended to reveal herself to him so she would awaken no doubts about her behavior.

Lucrezia tried on her costume first, a tight-fitting, flesh-colored sleeveless tunic. Angela giggled, Nicola pursed her lips and said it was indecent; Lucrezia pointed out that it would be well covered in flowing draperies. Then they all began to attach the nearly transparent veils Lucrezia had chosen, Lucia and the other maids hastily stitching them to the tunic and to other veils. Eventually Nicola was content and Angela began to frown—until Lucrezia started to move. Then the women's expressions began to change; both looked surprised, almost worried.

"Madonna," Angela said doubtfully, "I could almost swear you were naked under the veils."

Lucia held a mirror, lowering it slowly so Lucrezia could get some idea of how she looked. She shook her head. "I see only layers of veils that hide my shape better than any gown." She pouted slightly. "I look dull."

"Until you move," Nicola warned. "The veils are so light that they float away from your body, and that flesh-colored tunic looks . . . Lucia, hold the mirror so Madonna Lucrezia can see her arm. There. Now, madonna, move your arm gently right and left. . . ."

Lucrezia watched in the mirror and then giggled. She could not really see the skin of her arm at any time, but no one would doubt that there was no sleeve under the veiling. With the flesh-colored tunic on her body . . .

"It does look as if you can see my flesh," she admitted, then giggled again. "But you cannot. And I *am* wearing a tunic under the veils, even if it has no sleeves."

Her ladies continued to look worried, and Lucrezia sighed. "Lucia, go to the Palazzo Cortile and look at that painting showing Hebe serving wine to the gods. Do you remember where we were when I showed it to you in the grand sala?"

"Yes, madonna."

"Go and see if the goddess perhaps wore a golden girdle or something of that sort. Perhaps if I belt down the veils . . . not all of them, but some near my waist . . . then the others will show the gold when they move. We will see. Before you go, Lucia, help me out of this, and Nicola, put on your costume."

This consisted of a very thin white shift with voluminous, tight-cuffed sleeves and very full pantaloons that were gathered at the ankle. Since Nicola had chosen a soft but densely woven gold-colored silk, her legs were as effectively hidden as in an ordinary gown. Moreover, the body of the pants was loose enough that little definition of the crotch or buttocks showed. Still, the black band that surrounded her waist and was fitted over her upper hips gave the garment a decidedly sensual look, and the way the silk pants clung and swayed around her body was quite erotic.

Atop the thin shift, Nicola wore a tight black bodice liberally embroidered in gold thread. With her black hair loose on her shoulders and a wide gold band with a huge red stone in the center around her forehead to keep the hair out of her face, she looked very exotic indeed.

Lucrezia sighed. "I hate to make you wear that yellow wig with all its little braids. Your own hair is so much better suited to the costume."

Nicola laughed. "But it will puzzle everyone so much because the braids are so . . . so Ferrara. Everyone will try to think what silly woman would not give up showing her blond braids with a costume like mine. And I will only pin my hair up loosely and keep the headband with me so when we unmask, I can show how the costume should look."

"We will be dancing and making merry at least as long after the unmasking as before, probably longer," Angela said. "So Nicola's costume should have plenty of time to have its full effect."

"I suppose so," Lucrezia agreed as Nicola's maid began to help her take off the costume and replace her day gown. Lucrezia nodded to Angela's woman, who began to undo Angela's overskirt. "And we had better look at you in your shepherdess's dress before it is time for the midday meal. In case you realize you want something different after all. I don't know why you chose something so ordinary, Angela."

But when Angela had slipped on the short, full-skirted underdress with its very low-gathered neckline, lavishly embroidered in bright colors, and then put the dull blue gammura over it, pinned high on one hip as if to keep it out of damp grass and rough briars, Lucrezia knew that Angela's fine sense of what suited her had not abandoned her. The young woman's piquantly pretty face became utterly enchanting. Even Lucrezia was tempted to kiss her sweet, pouting lips. And there was a sense of such freshness about the milk-white bosom peeping—now more, now less—out above the bright embroidery of the blouse that the eye could hardly resist resting there.

Nicola offered a pretense of a sigh of exasperation. "Even with a black wig she will have every man under fifty chasing her. No one will be able to resist such sweet simplicity."

Lucrezia laughed. "I must admit I myself am tempted to kiss those lips . . . and perhaps that pretty breast also."

"It is my face," Angela said, grinning. "Something about the way the bones lie makes me look like a child. Sometimes Madonna Lucrezia can make herself look innocent also, but with me the face atop my body . . ."

"Yes, indeed," Nicola agreed. "You are delicious and—"

A determined scratching on the door interrupted her and she went and opened the door a bare inch. Adriano was standing there and over his shoulder Nicola could see a whole troop of helpers, including Innocenzio, his chief assistant. Nicola said to him, "Just a moment," and closed the door to tell Lucrezia that Adriano had decided they should eat a full dinner instead of the usual light repast. Lucrezia went out to talk to her cook—even a duchess does not offend a cook of Adriano's abilities—while Angela removed her costume and dressed in her ordinary clothing.

When her ladies emerged from her bedchamber, Lucrezia informed them that they were, indeed, to have dinner because there would be no time for a meal before the beginning of the ball. Of course, there would be food enough at the ball; Adriano and his staff had been deeply involved in the preparations and would be at the ball together with Alfonso's staff—Adriano sighed expressively, but he did not openly criticize the young and inexperienced cooks that served Alfonso—to help the duke's cooks serve.

"But that will be late, madonna," Adriano said, stepping aside so the ladies could advance on the elegantly set table. "If you do not eat enough now, you will be starved, and that, in your condition, is not wise."

So they ate and they ate and while they ate they addressed the question of how to hide their costumes once they were ready for the ball. There was no sense in walking out of Lucrezia's private rooms in their costumes—with or without the wigs. The ladies-in-waiting would immediately tell everyone they knew what Lucrezia and her "Spanish" ladies were wearing.

Various ideas were put forward and dismissed as too complicated or unlikely actually to hide the costumes and wigs until Nicola suddenly said, "Venetian cloaks!"

There was a moment of silence and then Lucrezia and Angela both began to laugh. Nicola and Angela knew that Giulio and Ferrante both had such cloaks and offered to ask to borrow them, but Lucrezia decided to buy identical cloaks for all of them. The maids were dispatched on that errand and Lucrezia and her women filled in the idle hours with small talk and silly games. Once or twice Lucrezia thought of Donna Bianca and wondered whether Correggio really believed Palagio innocent or was merely bowing to pressure, but she was unable to feel any strong conviction either way.

She sighed. She would see Bianca's maid Maria tomorrow and get a better idea of whether anyone could have been hiding in the apartment or have crept in while Maria slept. No, that was impossible. Palagio said Bianca was dead when he entered the room.

The cloaks arrived and proved to be perfect for their purpose. When the clock rang the next to the last hour of the day, the maids helped their mistresses into their costumes and combed their hair so it would not be too much disarrayed by the wig hiding it or the removal of that wig. Finally the voluminous Venetian cloaks were drawn over everything, the hoods lifted and pulled far enough forward to hide the masked faces within. The women looked at each other and smiled in satisfaction, until Lucrezia looked down to be sure her cloak was not dragging or exposing the hem of her veils.

"Shoes," she said. "Our shoes must be the same or we will be known by them."

They soon decided that black velvet slippers would fit best with all of the costumes. Of course, Lucrezia should have been wearing sandals and Angela wooden clogs, but it was too cool for sandals, Lucrezia decided, and Angela could not dance in wooden clogs. The maids brought the shoes and helped change them, gave a last look over their mistresses, and led the way into the private reception room. As they found seats, they heard the low murmur of voices through the portiere. It seemed that many besides Lucrezia's ladies had come to see what their future duchess would wear.

Alfonso did not keep them waiting long. He arrived soon after the clock had struck the last hour, his costume also concealed by a cloak but his head bare, his face unmasked. One side of the cloak bulged, as if he were carrying something in his arm. He looked at the three hooded figures and scowled. In the shadow of their hoods all three women smiled. Alfonso gestured toward the door. All three rose from their seats. Angela went first, then Lucrezia, then Nicola. Without hesitation Alfonso stepped forward and gave his arm to the middle figure.

"Oh, how did you know?" Lucrezia asked. "I thought we had been so clever."

"I doubt anyone else would know," Alfonso said, grinning with satisfaction, "but I . . . I know your body very well."

11

7 April,

Duke Ercole's grand sala

THE ROOM was bathed in golden light from hundreds of candles. It was bright as day, but the light fell mostly from the great candelabra hung from the rafters and was concentrated in the center of the room. Thus the paintings that lined the walls seemed less dominant and drew the eyes and the attention less. Also those static scenes had bright rivals.

The huge chamber was crowded already with men and women in brilliant dress ornamented with brilliant jewels. Every type of costume was there, from swaggering corsairs in gaudy red and blue to black-garbed priests. Multicolored harlequins pursued wide-skirted milkmaids. Knights clanked about in armor, crimson-garbed cardinals escorted ladies in every garb real and fanciful. Many of the guests were not even trying to conceal their identities, using only a thin black mask across their eyes. Others wore full-face masks: comedy and tragedy, gods and heroes, queens known to history.

Along the inner wall were tables for the food the cooks had labored over and would soon serve. Behind them screens had been set to provide space for the cooks to work, but those spaces could also give the guests privacy for the adjustment of masks and costumes. Lucrezia, who had dropped Alfonso's arm once safely up the staircase, watched with some amusement as he hurried ahead and down the room into one of the screened areas, ejecting the cooks.

His idea was excellent, however, and she and her women took possession of another screened space, much closer to the outer door. There they removed their cloaks, made sure their masks were in place and their wigs were not askew, and moved together out of their shelter, handing the cloaks to one of the servants who stood between the screened-off places.

Lucrezia had again been in the middle. Nicola glided away to the right, Angela skipped gaily off to the left. Through her nearly full-faced mask—not black but skin-toned and painted with flowers and butterflies by Master Giovanni Lateri—Lucrezia looked around the room. She was determined to recognize Alfonso as he had recognized her—but would he know her in the black wig? She wanted to go to him and take his arm and whisper his name in his ear, and see what response he would make.

At first she had no opportunity. Within moments of stepping past the screen, a gentleman came up to her, bowing and requesting that she dance. She agreed, and they walked up the room toward the dais, where the musicians played on one side and the duke's high chair occupied the other. Lucrezia was amused that her partner, after sliding his hand under the scarfs that hid her arms and finding flesh, tried to reach around her back to penetrate those that covered her breast. He was frustrated by the firm texture of her tunic, and by then she had recognized him.

Lowering her voice to a husky whisper, very unlike her usual light tones, she said, "Naughty, naughty, Don Cagnolo. If you do not behave, I will tell your wife."

He lifted his hand away from her back and laughed uneasily. "How did you know me?"

"I am not sure I should tell you because that would let you remove the telltale sign and free you to even greater mischief."

"A masked ball is a night for mischief," he responded.

"Well, perhaps." Lucrezia laughed. "It is the buckles of your shoes. A small vanity, but very beautiful, and most characteristic."

Don Cagnolo laughed aloud. "My wife bought those buckles and bade me wear these shoes. Oh, so she is jealous, is she? I will tease her life out of her for that."

They finished the dance with him guessing about her identity and trying to get her to confirm or deny. He was far enough asea that Lucrezia was delighted, and as they parted, after she refused a second dance with him, he accused her of looking for mischief too.

"No," she said, keeping to the husky whisper, "I merely want to surprise one person."

She slipped away from her partner before he could promise to tell no one and made her way closer to the dais. The duke was in his great chair, masked but not costumed more than an unusually gorgeous suit of clothing. She soon made out Ferrante in his lion skin and Giulio in the flamboyant dress of the Swiss guards. He was pursuing one of the several shepherdesses in the room, but it was not Angela. Lucrezia heard her high, sweet laughter from somewhere behind her.

Before she could turn toward the laugh, another partner presented himself. First she pretended reluctance, but then she allowed herself to be led to the dancing floor. This partner seemed more determined to discover who she was than to discover whether she was really naked under her veils, but he got no further than Cagnolo in either investigation.

Nor did Lucrezia come closer to discovering which of the men was Alfonso until nearly two candlemarks later, when she caught a glimpse of a Roman centurion striding across the lower edge of the dance floor toward the tables set out with food. She knew instantly who was under the Roman helmet, although it covered the upper half of the face completely. There was something in the way he carried himself, a heavy leonine grace that she had often watched through slitted eyes as he approached her bed. And she knew the legs under the short Roman tunic too; they were every bit as well shaped as those of Ferrante.

Now she had found him, she was able to relax. When the dance was over she would find him again and would make herself known. That would infuriate him and put the cap on the good time she was having. She had identified most of the important people of the Court as well as nearly all of her ladies. Don Niccolò da Correggio she knew as soon as he asked her to dance despite his monk's robe; and to her pleasure, he made no attempt to find flesh beneath her veils. Don Gian Luca Castellini da Pontremoli she recognized by his voice, as she recognized Count Ugoccione dei Contrari, who was married to Alfonso's cousin Diana.

The name reminded her of something that had made her uneasy, and she glanced over her shoulder at the bottom of the room, where chairs were ranged against the wall for those who grew wearied. She had seen Diana Altoviti's costume when they passed through her public reception room before the woman put on her mask, so she had had no trouble recognizing her in the sala. Earlier she had noticed Donna Diana seated in a corner and wondered if she was still almost hiding herself. Diana had been very quiet since the trouble on the stairway.

Lucrezia felt guilty over that. Perhaps she should try to reassure Diana that no blame was attached to her over the incident. But she did not want to encourage any of the Ferrarese women, so she was relieved to see that Diana was gone from the corner, and when she glanced over the dance floor, Lucrezia saw Diana dancing with a young man she did not recognize who was dressed as a cook. Both were laughing, and although Lucrezia raised her brows at the young man's choice of costume, she was glad to see Diana enjoying herself.

The same could not be said for the woman Lucrezia guessed was Donna Teodora, who passed through Lucrezia's line of sight as her partner turned her to face him in the dance. The woman was scowling so ferociously that the lines in her brow showed above the mask she wore and her mouth was turned down below it. Lucrezia remembered that it had been Donna Teodora who had actually pushed her—no, had fallen against her. And then because the idea that anyone would deliberately wish to harm her was so hurtful, she reminded herself that it had been an accident and Alfonso had saved her.

The memory of how tightly he had held her against him when he had kept her from falling down the long, marble stair restored her happiness and she looked over her partner's shoulder again to find him. Alfonso was still at the tables. She would go to him as soon as the dance was over; she would be safe with Alfonso. Then the movement of the dance turned her around again and she caught a glimpse of the entryway, where Sigismundo was just coming in the door.

That was odd, she thought, and then wondered why she should think it odd that Sigismundo should come to the ball, but Don Gian Luca said something and she had to ask him to repeat himself and then answer him. She was keeping to the husky whisper she had used from the beginning and it was obvious that Gian Luca had no idea with whom he was dancing. She forgot the chill the memory of the staircase had given her and began to be amused again.

He asked another question and another, but eventually Lucrezia was able to bow her thanks to him and remove her hand from his grasp. She smiled and shook her head, refusing to dance again, and then shook her head once more to reject the proffered escort to another part of the room.

"I want to surprise someone," she said, slipping away.

She just caught Alfonso, who had set down his plate and was starting to move away from the table. "Wait, Alfonso," she whispered. "I knew you as soon as I saw you. Did you know me?"

"Lucrezia? Balls of the Savior, you fooled me after all with that wig. I looked at the hair and never looked elsewhere. I thought maybe you were the harem girl, but the body wasn't right."

"That's just what we wanted you to think." Lucrezia giggled. "It's Nicola under those little blond braids."

He laughed with more good humor than she had expected and she began to fill a plate. Suddenly she paused and looked up at Alfonso. "Why didn't Sigismundo wear a costume?" she asked, realizing what it was she thought was odd.

When she saw him enter the sala, Sigismundo had been wearing a full-face mask, but he had been wearing ordinary clothes, his favorite black velvet jerkin over a bright green doublet topped by a green cape. He had even been wearing his favorite hat, a soft black velvet cap adorned with two bright peacock feathers.

"Costume?" Alfonso repeated, adding some pheasant's breast to her plate and putting another piece of it onto his. "Why should he be wearing a costume? As far as I know, he didn't intend to come to the ball. He has a famous guest."

"But I saw him come in," Lucrezia said.

Although she could not see much of his face, Lucrezia knew that Alfonso was frowning and his lips tightened with concern. "I wonder if Sigismundo's guest brought news that had to be given to my father at once," he said. But then he did not seem to know what he wanted to do. He glanced toward the dais and a muscle in his jaw tightened and jumped.

"Let us walk up that way," Lucrezia said, putting down her

plate of food untouched. "We can see if he is talking to your father. And he might not have come with news. You know Sigismundo. If his guest or Ercole decided they wanted to speak to someone like Correggio, Sigismundo would not hesitate to come fetch him from the ball."

Alfonso had turned his masked face to her; his lips, soft and full, seemed about to utter thanks. Instead they thinned and he asked, "Ercole Strozzi is with them?"

Lucrezia's brows lifted above her mask. "Well, there isn't much sense in his coming to a masked ball, is there? He cannot dance, and his crutch is identification enough. And no matter what you think, he is greatly respected as a scholar."

"Scholar."

The contempt in the word made Lucrezia bristle and begin a defense of the value of scholars, but it was plain that Alfonso was not listening. However, they had now made their way far enough forward to see that Sigismundo was not with the duke. Alfonso took Lucrezia's hand as if to lead her into the dancing, but he was looking around.

"I see him," he muttered, and suddenly dropped her hand. "Sigismundo, wait," he called, and began to make his way right through the dance set.

Lucrezia stood staring after him, furious at being abandoned as if he could not be bothered to dance with her. As far as she knew, there was nothing Alfonso needed to discuss with Sigismundo with any urgency. If he wanted to speak to his brother, he could have waited until morning.

"Alas, madonna, I see you abandoned, but the soldiers of Rome were always known to be cruel."

"And crude also," Lucrezia said with a last glance in the direction Alfonso had gone.

She could not see Sigismundo, and Alfonso had also disappeared. She smiled at the gentleman who was bowing over her hand. She did not recognize him, but the mellifluous voice was familiar. Surely she had heard it declaiming something . . . Suddenly she dropped a curtsy and bowed her head to conceal her grin. Yes, indeed, she knew the voice. It was the poet Ariosto—a really fine poet; she had read some of his work and Ercole Strozzi thought the world of him, but she had never been able to take him seriously after he had greeted her arrival in Ferrara with an overblown epithalamium in which he had addressed her as beauteous virgin . . . after three marriages and a son.

She had her mouth under control again when she rose and took his hand, but refused to dance, mentioning her abandoned plate and her growing appetite. The young man, graceful and witty now that he was not trying to make an impression, escorted her back to the table, where the presiding cook's helper solicitously began to fill a new plate for her. She was playfully asking Ariosto's advice about what to choose—starving poets frequently ate for a week at the duke's tables when invited—when a woman's piercing scream made her stop and turn her head.

She was not alarmed at first. She expected the shriek to change to laughter or into angry shouts, but it went on and on and Lucrezia abandoned her plate again and hurried toward the source of the sound. That was where Alfonso had been going when she last saw him.

Of course, by the time she tried to reach the place the crowd had closed into a solid block in front of her. She heard a hubbub of men's voices mingled with more than one woman's hysterical cries. Then the duke's stentorian bellow cut across the noise and Lucrezia backed out of the crowd blocking her way across the room and ran in front of the tables through an area now empty up to the dais.

"What is it?" she cried, taking hold of the duke's arm. He looked down at her as if to offer a sharp reprimand and she went on quickly, "It is Lucrezia. Where is Alfonso?"

"Doing something stupid, as usual, I suppose," Ercole d'Este growled, but he allowed her to accompany him as he bawled, "Make way! Make way!" and forged through the crowd.

"Have a care, my lord," Correggio said, turning away from a windowed alcove and blocking it with his broad back. "There's been murder done here." And then Alfonso was there beside Correggio, his hand on his sword hilt.

Lucrezia's breath caught and she could feel her eyes widen. There was blood on Alfonso's hand! Most of it must have been on the palm, but a streak, just starting to brown at the edge, could be seen along the skin between the thumb and the forefinger and along the opposite edge from the middle of the little finger to his wrist.

"Murder?" the duke bellowed. "You mean a duel was fought here in my sala?"

"No, my lord." Correggio pulled off his mask and pushed back the monk's hood. "A man was murdered. He was stabbed in the throat, and not by any dueling sword."

For a moment Ercole d'Este simply gaped at his trusted courtier, speechless with outrage, then his eyes slid sideways toward his eldest son, who had removed the centurion's helmet. Lucrezia swallowed back a soft sob. Alfonso's face was as pale as his swarthy complexion could get. Because she could not help it, her glance fixed on the sword hilt he had been clutching. Once it had been bright gold; now it was discolored.

"Guards!" the duke bellowed.

"No!" Lucrezia whispered, her hands covering her mouth.

Ercole d'Este did not appear to hear her and did not glance her way. When the guards arrived, he merely told them to cordon off the area in which the dead man was. Then he called for his mae-stro di sala and told him to apologize to the guests and see that they left.

"And make them all unmask as they go," Alfonso said. "If there is anyone there you do not know or who was not on the list of guests, make sure to discover who that person is. Get a name and a direction. If you have any suspicion of any persons, put them in a room under guard."

"Alfonso?" the duke said softly, but Lucrezia could hear the sur-prise and doubt in his voice.

"Well, I did not kill the man," Alfonso said irritably. "Why are you looking at me so strangely? I never touched him—"

"Then why is there blood on your hand?" the duke asked.

"Blood . . ." Alfonso lifted his hand and stared at it. His jaw clenched. He unclenched it with an effort. "I will explain later. I did not kill the man," he repeated. "I do not even know who the devil it is. I thought he was just asleep in that chair. I didn't know he was dead until the damn woman started to scream."

"Where is the woman?" the duke asked.

"Here, my lord," Count Ugoccione said, gently turning a woman who was weeping on his breast toward Duke Ercole. "This is Beat-rice Tisio, a distant kinswoman. She found the dead man."

"Beatrice," Lucrezia breathed.

Beatrice, who hated Bianca for not giving her the money to save her brother a beating. And the beating was because of a gambling debt. Could the brother have been gambling with the dead man? Who was the dead man?

"Who is the dead man?" Lucrezia asked, voice echoing thought.

Her voice was her own, high and clear. Both Count Ugoccione and Don Gian Luca stared at her. She had spoken to both as they danced in a husky whisper. She pulled off her mask and then her wig, distracted for an instant by regret that she could not enjoy their surprise, but her doubt drove her to repeat, "Who is it?"

One of the guards stepped forward at Duke Ercole's gesture and gingerly removed the mask. Beatrice screamed again and was abruptly silenced by the count.

Lucrezia gasped, "Palagio!"

She then looked hastily away, swallowing hard and very grateful that she had had no chance to eat anything. Below the man's chin, a gaping wound had released a waterfall of red, which had soaked the front of his costume.

"You know this man?" the duke asked.

"Yes," Lucrezia replied. "He came to me on the recommendation of Madonna Isabella. She said he was a poet. . . . I can only suppose she never heard any of his verses. Because of her recommendation I did not feel I could forbid him my public room, so he was often there, but I had nothing to do with him after the first—and last—reading he inflicted on me."

She heard her own voice, too high, and knew she was babbling. She swallowed hard and fixed her eyes on the duke's face. Then she took a deep breath and said slowly, "The ladies you appointed to serve me knew him far better than I."

"You are accusing my daughter—"

"Do not be silly, Your Highness. I am accusing Madonna Isabella of nothing besides wanting to be rid of a very bad poet. And he kept saying he was from Naples, so perhaps she thought I would like to talk to him."

"From Naples? He was of Aragon?"

"In fact, he was not. He did not even know as much about Naples as a common visitor and his speech had no touch of a Spanish accent."

"He could still have been a Spanish spy," the duke growled. "It is more likely if he was not himself Spanish."

"I suppose so," Lucrezia agreed doubtfully, "but if so, what was he doing wasting his time in my apartment? I know nothing any spy could wish to hear."

The duke's eyes flicked toward Alfonso, then back to Lucrezia, but all he said was, "No hint of Cesare's plans?"

Lucrezia also glanced toward Alfonso, who stood pale and silent, then she laughed. "My brother knows what I think of most of his plans and he never speaks or writes to me about them. Sometimes he asks me about a matter of administration, for you know I ruled Spoleto for a year, but I cannot imagine why Palagio should be interested in minor legal disputes and I cannot remember ever speaking about such matters in my public reception room."

"Then perhaps he came there to meet someone."

The duke's eyes again moved toward Alfonso, who stood silent, his head turned toward the window, but he did not seem to be aware of his father's suspicion.

"If so, I am not aware of it," Lucrezia said. "It would not be one of my intimates, like Nicola or Angela or Alfonso; they almost never went into the public reception room, and even Giulio, Ferrante, and Sigismundo only passed through. But I can ask my women—"

"Your Highness," Count Ugoccione interrupted, "I think you had better hear what Donna Beatrice has to say. It is important."

The count glanced around as he spoke, and so did Lucrezia, who realized that almost all the guests were gone now, only a few still unmasking before the maestro di sala near the entrance. The group around the body, all looking elsewhere, consisted of four guards, Count Ugoccione and Beatrice, Don Gian Luca, Correggio, herself, Alfonso, and the duke.

"No, no," Beatrice cried hysterically, trying to turn away. "It is all a mistake. I saw nothing. I was only frightened and . . . and babbled what could not be true . . ."

Lucrezia examined the woman from head to toe just as Duke Ercole was examining her, but her hands and her costume were clean of any spots or stains of blood.

"Ugoccione?" Duke Ercole asked uncertainly, again glancing at Alfonso.

The count shook his head infinitesimally while patting Beatrice gently on the shoulder. "I think we could all talk more easily if the guards disposed of the body and the servants cleaned up the floor."

Lucrezia could not prevent herself from looking and saw that the floor in front of the chair in which Palagio still sat had a very small puddle of blood between the corpse's feet and spatters on its shoes and beyond them on the floor. She looked away hastily.

"Of course," the duke said. "Let us go to my apartment. We will be more comfortable. Lucrezia, I am sure your women are waiting for you just outside the door. If not, the maestro di sala will arrange—"

"Oh, no, Your Highness. I am coming too. Beatrice is one of my ladies-in-waiting and, although I did not appoint her and do not want her, neither will I leave her to the tender mercies of five selfish and angry men. Besides that, Palagio's death may not have anything to do with politics at all. He was the one who had the best opportunity to murder Donna Bianca, but if he was not guilty—as Don Niccolò insists—then he had the best opportunity to see who did murder the poor woman . . . which would give that person a very good reason to murder him."

"Let her come," Alfonso said, "or the whole world will be told that we are trying to cover up murder and other shameful crimes."

The duke cast an odd look at his son, but said no more, shrugging and turning away to lead the party to his apartment on the next floor of the palace. Servants ran ahead to light candles and to put more wood on the fire. When wine and cakes had been brought in and set on a handsome table between the windows, the servants were dismissed and the duke turned to the woman Count Ugoccione still held with an arm around her shoulders.

"Your name is Donna Beatrice Tisio?" the duke asked.

Beatrice swallowed and nodded. "Yes, but I saw nothing. I swear I saw nothing."

Lucrezia got up from the chair she had settled into and poured a glass of wine, which she brought to Beatrice. "It is too late to say that," she said, offering the glass. "Here, take some wine and tell us what you told Count Ugoccione. I know you think it a terrible thing, but perhaps what you saw was not what actually happened."

"I was hysterical. I was . . . I . . . I . . ."

"Donna Beatrice, was Palagio the man who gambled with your brother?"

"No!" Beatrice shrieked, breaking free of Ugoccione's hold. "No! My brother has nothing to do with this. He was not here tonight."

"I am sure he was not," Lucrezia said silkily, "but you were. Now, will you not tell us what you saw?"

Beatrice's dark eyes bulged and her lips drew back to show her teeth. With her sharp nose and pointed chin, she looked like a vicious rat at bay.

"Oh, yes, I will!" she cried, rage overcoming fear. "I will tell you! You will not accuse me of murder, nor put the crime on my poor brother. I will tell you what I saw. I saw Don Sigismundo stab Palagio to death. That is what I saw!"

12

"SIGISMUNDO?" Lucrezia's voice scaled upward in a crescendo of disbelief.

"Ridiculous!" Don Gian Luca said.

"Nonsense!" Correggio exclaimed.

"Sigismundo?" the duke echoed Lucrezia, with an equal amount of disbelief in his voice.

The only one who had not exclaimed was Alfonso. He stood by a window, which was glassed, and stared out into the dark.

Now the duke turned his eyes on Lucrezia. "Now you see what you have accomplished! Why did you say you suspect her? Because she found the body? All you have done is made her lie."

"I did it to make her speak," Lucrezia said. "Because she could not lie. Remember, she had already told Count Ugoccione what she saw." Lucrezia turned to the count. "Is that what she told you when you first reached her?"

"Yes," Count Ugoccione said. "That is what she said. She was screaming so much that at first I did not understand her, but I heard 'Sigismundo,' and when I turned her away from the body, she said, 'Don Sigismundo did it.' I had not yet seen the body because I was looking at her. I should have realized no one could sleep through such shrieks, but I was annoyed because the man in the chair offered no help and I shook her hard and asked, 'Did what?' and she said, 'Stabbed him,' and pointed."

All of them except Alfonso stared at Ugoccione in silence for a few long moments.

"I could not believe it either," the count said, "but I had no time to question her. Her shrieks had brought a crowd about us. Some other women noticed and began to scream. . . . I silenced Beatrice, but—"

The duke held up a hand and walked to the door, where he bade his page run and fetch Sigismundo. "Have him waked if his servant says he has gone to bed. He must come, and at once."

Count Ugoccione steered Beatrice to a chair and refilled her wine glass, but he did not speak to her. Lucrezia filled another glass with wine and carried it to Alfonso.

"Go and wash your hand," she said softly to him.

She remembered now that although his hand was stained and the hilt of the short Roman sword was bloodied where his hand had gripped it, his clothes were not spotted, nor his shoes. The shock/relief—relief because, despite what Beatrice thought she saw, Lucrezia could not believe that Sigismundo would kill anyone—of hearing Sigismundo blamed had reduced her fear that Alfonso had killed Palagio to prevent him from telling the duke his son had been making overtures to the Spanish.

Lucrezia shuddered, remembering. She had seen a man killed, stabbed in the throat as Palagio had been, and his blood had sprayed out when the dagger was draw. Alfonso might have touched the dead man, but whoever killed Palagio must have been spattered with blood, if not drenched with it, and Alfonso was not. He looked down at her, his black eyes utterly blank. Something had shocked him deeply. She shuddered again. Could Alfonso also have seen Sigismundo kill Palagio? He had been calling out to his brother when he left her. She offered the glass of wine.

"Drink it," she urged. "Then go and wash your hand."

"He was running away," he muttered, whether to her or to himself, Lucrezia could not tell. "And his cloak was on the terrace outside the window. I picked it up. It was . . ." He swallowed, then took the glass of wine from her and drank it down in three gulps.

"Not Sigismundo," Lucrezia said. "I cannot—I will not—believe he would commit murder."

"For me? To save me? I never let Ferrante or Giulio torment him."

Lucrezia took the empty glass from Alfonso's stained hand. "No," she said. "He is too clever. He would have found another way. Go and wash yourself, and the hilt of that sword also."

Alfonso had barely returned when Sigismundo arrived. He looked decidedly cross.

"What is it, Father? Why did you call me away from a guest who is so important and has so little time?"

"For another matter, equally important," the duke said sharply. "Why did you kill Guido del Palagio?"

Sigismundo simply stared at his father for a long moment. Finally he said, "Why did I do what to whom?"

"Kill Guido del Palagio," Ercole d'Este repeated, his voice harsher.

"You cannot be serious," Sigismundo said, looking utterly bewildered.

"I am perfectly serious," the duke said, obviously growing angry. Then he said, almost pleading, "Give me a reason, Sigismundo. Give me a reason for this killing."

"I do not believe I have ever killed anyone," Sigismundo said, "and I do not think I even know this . . . this Palagio. Why are you accusing me of such a terrible crime against a man I cannot remember meeting?"

"Someone saw you," Duke Ercole said. "Someone saw you stab Palagio to death."

Sigismundo looked even more bewildered and turned his eyes toward his brother. Lucrezia looked from one to the other. There were tears in Alfonso's eyes, but he did not speak.

"When am I supposed to have done this thing?" Sigismundo asked.

"Tonight during the masked ball. This woman"—Ercole d'Este gestured toward Beatrice—"saw you stab Palagio in the throat."

"Madonna, you are mad," Sigismundo said, shaking his head. "I was not at the ball. I was sitting in my own apartment with Master Leonardo da Vinci and Ercole Strozzi—"

"I saw you!" Beatrice shrieked, leaping to her feet. "I saw you! You were wearing your favorite clothes, that black jerkin over a green doublet with a green cloak and that big soft black hat with the peacock feathers. You walked right over to Palagio and spoke to him and raised your hand and stabbed him in the neck."

Sigismundo blinked. "You are saying that I wore my favorite clothing, a suit everyone has seen me wear, and a hat with peacock feathers, which everyone knows I love, to stab a man in the neck in public? Madonna, I resent that. It is bad enough to try to make me out a vicious killer, but to add to that that I am a total idiot is too much."

There was one moment of breath-held silence, and then Lucrezia began to laugh aloud. She jumped to her feet and ran to embrace Sigismundo. "Oh, I knew you did not," she cried. "I knew . . . and yet I was too stupid to realize that a man bent on murder does not scream his identity aloud."

"You were too shocked, sister," Sigismundo said, and kissed her cheek.

"But *I* did not kill him!" Beatrice Tisio screamed. "Just because he wore his own clothing you will call him innocent and blame me?"

Count Ugoccione put his hand on her shoulder and Lucrezia shook her head. "No one is blaming you," she said. "The duke and I both looked at your clothing while we were still in the Sala Bianca and there was no blood on it. I do not believe whoever killed Palagio could have escaped being spattered with blood."

"More than spattered," Alfonso said, coming to join Lucrezia and his brother. "I found your cloak on the terrace outside the window near where Palagio was killed, and the front was soaked with blood." He looked at Lucrezia. "That was where I got blood on my hand."

"You found *a* green cloak on the terrace," Sigismundo said sharply, "not *my* green cloak. Mine is, I suppose, in my apartment with my other clothes."

"You suppose," Correggio said, "but we need to know, Don Sigismundo."

"Are you saying that you believe I am such a fool that I would wear my own clothing to murder someone at a masked ball when I could have worn any costume at all?" Sigismundo turned eyes full of affront on his father's counselor.

"No, of course not," Correggio said with a short laugh. "I want to know whether your own cloak was stolen and, if it was, how it was stolen. That will tell us whether your servants are trustworthy. If it was not stolen, we may be able to trace who made a copy of it and through the tailor discover who ordered the copy made."

"Ah!" Sigismundo sounded satisfied.

"And we will need the evidence of Don Ercole Strozzi and Master Leonardo da Vinci," Ercole d'Este said.

He had sunk rather limply into a chair when Sigismundo denied any guilt. Now he was erect again and angry-looking. "There must have been guests who heard this idiot woman's accusation. Most will recognize the truth of Sigismundo's remarks that no sane man would wear his own favorite clothing in which to commit a murder, especially at a masked ball—"

"Not to mention," Sigismundo said with a grin, "that if Alfonso's remark about the blood on the cloak is correct, it would be the ruination of that favorite suit."

The duke glared at his youngest son. "This is not a joke."

Sigismundo continued to grin. "I am very sorry for my levity, Your Highness, but I cannot take seriously the idea that I would be stupid enough to go to a masked ball to stab a man I do not know, wearing my favorite suit of clothes."

Ercole d'Este snorted. "Idiot," he said, but fondly. Then he frowned. "I will send for Ercole Strozzi and Master Leonardo and I hope they can testify that you were in their sight and not absent from them at any time this evening. Then we will have to set about discovering why anyone should wish the blame for this crime to fall upon you. Unless"—he turned on Beatrice—"you lied about seeing my son—"

Beatrice shrank back in her chair and whimpered.

"No, Your Highness," Alfonso said. "I saw Sigismundo—I mean, the person pretending to be Sigismundo—also. I thought perhaps he had news of importance and I called out to him, but instead of coming to me he stepped out the window."

"I saw whoever it was too," Lucrezia said. "But I do not think you should summon Master Leonardo and Don Ercole. I think we should all go to Sigismundo's rooms. There we can not only question his guests but examine his clothing and ask his servants whether there had been the need to clean anything or discard it tonight."

"Do you not believe me?" Sigismundo asked Lucrezia, his eyes wide with shock.

She leaned over and kissed him, then pulled his arm through hers. "Of course I believe you. I say this because of my desire to make sure everyone will know that this is a calumny against you, that, perhaps, there has been an attempt to blacken not only your name but that of Duke Ercole for refusing to apply justice to his own son. I do not want any detail omitted that might later be questioned or said to have been deliberately ignored or falsified." She turned to Count Ugoccione. "By any chance do you remember anyone of note who was close enough to you to have heard Donna Beatrice's accusation?"

"They were all masked and I did not bother trying to discover who was who. Why do you want to know?"

"Because we here are all of the duke's family or in his closest confidence. We need an outsider. A man or woman of known probity who will support our evidence."

"Ah." Count Ugoccione nodded, his face wearing an expression of strong approval. Then he frowned in thought and said slowly, "The priest of Corpus Domini was there." At the expressions of surprise on everyone's face, he added, "I do not believe he was attending the ball, but he came running at Beatrice's screams and gave last unction to the dead man. He was not costumed or masked and I am not sure he heard Beatrice naming Don Sigismundo, but he is a witness everyone will believe."

Duke Ercole nodded agreement and said, "And Corpus Domini is no great distance. I will send for him at once."

"I will go," Don Gian Luca said. "I will be able to explain to him what happened so we do not all need to repeat our stories."

He suited his actions to his words. Sigismundo was clearly annoyed about losing so much time with his busy visitor, but understood without saying that he would not be allowed to go back to his apartment. He took a glass of wine and some cake and went over to talk to Correggio. The duke beckoned to Count Ugoccione, who left Beatrice's side and went to join him. Alfonso went to the table and refilled his glass, then filled one for Lucrezia and brought some cakes. They both sat down on the rug-covered chest under the window.

"I have been lucky in being unable to meet Palagio," he said in a low voice to Lucrezia.

"You think this is a political murder?" she asked.

"What else? Unless it is a purely private matter and someone killed him because he was Palagio rather than for being a Spanish spy . . . or not being one."

Lucrezia giggled. "Well, his poetry was *very* bad, but not so bad as to invite murder." She hesitated, then added judiciously, "Although if I had had to listen to it for any length of time I might have considered killing him to silence him."

Alfonso snorted, a sound so much like that his father had made that Lucrezia looked at him sharply. Outwardly he wasn't much like Duke Ercole, although both were clean-shaven. The duke's hair was mostly gone and what remained was lank and gray; Alfonso's hair was black and curly and he wore it long, down to his shoulders. His nose was less well defined than Duke Ercole's and his eyes were larger and darker. Still, there was something about the way his eyes were set . . .

Lucrezia glanced at him. Mostly Alfonso looked at nothing, out into the distance or down at the floor, as if to hide what he was thinking. Yes, as if to hide what he was thinking. As if he did not want his father or anyone else to know how clever he was. And he *was* clever. Much cleverer than he acted. He had been the one to tell the maestro di sala to have the guests unmask. She had been so much shocked by Palagio's dead body that she had completely forgotten the murderer could have walked out masked, after having got rid of the bloodstained cloak.

"You do not think he could have been killed for seeing more than he should in Donna Bianca's apartment?"

He looked down at her. "You think those deaths are linked, that

Palagio's is not a completely separate matter?" He shook his head. "Then why choose Sigismundo's clothing as a disguise? It was a masked ball. The person could have come in any guise at all. No, there must have been some purpose to that."

Lucrezia sighed. "I suppose so, but I just feel . . . Donna Bianca's death is so recent, and to have another murder so very soon . . . If it were not connected, it would be strange. I recall someone telling me that Ferrara was not like Rome, where one death was followed quickly by another."

Alfonso shrugged but said no more and they sat in silence. After a while, suddenly remembering how Beatrice had gobbled the breakfast she had offered, Lucrezia got up and filled a plate with cakes for her. The woman thanked her but without any particular warmth. Lucrezia was annoyed and then remembered that it was she who had forced Beatrice to tell the duke that she had seen Sigismundo; likely she feared that Duke Ercole would resent her accusation. She shrugged and return to her seat beside Alfonso.

Not long after, Don Gian Luca came in shepherding the priest of Corpus Domini. Duke Ercole thanked him for coming and assured him that none of them had left the room since Gian Luca had gone to fetch him. The priest shook his head.

"I am only glad that the murderer is being sought with honesty and diligence." Then he walked over to Beatrice and took her hand. "I hope you are recovered from your terrible fright, madonna."

"Yet now it seems I have brought a false accusation against an innocent man," she said with a sob.

"You told honestly what you saw. There is nothing to blame in that. Now we will go and see whether Don Sigismundo is, as he says, innocent." The priest smiled over his shoulder at Sigismundo, who had drawn a sharp breath. "Yes, yes, my son, I realize you resent being thought stupid, but to wear your own clothing could also be very clever. You are known for your sharp wits. Then who would believe you could act so stupid? Did not your first protest convince everyone that you were innocent?"

"My son would never—"

"Stoop to a lie? Murder an enemy?" The priest nodded sharply. "I think in this case you are probably telling the truth because I have some knowledge of Don Sigismundo, but I came to bear honest witness, and it would be wrong in me not to consider every side of the question."

"Indeed, Father, that is so," Ercole d'Este said. "So let us go to Sigismundo's rooms and uncover the truth."

Lucrezia was not at all surprised upon entering Sigismundo's apartment. If she had given it any thought, she would have imagined it just as it was, with good paintings on the walls, handsome rugs underfoot, comfortable chairs, a large clear fire—because evenings in early April grew chill—and very well lit.

When Sigismundo opened the door, Ercole Strozzi, who had been saying something in an animated voice about body proportions, only turned his head casually and said, "That was a very long few minutes you were away. But I have taken notes about everything I asked Master Leonardo and—" He stopped speaking abruptly when the duke followed Sigismundo into the room, and scrambled to his feet, grabbing for his crutch.

The duke nodded kindly and said, "Sit down, Ercole, there is no need for you to stand." He bowed to Leonardo, who had also risen. "You honor our house, Master da Vinci. Had my son not kept your visit a secret, I would have invited you to our ball and offered our hospitality."

"Don Sigismundo and I have been in correspondence for some time, and when this opportunity to visit arose, I begged him not to mention it to anyone." His eyes moved to the two women, settled on Lucrezia. "Your brother is well, Madonna Lucrezia, and often indulgent to me, but I did not want any long delay in my rejoining him to try his patience."

"Give him my love when you see him again," Lucrezia said, smiling. "And I do not blame you for not wanting to try Cesare's patience. He does roar so."

"Enough," Sigismundo said. "I have more important matters to discuss with Master Leonardo. Let us leave the small talk and come to business. Master, would you mind telling my father and these others when you arrived?"

Leonardo blinked. "Not at all. Since I was riding south to Cesena, according to my agreement with Don Cesare, Ferrara was right in my way. I arrived at the twenty-first hour or before, not long after noon . . ." He looked at Sigismundo, who nodded confirmation. "Yes. Sigismundo was kind enough to order a midday meal for me and then to send off a note to Don Ercole, whom I had wanted to meet."

"Did Sigismundo go to fetch Strozzi?" Correggio asked.

"No." Leonardo smiled. "We had already fallen into a small disagreement about the effect of a strongly flowing stream on the stones in its bed and why a substance as soft as water could wear away stone."

"I sent my maestro di sala," Sigismundo said. "He is not here now. You can question him later."

"Question him?" Leonardo's voice rose in surprise.

"Just answer one question more before I answer yours," Correggio continued. "Did Sigismundo leave you at any time during the afternoon or evening?"

"Yes, of course." Leonardo was frowning, half irritated, half puzzled. "He was summoned by a page to go to his father's apartment perhaps a candlemark ago. There he is. He came back with you all."

"I meant at any time before that."

"No, I do not believe he did." The frown grew darker. "He went out of the room to use his close stool. I used it too, but by then Don Ercole was here." He hesitated and then said strongly, "I would like to know why I am being asked these questions before I answer any more of them."

Duke Ercole breathed out a heavy sigh of relief. "Forgive us, Master Leonardo. This lady"—he gestured toward Beatrice—"believed she saw my son stab a man to death at the masked ball that was taking place in the Sala Bianca—"

"Don Sigismundo?" It was a ragged chorus replete with disbelief from both Strozzi and da Vinci.

The duke smiled and then went on to tell the whole story, after which both Ercole Strozzi and Leonardo da Vinci repeatedly affirmed that Sigismundo had never been away from them for more than a few minutes and, during the pertinent time, from the fourth hour of night through midnight, that they were all sitting together at Sigismundo's table being served an evening meal and drinking a few glasses of wine while they talked.

Sigismundo's body servant was then summoned and asked to produce his master's green doublet, black velvet jerkin, green cloak, and black velvet hat with the two peacock feathers. He did so promptly. The cloak was passed from hand to hand and all agreed that it was not stained with blood, nor had it been washed that evening.

Alfonso then described where he had hidden the bloodstained cloak and a page was sent to fetch it. Sigismundo grinned at his older brother. "I thank you, I think," he said wryly. "I know you were trying to protect me, but wearing my own cloak?"

They both laughed and Alfonso said, "I don't think my head was working very well. If you had seen that body, with the hole in its neck and the blood all over . . . When I found that cloak, also drenched in blood, I just needed to get it out of sight so no one else would see it."

Sigismundo was not so jocular when the cloak was brought and spread out. He paled at the broad, nearly black stains and shrank back, away from the smell of the dried blood, after he had bent down to look more closely at the cloak. Alfonso did not approach it again, but the other men, experienced soldiers all, examined it closely. So did Lucrezia, although she had to force her fingers to take an unbloodied edge and lift it to examine the stitching more closely.

"What are you looking for?" the duke snapped.

Lucrezia immediately dropped the cloak and stepped away, feeling the blood drain from her face. Doubtless her father-by-marriage felt her examination was unwomanly or ghoulish and that she had paled at his reprimand, but she had hardly heard him. She had seen something none of the men would notice, something that suggested a horrible notion to her mind. She shrank back, away from the men examining the cloak, until she was nearly touching Alfonso. He did not seem to notice her, but his sturdy bulk was comforting.

The stitching of the cloak was not like that of a tailor-made garment. It was the stitching of a woman, and a woman in haste. Had a woman made that garment for a small man who hated Palagio or had she made it for herself? Could it have been that Sigismundo was chosen more because of his slight height and slender figure than for any particular animosity toward him? If the murderer was also short and slender compared to a man . . . if the murderer was a woman . . .

It was the first time Lucrezia had seriously considered that a woman might have poisoned Bianca, even though four women had profited from her death. Poison was said to be a woman's weapon, and she had questioned the women; however, they all seemed to be cleared by being together in her apartment until after Bianca was dead. Also, she would rather have believed Palagio guilty. Only now he was dead. Did that necessarily make him innocent? Only if his murder was because he had seen someone or knew something about Bianca's death that made him a danger to the true murderer.

She shivered slightly and Alfonso put a hand on her shoulder, but his eyes were on the group surrounding the cloak. When that had been thoroughly examined, there seemed no doubt that if Sigismundo had murdered Palagio, his clothes would have been bloodstained too—and they were not.

They began to discuss why anyone should want to incriminate Sigismundo, the duke pressing his youngest son about whom he could have offended or insulted. Sigismundo just kept shaking his head and insisting that by his will he had troubled no one and if the murder of Palagio was a result of his accidentally annoying the murderer, he could be no help because he was totally unaware of it.

Lucrezia could see that Sigismundo was not at all troubled by the idea that anyone hated him enough to try to make him look guilty of murder. He also seemed indifferent to the fact that it was purely a lucky accident that da Vinci and Strozzi had been his guests and proved he could not have committed the crime. Clearly he was growing more and more impatient with the discussion. To Sigismundo the scientific talk Leonardo da Vinci could provide was of paramount importance. Finally he said aloud that he did not want to seem discourteous and he knew the murder was important, but it was not important to *him* in comparison with the instruction he could obtain from Master da Vinci if everyone else but Ercole Strozzi would *go away*.

Lucrezia and Alfonso laughed aloud. The duke growled and shook his head. But all of them were accustomed to Sigismundo's skewed views and they all trooped back to the duke's apartment, carrying with them the bloodstained green cloak. Duke Ercole arranged for the priest to be transported back to his home and the rest of them continued to talk about the murder; however, it was soon apparent that no one had anything new to say. Lucrezia tried to restrain a yawn and failed, which, of course, caused everyone else to yawn also.

"I think we have done all we can tonight," Ercole d'Este said.

There was a general murmur of approval and Correggio came forward to pick the cloak off the back of a chair where it had been draped. "I will try to find the tailor who made this," Correggio said, "and I will try to discover what Palagio was doing and why he should be a target. And, of course, why anyone should try to make Don Sigismundo seem guilty."

Lucrezia made no protest, nor did she reveal that she did not think any tailor had made the garment. There was always the possibility that whoever had ordered the copies of Sigismundo's clothing had not left time enough for the clothes to be properly made and had told the tailor the garments were for a costume that would be worn once and discarded. Any tailor would remember that, and if he did, Correggio would soon have the person.

It was best, also, for Correggio to pursue any political cause for the murder, as Lucrezia was determined not to be involved in any political faction. If Correggio found a political cause, Lucrezia could dismiss Palagio's death as irrelevant, although he might still be guilty of poisoning Bianca. If Correggio could not find any political or personal cause for Palagio's death . . .

Alfonso took her arm to lead her from the duke's apartment. She started, but did not pull away, and he said, "You are thinking very hard. About what?"

"That I will need to speak again to Bianca's maid, Maria, and to Guadaruzzi also."

"Guadaruzzi? Who is he?"

"The man . . . or half man . . . who was watching Bianca's door from an edge of the corridor."

"Oh, I remember. My servant warned me that someone was watching, but I did not remember the name."

"Yes, well, Guadaruzzi told Giulio or Ferrante of Palagio entering Bianca's apartment and of the cloaked and hatted man. But I think it possible that Giulio and Ferrante did not get everything he knew from him. I will do better."

"You will not leave that death alone, will you?"

They came to the head of the stairs and Lucrezia gripped Alfonso's arm tightly. He stopped and shifted around her so that she could hold the banister with one hand. She looked up at him, wondering suddenly if he did not want her to hold his arm because he had more secrets than he had told her and he feared his muscles would betray him. Then he offered his arm again, and she put the thought aside, pleased and grateful for his allowing her the double security.

At the foot of the stairs, she said, "No, I will not leave it unsolved. Perhaps you meant me no harm, but as long as Bianca's poisoner is in doubt, there will be whispers. And Palagio's death will not improve matters. Remember, I was at the masked ball."

"Nonsense. If there are rumors about that, they will concern Sigismundo. Likely enough Bianca's death will be forgotten."

"Until someone wishes to find ill to say of me." Lucrezia's jaw set hard. "No, I will not cease from seeking the murderer."

13

AS SOON as she was awake and dressed the next morning, Lucrezia sent Lucia for Maria and asked her to send in Ascanio the page on her way out. The boy came in, rubbing sleep out of his eyes, and she sent him off with two hastily penned notes to Giulio and Ferrante asking them if they would break their fast with her or, if they were already pledged, to come and visit as soon as they were free.

The boy was hardly gone when the cook's helper came in with another servant who worked for the maestro di sala. The table was set and spread with dishes, the servants dismissed until called. Lucrezia went back into her bedchamber and stretched out on her daybed, until Lucia came back with Maria. The maid curtsied to the ground and then asked faintly if Lucrezia would be keeping her long.

"That is up to you. If you tell me quickly what I want to know, you can leave the sooner. If I think you are keeping secrets and I must question you in different ways to find the truth, it will take much longer. I presume that Madonna Adriana Castelli was pleased with your work and desired you to come to her again?"

"Yes, madonna," Maria whispered.

"I understand how important it is to you to find a new place and how much simpler your life will be if your new mistress knows that your old mistress was murdered. It is just as important to me to discover who killed Donna Bianca. Now, the man who had the best chance to do this thing was himself murdered last night. Did you hear?"

"Oh, yes, madonna. The whole city knows of it, I think, because of the people who were at the ball."

"Yes, well, it appears that Palagio was innocent of killing Donna Bianca. Thus someone else must have entered Donna Bianca's apartment either before she came back to it or while you were asleep."

Lucrezia was by no means as sure of this as she sounded, but she wanted Maria to think Palagio was innocent so her mind would be clear to seek other possibilities.

"Oh, no, madonna. That is not possible."

"Which is not possible?"

"Both are not possible, madonna. You see, the back door opens right into my little closet, so anyone who came in would surely wake me."

Lucrezia lifted her brows. "Maids work hard," she said. "They are awake before their mistresses and cannot go to their beds until their ladies are already asleep. Thus a maid sleeps hard. I know you *think* you would wake if someone entered your room, but I am not sure."

"Oh, please, madonna," Maria whispered. "The room is so small that the door hits the bed when it opens. Anyone who comes in must walk along the bed to close the door before getting around the bed. I cannot have slept through that. I swear, madonna, I was more bored than tired. I would have wakened if anyone came in."

But would not anyone who knew of the back door also know the door would hit the bed? Lucrezia knew better than to voice her doubts. They would only frighten the maid and make her more guilty so that she would cling even more stubbornly to her story.

"Well, then, someone hid in one of the rooms, either in Donna Bianca's bedchamber or her public room before you and she came in that evening."

Maria began to weep. "There is nowhere to hide, madonna. The walls of the public room are bare. They are painted, but there are no hangings, no niches in which to hide. The bedchamber too. There are chests up against the bed. I swear they are too heavy to move without being emptied, so no one could hide under the bed."

"In the chests?"

"No, madonna. They are too small for anyone to hide inside them. And Donna Bianca had no great wardrobes for her dresses. They hung in my little chamber with no more than a sheet over the rack to keep away dust. Nor were there so many that I could not see around and behind them. She kept many gowns at her estate. The maids and seamstresses there cared for them and she sent back those she had worn and brought fresh ones week by week."

Lucrezia stared at the girl for a moment, then shook her head. "If there was no one in the apartment before Palagio came and Palagio found her dead, as he claimed, then Donna Bianca was not murdered at all. Somehow she killed herself. She is safely buried in consecrated ground now. You can tell me how and why she ended her life."

"No! No! I swear she did not." Maria sobbed bitterly. "She was happy that day. She was pleased with herself because she was going to help two men accomplish something. She did not tell me what men, nor what they wished to do, only that she was going to help, which always made her happy."

"She was easy to please," Lucrezia said.

Maria nodded. "Yes, and she was not the kind to kill herself. When things went wrong, she would cry for a bit, but then she would cheer up. Even when she needed to care for Don Celio—and he was in agony and rotting away under her hands—still she found things to be happy about."

"Did she miss her husband greatly?"

"After Don Celio died," Maria said slowly, "she was sad. But she never said a word about ending her life. And when the French ambassador got her a place as your lady-in-waiting, she was ready to fly away with joy." Maria's sobs had stopped and now she looked mulish. "She was enjoying herself so much. Why should she kill herself?"

It was what Lucrezia herself believed about Bianca, yet she was faced with an impossible situation—a woman who was murdered by an invisible enemy. A chill passed over Lucrezia and she thought of witchcraft, but no, the means of death was clear. It was poison. From witchcraft the victims wasted away or fell down in a fit foaming at the mouth or suddenly clutched their chests in agony when a moment before they had been well.

Aconite was a real thing, not a witch's curse. The only question was, if she had eaten and drunk nothing and no one had been in the apartment and forced her to swallow it, how did the aconite get into Bianca? She must have taken it herself—but not on purpose, not meaning to kill herself, and not in food or drink. An accident?

Something tickled Lucrezia's mind. Something dei Carri had said about Donna Bianca's mouth not looking like those of the people in the mountain cabin who had died of aconite poisoning. But how else if not by mouth? And then she remembered him mentioning that aconite was used in salves to ease aching joints. He had said he never used such salves because they were too dangerous. Surely that meant aconite could pass through the skin. If Bianca had used a salve with aconite in it, no one needed to give it to her at the moment when she died. It could be something that she had received days or weeks before that she happened to use that day.

Lucrezia was so intrigued by the revelation that she did not realize how it applied to herself. She asked eagerly, "Did Donna Bianca use a salve to ease aching joints?"

Maria looked astonished. "Aching joints? But she was young. Her joints did not ache."

Lucrezia frowned, now remembering that she had had a discussion about Bianca's joints with someone, possibly dei Carri, and come to the conclusion that Bianca was unlikely to have suffered from joint-ail and used a salve for it. They had then dismissed the idea of aconite in a salve. Lucrezia shook her head at her stupidity. Salves were used for other things than aching joints. All women used salves. She herself used several to protect and soften her skin.

"What salves and creams did Donna Bianca use?" Lucrezia asked sharply.

Maria suddenly looked frightened, but shook her head in denial. Lucrezia now remembered the last time she had talked to the maid, Maria had been hiding something.

"Enough," Lucrezia said sharply. "If you lie to me now, I will send to Donna Adriana and tell her you are not fit to be her maid."

"It is not true!" Maria cried, bursting into tears again. "I am fit. I am. It is out of loyalty to my mistress that I am silent." Then she clapped her hands to her mouth looking even more frightened.

"Your mistress is dead," Lucrezia said more gently. "Nothing can hurt her now, and it has occurred to me that if it is true she ate and drank nothing and that Palagio found her dead, the poison must have got into her in another way. Master dei Carri told me that the poison that killed your mistress was sometimes used in salves for aching joints."

"No," Maria breathed, looking relieved. "She never used a salve for aching joints, never. I swear it on my soul."

"I know that, but she used lotions and salves for something else. Something you will tell me right now!"

More tears spilled down Maria's cheeks. "She had buboes," the girl whispered. "Oh, she made me swear I would never tell, never tell anyone. She was so ashamed and so afraid. She thought the sores marked her as . . . as not a good woman, but until Don Celio died she never had another man. And she thought she might die as he died, rotting." Maria hiccupped with grief.

"I never saw a sore on her," Lucrezia said.

"They were near her private parts," Maria whispered. "Just where his began. Oh, she tried everything to cure them, everything except go to a physician. All kinds of salves and creams and lotions."

Lucrezia's eyes lit. "And she tried a new one that night, did she not?"

"I . . . I think so. I am not sure. Mostly she did not let me see, so likely she waited until I went down to the kitchen before she applied it, but I did notice her take a small flask from the secret drawer in her dressing table."

"Did you find it?" Lucrezia asked eagerly. "Do you have it? We might be able to discover who made it or ordered it and from where it came."

"No, madonna, I did not find it. And I did look for it first in her pocket—because her hand was curled as if she held something in it—and then in the dressing table drawer. I wanted to throw all those things away so that no one would know." Maria shivered. "How could I guess anyone would put poison in a medicine?"

"You could not guess. I did not think of it and dei Carri and I even talked about using the aconite as a medicine. But we spoke of joint-ail. I never thought of treating buboes." Lucrezia hesitated, frowning. "You are sure she took out a flask?" Maria nodded. "Did you see what it looked like? Can you describe it?"

"Only that it was very, very pretty . . . like yours, madonna. Like those Lucia showed me on your dressing table. It looked just like those."

Lucrezia drew a sharp breath. Did Maria make that comparison deliberately? But even if the maid did not make the connection, why was the aconite put in a flask like those Isabella sold her? To incriminate her? To incriminate Isabella?

"You did not find it?" Lucrezia asked sharply. "Be very sure, Maria. What is in it will kill you if you try to use it, even if you try to clean it out. The Mother of Poisons is very dangerous. If you have that flask, do not remove the stopper, wrap it in a rag, and bring it to me."

"I never found it, madonna, I swear." Her mouth firmed. "If I had found it, I would have thrown it away as I know my poor lady would have wanted me to do."

What more could she ask the girl? Lucrezia could think of nothing and she did not want Maria to lose her chance of employment. It would be better to have her remain in the palace as Adriana Castelli's maid in case her evidence was needed. She dismissed Maria to her new duties but warned her that she should not leave the Castel Vecchio without telling Lucia.

Should she tell Correggio what she had discovered? No, not until she could speak to Master dei Carri and be sure her vague memory that he had said aconite was dangerous even when rubbed on the skin was correct. She rose from the daybed and went into the private reception room. Giulio, Ferrante, Angela, and Nicola looked up from their plates. Her chair had been left empty and there was a plate before it, but it did not look as if anyone had missed her.

"Just leave some for me," she said as she bypassed the table and went to her writing desk. There, after a proper salutation to the physician, she wrote. "I have just discovered that Donna Bianca suffered from buboes which were near her private parts. Her maid tells me that she used many different salves and lotions in an attempt to hide and cure the sores. If aconite was introduced into a salve or lotion and she anointed the sores with it, would that have killed her? This would explain how she was poisoned without eating or drinking anything."

Having addressed it and rung for her page, she sent it off to dei Carri. When the boy was gone, she took her place at the table and filled her plate.

"What do you think of Palagio's murder?" she asked. "Did any of you recognize him?"

"Easily," Giulio said. "He was not trying to hide who he was. The mask he wore barely covered his eyes. Anyone who knew him would recognize him immediately."

An idea occurred to Lucrezia and she cocked her head inquisitively. "Apurpose, do you think? I mean, did he want to be recognized? Was he making it easy for someone to find him?"

"That could be," Ferrante said. "I spoke to him and asked how he was enjoying the ball, and he said it was perfect to while away the time and for meetings that would have been difficult in private."

"He didn't seem worried or frightened?"

"Not at all," Angela chirped. "I danced with him early, before the cooks had set out the food on the tables, and he was in a very good humor. He told me he was sorry that you could not appreciate his work, but since that was so he felt it best for him to move on and the ball conveniently would allow him to finish some profitable business. He was fingering something in his pocket and I wondered if he was being lewd, but it seems to have been a charm or talisman . . . a perfume flask, I thought. But he said it was something that would bring him success."

"It does not seem to have been very effective," Nicola remarked.

Lucrezia shuddered, remembering the ugly hole in the man's neck and the blood. "Could Guadaruzzi have killed him?" she asked.

"Guadaruzzi? Lord, why should he?" Ferrante asked. "And I know he didn't because he was dressed as Pan. He also was not trying to hide his identity. I recognized him quite early. I thought Sigismundo—oh, I mean someone dressed as Sigismundo—was the one who did it."

"Well, have you thought how that limits those who could have killed Palagio? Think of Sigismundo. He is no taller than I and very little heavier. How many men, even wearing his clothes, could be mistaken for him? Yet Alfonso thought the person was Sigismundo. He only saw him for a moment, but if either of you had been dressed in those clothes, would he have made that mistake?"

"Don't be ridiculous," Giulio said. "I couldn't get into Sigismundo's clothes. They would split on me."

Lucrezia sighed. "The clothing would have been made large enough to fit you, Giulio, but even so, would Alfonso or I have mistaken you for Sigismundo? Of course not. You are much too tall and broad."

"Well, thank God for that," Giulio said. "Who would want to be a weakling like Sigismundo?"

Lucrezia sighed again, thinking that if Sigismundo had a bit of Giulio's bulk and Giulio a bit of Sigismundo's brains . . . Then she had to swallow a chuckle. Sigismundo would not thank her for such a wish.

"No, Giulio, you aren't thinking . . . if you can think," Ferrante said. "Lucrezia means that it had to have been a small, thin man who stabbed Palagio or no one would have thought it was Sigismundo no matter what clothing he wore. Who do we know who is small and thin like that?"

"Sigismundo," Giulio said.

"But it was not Sigismundo," Angela said patiently. "We know that. Who else?"

"Ah, now I understand why Lucrezia asked whether Guadaruzzi could have killed Palagio," Ferrante said. "He is small and frail." But then he shook his head. "You want to know whether he could have run out, changed his clothes, killed Palagio, run out again, then changed his clothes again, and come back in time to leave with the rest of us." He shook his head again. "No, I don't think so. I saw him not long before the screaming began, talking to one of those big soldier types. And after, when we were all leaving, he was still with that man."

"Then we can forget Guadaruzzi."

Lucrezia was no longer interested in seeing if she could extract more information from Guadaruzzi. If Bianca had been killed with a poisoned salve or lotion, exactly who entered her apartment the night she died was no longer important. A chill passed over her at that thought, but she was distracted by the realization that she could not really forget Guadaruzzi, not without proof of Ferrante's statement. Guadaruzzi was the right physical type to have killed Palagio.

"Still, I would like to make sure," she said to Ferrante. "Do you think you can discover to whom he was talking and ask the man how long before the screaming began, and how long after, Guadaruzzi was with him?"

Ferrante looked at Giulio, who shrugged.

"The easiest way would be to ask Guadaruzzi," Giulio said, and his lips twisted. "After we know the man's name, we can both say we recognized him. Many men are shy of admitting that they know Guadaruzzi well."

"However you do it is fine. Just make sure the man really was with Guadaruzzi and is not some scapegoat Guadaruzzi decided to mention. As you say, I can see no reason for Guadaruzzi to have killed Bianca, but I can see no reason why *anyone* should have killed her."

They had all long since agreed on that, so after assurances from Giulio and Ferrante that they would do their best to get the information she wanted, the talk drifted away to other matters. Breakfast finished, Lucrezia rose in polite dismissal and bade the gentlemen good hunting. When they had gone out, accompanied by Angela and Nicola, she went to her writing desk; however, before she had begun a letter to her father, the page slipped around the portiere and asked whether she would see Master Ludovico dei Carri. Lucrezia agreed at once, standing up to greet the physician in her eagerness to know whether her deductions had been correct.

After bows and salutations and formal thanks for receiving him so promptly, the doctor said, "I must thank you for your note this morning. It may have saved my life, madonna."

He smiled as he spoke, not as if what he said was a jest but as if he did not want to frighten her. Still, Lucrezia sank back into her chair and echoed, "Saved your life?"

He nodded, still smiling. "There was not much doubt about the cause of Don Guido del Palagio's death, but this morning to be on the safe side and also to prepare the body decently for burial, I had his clothing removed. There was no other wound, nor sign of poison. He did die of having his throat cut."

"There was so much blood," Lucrezia said faintly. "That must have been the fatal wound."

"Yes, well, I did not really suspect poison, you see, so when we examined what was on his person and I found this little flagon, I opened it. I had smelled it and the odor was pleasant but not strong enough for perfume and I wondered why a man would be carrying such a flask. I was just about to pour some out into my hand to examine it more closely so I could determine what it was when your note came. Perhaps it would not have killed me"—he smiled at her—"a physician is by nature cautious, but I prefer not to be as ill as that might have made me."

"You mean that flask holds the Mother of Poisons?"

"Yes, mixed with a lotion. I have not yet had it tested, but I believe it is mostly a solution of aconite. Far more than should be mixed with salve or lotion to be used for relieving joint-ail."

Lucrezia shook her head. "It was not for joint-ail. I fear that what was in that flask was what killed Donna Bianca—if rubbing it on her buboes would kill her."

"Indeed it would, and faster than if she swallowed what was in the flask. But what was Palagio doing with the poison? Had he given it to her?"

"I doubt that. When Don Correggio questioned him about being in Donna Bianca's room—someone saw him enter and leave—he said he had found Bianca dead. But he did not run out and call for help. He was in her chamber for half a candlemark or more. I think he was searching for compromising letters so he could extort money from those who wrote to her, and he must have searched the body as well as her writing desk and drawers. He found the flask, possibly on her body. I think he recognized it and guessed or knew who had given the flask—and presumably its contents—to her."

"How did he know it was poison?" dei Carri asked.

Lucrezia shrugged. "He found her dead and she had been perfectly healthy earlier in the day. You suspected poison at once. Likely he decided to show the flask and judge by the person's reaction."

"So he took the flask and accused the person he suspected . . . and then he died."

"Yes. I think so."

The physician stared at Lucrezia and her glance met his. "And do you recognize the flask?" he asked.

She was silent for a long moment while the fear she had suppressed rose full-formed into her mind. Then she said slowly, "It looks like one of mine." Her lips trembled and she firmed them. "But I am sure there are other women who have similar flasks. I buy my perfumes and lotions from Madonna Isabella, and so do other ladies of the court."

"Many," dei Carri agreed.

Lucrezia bent her head and sighed, shivering as she voiced the fear that chilled her. "But after the accusation Don Alfonso made, I cannot say I am happy that the flask looks as if it comes from my collection. By this method I could easily have killed Bianca even while I was praying in the convent of Corpus Domini."

The physician shook his head. "But you did not kill Palagio. You were in plain sight when the man dressed as Don Sigismundo stabbed him. And if Palagio was killed because he confronted the murderer about this flask, then you are not the murderer."

Lucrezia shivered again and clutched her arms around herself. "But how many will think this through as you did? I must find out who did this. I must! And how can I, when the man who knew the answer is dead? And how did the murderer get my perfume flask?"

"That at least will be easy to determine, madonna," dei Carri said. "What do you do with the flasks when you have emptied them?"

"I?" Lucrezia stared at him, uncomprehending. "Nothing. I suppose my maid Lucia throws them away."

Master dei Carri chuckled softly. "I would doubt that very much, madonna. A finely blown and decorated flask like this is expensive—oh, not expensive in terms of gold or jewels, but costly in terms of a peasant girl's clothing. It might be worth a pair of shoes or more." He smiled. "Ask your maid. You might find out who bought the flask from her and, from that person, who filled it."

"Yes, of course!" Lucrezia exclaimed, sitting more upright and reaching for the bell on her writing desk. As she rang it she said, "Thank you, Master dei Carri. I was so frightened when I felt my proof of innocence slip away that I could not think."

The physician came forward and patted her shoulder gently, but before he could speak, Lucia came from the door of the bedchamber. He turned from Lucrezia to the maid and held out the flask. Lucia reached for it without any hesitation, smiling at the physician.

"Shall I put this with the other bottle of medicine Master dei Carri sent?" she asked Lucrezia.

"Other bottle of medicine?" dei Carri echoed.

Puzzlement spread over Lucia's face. "Yes, the bottle of lotion your page brought yesterday." Then she began to look frightened. "Did you not see it, madonna? I put it on the dressing table with the note from the doctor. I think I mentioned it, but we were so busy making ready for the ball—"

She stopped speaking and backed away as Lucrezia jumped up from her chair and hurried into her bedchamber, with dei Carri hard on her heels. They both stopped before the dressing table and stared. And there the bottle was in the midst of other flasks and handsomely painted ceramic jars. Larger than the flask dei Carri still held and without decoration, although its sides had an elegant curve and the wax-covered stopper was a beautiful rendition of a fan of feathers, it was filled with a pale pink liquid. Beneath the bottle was a folded sheet of paper.

Lucrezia drew the note out, lifting the bottle carefully by its sides, her hands away from the stopper area, although that seemed quite dry. The paper fluttered slightly as her hand trembled, but she managed to open it.

Skipping the elaborate salutation, Lucrezia read, "'For your lovely skin, madonna, which I would not like to see stretched and marred by your coming joy. If you will apply this lotion liberally every evening before bed, rubbing it well into your entire abdomen, you will have less discomfort as your body swells and no marks on your skin when you are, I hope, joyfully relieved of your burden.'"

"I never wrote that," dei Carrie exclaimed indignantly. "What nonsense! As if I could guarantee how large a babe a woman will carry! Or what effect a pregnancy would have on her."

Lucrezia gave no sign she had heard him, but the hand that held the note had stopped trembling. She stood with the sheet of paper in her hand, her eyes fixed on the bottle on her dressing table.

"Oh, I think you could guarantee I would have no stretch marks if I followed the instructions in the note," she said, smiling grimly. "I would have been dead and in no danger of having my skin marred by my pregnancy."

The physician sputtered with rage, and Lucia, who had followed them into the bedchamber, uttered a faint cry.

"I did not know," the maid said, falling on her knees and taking her mistress's free hand.

"Of course you did not know," Lucrezia said, her smile softening. "How fortunate that we were so busy getting ready for the masked ball yesterday that I did not hear you mention the lotion. I might have been curious enough to try some."

Lucia shuddered and clung to her mistress's hand. Dei Carri snorted.

"Well, I hope you are more sensible than to try anything that I do not give you myself," he said. "Or at the very least send for me and ask why I prepared for you medication you did not request." Then he cocked his head inquisitively and added, "You seem remarkably indifferent to this attempt on your life, madonna."

"Yes." Lucrezia tugged at Lucia so she would rise to her feet. "First, I think this is proof that *I* did not send Bianca the poisoned lotion. Second, I think this attempt to be rid of me indicates that I am a threat to the killer, perhaps coming closer to discovering his identity. And last"—a smile of great sweetness and confidence brightened her face—"does not the whole circumstance about this threat show that the Blessed Virgin and Lord Jesus Himself are holding out their hands to protect me?"

"Very likely," dei Carri said, smiling gently, "for you are good and innocent and love God and the Holy Virgin. Nonetheless, do not count too much on such protection. God and His Mother expect their children to use their wits."

"Oh, yes," Lucrezia agreed heartily. "That I can see is part of their saving me this time. I am sure if the poison had been made to seem as if it came from my sister-by-marriage, Madonna Isabella, Lucia would have insisted I look at it, because a new perfume would have been an ideal part of my disguise. And I would have tried it at once for the same reason. No, no. I will trust nothing that does not come from the very hand of the donor. But that does look like one of your bottles, Master dei Carri."

The physician nodded. "Very likely it is one of mine. It looks very like a bottle I used for a lotion that I made up for Don Alfonso. You know he is forever burning his hands in that foundry and getting paint on them and scrubbing them raw to get it off." He stopped speaking abruptly, then added, "Hmmm. That is interesting."

"No," Lucrezia protested. "Alfonso would not—"

"Of course not," dei Carri said on an impatient note. "But perhaps whoever did use the bottle got it from the same source as the flask that may have belonged to you." He turned on Lucia. "Well, my girl, to whom did you sell your mistress's empty perfume and lotion bottles?"

"Oh, forgive me, madonna! Forgive me," Lucia cried, slipping down on her knees again. "All the maids sell empty flasks and jars. No one ever forbade us. It seems such a terrible waste to cast away such beautiful bottles."

"Get up, do, Lucia," Lucrezia said. "No one is forbidding you to sell the bottles or blaming you for doing so. It just never occurred to me that they were of any value. I know you either use or sell my old clothing or shoes. Master dei Carri and I just want to know to whom you sold them."

"I do not know," Lucia whispered, eyes wide. "She is always called La Vecchia. She is just an old woman who comes to the palace about once a week. I do not believe she uses the bottles herself. I think she cleans them and then sells them to others. I am pretty sure that Anna Peruzzi buys some from her—"

"Peruzzi?" Lucrezia repeated. "Why does that name sound familiar to me?"

"You were in her shop the day before yesterday," Lucia said. "She was the woman who sold perfumes and lotions."

"Of course, I remember now."

"But I never saw a bottle as fine as the one Master dei Carri has in her shop," Lucia said doubtfully.

Lucrezia sighed. "There must be many perfume shops in the city."

"Perhaps your ladies will know," dei Carri suggested.

"They might indeed," Lucrezia said, smiling now. Then she turned to Lucia. "When La Vecchia comes again, you must bring her to me. Be careful to say nothing about poison being in any bottle she might have had and assure her that she is not in any trouble for buying the bottles. If she wants to know why I want to speak to her, tell her . . . tell her that it is a private curiosity about my own perfumer who does not live in Ferrara and cannot have bought from her."

"I will speak to my manservant and my apprentices, too," dei Carri said. "Between us, we are sure to lay hands on La Vecchia so we can question her."

"But you will be careful about what you tell them?" Lucrezia asked anxiously. "I think it is important that no one except ourselves and my two women know the truth of how Donna Bianca died."

"Why?"

"Perhaps it is only a selfish fear. If it does not matter when the poison was delivered, I could easily have given it to her before I left for Corpus Domini. She might simply have put it aside . . . out of spite? . . . and not—"

"You are too sensitive, madonna, but I will certainly do as you ask nonetheless. For now all attention will be on Palagio's death, and since this flask was not the instrument, I simply will not mention it."

"And will you take this one"—Lucrezia gestured at the still-sealed bottle of lotion—"and keep them safe in case we need them with which to confront the murderer?"

"I will, and have it tested to make sure we have not leapt to an unfounded conclusion. It is possible that someone has used my name simply to get you to try an innocent lotion so that you would speak well of it in the future."

Lucrezia smiled. "I hope it may be so."

The physician shook his head and sighed as he came forward and carefully took the bottle of lotion. Lucrezia thanked him, and he bowed a farewell, following the maid from the chamber. Lucrezia stood staring at the dressing table and shuddered once before rearranging the items on it to cover the empty area the bottle of poisoned lotion had occupied.

14

NICOLA and Angela hurried into Lucrezia's bedchamber as soon as the door had closed behind Master dei Carri.

"What is wrong?" Nicola asked, large-eyed, slipping her arm around Lucrezia's waist.

"Oh, sit down, love, do," Angela cried, turning the chair near the dressing table so that Lucrezia had only to lower herself into it. "Or would it be better for you to lie down in your bed? Are you ill, dearling? Why did you not tell us?"

Lucrezia looked from one to the other in amazement. "Ill? Of course I am not ill! Whatever gave you such a silly idea?"

"We saw Master dei Carri come out of your bedchamber and he was carrying something wrapped in his kerchief," Nicola said. "What could that be but samples of your urine?"

"Bottles of poison," Lucrezia said, grinning at the expressions of horror on her ladies' faces. "And no, I did not use any of it . . . by the grace of God and His Merciful Mother."

Her smile had vanished by the last phrase, which was spoken with utter seriousness and gratitude. Then, of course, after the exclamations of pleasure that she had not called the physician because of any illness and exclamations of horror over the idea of poisoning Bianca and, far worse, trying to poison Lucrezia, she had to repeat to her ladies what had passed between her and the physician and what Lucia had told them both.

"La Vecchia," Nicola mused. "I think I once saw an old woman in poor but respectable clothing going into Teodora Angelini's rooms."

"That must have been the person my maid was talking to in the closet behind my bedchamber," Angela said. "I once saw her leaving, I think. Gray hair and a skirt of fine cloth, but mended." Angela sighed. "My maid gets little enough of castaways, poor thing. Do I have to tell her that she must not sell my empty bottles?"

"By no means," Lucrezia said. "Only tell her to bring the woman to me. Or, even better, let her call you if you are in your apartment, and you bring her to me. She is less likely to ignore you or refuse you. Assure her she is in no trouble, that I merely wish to question her about her business out of curiosity."

"I will tell my maid the same," Nicola offered. "And if La Vecchia says she is busy, I will tell Filameta to get her true name and direction. Shall I offer her money to speak to you, madonna?"

"Oh, yes, of course. Anything reasonable. If the poor woman must work for her living, I must not take up her time without recompense." Both women nodded, and Lucrezia smiled at them. "And now I have work for *you*."

"Who do you want me to seduce?" Angela asked, giggling.

"Perfumers and apothecaries," Lucrezia replied.

Angela wrinkled her nose and Nicola laughed.

"Yes," Nicola said, "it makes good sense to work the problem from both ends. If La Vecchia is hard to lay hands on and is reluctant to name her customers, we can find out from the customers themselves. And for the apothecaries, of course, we will have old mothers or fathers or uncles who have painful joints, but they will be fussy and only want a joint-ail that contains aconite in a lotion, not a salve."

Lucrezia's glance was full of approval. Angela kept her spirits high and made her laugh, but Nicola understood the way her mind worked.

"Exactly," she said. "You can take one of the older perfumes that Madonna Isabella gave me and ask the perfumers if they can copy the scent and supply it in the same elaborate bottles. You can even buy, if the perfumer has the right bottles. I will then have the bottle for proof . . . and you will have the scent."

"What about the dinner at Count Ugoccione's palazzo this afternoon?" Angela asked. "If Nicola and I go out to the shops, who will help you dress?"

"Lucia can dress me," Lucrezia said, smiling at the worried frown on Angela's face, "but we can pick out the gown now, and then have a midday bite before I order the carriage for you. And I can tell Adriano to bring dinner to you. Where do you want it served?"

"My chambers, please," Nicola said. "They are so musical here that Angela and I will practice some songs after we eat."

Lucrezia applauded this program, which would help avoid a repeat of the embarrassment when they had been asked to perform at a family gathering in the duke's apartment. Although Nicola could play the lute and Angela had a sweet singing voice, neither had practiced in some time because of Lucrezia's wedding journey and all the upheaval surrounding her arrival in Ferrara. They had had to refuse the invitation to entertain and had been put to shame by the elegant performance of Lucrezia's Ferrarese ladies.

The immediate need, however, was to decide upon which gown

Lucrezia would wear. She wished for something different from what she had been wearing to the functions in the Palazzo Cortile, something that indicated her indifference to Palagio's death. Eventually they chose a dress she had not worn since she left Rome, a gammura of gold brocade over an underdress of red velvet. The sleeves, slashed from shoulder to elbow to show the underdress, were loose and trailing below. Her jewelry would consist of a pearl necklace with a pendant of an emerald, a ruby, and a large pearl, and she would wear her hair loose, simply confined with a black ribbon.

By the time all the details were decided, Adriano was waiting impatiently for them, ready to serve the midday meal. Although it was delicious and abundant, Lucrezia ate little. She laughed at Adriano's protests and pointed out that no matter how much he wanted her to seem less than satisfied by the food provided by a rival cook, it would be very bad manners indeed for her to so insult her host.

"I am sure you *are* a better cook," she said to Adriano, "but I dare not offend the premier count in the duchy the first time I am his guest."

Eventually the remains of the meal and the service were removed. Shortly thereafter, the captain of Lucrezia's guard asked admittance to report that the carriage was ready and four guards had been assigned to accompany it and to protect Donna Angela and Donna Nicola. Angela ran into Lucrezia's bedchamber to select a nearly empty bottle of perfume, making her choice more by the elaborateness of the bottle than the scent. Then both women kissed Lucrezia, wished her great enjoyment of her evening, and went away to get their cloaks.

Lucrezia rested for about a candlemark after her ladies were gone and then proceeded to allow Lucia to ready her. She washed carefully and rubbed her skin with a soothing lotion—although both she and Lucia looked with suspicion on the creamy substance and Lucia rubbed one fingerful onto her wrist to be sure it caused no tingling. Then they both laughed, rather shamefaced; the bottle was almost half empty and Lucrezia had used it several times without hurt.

After she slipped into her shift, her brows and lashes were darkened, her cheeks brushed delicately with rouge on a hare's foot, and a light dusting of powder applied. Then the underdress, the gammura, and finally the sleeves. Lucia stood back while Lucrezia revolved slowly in place. The maid tweaked this, pulled a fold, tightened a tie. She was just nodding in satisfaction when Alfonso walked through the door that opened into the inner corridor.

He looked Lucrezia's dress up and down. "Now, if I could only put you in an oven and mint you into coin, we would be the richest duchy in all of Italy."

"For what you wrung out of my father as dowry, you already are the richest duchy in Italy—without coveting my gown. Besides, it is only a particularly successful dyeing of Eastern silk. There is very little gold thread in it."

He laughed. "Well, you look very grand and Count Ugoccione will be pleased. He likes his importance to be recognized, and your dress implies his dinner is a state occasion."

"That was my intention," Lucrezia admitted. "I need all the friends I can get."

"Speaking of friends, Don Niccolò reports that he could not find a tailor in the city that would admit making the cloak or any other clothing to match Sigismundo's suit. He intends to widen his search tomorrow to the nearby villages."

Lucrezia widened her eyes. "Don Niccolò asked you to tell me what he learned about Palagio's death?"

Alfonso gazed back and Lucrezia could have sworn there was a twinkle in his usually flat black eyes. However his voice was gravely sober when he said, "He told me. I assume he knew I would tell you because you were there and much interested."

"Whether he intended it or not, I thank you, but I must tell you that I am not at all surprised. I looked at the stitching on the cloak and I think it was done privately either by the murderer or by some relative. Unless it was the murderer, whoever did the work probably did not know they were copying a favorite suit of Sigismundo's."

Alfonso shook his head at her. "Why didn't you tell Don Niccolò right away? Why waste a dozen men's time going to tailor shops?"

"Because my guess might have been wrong and if a tailor had made the clothing, the murderer could have been identified. I hope you will not discourage Don Niccolò from asking questions in the nearby villages. There is still a chance that the murderer had the work done outside the city in the hope that no one would seek so far, and the kind of stitching that made me think no Ferrarese tailor had done the work might be what a village tailor would do."

"I see," Alfonso said, then frowned. "But you said the murderer did the work himself. What man could . . . Ah, you think a woman . . . A *woman* stuck that knife into Palagio's throat? No. I do not believe it."

Lucrezia shrugged. "I find it hard to believe myself, but how many *men* would you or I mistake for Sigismundo, even in a quick glance? There are few who are so short and slender. And how many men would think of putting poison into a lotion—" She stopped abruptly, remembering that she had not intended to tell anyone how Bianca had been poisoned.

Alfonso had started to lead her toward the door to her private reception room, but he stopped and turned to stare at her. "In a lotion? Was that how Donna Bianca was killed? But then . . . then it does not matter who was in her rooms the night she died." His brows knitted. "How do you know this?"

"Master Ludovico dei Carri found the flask in Palagio's purse. He and I believe that Palagio had taken it from Bianca's body and was using it to extort money from the murderer, and he was killed to silence him."

"Then Palagio's death *is* tied to Bianca's." He was silent for a moment and then said, "I am glad to know that."

He did not need to say that he preferred no investigation of Palagio's political connections be made. Lucrezia understood quite well. Their glances locked for a moment and then Alfonso began to move toward the door again.

Just before he opened it, Lucrezia said, "I hope you will not tell anyone about the poisoned lotion. Master dei Carri and I felt it would be better to keep that knowledge to ourselves."

Alfonso paused with his hand on the door latch, again meeting her gaze. He shook his head. "I must tell Correggio to stop him from pawing over Palagio's every move and meeting, but I understand why you do not want word of this spread around. I will tell Don Niccolò that to find the murderer the secret must be kept. He can be trusted. Word of the poisoned lotion will go no farther." Then his lips curved in what was not really a smile. "Even though it means you could have killed the woman as easily as any other."

Lucrezia drew a sharp breath, but he opened the door and ushered her through it. She had no idea whether the door to the public reception room was open; the portiere was down, but she was not going to attempt to discuss Bianca's death where keen ears might be attuned to any conversation in her private reception room.

Alfonso did not follow up his provocative remark. Instead he said, "But why dress as Sigismundo?"

"About that I have no idea," Lucrezia admitted. "It might have been simply because Sigismundo is small and slight, but it was a masked ball. The murderer could have dressed as a woman, as anything."

"True enough, only if it was a woman, dressing as a man might seem more protective." His voice went cold and flat. "If the murderer is caught, I will wring an answer to that out of him . . . or her."

Lucrezia shivered. She did not know, or want to know, the depths of cruelty of which Alfonso was capable, so that it was a relief when his voice took on its normal tone and he told her, as he led her toward the door to the outer room, that Count Ugoccione had asked him to bring with them Teodora Angelini, since she had no carriage and was Lucrezia's chief lady-in-waiting.

Lucrezia suppressed a groan. The last person whose company she wanted was Teodora Angelini, and the thought that the duke might consider giving Teodora a ride as a sign Lucrezia was weakening in her rejection of the Ferrarese ladies was infuriating. However, Alfonso was already holding the portiere aside for her, so she could not protest. She wondered if it was truly Count Ugoccione who had asked that Teodora be transported or whether Duke Ercole had suggested it. At least they would be traveling in Alfonso's carriage, so Lucrezia could insist she was simply obeying him.

The lady was already in the public reception room when they entered. She was dressed in a handsome black velvet gammura embroidered with gold arabesques and flowers over a cream-colored underdress. Lucrezia nodded to her; Alfonso inclined his head.

Annoyed though she was, Lucrezia was determined to be civil. "Alfonso tells me that you are going to Count Ugoccione's dinner, Donna Teodora," she said.

"Yes, Madonna Lucrezia."

"Would you like to accompany us?" Lucrezia offered. "It seems silly to use two carriages when Alfonso's is already waiting and we are only three."

"Thank you very much," Donna Teodora said, her voice and face totally expressionless.

Lucrezia was not certain whether the woman was angry or simply embarrassed, but she was annoyed all over again. She had done her best to spare Teodora's feelings, making it clear that she had been invited to an important function. She had even avoided implying that she knew Teodora had no carriage, although she suspected that the other ladies in the chamber did know. Thus, she could see no reason for Teodora to be so ungracious. That made it easier for her to decide not to bother with any polite nothings. Once they were seated in the carriage—Alfonso, who liked his comfort, having skillfully arranged that he and she would face forward and Donna Teodora have her back to the horses—she asked directly for the information she wanted.

"Angela mentioned to me that she saw the woman called La Vecchia enter your apartment a week or two ago," Lucrezia said after the horses had started. "I would like—"

"La Vecchia?" Donna Teodora interrupted. "Who is that? I have no idea of whom you are speaking." But the woman's sallow skin was now a dull red.

Again, Lucrezia could not decide whether the flush was owing to rage or embarrassment. She replied as if she had not noticed the telltale color. "La Vecchia is an elderly woman, gray-haired, who wears fine but much-mended garments. She buys used perfume bottles and ointment jars—"

"Oh?" Donna Teodora interrupted again. "And how do you know about this woman?" Her glance flashed toward Alfonso.

If she had expected him to react to the hint that Lucrezia was selling her emptied bottles, she must have been disappointed. Stony-faced, he looked out of the window as if neither Lucrezia nor Teodora Angelini existed.

Because she was amused by Alfonso's seeming stolid indifference—Lucrezia suspected Alfonso would sell bottles without the smallest hesitation and see no shame in it if it would bring more money for his cannon—she answered good-humoredly, "My maid, Lucia, told me about her."

Having gone that far, Lucrezia realized she had to explain why she had been asking her maid about perfume bottles. Since she was certainly not going to include Donna Teodora in the small circle that knew about the poisoned lotion, she quickly decided on a blatant lie.

"When we went to get the wigs for our costumes for the masked ball, we were told about a perfumer. Nicola and Angela wanted to go and our maids pleaded for the treat, so we went. I thought I recognized several bottles, but we were all busy with the costumes for the masked ball and I never mentioned it. Today while I was dressing it just happened that I emptied a perfume bottle and remembered and finally got around to asking Lucia about the bottles in Peruzzi's shop. Lucia confessed that they might have been my bottles because she had sold emptied bottles to La Vecchia, who presumably cleaned them and sold them in turn to Anna Peruzzi, the perfumer."

"As I said, I know nothing about La Vecchia, and I am surprised anyway that your maid did not sell to Peruzzi's daughter, who is also a maid."

"You mean Anna Peruzzi could have bought the bottles directly and would not have to buy from La Vecchia? But Lucia said . . . Oh, I suppose I had better talk to her again. Do you sell directly to Peruzzi's daughter?"

Donna Teodora seemed to swell with rage, but her voice was icy cold. "I do not need to peddle empty bottles."

Lucrezia had not the smallest doubt that if Teodora had had a knife and had any hope of escaping the consequences of her crime, the woman would have been quite capable of plunging it into her throat. She did not like Donna Teodora, but she had not intended to offend her. Lucrezia shook her head.

"I meant no insult. I do not think there is any shame or wrong in selling the empty bottles. They are so pretty and some artisan worked very hard to produce them. Surely it is more sensible to clean them and use them again than to destroy them?"

"This is a very boring conversation," Alfonso said. "It is very likely that my man sells my empty bottles. . . . So what?"

Donna Teodora took a deep breath and shrugged. A person in her position did not contradict the duke's son. "Perhaps you are right, madonna. My maid might have done business with this La Vecchia, but I would not know about that."

"It does not matter," Lucrezia said. "I merely wanted to speak to the woman to assure myself that the bottles were not identified as to their first owners . . . that is, I did not want any scent or lotion put into a bottle I received from Madonna Isabella attributed to Madonna Isabella. I do not wish to interfere with the woman's business, only to warn her about that."

"Enough," Alfonso said. "Donna Teodora, you have an uncle at the French court, do you not? What do you hear from him about the health of the king and other such matters?"

"I am afraid my uncle does not write to me directly," Donna Teodora said, but now Lucrezia noticed she had turned quite pale.

"Perhaps not. Perhaps not." Alfonso looked past her. "But did not Donna Bianca carry some letters to you from France? Don Correggio let her do that if he did not wish to intrude on the recipient. She was very faithful in doing as she promised, I understand."

"Possibly . . . possibly I did receive a letter, from my aunt. It would be about dress and such light matters. I do not really remember when I last had a letter from her."

"Ah, yes, fashion. That would certainly merit being sent in a diplomatic pouch. Nothing stales as quickly as fashion, and I am sure your aunt—"

The carriage came to a halt. Alfonso glanced out of the window, then turned his head toward Donna Teodora, who said, too quickly and too brightly, "Well, here we are. I thank you for carrying me with you, Don Alfonso. You have a fine carriage. It is so very well sprung that I was hardly aware of any unevenness in the road. I hope——"

What she hoped was lost forever when a footman opened the carriage door and set the small steps that permitted easy descent. Regardless of protocol—if there was one for exiting carriages—Donna Teodora nearly leapt out of the door and hurried up the wide stair toward the portico and the open front door of Count Ugoccione's palazzo. Alfonso stared after her, then got down himself and extended his hand to support Lucrezia as she descended.

As they followed Donna Teodora toward the steps leading to the portico, Alfonso said, "That was very interesting. I wonder why she was afraid to acknowledge her uncle wrote to her—or her aunt at his dictation. Or why she was so agitated about selling empty bottles to . . . whoever."

"I don't know anything about her French relations. She never mentioned them that I remember," Lucrezia replied. "But as far as selling the bottles, I suppose she is ashamed . . . oh, dear. She would not be ashamed if her maid were selling the bottles. After all, the poor girls need every extra lire they can gather. She must be selling them herself, which is why she did not want me to question La Vecchia." She sighed. "Oh, dear, why does your father have to be such a miser!"

"It makes little difference, since you would not support Donna Teodora as your lady even if you had what you think you deserve. But I think she knows something about the perfume bottles, and she does not like you, my little bird." He laughed. "Oh, yes, I saw the look in her eyes. It is just as well that you were not sitting in Palagio's chair and she the one with the knife. I take back my doubt about a woman using the weapon."

Lucrezia gripped his arm tighter as they climbed the stairs, and Alfonso looked around to be sure no one was close enough to play any tricks.

"She was the one who 'fell against' me on the stair," Lucrezia said faintly. "What if that was not an accident? But why, Alfonso? I cannot think of any reason she could wish to kill Bianca."

"For the money? Because of something Bianca saw or heard about the letters from France?" He made a whooshing I sound and added, "Allowing Bianca to deliver letters was a sad mistake on Correggio's part."

"Perhaps for Bianca, poor creature. She is dead. Do you truly think that her death had something to do with the letters she carried? I am sure Don Niccolò would not entrust her with anything of real importance. In fact, I remember his telling me that he only gave her letters to women."

"I have not really thought about it. I cannot see that it is so important."

"Well, if you had not publicly called me a poisoner, I might think it was less important too," Lucrezia snapped.

He shrugged indifferently. "It was impossible. No one believed it."

As they reached the top and started across the portico, Lucrezia said into his ear, "But now that her poisoning is no longer so impossible for me, I *must* find out who is guilty. It is your fault. You should not have been so prepared to sacrifice me so your father would never hear you were meeting Palagio in Bianca's apartment."

He stiffened as her breath tickled his ear and pulled away, but when Lucrezia looked into his face she saw lust there rather than anger, and she laughed. After a moment Alfonso laughed too, and they passed through the door into the grand sala of Count Ugoccione's palazzo. He came forward to greet them, abandoning Donna Teodora, who slipped back into another group of guests.

"It is good to see you both so happy," Ugoccione said, which of course made both of them laugh harder.

Nonetheless, they both thanked him and each made some platitudinous remark, Alfonso about the weather and Lucrezia about the grand sala, which was beautifully decorated and lit. Lucrezia spoke with considerable warmth about several of the newer paintings, since she had recommended the young artist Giovanni Lateri to the count. Other guests coming forward to greet them supported her remarks, however, and Ugoccione smiled at her.

"You have an eye, madonna," he remarked. "And I understand that Master Giovanni is taking on a most talented apprentice, owing to you. I happened to be in his studio and heard him ordering a servant to make a place ready for the boy to sleep. When I asked, 'What boy?' he showed me the sketches the child had made. They were very good."

"It was really nothing to do with me," Lucrezia said, smiling. "His grandmother accosted me in the street and begged me to find a master for him. Fortunately she had brought along that sketch of people around a fountain. Once I had seen it, I knew such talent should not be wasted."

"Yes, but it was clever to put him with Master Giovanni, who will not insist that he paint flat figures on a flat surface," Ugoccione said.

"I did think of that," Lucrezia said with a laugh, "but I am afraid it was mostly that Master Giovanni is young and not yet very famous, so his fee for taking the apprentice and keeping him would be more modest than that of a more recognized painter."

Alfonso uttered a short, hard chuckle. "You have money enough to support artistic apprentices, but not for your own ladies."

She turned on him. "*My* ladies lack for nothing, and had I been allowed to keep those women I wanted to serve me, *they* would have lacked for nothing, even if I had to go without a new gown for ten years. If my household is to be a refuge for indigent—"

"Peace!" Alfonso exclaimed, holding up both hands with palms out in a gesture showing himself disarmed. "I will not become a kernel of wheat between the upper millstone of my good father and the nether one of my stubborn wife. I take back my words about the apprentice."

"No, no, Don Alfonso," Count Ugoccione put in, diverting their attention to himself, "your lady wife was right about the boy, and if a few florins will help with his support, I would be willing to provide them. You should go to Master Giovanni's studio and see the child's sketches. They are quite remarkable."

Alfonso shrugged indifferently and the count began to urge them up the length of the room toward the dais holding one long table. Other tables to the right and left of the room were set perpendicular to the dais, permitting everyone to see those seated at the high table, and those at the high table to see the other guests. Mostly conversation was kept to those at the same table, but if the host wished to include anyone from a lower table, he could see and call out to that person if he wished.

The count perforce placed Alfonso and Lucrezia at the center of the high table. Ugoccione's wife, right on his heels, drew Alfonso's attention, and Alfonso seated her beside himself while Ugoccione seated Lucrezia. Everyone else was also guided to the proper seat by servants, and the musicians in the gallery above began to play.

"I am sorry you still find the loss of your Roman companions so distressing," Ugoccione said when he could be heard above the scraping of benches and the music. "Duke Ercole meant it for the best. He thought that a circle of Ferrarese ladies would soon provide you with a wider acquaintance and that keeping your Roman servants would isolate you from the Ferrarese people."

Lucrezia's brows lifted. "Do you really feel that Donna Teodora is likely to provide me with a large and *congenial* circle of acquaintance? Why in the world did you invite her and ask Alfonso to bring her?"

It seemed at first that the count was not going to answer Lucrezia's question. He looked around, and seeing that nearly all his guests were safely seated, he signaled for the maestro di sala to order the cooks to begin serving. Almost immediately succulent appetizers displayed on large platters were carried around the room. Servers appeared with flagons of wine and filled the fine, stemmed glasses before each place. When he had urged Lucrezia to try this and that, however, he returned to the question she had asked.

"You know that Donna Teodora has relatives at the French court?" he asked, and when Lucrezia nodded, her mouth too full to reply, he added, "the duke is concerned over the . . . ah . . . coolness between you. I think he might have considered dismissing her, except for those connections. I will make a chance to talk with her later in the evening and warn her about writing untrue and unpleasant tales about you to her uncle. It is just as well that you did not encourage that Palagio, who, it was hinted, was a Spanish spy."

"He may have been, for all I know," Lucrezia admitted, "but *he* was not Spanish, nor Neapolitan either."

Count Ugoccione shuddered. "Well, whatever he was, he is no longer. It was an ugly way to die."

"Perhaps worse for us than for Palagio," Alfonso said, turning his head from the countess for a moment. "He was likely dead in ten or twenty heartbeats, but the rest of us had to look at him for much longer."

Alfonso turned back to the count's wife before Lucrezia could respond to his remark, but she was smiling when she looked at Ugoccione. Then she sighed. "I wonder how *that* tale will be related to the French court."

"It can only be related as hearsay," the count said, swallowing hastily. "Donna Teodora was not there. I have seen the list of those who unmasked before the maestro di sala, and her name was not on the list."

"It was not?"

Lucrezia blinked as she bit into a cracker spread with a delicious pâté. She was sure she had seen Teodora with her other women when she had left for the Palazzo Cortile, but they had all been masked and there were several whom she hardly knew at all who were also tall and thin, like Teodora. Perhaps she had mistaken one of those for the chief lady.

"Unless she left early," the count remarked, "or ran off when she heard the screaming."

He then devoted himself to finishing what he had taken on his platter and Lucrezia also ate without interrupting him, sipping her wine between bites. The cook's helpers made a second round with the platter of appetizers, but Lucrezia refused another helping, smiling at the count and saying that she did not want to blunt her appetite too much before the first course arrived. When it had been served and the first few bites taken and appreciated, she went back to a subject that puzzled her.

"It is certainly possible that Donna Teodora left before the excitement started," Lucrezia said. "She and any number of others may have slipped out before Alfonso bade the maestro di sala to ask the guests to unmask and note down their names. Do you remember Elizabetta Dossi? And Diana Altoviti? And, of course, we know Beatrice Tisio will not be on the list because she was with us and did not leave with the other guests."

Count Ugoccione shook his head. "I do not remember. . . . It was only because the duke was talking to me about Teodora that I remembered not seeing her name. The others . . . Wait. Dossi, yes, she was there. She came and tried to comfort Beatrice but nearly fainted when she saw Palagio, so I sent her away. Diana Altoviti . . . Altoviti . . . no, I cannot remember whether I saw her name or not, but I hope you are kind to her, poor thing."

"Oh, my dear count, not another cousin!"

He laughed easily. "No, no relation at all, not even as distant as Beatrice. It is just that I am sorry for the Altoviti women—all the men are dead now, I think. I saw Donna Gabriella Altoviti—she is Diana's mother—just yesterday in the Palazzo Cortile. I stopped to say good day to her, but she was so shabby and so terribly uncomfortable that I did not keep her long or ask what she was doing."

"I did not even know Diana had a mother. She never mentioned her—although, to speak the truth, I do not encourage conversation with the Ferrarese ladies. But I cannot see why the mother should be shabby. Diana dresses well and does a good business with her perfumes and lotions."

"Perhaps not as good as she claims," Ugoccione said. "In that case, likely the mother is shabby so that the daughter can keep up appearances."

That might well be true, Lucrezia thought, and felt a pang of guilt. Perhaps she should inquire and offer a little help. She thought of her own mother in need . . . but that could never happen. Her father had long ago arranged for Vanossa's generous income. And the thought of income reminded her that Diana would have a very nice income from Bianca's bequest. Relief washed out her guilt, and free of that she had to bite her lip to keep from laughing.

Count Ugoccione had almost caught her in his little trap. That sad comment about the shamed and shabby mother must be another device to weaken her resolve to refuse to support the Ferrarese ladies. Lucrezia made a sympathetic *tsk*ing noise while she gave her attention to a whitefish fillet in a really remarkable sauce.

"They were Florentine, just like the Strozzis," Ugoccione was saying, "and were also driven out of Firenze because of some political difficulty. I am not sure whether they were simply not as clever—as you know, Ercole Strozzi's father did very well for himself in Ferrara and Ercole is quite comfortable."

Lucrezia swallowed the remainder of the fish and smiled. "I suppose so. At least he never hints to me of any need for money."

The count laughed. "If he does, you just rap his knuckles. That estate at Ostellato is a mark of the Strozzi well-doing." Then he sobered. "The Altovitis were a different case. Although there were several substantial estates actually outside Firenze, Gabriella's father-by-law was a stubborn man and would not sell. He believed he would get his lands back when the Medici were cast out . . . but it did not happen. I believe Gabriella's husband returned to Firenze to prosecute the case, but he died there, and most of the property is still in contention."

"That is a sad tale, indeed," Lucrezia said, "but surely it would be more practical for the duke to try to secure the good services of some highborn Florentine family to negotiate the restoration of at least part of the Altoviti lands than to expect me to support the family."

The count grimaced at her recognition of his device, but he only said, "You are a hard case, Madonna Lucrezia."

For a moment Lucrezia dismissed all pretense, and the gray steel showed behind the blue of her eyes. "I do not like to be cheated, Count Ugoccione. I do not really like most of the women the duke selected to be my ladies. Also, I would prefer to choose my attendants for myself. However, if I had the full income to which the dowry I brought entitles me, I would make do to support the duke's charity cases. Since I have neither income nor great delight in the company of the women, I will do nothing."

Ugoccione sighed and returned his attention to his plate. Lucrezia, feeling she had acquitted herself very well, also applied herself to her dinner with good appetite. She heard Alfonso's deep chuckle, but he said nothing.

They had eaten steadily until the first course was only odd lumps and gravy and sticky bits on the fine platters. A glance around the room showed Count Ugoccione that all of his guests were leaning back and that some were surreptitiously loosening belts. He nodded to the servers and rose, holding out his hand to help Lucrezia rise also. Behind her, Alfonso was repeating the actions with the countess, who was giggling over something he had said.

The count's rising was the signal for all the other guests to do so. Then those at the high table descended from the dais and mingled with those from the side tables. Servers came to clear away, to remove everything on the tables so the cloths could be replaced and the tables set for the second course.

Lucrezia accompanied the count around the room, smiling and nodding and even exchanging small politenesses with the other guests. Eventually they came to a stop again near the dais. For a moment Lucrezia watched absently as finishing touches were put to the tables.

"You know, Count Ugoccione," she said, "I cannot completely dismiss the case of the Altoviti from my mind." She laughed lightly and shook her head as the count looked at her hopefully. "Oh, no, I am not offering any support, but I cannot help but wonder why Donna Gabriella does not herself go back to Firenze and appeal for restoration."

"Perhaps she feels it would not be safe," the count remarked, leading her slowly toward the step to the dais. "I am not certain how her husband died. Perhaps it was no natural death."

"Even if *he* had been murdered," Lucrezia persisted, "I am sure that Piero Soderini, who is now gonfaloniere in Firenze, would scarcely attack two women who are not likely to make political trouble."

"It depends on the women," Alfonso put in, having also stepped up on the dais, with the countess clinging to his arm. "Some of them are incredibly stupid." Lucrezia drew a sharp breath, and Alfonso touched her shoulder. "Not you, madonna. You show uncommon good sense in avoiding political trouble and could probably cozen the gonfaloniere and the entire Signory into doing whatever you want."

"How unfortunate, then, that I cannot cozen your father into paying me my proper appanage, nor you into supporting my demands."

Alfonso rolled his eyes. "The mills of God grind slow, but they grind exceeding fine—and I have not the smallest impulse to be rendered into dust."

Count Ugoccione spoke hurriedly, wishing to avoid any argument between his guests of honor. "The covers are restored. Let us take our places for the second course."

Apparently either having learned his lesson or come to the conclusion that his attempts to influence Lucrezia were hopeless, the count introduced only impersonal topics and invited participation in the conversation from the other guests at the high table and even from a few seated at the side.

Ariosto was induced to recite from a current work during the second change of covers, and Lucrezia was impressed. She began to realize that he was a great talent, but not one that could resist sycophancy. Hiring him to write epithalamia produced bathetic and ridiculous tripe; on the other hand, his own work on epic subjects was wonderful. She must consider, Lucrezia thought, how she could help him but without producing any foolish effusions in her honor. It was one of the things she valued so highly about Ercole Strozzi. He managed to flatter without making the subject of his flattery ridiculous.

For the rest between the third and fourth courses, a marvelous soprano, who had been seated modestly toward the very end of the second table at the left side of the room, sang. Lucrezia was thrilled with her voice and drew Count Ugoccione to where she stood. It was with some chagrin that she discovered the singer was not a professional but the wife of a minor nobleman. Still, the lady was flattered by Lucrezia's genuine appreciation and promised to come to a private dinner in Lucrezia's apartment and sing. The quality of her performance was also attested to by Alfonso, who even offered to play for her.

The light was beginning to fade by the time the fourth course was consumed and Lucrezia said playfully that she was so full she would have asked Alfonso to carry her to his carriage if she had not believed she had taken on so much food she would need a four-man litter to move her. The count expressed his regret that his cooks had been so successful. He had intended, he said, to ask her to dance to round out the entertainment. Lucrezia said she was sorry she had not known, that she would have eaten less, but as it was she did not think she could do anyone any credit by trying to dance.

A few more pleasant nothings were exchanged. Those from the high table spent another half candlemark circulating among the less important guests. Finally Alfonso ordered his carriage, thanked Count Ugoccione again for a wonderful meal and a pleasant afternoon, a page was sent to collect Teodora Angelini, and they made their way out of the palazzo.

The steps were negotiated safely, Alfonso having simply turned around and ordered the area to be cleared and that Donna Teodora go down first. When they reached the carriage, Alfonso again placed his ladies where he wanted them and got in beside Lucrezia. At first no one spoke. Alfonso had closed his eyes. Lucrezia also closed her eyes and rested her head on the cushion behind her, but when the carriage started, she opened her eyes slowly. Donna Teodora was sitting upright, wide awake. Between her hands was a thin, gleaming round of steel.

15

"WHAT IS THAT in your hands?" Lucrezia cried, her voice thin and high.

Alfonso jerked upright, his hand going to his knife.

Donna Tedaldo's face changed color so violently that the dull brick red could be distinguished even in the dim light. Her hands moved convulsively as she tried to pull a fold of her skirt over them.

"Nothing," she breathed. "It is nothing, a bit of woman's foolishness."

"For God's sake, Lucrezia," Alfonso said, looking disgusted, "you have murder on the brain. Whoever killed Bianca and Palagio is clever. Do you think it would be clever for Donna Teodora to stab you while we three are in the carriage and there are footmen behind us and outriders all around?"

"No, of course not," Lucrezia said, her cheeks now feeling as red as Teodora's had been a moment before. "I do beg your pardon,

Donna Teodora. I was half asleep, and when I saw the metal in your hand . . . I cannot tell you how horrible it was to see that hole in Palagio's throat and the blood . . . so much blood." She shuddered. "The vision comes back to me, and the horror of it all. I hope you were spared that terrible experience."

"I was, indeed," Teodora said. "I did not attend the masked ball at all."

Lucrezia hoped she retained only an expression of mild concern, but she was shocked, remembering a tall, angular, masked woman in an unsuitably provocative gown she had been sure was Teodora. Still, the person who came in dressed as Sigismundo would claim not to have attended the ball. And Teodora could have stripped off the skimpy gown quickly and redressed to pass as Sigismundo. Only there did not seem to be any reason for her to have killed Bianca . . . unless she needed the money far more than she admitted.

"I hope you were not ill," Lucrezia said.

She thanked God as she spoke that the darkness was even more complete than it had been a few minutes ago. Teodora would never see her expression or that her eyes were straining sideways, trying to see what was now concealed by Teodora's skirt.

"No, I was not," Teodora said sharply. "I do not approve of such entertainments as masked balls. They are no more than an open invitation to misbehavior. I am surprised and saddened that the duke so indulges the very worst aspects of his courtiers' characters."

"But I did not see any misbehavior at the ball," Lucrezia said rather plaintively.

That was not strictly true. Most of the men who danced with her had tried to get their hands through the swaying veils she wore. But Lucrezia did not really consider such playful nonsense as wicked, and in any case she was far more interested in keeping Donna Teodora concentrated on lecturing about morality. In her agitation, her grip on the fold of her skirt had loosened. Lucrezia was careful to hold her head so that it would appear she was looking at Teodora's face, whereas her eyes were fixed on Teodora's lap.

"It is not so much what is actually done at the ball but what is said behind the protection of the mask. Who knows what temptations are laid in the path of innocent maidens and dutiful wives?"

Lucrezia shook her head, taking the opportunity to look more openly at what Teodora held, and said, "If the maidens are truly innocent, they will not even recognize the temptations, and a dutiful wife, if she is truly devoted to her husband, simply would not *be* tempted. Do not make women out to be less than they are, Donna Teodora. I assure you the temptations thrown out to me at the ball struck me as comical or even ludicrous rather than dangerous."

If Lucrezia's voice was sharper than it had been, that was owing partly to disappointment. She had finally been able to see enough of the shiny thing Teodora held. It was not metal at all, but polished white bone—no more nor less than a pair of knitting needles. And she understood perfectly why Donna Teodora was hiding them. No elegant court lady would dare to be caught knitting; she would be laughed out of her position. Knitting was an activity reserved solely for the lower classes.

Since Donna Teodora did not deign to answer Lucrezia's defense of the masked ball with more than a sniff, Lucrezia leaned back and closed her eyes again. Why in the world would Donna Teodora be carrying knitting needles? From what Lucrezia had heard from Lucia, Teodora was not the kind to obtain things for her servants. So they were for herself and something she would not willingly ask a servant to get for her lest the servant talk.

Lucrezia resisted frowning. Admittedly Teodora had no place to conceal the knitting needles—except perhaps down the front of her dress, and then she would risk stabbing herself in the stomach, *but what did she want them for* if it was not to stab . . . ? No. Alfonso was quite correct. Only a madwoman would stab one of her fellow travelers in a coach, and Donna Teodora was not mad, no matter how silly her actions seemed. And then Lucrezia suddenly guessed the answer to a lot of questions about Donna Teodora and she very nearly opened her eyes to look at the woman with sympathy.

Teodora was poor. Much poorer than she allowed anyone to guess. The knitting needles were for her to make a warm garment to wear under her gowns. She denied knowing La Vecchia because she herself sold her own empty bottles to the woman. She had not gone to the masked ball because she could not afford to buy or even make a costume. Poor thing.

Yes, poor thing, but did that not make the bequest from Bianca a matter of greater importance? And Teodora must have known Bianca's light-mindedness, her fatal flaw of allowing herself to be convinced by the last person to whom she spoke. Had that truly been a *fatal* flaw? Had Teodora convinced Bianca to make the bequests in a new will . . . and then given her, perhaps as a thank-you gift, a flask of poisoned lotion? And had that led to the bleeding hole in Palagio's throat?

The slight jostling as the carriage stopped allowed Lucrezia to open her eyes, but it was too late to ask any questions . . . if she had been able to think of any. Donna Teodora was out and away as quickly as she had been when they arrived at Ugoccione's palazzo. Alfonso followed her retreating back until it disappeared under Castel Vecchio's deep gateway.

"The lady does not seem to enjoy our company," he said.

Lucrezia could not see his expression in the dark, but there was nothing in his voice, and she made no reply, simply allowing him to lead her into the building and to her apartment. There, she told Lucia not to summon Angela and Nicola but to help her into a warm bedrobe. If it were not that she knew Alfonso would be back to do his marital duty—she could not call it making love, although perhaps he was not quite as brusque as when he first took her—she would have gone to bed. But he would only wake her later. She shook her head and went into her study, where she selected a book of Giovanni Boccaccio's wicked tales. They might divert her mind from thoughts of murder . . . and make her more welcoming to her husband.

9 April, Ostellato and Lucrezia's Apartment

By the morning, Lucrezia's lingering horror was gone. Over breakfast in her private reception room, she first inquired from Angela and Nicola about the success of their mission among the perfumers. They had nothing to report but frustration. Not a single perfumer among the shops they visited had admitted ever buying used bottles and flasks, and every one had been shocked (or claimed to be) at the idea of refilling a bottle supplied by a customer.

"We were the wrong ones to send," Nicola sighed. "We are too obviously ladies of the court. They could not admit to us practices that would cheapen their wares."

"I will have to find another way," Lucrezia said.

She was disappointed, but since she had not really expected any major revelation, when Angela asked about Count Ugoccione's dinner, Lucrezia was able to recount to her and Nicola the count's attempts to make her guilty over refusing to support Duke Ercole's choice of ladies-in-waiting. She did not tell them about Donna Teodora's knitting needles. After all, the woman had not brought them to stab anyone with and she had a right to keep the shame of her poverty private. She did, however, tell her ladies that Teodora claimed she had not attended the masked ball.

"Then she could have come as Sigismundo and slipped out through the window, discarding the bloodstained cloak where Don Alfonso found it," Nicola said. "It is possible that the rest of the clothing was only spotted with blood, and that would not be noticed in the dark."

"Especially if she had another cloak, a long one, concealed nearby to cover herself," Angela added, and then shook her head. "But why? Why should she kill Bianca?"

"I suppose for the money," Lucrezia said, but without any emphasis that might reveal Donna Teodora's urgent need.

Still, she was relieved when Ascanio came through the portiere and said that Ercole Strozzi was requesting the favor of an audience with Madonna Lucrezia. She agreed to see him and Nicola rose from her seat to fetch an extra stool for Don Ercole, while Angela went to the sideboard and got a fourth plate. Breaking the fast was not a formal meal, and the cook and maestro di sala did not remain to serve while Lucrezia and her women ate.

All greeted Don Ercole with pleasure and he responded with equal pleasure and with thanks for the seat and the place at the breakfast table. "However, I did not come to eat," he said—and then, after eyeing the dishes, added, "although I will, with pleasure. You are well served by your cook, madonna."

"Thank God the duke could not dismiss my personal servants," Lucrezia said. "Not that there is anything wrong with Ferrarese cooks; the duke's kitchen staff leaves nothing to be desired—except any knowledge of Roman dishes. I am not saying they are better or worse than Ferrarese dishes, but they are what I am accustomed to."

"Of course," Strozzi said, filling his plate. "And as you can see, *I* have no objection to Roman dishes. But, as I said, I did not come to eat, despite the fact that I am doing so with great pleasure. I must admit I came for gossip. I was invited to Ugoccione's dinner, but I had a previous engagement and I could not go. So, madonna, did anything of note happen?"

Lucrezia made a wry moue. "Aside from Ugoccione doing his best to weaken my resolve to refuse stipends to the ladies the duke appointed, not much. Ugoccione told me a sad tale about how Diana Altoviti's family lost their Florentine estates, and also hinted that I should moderate my attitude toward Teodora Angelini because she has relatives at the French court and she might write them nasty tales about me."

Strozzi sighed. "That last is, unfortunately, true. Of course, I am not sure how much influence her uncle has or how close he can get to the king. I would not let it worry me, madonna. You are now well established here. Not only are you carrying Don Alfonso's child, but you are greatly beloved by the people for your kindness and the good you have done. The duke is deeply fond of you too."

"But not fond enough of me to pay me a fair appanage!"

Strozzi sighed again. "That does not mean he is not fond of you, madonna. That is merely his nature, and it is not directed at you. It is the same for everyone."

Lucrezia huffed out an exasperated breath. "I know it, but I wish he would not try to cozen me or trick me into supporting his charity cases. When Count Ugoccione was trying to arouse my sympathy for the Altovitis, I asked why Duke Ercole did not approach some wellborn Florentine—I know Firenze and Ferrara are often at odds, but Florentines do come here—and ask that person to intervene for Gabriella Altoviti."

"It is not so easy as you think," Strozzi said. "To do that might well involve Duke Ercole in Florentine politics and he might not even know on which side . . . provided there was any clear distinction between the sides." He laughed bitterly. "Even you who probably understood the convoluted politics of Rome would find those of Firenze bizarre."

"Are there *no* neutrals?" Nicola asked.

Strozzi shrugged. "My father thought *we* were neutral." He laughed again, not bitterly this time. "The trouble is that papa was already a man of prominence, admired for his learning and his eloquence. Such a man who did not sing your praises did you harm just by his silence. Thus . . ."

"But you are at home here now, are you not?" Lucrezia asked anxiously, covering one of his thin hands with hers.

He smiled easily. "Oh, yes, madonna, and since your arrival, this home has taken on a warmth that makes it the only place I could call 'home.' But I do not want you to think ill of my family's birthplace. Those who are . . . ah . . . nonentities mostly live in peace. There are some really old noble families, like the Palagios, who have lost all their influence and most of their money, who—"

"Palagio?" Lucrezia repeated. "Could the murdered man have belonged to a noble Florentine family?"

"I never thought about it," Strozzi admitted. "You know the way retainers will take the name of a family. I just assumed . . . Perhaps because his poetry was so awful. But you are right, madonna. Some investigation of the possibility that he belongs to the Florentine Palagios must be made." His brows knitted. "I will talk to Correggio about it. If Guido del Palagio was a scion of the family, Don Niccolò will be able to write to them and express our regret over his death and explain what we are doing to try to bring the murderer to justice."

Now it was Lucrezia who sighed. "We do not seem to be able to escape that horrible event, do we?"

"We certainly come back to it too frequently," Strozzi admitted. "Come, let me reciprocate for this delicious breakfast you have provided. Let us all ride out to Ostellato, where I will provide a midday nuncheon and you can advise me on the most romantic way to lay out the gardens around the house."

The invitation was accepted with delight, Ostellato being far enough outside the city to feel like the country and close enough to go there, stay some hours, and return in good time for dinner. Lucrezia rang for Ascanio and bade him send for a coach and outriders before she went into her bedchamber to dress. Nicola and

Angela also hurried away to dress, pausing in the public reception room to announce that Madonna Lucrezia would not be giving any audience that day because she was riding out. In a remarkably short time—proving how much a pleasant purpose can influence the speed of a woman's dressing—they were all in Lucrezia's carriage and on their way.

Determination also has an influence. No one mentioned Donna Bianca or Palagio the whole afternoon. Strozzi exerted himself to be amusing, and no one was more so when he did. They spoke of poetry, of music, of art, of the fine art of dressing. They had a delicious meal, not with the refinements that Lucrezia's Roman-trained cooks would have provided but appetizing for its very plainness in which all the ingredients could be identified.

Over the meal and as the servants cleared away, they discussed politics and religion, until deterred by Angela's sighs of boredom. They walked out to examine Ostellato's fine herd of milch cows, the vineyards just coming into bud, the orchards where perfume was beginning to waft from the earliest blooms on the branches. They did not, however, play games of tag or hide-and-seek in the gardens or race on the lawns and paths. For one thing, Ercole Strozzi, crippled as he was, could not have joined them. For another, Lucrezia remembered all too vividly how she had tripped and fallen during a race on a visit to Cardinal Lopez's vineyard. The fall had caused her to miscarry the first child she and her first, beloved Alfonso had conceived. That had been sad, but to lose this Alfonso's baby for such a cause would be a disaster.

Despite that unhappy memory, color had come back to Lucrezia's cheeks and her voice lilted as she spoke. Still, the memory made it easier for her to remind everyone that they were all invited to eat at the duke's tables, and, regardless of everyone's sighs, to say it was time to return to Ferrara. They left Strozzi at his house in the city to dress and returned to Lucrezia's apartment, which was strange but peaceful with no attendants or curious visitors in the public room.

Having delivered their lady safely to her bedchamber, Angela and Nicola went to their own rooms to dress and Lucia began at once to remove Lucrezia's clothing.

"I hope you are not too weary," the maid said, while she untied points and stripped off Lucrezia's sleeves.

"No. In fact I feel refreshed by the country air. And we only strolled about quietly. Don Ercole is not fit for any strenuous exercise and"—she put her hand to her belly—"I was mindful of my little one."

They spoke briefly then about what Lucrezia would wear, and Lucia poured a glass of wine for her lady, which she carried to the daybed where Lucrezia was resting. Lucrezia sipped at the wine while Lucia laid out the clothes.

"About La Vecchia, madonna," Lucia said, as she brought a tray of perfume bottles from the dressing table for Lucrezia to choose among. "I saw her this afternoon and told her that you wished to speak to her. I tried to get her to promise to come back just about this time when I knew you would be dressing, but she would not."

Lucrezia looked up from the selection of perfumes and saw that her maid looked troubled. "What is it, Lucia?"

"I did my best not to frighten her, madonna, I swear. I never mentioned that a bottle she sold had held poison. I told her that you only wanted information about who she sold to and that you would pay for it, and I assured her that you did not mind my selling the bottles, that you had even spoken well of using the pretty things again instead of throwing away the hard work of some artisan . . . but she was frightened nonetheless. The moment I mentioned that you wanted to know who her customers were, she began to look sidelong, as if she wanted to escape."

Lucrezia sighed. "I am not surprised. When those who live off the leavings of the nobility are noticed at all, it usually means trouble for them. I was hoping to spare her trouble. Now I will need to alert the guards to hold her for me, and that will mark her so they will be suspicious of her. I am sorry. . . ."

"Not yet, madonna, please?" Lucia pleaded. "I have thought of one thing more we can do if La Vecchia does not come here as I asked her to do. I could go to Anna Peruzzi's perfumery and ask for La Vecchia's direction. I know Anna buys from her. I hope she will know where the woman lives."

"Yes, do that." Lucrezia smiled at her maid. "When we know where she lives, I can send a man to fetch her quietly so that her little business will not be damaged. Poor creature, she must find it hard enough to make a living out of cleaning and reselling bottles. I would not want to take that from her, but I really do need to know to whom she sold that bottle. Even if the buyer was not the one who filled it with poison, eventually, going back along the trail the bottle left, we will discover who did."

Lucia kissed Lucrezia's hand. "You have a good heart, madonna. There are not many who would care if they destroyed one of the little folk who nibble around the edges of the Court."

Lucrezia smiled at her and chose a bottle of perfume. "That one, I think, but perhaps we had better wait for Angela, who will know exactly which scent will go best with the dress I have chosen."

"I am sure she will choose the same, madonna," Lucia said just a little stiffly, "but I am also sure that your taste is as good or better than Donna Angela's."

"In some things a great deal better," Lucrezia said, laughing. "For example in poetry or art, but in matters of dress Angela is always perfectly right."

Lucia sniffed but did not argue, merely carrying away the tray of perfumes and asking if Lucrezia wanted her wine glass refilled. Lucrezia shook her head and bade the maid make ready washing water. It was too late to take a bath, but that could wait for the next morning; a thorough sponge bath would do for today.

Much refreshed, Lucrezia came from the bathing room to find Angela and Nicola waiting. To Lucia's nose-tilted approval, Angela chose the same perfume that Lucrezia had, and when it had been applied, Lucrezia was quickly dressed. Alfonso arrived soon after to escort her to the Palazzo Cortile, but he was in a foul mood, apparently because he had heard of her excursion to Ostellato.

Lucrezia raised a brow at Nicola, who promptly told him exactly how the little expedition had come about, what they had done, and where they had gone on the estate. She mentioned that Lucrezia had *never* been alone with Don Ercole; not counting herself and Angela, there had always been many servants—herders, gardeners, workers in the vineyards. Lucrezia said nothing herself, and would not have indicated that Nicola should tell him except for Strozzi's sake. Alfonso already disliked poor Ercole and she did not want him complaining to the duke about Ercole misbehaving with her.

By the time they had gathered up the ladies-in-waiting, none of whom, except for Teodora Angelini, Lucrezia knew except in the vaguest way, and set out for the grand sala, Lucrezia had decided she had better immediately tell the duke about her visit to Ostellato. She was forestalled, however, by seeing Ercole with the duke. He had slipped away, surprisingly agile in spite of the crutch, when she and Alfonso reached the duke, and since Duke Ercole's opening remark was about how much her few hours in the country had benefited Lucrezia, Alfonso's mood was not improved.

Fortunately, Alfonso always curbed his reactions in his father's presence, so there was no shouting or threats. Dinner was quiet and dull; still, it was not exactly pleasant or restful to be seated beside a bubbling and smoking volcano all though the meal. Before the fourth course was completed, Lucrezia felt like consigning Ercole Strozzi to one of Dante's hells. She knew Ercole had meant well, that he had probably intended to spare her needing to explain her visit to Ostellato to her father-by-law, but she now realized that depriving Alfonso of the opportunity to complain had merely guaranteed a later and more violent explosion.

Lucrezia herself was in a foul mood by the time she was able to return to her own apartment and barely prevented herself from gritting her teeth when one of the ladies asked a perfectly innocuous question. She managed to answer politely and then slipped away to her private reception room, where she dismissed Angela and Nicola also. Both offered to remain as buffers against Alfonso, but Lucrezia merely shook her head.

"Let him roar. It was a mistake for Ercole to explain the expedition to the duke. If Alfonso had been allowed to complain, I could have justified myself to the duke and most of Alfonso's ill temper would have been blown away. To keep him from expressing himself still longer will be worse."

She saw Angela and Nicola consult each other silently in a meeting of glances and suspected that one or both would remain in the private reception room to rush in and bear witness if Alfonso should threaten physical harm to Lucrezia. She did not protest, although she was not at all afraid that Alfonso would beat her. It was odd not to be afraid, she thought. Alfonso was a violent man and his patience had been sorely tried, but somehow . . .

She entered the bedchamber, and Lucia, who had been seated on one of the chests around the bed, leapt to her feet.

"Oh, madonna, I have such interesting news," she said, her eyes wide with excitement.

"You learned where La Vecchia is? Who she is?"

"Both, I think," Lucia replied.

"Anna Peruzzi knows her well, then?"

"I never asked Anna Peruzzi about her. Oh, let me help you undress while I tell you, madonna, and then you can be comfortable."

Lucrezia nodded and seated herself at her dressing table to allow Lucia to remove the jewels and pins from her hair, and begin to unfasten Lucrezia's sleeves. When that was done, Lucia brushed and braided the hair very loosely, talking all the while.

"La Vecchia came into Mistress Peruzzi's shop just after I did, and she was surprised and not too pleased to see me. So I bought the lotion I was looking at quickly and went out, but I only pretended to walk away. I went to the other side of the road and walked along a little way. Then I crossed again and went alongside where there was a cloth banner hanging that I could pull over to hide me—only I held it away at first so I could see into the shop."

"That was very clever, Lucia."

The maid nodded to the compliment, but she was so excited about telling her tale that she continued almost without hesitation. "By the time I could see in, La Vecchia had taken two large flasks, half a dozen smaller ones, and a whole array of empty little perfume bottles from her basket and set them on the counter. Mistress Peruzzi was pouring a little out of one flask and was rubbing it into her hands. She smelled her hands and then wiped them dry and said something to La Vecchia, but I could not hear the words."

"Too bad," Lucrezia said. "But go on."

"After that she tested the other flask and sniffed the smaller ones—they held perfume, I believe. Then they went into the back room together. I was so afraid La Vecchia would go out the back way, but fortunately she did not. She and Mistress Peruzzi came back to the front of the shop together. La Vecchia picked up her basket—I could see that it was empty—and I guessed she would leave, so I ran across the street and turned my back while I pretended to look at scarfs." Lucia sighed. "She stopped in the doorway to say that she would come again on Monday and took so long about it that I had to buy a scarf."

"If you discovered where that woman lives, I will pay for the perfume and the scarf," Lucrezia urged.

"I did," Lucia said eagerly, but it was quite plain that she was more interested in explaining her cleverness than in obtaining the money. "I put the scarf over my head and tied it under my chin so that it would shadow my face, and I followed her. She never turned to look. I think whatever arrangement she made with Perruzi pleased her, because she walked quickly."

"Did she go directly home?" Lucrezia asked, trying to move the maid's narrative along.

"I think so, but I cannot be sure. The house was not far from the market, only two streets back, and it was a large house, sitting in its own garden, not a large garden, but enough land to be called one. From La Vecchia's clothing, I would have guessed that she lived in a room or two in a low warren. This was nothing of the kind, it was one of the better houses in a neighborhood of successful tradesmen."

"Perhaps she was only delivering—no, you said her basket was empty—picking up bottles or—"

"No, madonna." Lucia was so eager that she interrupted. "It was Diana Altoviti's house!"

"Diana Altoviti? How could you know that?"

"Because I saw her! La Vecchia did not go in the front door but went around the back of the house, where there was a shed—I could see it through the gate. Donna Diana came out of the shed and they spoke, but I could not hear. I could see that Donna Diana was not pleased, but La Vecchia was stubborn and soon Donna Diana sort of shrugged her shoulders as if she agreed because she had no other choice. Then they started toward the house together."

"Yes, but how did you know it was Diana's house? She could have been visiting a friend or . . . or . . ."

"I thought so too, madonna. I thought maybe she was going to take La Vecchia inside and introduce her to the lady of the house, but then a manservant came out of the back door. They were closer to me then and I could hear him. He called Diana 'madonna' and bowed to her."

Lucrezia was silent for a moment, then nodded. "Diana always said she had no need for Donna Bianca's bequest, that she was doing very well with her business. It seems she was telling the truth. Likely she does not care whether or not I pay a stipend either. She needs to be at court to sell her lotions and perfumes." Then she looked at Lucia again. "But why do you think La Vecchia lives in the house also?"

"Because she never came out. I waited, madonna. I found a place across the street where I could sit, and I waited until it was nearly dark, and La Vecchia never came out. She must live there."

The last sentence was said anxiously, as if she feared she would lose Lucrezia's good opinion of her, so Lucrezia smiled at her. "Likely she does. Perhaps Diana rents a room or two to her where she can wash her bottles—or perhaps she does it in the shed. It would be convenient for Diana to have the supplier of bottles and flasks right in her own house. However, even if La Vecchia does not live there, it doesn't matter. Diana will know where she lives and be able to bring her in whenever I want to speak to her."

"Of course, madonna. I did not think of that."

They had been so busy talking that they had not gotten much forwarder with removing Lucrezia's clothing, so Lucrezia was barely undressed and wrapped in her bedgown when the door to the inner corridor slammed open so hard it bounced back and hit Alfonso's chin, which he had thrust forward in his rage. Lucrezia had to bite her lips hard to keep from laughing. In general she did not fear her husband, but to laugh at this moment might well have been too much.

Lucia backed against the wall farthest from the enraged man and began to sidle toward the door.

"How many times do I have to tell you that I do not like Ercole Strozzi and you should avoid him?" Alfonso asked in a low, dangerous voice.

"You can tell me as many times as you like," Lucrezia replied calmly. "I *do* like Ercole Strozzi. He is clever and amusing and his poetry is not a mixture of bathos and imitation. He has, moreover, some very interesting ideas in his head that have nothing to do with either sex or money. Finer minds than mine have praised him, and your own father thinks the world of him."

"You mean you will not obey me?" he bellowed.

Lucrezia's brows went up, but her voice did not. "Certainly not in the choice of my friends, so long as the friendships are innocent and cause no political embarrassment. If you can show me that Ercole Strozzi offends against either of these conditions, I will inform him that I can no longer receive him."

For a moment Alfonso actually sputtered with fury and Lucrezia could not help wondering why her husband disliked Ercole so much. He did not dislike his brother Sigismundo, who had many of Ercole Strozzi's characteristics—the same soft voice, the same gentle way, the same clever mind and sharp wit.

A notion came to Lucrezia. Could Alfonso be jealous of Ercole? Not physically jealous, of course—Lucrezia took great care never to be in a compromising situation with any man—but jealous of Lucrezia's preference for and pleasure in Strozzi's company? The notion was somehow pleasing and for that very reason not to be indulged. Nonetheless, it made Lucrezia eager to divert Alfonso rather than infuriate him until he flung himself upon her with a mingled passion and rage that always brought her to the most violent climaxes.

"Never mind Ercole Strozzi," she said. "We will likely never agree about him and I have something far more important than Ercole to discuss with you."

"I did not know there was anything more important than Ercole Strozzi," Alfonso snarled.

There was a faint click in the background. Alfonso's eyes glanced toward the sound, but Lucrezia knew it was the door closing, marking Lucia's escape, and did not hesitate.

"Do not be ridiculous. Ercole is an amusing friend and occasionally very useful. For example, he mentioned to me that Palagio is the name of a very old and very noble Florentine family. We are not certain that the Palagio who was murdered actually belonged to the family, rather than being the offspring of some retainer who had taken the name, but—"

"If you had asked me, I could have saved you the trouble of wondering," Alfonso said, his full lips curving slightly with satisfaction.

"What do you mean?"

"Palagio *was* of the family, and in the direct line too. A younger son. Correggio found letters from his parents—I suppose under the circumstances it is just as well that they were not fond letters. Sometimes I can be more useful than Ercole Strozzi."

"You well might be, if you were the least bit interested in being of help to me about anything."

Alfonso looked away and shrugged. "I did not withhold the information apurpose. I . . . it did not seem of any importance. The family has lost most of their influence and nearly all their wealth. And from what Correggio found in Palagio's papers, it really does not seem likely that politics played any part in his death. Besides, he was carrying the flask that had the poison in it. I told Correggio about that, as I said I would, and now he too thinks that Palagio was trying to extort money from the killer—especially since one of the letters from his father was a refusal to send him money despite his—Palagio's I mean—expectation of marrying a wealthy woman."

Lucrezia drew a quick breath. "So he did intend to marry Bianca. That, I suppose, is the final evidence that he did not kill her."

"Unless she refused him," Alfonso pointed out. "He might have taken the flask from her body because it could be traced to him."

"And carried it to the ball days later? No." Lucrezia shook her head. "For one thing, Bianca was known for volatility. She might say no one day and yes the next. He would have believed he could change her mind had she refused. It would still be pointless to kill her. In fact, I do not believe he had yet asked her, but it might have been expected. Maria said Bianca was in very high spirits that night. But you are right in thinking the flask might be traced."

"Can it be? If we could find out who gave Bianca the poison, we would have our answer."

"Yes. That was what I wanted to tell you when you rushed in to scold me about liking Ercole. We know who bought the empty bottle from Lucia—that woman known as La Vecchia—and now we need her to tell us to whom she sold it. Lucia tried to get her to come here, promising that I would pay for information, but the woman would not agree and left the castle in a hurry. Lucia said La Vecchia seemed frightened."

"Frightened? Perhaps she filled that bottle herself."

"Heavens, I never thought of that. But, Alfonso, as far as I know, she does not herself sell perfume. The maids would know if she did."

"Perhaps she does not compound and sell scents herself, but I would lay a wager that she knows all the perfumers and could have had that bottle filled, likely without cost—and then added her own seasoning."

"But why, Alfonso? Why should she kill Bianca? She was not one of those named in the will."

He shrugged. "That has been the question from the very beginning, has it not? Bianca was simply not the kind of person to invite murder."

"Except for her estate," Lucrezia said slowly. "Two, at least, of the ladies who served with her and would have benefited by the bequest are in dire straits, and the third may be equally in need but is hiding it better."

She shivered. If it was one of her ladies, she was so close again to a killer. Again . . . she thought she had escaped that. Alfonso took her arm and steered her toward the bed; his hand was hard, burned and callused, but his grip was gentle. Lucrezia went willingly. Alfonso might be brutal and boorish, but he was not a murderer.

16

 ALFONSO put his hands behind his head and stretched his body languorously. "It should be easy enough to discover whether La Vecchia had someone fill that bottle for her," he said over a yawn.

Lucrezia barely withheld a start of surprise. This was the first time since their marriage that Alfonso had actually said something to her after their coupling. Usually he just got out of bed and walked out. Rarely, he would make a brusque remark as he left the room. Never before had he stretched as if he were settling in for a conversation and said something significant. With an effort she kept her voice low and conversational, with no hint she was aware the situation was at all unusual.

"We must ask the perfumers, I suppose," she said, "but I am not at all sure where the shops are . . . if they all have shops. Diana Altoviti does not; apparently she compounds the perfumes in her own home. And I cannot put out a notice inviting all perfumers to present their wares so I can choose among them, because it is well known that I buy my scents and lotions only from your sister."

"Hmmm . . . That need be no impediment. Write to Isabella and tell her the whole tale."

Including your accusation? Lucrezia was tempted to ask, but she did not want to spoil their rapport, even if it was only temporary, so she said nothing.

"She will be entranced by the idea that you are trying to solve the murder and readily forgive you for indicating you were about to add another perfumer to your list," Alfonso continued. "The notice should bring in the noble ladies who do perfuming as a hobby and the other amateurs. Meanwhile, I'll have Correggio send his men around the shops. What do you want them to ask?"

"It is very good of you to offer to help," Lucrezia said, smiling, knowing her voice would carry her expression.

She could feel Alfonso move his heavy shoulders uneasily. "I am afraid several people now know about the flask of poison," he said, "and more will soon know. I think we need to find the poisoner and expose him."

"Or her," Lucrezia said slowly. "I am not guilty, but I am not blind to the fact that poison *is* often a woman's weapon. And if Palagio was killed because he was trying to extort money from the poisoner—"

"I still find it hard to believe that a woman was capable of that knife thrust," Alfonso said, then sat up and swung his legs out of the bed.

"Wait." Lucrezia also sat up and put a hand on his arm as he reached for his bedrobe. "I would prefer if Correggio's men would only seek out all the shops and give Nicola a list. I am afraid if guardsmen ask where perfumers get their bottles that the answers they receive might be less than the complete truth."

"We will get no answers if we do not send someone."

"I think what I might do is send Lucia around to the shops with two or three cleaned-up bottles to ask if the shopkeepers would like to buy them and, of course, others that she did not bother to bring. Most of them, I hope, will refuse because they already have an adequate source."

"As you like," Alfonso said indifferently, standing up and pulling the bedrobe around him. "And I will let you know if Palagio's parents or Correggio's other sources have anything of note to say about Palagio's death."

"Thank you, Alfonso," Lucrezia murmured, lying down again and letting her eyes close.

There was a warmth in her and a pleasure that followed her into her sleep and gave her a very restful night. The next morning she wakened before her maid came to pull back her bedcurtains, but she lay quietly, thinking about the previous night. First she reviewed Alfonso's behavior with some satisfaction. If the result of this murder inquiry was a better relationship with her husband, she would have profited mightily by poor Bianca's death. Had she known it would be the result—Lucrezia chuckled softly—there might have been good reason to suspect her. Then she sighed and warned herself she could not expect Alfonso's good humor to continue; after all, he had been known for his sullen nature before she married him. She could not expect him to change his whole character.

Still, she was pleased enough to be very surprised when Lucia opened the bedcurtains with exaggerated care and presented a face wearing an anxious expression. Lucrezia blinked at her, recalling now the meat of the conversation she had had with Alfonso rather than the simple fact that he had stayed to talk at all. But that could not make Lucia anxious; she did not yet know the role Lucrezia had designed for her. Then Lucrezia smiled. Lucia had slipped out while Alfonso was still raging on about Ercole.

"You need not be afraid, Lucia," she said. "Don Alfonso and I parted on better terms than we started. He is very silly about Don Ercole."

The maid shook her head. "He is envious," she said, briskly pulling the curtains back the rest of the way.

"You mean jealous." Lucrezia laughed.

"Oh, no, madonna. If he were jealous of your body . . . Oh, that would be terrible. He would be terrible. No, he is envious of Don Ercole's ability to amuse you and make you laugh. He does not take it so ill from Don Sigismundo, because . . . I suppose because in some way he feels that Don Sigismundo is part of himself."

Lucrezia stared silently at her maid for a moment. She too often forgot how clever Lucia was. "But he does not feel that way about Don Ferrante or Don Giulio," she remarked.

"No, but he knows you do not really like them much."

"You have sharp eyes and ears, Lucia."

The girl smiled. "I did not get to be *your* maid by being stupid, madonna."

As she spoke, Lucia helped Lucrezia out of bed and slipped her bedrobe around her. Lucrezia went at once to the screen that concealed her close stool and relieved herself. She was smiling as she thought that Lucia had come to the same conclusion she had come to herself regarding Alfonso's reaction to Ercole Strozzi, but by the time she had finished and come out to wash her hands and face and work a frayed green twig around her teeth, she had put aside her thoughts about Alfonso for those of Lucia's cleverness. She would be ideal for her role, if she were willing.

"Lucia," she said, as the maid began to brush out her hair, "if I had a list of all the perfumers in the city, would you be willing to take to them several emptied and cleaned bottles and ask whether they would buy from you?"

"Of course, madonna, but *all* the perfumers? I do not think I could do that and still perform my duties to you."

"I can forgo your services for one day, Lucia," Lucrezia said, smiling. "I can get . . . Oh, I forget her name, the girl with the crooked teeth . . ."

She saw the pleasure go out of Lucia's face and a tension rise in her, and she remembered how the maid said she had not gained her position by being stupid. Suddenly Lucrezia realized that Lucia never missed a day at her duty; sometimes she came to serve pallid to greenness with illness, and Lucrezia had to send her away to see a doctor and rest. But by then Angela and Nicola had already been on duty and had taken Lucia's place for such personal duties as combing her hair and helping her dress. Lucia, it was clear, never let another maid attend her mistress personally.

Lucrezia put out a hand, touched Lucia's wrist, and smiled at her. "Very well, since I want you to give all your mind to dealing with the perfumers, I will not have that maid . . . although I do not think I would like to have someone with crooked teeth about me all the time. Still, we will wait for Angela and Nicola to arrive to attend to me."

Lucia raised her hand so she could kiss the fingers that still rested on her wrist. Her eyes now sparkled with interest. "Thank you, madonna. Now, what is it that you want to know about the perfumers?"

"First, whether any of them bought the bottle that held the poison." Lucrezia frowned in thought. "Do I have another of the same kind?"

"Not exactly the same, madonna, but very close. If I remember aright, that bottle had vines and leaves. You have one that only differs in having flowers amid the leaves."

"Is it near enough empty for you to clean it and use it as an example?"

Lucia went to look at the perfumes on the dressing table. "There is enough for three or four uses, I think, madonna."

Lucrezia sighed. "We all must make sacrifices in a good cause. I will wear that perfume today and we can discard . . . No, run and offer it to Angela and Nicola. We will all smell the same today. Then you can clean the bottle and see if you can find two or three others to clean and take with you."

When Lucia returned from her short excursion to the rooms of Lucrezia's ladies, she asked, "Should I ask if any of the perfumers know where La Vecchia lives?"

"Oh, yes. In case Diana Altoviti does not want to admit the woman lives with her and pretends or is truly ignorant of where she does lodge. I don't know why Diana should deny having the woman as a lodger, except for spite, but one can never tell. She might think it unsuitable to her pride to rent rooms to a washer of bottles, or something of that sort. Oh, and if the perfumers say they never bought such a bottle, try to discover if one of them filled a flask like that with lotion as a gift or a favor for anyone."

By the time a gown had been chosen and put on, Lucia was eager to get on with a mission that had the promise of more interest and excitement than her ordinary service. Instead of waiting for Correggio to collect a list of perfumers, she suggested going to the perfumers she knew of during the morning. She could ask at each shop for any others in the vicinity and go to them. Then she could return to the Castel Vecchio for her noon meal and to discover whether the names of any other perfumers she had not spoken to were on Correggio's list or Lucrezia had some other task for her.

Lucrezia agreed readily with this plan, and sent Lucia off when she walked into her private reception room and found not only Angela and Nicola but a lavish breakfast. She and her women discussed Lucia's expedition with considerable interest while they broke their fasts, but the topic could not last forever. Unfortunately, a quiet day stretched before them and they were growing quite impatient for answers to the questions Lucia would be asking— despite the fact that they all knew it would be some hours before their curiosity could be satisfied—when Ascanio slipped through the portiere to ask if Lucrezia would admit Don Giulio and Don Ferrante.

The women consulted each other with silent glances, agreed, equally silently, that the young men would serve as a distraction, and Lucrezia nodded to the page.

"Yes, let them come in."

Places were made for them at the table, dishes and goblets fetched from the sideboard. Food there was more than plenty, but neither young man reached for it immediately.

"Had you heard that Palagio was that Guido who was the youngest son of the Florentine Palagios?" Ferrante asked.

"Yes," Lucrezia replied. "Alfonso told me last night. I had not known there was a Florentine Palagio family. They had never come to my father's notice in any way."

"Too poor. Too unimportant," Giulio said, as he poured wine into his goblet. "The family can't have anything to do with his death. They have no political influence at all."

"Oh, well, you can't say that," Ferrante protested mildly. "I suppose they still have friends in the Signory."

"Yes, but Correggio didn't say anything about politics," Giulio insisted. "In fact, he seemed of your mind, madonna, that Palagio's death was because of Donna Bianca's. He was on about a flask of poison that Palagio was carrying. He didn't say Palagio did it, though."

Ferrante made a face. "Of course not. If he poisoned Bianca on the night of the play and took the flask away with him, why would he be carrying it almost a week later when he himself was killed? He brought it to show to someone, didn't he, Madonna Lucrezia?"

"That is what I believe," Lucrezia said. "And when he showed the flask and probably asked for money to keep silent about it, the person killed him."

"He needed money," Giulio said, pausing in stuffing his face with the various viands from the selection on he table. "Correggio found letters from his father, refusing to give him more money. He said Guido's previous claim that he would marry a woman with a good business had come to nothing and that money had been wasted—"

"Could that be why Madonna Isabella sent him here?" Nicola asked. "Could he have been courting a girl whose family objected?"

Lucrezia laughed. "I would rather believe that than that Madonna Isabella sent him to me because she believed I would like his poetry . . . or welcome a Spanish spy. Alfonso told me that Palagio's latest attempt to wring some money from his family was to claim that he was going to marry Bianca."

Ferrante nodded. "Yes. How did you know? I thought we were going to bring you news."

"Alfonso told me. He wondered if Palagio had killed Bianca because she refused him."

"Nonsense," Nicola said, wrinkling her nose. "One does not carry around a flask of poison in case the lady you ask to marry you refuses."

Lucrezia chuckled. "No, but more important than that, if Palagio knew Bianca at all, he would know that changing her mind was not at all unusual or difficult. Why kill her when he could get her to agree on another day?"

"There is that," Giulio agreed. "And, although he was a nitwit, one does not kill a man for that. If he killed Bianca, who killed him?"

Nicola choked at hearing Giulio call anyone else a nitwit and hastily changed the laugh to a cough as Lucrezia hurriedly raised her goblet and drank.

"One of Donna Bianca's other lovers who blamed him for her death?" Angela suggested.

"Not Guadaruzzi again!" Ferrante said. "Oh, I almost forgot to tell you that I did chase down that guardsman type to whom Guadaruzzi was talking. He was. The man remembers clearly because he was annoyed. He had his eye on a particularly delicious shepherdess and he could not shake off Guadaruzzi to pursue her . . . and then the screaming began."

"Thank you," Lucrezia said. "I never thought seriously it was Guadaruzzi. From everything you have told me he is not the type to stick a knife in a man's throat."

Giulio laughed with a coarse leer. "No. He was more likely to stick something else in."

Lucrezia raised her eyes to heaven, but found no help there and simply continued as if Giulio had not spoken. "Besides, there simply was not enough time for him to run out, change his clothing, murder Palagio, and then change his clothing again. But I must admit I cannot think of another man who could disguise himself as Sigismundo."

"A woman, then?" Ferrante asked.

Giulio, who had begun to eat, shrugged off the question. Apparently he had expended all the interest he had in a murder two days old. After a few mouthfuls, he complimented Lucrezia on her cook. The talk drifted away to the differences between Roman and Ferrarese cooking and then to more common topics of gossip. Finally the maestro di sala's servants arrived to clear the table and Lucrezia led her favored companions into the public reception room.

She could have wished that the men and women gathered there shared Giulio's lack of interest in the murders. Marino Sanuto asked curiously how Sigismundo had reacted to someone using his clothing as a costume to commit murder.

"With irritation," Lucrezia replied. "He was offended by the insult to his intelligence to suspect that he would wear his own favorite clothing to kill someone, particularly at a masked ball during which he could have worn any costume at all."

That drew laughter from everyone, but unfortunately her light answer also encouraged more questions, many of them very morbid. When Bernadino Zambotto pressed her for a more detailed description of Palagio's corpse for his chronicle, she shuddered, closed her eyes, and said she had tried her best not to look. Her clear disapproval closed off more questions about Palagio, but opened the topic of whether his death was related to that of Bianca. And one of the women—Lucrezia was not sure of her name, only certain that she was related to Gian Luca Castellini da Pontremoli, one of the duke's favorites—mentioned the flask of poisoned lotion.

Lucrezia was disappointed but not surprised by the woman's knowledge and resigned when the woman was at once surrounded and pressed for details. Lucrezia said nothing, grateful at least that the woman did not know of Bianca's sores. Apparently all she had heard from Gian Luca was that the poison could be taken in by the skin. Unfortunately, Marino Sanuto was not only curious as a monkey but clever with it. It did not take him long to come to the conclusion that anyone could have sent Bianca the lotion at any time and she might have used it days or weeks later.

"Oh, goodness," Marino said, "if we are not bound to consider only those who are free to come and go in the castel, anyone in the whole world could have sent that poison to poor Donna Bianca."

"That has been considered," Lucrezia answered calmly. "Don Niccolò da Correggio has set his men to look through the lady's papers, both here and at her estate in the country, and to ask questions of those who knew her. He will discover if any hated her or would benefit by her death."

"We already know of those who benefited by her death," a shrill-voiced woman said. Lucrezia knew her to be one of the ladies-in-waiting, one of Teodora Angelini's relatives and also an Angelini, but Lucrezia could not recall her first name. "Those ladies served with her and could easily have offered her a little gift of a flask of lotion at any time."

Lucrezia waited a heartbeat's time for Donna Teodora's voice to reprimand the woman and suddenly realized that Donna Teodora was not there. "So could I have done," she said in answer to the woman's remark, "but I did not. Fortunately, we have the flask, and the question of where it came from is also being pursued. The bottle originally held a perfume or lotion mixed by Madonna Isabella d'Este da Gonzaga, from whom many of the Court ladies—myself included—buy our scents and lotions."

"Madonna Isabella could have no part in Donna Bianca's death," Gian Luca's relative snapped.

"No, indeed," Lucrezia agreed, raising her brows. "I have learned there is a common practice of selling the empty bottles to a woman who is only known to me as La Vecchia. I expect to discover from La Vecchia to whom she sold the bottle, and from that person who bought it, filled it, or ordered it filled, with lotion, and added the poison."

"Then you are still determined to discover the killer?" Bernadino Zambotto asked.

"Of course. It does not matter how Donna Bianca died, she was my lady and someone did her harm. I will see her avenged and suspicion removed from the innocent." She looked around and her lips thinned. "Me among others. Is there anyone who can help? Anyone who has dealt with La Vecchia? Has anyone bought any lotion or perfume from her?"

"I will speak to my maid," the tall, thin, shrill-voiced lady said. "The idea of her filling her purse at my expense and not even telling me!"

"How can it be at your expense?" Nicola asked sharply. "I am sure you believed the woman had thrown the bottles away, and you did not blame her for that. Why should you care if she sells them?"

"I would be very sorry, indeed," Lucrezia said coldly, "if I heard that your maid had lost her position or suffered in any other way because of something I said. My Lucia did not ask my permission either—not because she thought I would deny her, she knows me better than that. She did not ask because it never occurred to her that I would care."

"Oh, who cares what the maids do with old bottles," Angela said, sounding thoroughly disgusted. "The important thing is whether anyone knows La Vecchia."

Two of the ladies-in-waiting admitted knowing *of* her and of being aware of the traffic in bottles. One said timidly that she was glad her maid had a little extra money because she could not afford to pay more and the maid helped her family; the other, Lucrezia assumed because of her evasive manner, sold the bottles herself. Both denied knowing La Vecchia's true name, having any knowledge of where she lived or dealt with the bottles, and both denied ever purchasing anything from her.

The timid girl said she had never been offered anything and would have been afraid to buy from someone so obviously poor because she would have doubted the quality of the ingredients the woman used. She bought from Diana Altoviti, she said, and Diana's products were always sweet and pure. The evasive one admitted to having asked—she did not say why, but Lucrezia assumed it was in hope of cheaper products—and being told that La Vecchia did not sell anything.

Those confessions loosened other tongues. Nearly all the ladies and Zambotto as well recalled seeing La Vecchia in corridors and other public areas . . . but not for the last day or two. After some argument, all agreed to that. No one had seen her all day yesterday or this day. A faint chill passed over Lucrezia. La Vecchia seemed to have disappeared soon after Lucia had spoken to her about her mistress's interest in her bottles. Surely that meant the woman knew something. Lucrezia could only hope that she had not tried to use that knowledge and was now lying dead somewhere.

It was a relief to remember that Lucia had seen her hale and hearty in Anna Peruzzi's shop late the day before. And then with Diana Altoviti . . . and had not Lucia said that Diana did not seem pleased with what La Vecchia said to her? Lucrezia wondered with a clenching of the heart whether she should send some of her guards to Diana's house and demand to see La Vecchia. But she did not know where the house was! Only Lucia knew, and Lucia was heaven knew where in the city.

17

10 *April,*

Lucrezia's apartment

 THE ARRIVAL of Roberto Malaleone and his staff to set up the table for the noon meal in Lucrezia's private reception room finally freed her from the "guests" in her public room. When she Angela and Nicola were seated and Adriano had finished serving small portions and retreated against the wall, Lucrezia told Nicola and Angela about her fears for La Vecchia. Angela was horrified, but Nicola calmly shook her head.

"If La Vecchia went to Diana's house to extort money, she is now beyond your help. Whatever happened must have happened soon after she entered the house. Unfortunately, there has been a whole night for Diana to be rid of the body and a whole morning for her to flee, if she wished to flee. She should be on duty tomorrow, I believe. If she does not appear, it will be soon enough to send your guardsmen to her house and to tell the duke to send men after her. After all, where could she go? I doubt she has anyone in Ferrara she would trust to hide her against a charge of murder. I think you told us she was Florentine; she might have relatives there, but it would be days before she could reach Firenze. You would gain little by trying to find her now . . . and if the woman is innocent, you will have done her great harm."

Lucrezia sighed. "Thank heaven for your good sense, Nicola. You are quite right. All I have to go on is Lucia's impression that Diana was not pleased with what La Vecchia told her. For all I know, that was about the price of bottles and had nothing at all to do with poison. But I am so uneasy. I hate to have to wait another day. . . ."

"So ask Teodora Angelini to send a page for her," Angela suggested. "That would not do Diana any harm, and if she was not there . . . well, if her servants said she would soon be back, the page could wait. If the house was closed up and the servants gone or she refused to come, you could tell the duke a day earlier."

"Teodora Angelini is not with the other ladies," Lucrezia said. "Did you not notice that her niece or cousin . . . oh, some relative, was a lot freer with her tongue than she ever is when Teodora is there to curb her?"

"I have never known Teodora to miss a day without sending you a note to tell you she would be absent," Nicola said, her voice flat.

"Oh, she often leaves about midday and does not return," Angela said.

"Yes, but not until she knows what you intend to do for the day, madonna," Nicola insisted. "She is always in attendance in the morning."

Lucrezia had a sudden vision of the gleam of knitting needles in Teodora Angelini's lap. The points were as sharp as those of any knife, and bone could be used to stab as well as steel. Nonsense. Alfonso was right. Teodora could not use a weapon when they three were alone in the coach. But some other time? *What if she had one of those knitting needles in hand when she stumbled against my back on the stair?* Lucrezia wondered. *The hole a needle would make would be so small; there would be so little blood; she could hide the weapon so easily.* And why had Donna Teodora denied all knowledge of La Vecchia?

Lucrezia nodded, then asked, "Are you sure you saw La Vecchia go into Donna Teodora's apartment? Did you see who let her in?"

"No one let her in. La Vecchia was with Donna Teodora," Nicola replied. "I noticed because her gown was in very much the same style as Donna Teodora's, only La Vecchia's was darned and even seemed to have some patches on it. I thought how old-fashioned Donna Teodora's gown was."

"Yet she denied to me that she knew La Vecchia," Lucrezia said. Angela shrugged. "Pride?"

"Yes, I suppose so," Lucrezia agreed, but her voice was uncertain. "You know Donna Teodora has relatives at the king's court in France. And Don Niccolò allowed Bianca to deliver letters from the diplomatic mail bag to ladies of the Court. Alfonso made a remark about Bianca learning something Donna Teodora might consider it dangerous to know."

"Something worth killing Bianca for?" Nicola asked, sounding very doubtful.

"It doesn't seem very likely, does it? But it would explain why she denied knowing La Vecchia. And she told me she had not been at the costume ball, but I could swear I saw her when we passed through the public reception chamber. Why should she deny being there, unless it was because she fled through the window after killing Palagio and could not unmask with the others before the maestro di sala?"

Nicola shrugged. Angela shook her head. Both were patient, but had nothing more to say. Lucrezia sighed and signaled the cook's and maestro di sala's helpers to clear the table. She and her women withdrew to the chests, padded with carpets, that provided seating under the windows. Lucrezia sank down on a chest at an angle that would permit her to look out of the window at the hanging gardens, which were becoming more lush by the day.

"I am glad we will be dining here in my chamber tonight," Lucrezia said. "I simply cannot make light conversation, and I would be sure to say something unacceptable if we dined with others. I do not want to talk about these murders, yet I cannot seem to fix my mind on anything else."

Nicola smiled. "Send for Ercole Strozzi and Don Sigismundo to dine with us. You can say anything you like to them with no offense taken. Besides, you know how they are when they get together. Something is sure to set them off about literature or art or science and no one will be able to get a word in edgewise about the murders."

"*No* one will be able to get a word in about anything!" Angela exclaimed.

Lucrezia and Nicola laughed, but Lucrezia promised as she sent off her notes that she would not allow her two learned guests to dominate the conversation totally. She offered to invite one of the better musicians, who were often asked to play with the family when the duke gave a concert. With the invitation, she would send some music to which they all could sing.

They were still absorbed in the discussion of which musician to ask—there was an abundance of fine instrumentalists in the court of Ferrara—and making a list in order of preference, in case their first choice should be engaged elsewhere, when Lucia arrived, rather tired and breathless and full of apologies for not returning earlier as she had promised.

"I was all the way at the other end of the city," she sighed, "and I had a whole list of shops to visit. If I had come home for my noon meal, I could never have got back before most of them closed and I would have needed to be away another day. And the worst of it is that I have nothing to offer you."

"Get a stool and sit down," Lucrezia ordered. "Your feet must be very tired. And you really do not know whether what you learned will help us find the killer. From what you say, I suppose everyone denied buying Madonna Isabella's bottles or even filling one for a friend or client."

"Just so, madonna," Lucia said as she set drew over a stool and sank down on it. "But I think some of them lied."

Lucrezia smiled. "See, already you have some interesting information. Did they lie about buying or filling?"

Lucia smiled back, the anxiety fading from her face. "Oh, about buying. No one seemed in the least troubled when I asked about filling La Vecchia's bottle. All denied doing so, but most with scorn or laughter, saying she would know better than to ask. I asked, most innocently, why they would begrudge her a small flask of lotion—acting as if I would expect such a courtesy. Some said she would have no clients who could afford their wares, so it was useless to give her a sample. Others claimed they feared she might use their perfumes or lotions to convince someone to buy and then actually sell bad, inferior products."

"And you think they were honest in their denials? If so, she did not get the flask filled by a perfumer."

"I could see no sign of hesitation or doubt. One—no, two—actually seemed a little annoyed that she did not ask for samples, saying she could have made some extra money by offering, say, their lotions to other shops that sold only perfumes, but La Vecchia said she only sold bottles."

"Ah, yes, and it was about buying her wares that some lied?"

"Three shops, all dealing with rich merchants, I think. They hustled me into the back as soon as they understood I was not a maid buying for my mistress. Although they told me they used only new bottles, all three were clearly interested in the finest flasks and one asked the price of the one with leaves and flowers." She uttered a little sour laugh. "They said they never did business with La Vecchia, but all recognized my description of her. In one place a serving girl complained that 'the old one' had not come yesterday as usual. The man who was speaking to me hushed her and bade me come back on Monday when some person with more authority would be in the shop, but I think it was to see whether La Vecchia showed up."

Lucrezia suffered another pang of anxiety when Lucia mentioned that La Vecchia had not appeared to do business as usual, but she suppressed it and urged the maid to continue. There was, however, very little more she had to tell—except that several shops complained of La Vecchia's nonappearance and said that if she did not come soon, they would definitely consider Lucia's offer.

Fortuitously, a page from Correggio with the list of perfumers shops gleaned from the tax rolls arrived just before Lucrezia sent Lucia away to rest. Nicola read out the names and directions aloud. There were only three that Lucia had missed, two hidden in back alleys—one of which was Anna Peruzzi's shop—and one Lucia had somehow not visited. It was not such a very long list, some sixteen names. Perfumeries were not, fortunately, as common as grocers or mercers.

"I do not understand," Angela said when Lucia had gone off to get a belated meal and change her gown.

This was a sufficiently common remark by Angela to arouse little interest in her companions. Lucrezia smiled in a long-suffering way at her handmaiden and Nicola sighed gently.

"What, love?" Lucrezia asked, since Angela was looking at her with a puzzled frown.

"Why La Vecchia refused to offer samples of lotions and perfumes from the shops that offered her that chance." Angela cocked her head in thought. "I saw myself how worn her skirt was, even darned and patched. Surely the opportunity to make a few more coins should have been of interest to her."

Lucrezia stared at her "silly" lady. "Out of the mouths of babes . . ." she breathed, not for the first time. "Indeed, Angela, now that you point it out to me, I do not understand it either."

She pursed her lips and rolled them against each other, feeling the dryness of the tissue, something telling her she *did* know the answer if she could just remember it.

A moment later she burst out, "Oh, wait! I think I do know why. Yesterday Lucia went to Peruzzi's shop to ask if she knew were La Vecchia lived. While she was there, the woman herself came in. Because La Vecchia had virtually run away when Lucia told her I would pay for information about those who bought her bottles, Lucia bought some lotion or perfume and went out, lest La Vecchia run away again."

"She is a clever girl," Nicola said.

"Indeed she is, and trusts me enough not to hide it. In fact she told me that she did not get to be my maid by being stupid."

Nicola chuckled, but Angela said impatiently, "Never mind Lucia. Tell me why La Vecchia refused what might have been a lucrative side business."

"Because she already had such a business," Lucrezia said triumphantly. "Lucia told me that when she watched La Vecchia in Peruzzi's shop, the woman put several filled flasks on the counter as well as the empty perfume bottles. Peruzzi tested what was in the two larger flasks by rubbing it on her hands—that must have been scented lotion. The smaller bottles she only opened and smelled."

"Mmh-huh, perfume." Nicola nodded. "So La Vecchia had a regular supplier already." She frowned. "Not one of the perfumers that Lucia had questioned, though. All of them seemed agreed that La Vecchia did not sell anything."

Lucrezia cocked her head. "Perhaps she sells only to Peruzzi, who is not truly a perfumer but only an outlet for products of some private perfumer—a lady or gentleman with a *very* high sense of his or her position, because Madonna Isabella does not hesitate to sell what she has produced."

Angela laughed. "Madonna Isabella's position is unassailable. Other ladies and gentlemen might well be more sensitive."

"I suppose," Lucrezia agreed, and then said with a shiver, "I do hope that La Vecchia will still be able to answer our questions when we find her . . . if we find her."

Nicola rose to her feet. "You are worrying yourself entirely too much about this. If Teodora Angelini is still not in attendance, I am going to get the direction of Donna Diana's house from Lucia and send a page to ask Diana to come to you and to bring La Vecchia with her. Then I will go and dress. Angela, stay and help Madonna Lucrezia make ready for our dinner guests."

Since Lucrezia knew it was impossible to focus Angela's mind on anything besides clothing when she was dealing with it, she let the subject of the murder rest, but only with the greatest difficulty. She had the feeling that she knew the answer, that all the pieces were in her mind and she only needed to assemble them. Yet they would not come together and she tried to pay attention to Angela, who had picked out a white velvet undergown and a soft pink gammura and matched them to pink-and-white-striped sleeves. She knew Angela's purpose was to lighten her mood and, indeed, the gay dress did cheer her up, as did a lighter and more flowery scent, with less cutting citrus edge to it.

While she was dressing, three notes of acceptance to her invitation arrived and Ascanio was sent down to the kitchen to warn

Adriano there would be six for dinner. Wryly she told him that the cook would doubtless shout at him for the unnecessary warning.

"But better he should shout at you than pout at me for not telling him when I have noble guests so that he can make an extra effort."

Nicola came back, having changed only her sleeves to make her gown more festive. Angela left to change her own gown in honor of their guests, and Nicola told Lucrezia that she had asked the ladies-in-waiting, just leaving to dress for their own dinners—or undress and eat what they could get if they were not dining out—for Donna Teodora. She had been told that Teodora had never appeared that day, nor sent any message. A few discreet questions had received no real replies, so she had sent the oldest page to get directions from Lucia while she penned a note requesting Donna Diana to come to Madonna Lucrezia bringing La Vecchia at once.

Lucrezia and Nicola went out to the private reception room, where Roberto Malaleone and his minions were setting up the table. Because there would be guests, Adriano would bring the food in a more formal procession when everyone had arrived.

They seated themselves well out of the way, and after a few moments of silence, Lucrezia said, "It is just in the back of my mind." Her voice was redolent with impatience. "But I cannot put the pieces together and draw it forth."

Nicola did not need to be told what "it" was. Lucrezia was still thinking of the solution to the murders. "You need not to think about it," she said. "You need to think about something equally irritating. Consider instead what Don Alfonso will say when he hears that you invited Strozzi to dinner only one day after he *again* told you he does not favor your friendship with Don Ercole."

Lucrezia laughed dutifully, but only half her mind was on Nicola's question. "Oh, he will roar a bit, but he is interested in finding the killer himself. You know, he is not nearly as stupid as he acts most of the time."

"I never thought Don Alfonso stupid, only honest enough not to pretend an interest in subjects he thinks unimportant. Not that he cares about being *thought* honest." Nicola shrugged. "He does not care what others think of him."

"Yet Lucia said he was envious of Strozzi for being able to make me laugh and talk about things that interested me."

"Lucia is very perceptive about people," Nicola said. "I think all the servants who come into contact with their betters are astute judges of character—at least those that remain in their masters' employ." She smiled. "I did not say that Don Alfonso did not care what *you* thought about him. He does, you know."

"I have begun to think so myself," Lucrezia said. "Believe it or not, last night he lay in bed and talked after we coupled. He did not just get up and leave as he usually does. He talked about the murders. He is interested in solving them."

Nicola laughed gently. "Solving a murder is practical. I would imagine that is far more impressive to Don Alfonso than how well you understand art or literature."

Lucrezia widened her eyes. "Oh, yes? Well, I absolutely refuse to encourage murders to happen just to impress my husband. Or were you suggesting—"

She broke off as Ascanio entered the room escorting one of the older pages, of whom Lucrezia did not make pets. The young man bowed deeply, first to Lucrezia, then to Nicola.

"Were you able to deliver my note?" Nicola asked.

"No, madonna, I am sorry, since you said to deliver it to the hand of Donna Diana Altoviti. She was not at home."

Lucrezia heard herself draw in a sharp breath, but Nicola gave no sign of having noticed, and her voice was even as she said, "Oh? To whom did you speak?"

"The maestro di casa, madonna. He said that both ladies had gone out. He did say I could wait for them and—"

"*Both* ladies?" Lucrezia interrupted. "Is that what he said exactly? Both *ladies*?"

The page bowed, puzzled and anxious over the sharp questions. "Yes, madonna. He said both ladies had gone out but that he expected them back soon, and he said I could wait and deliver my note when they returned, but I thought I had better come back and tell you."

"Yes, indeed," Lucrezia said, smiling at him and gesturing for Nicola to find a coin for him. "I cannot tell you how pleased I am to learn that both ladies were expected to return." She watched as Nicola found a coin and handed it over, then said, "Well, shall we send him back to wait for them?"

"I think not," Nicola said. "The likelihood is that they would get back in time for dinner, which would bring them here right in the middle of our meal. Since you now know La Vecchia is safe, why not leave the whole matter until the morning? If the page does not return, either the maestro di casa will not even mention him or Diana will think the matter of little importance." Then she frowned at the page. "Were you asked who sent the note? Do you believe that the maestro di casa knows you came from Her Highness?"

"No, madonna. The maestro di casa asked me nothing. He must know the livery, but from his manner I would believe that notes often come for the ladies of the house."

"So they might. You are right, Nicola. Now that my mind is at ease about the old woman, I can wait to talk to her until tomorrow." She sighed. "Perhaps by then I will have discovered what is nagging at me and I will know better what to ask."

She smiled at the page again and nodded a dismissal. Nicola took back the note and folded it away. Lucrezia had just parted her lips to comment with satisfaction that they now knew two new things—that La Vecchia did live with Diana Altoviti and that whatever had displeased Diana when Lucia saw the women talking was unlikely to be that La Vecchia was threatening her hostess. Her remark was aborted by Angela's entrance and, hard on her heels, that of Don Sigismundo.

He was in high good spirits, still recording what he had learned from Master Leonardo da Vinci and gathering arguments for a letter disputing some points. When asked about the night of the murder and what happened to the rest of his clothing, he at first blinked in a confused manner and said it had nothing to do with him. But then he remembered that he had been told Don Niccolò's men had discovered at the stall of a secondhand clothes vendor a black jerkin and green doublet that could be mistaken for his at a distance especially when half covered by a cloak. The garments had some spots and smears of blood, although the stains were noticeable only on close examination.

"And from whom did the clothes vendor buy the garments?" Lucrezia asked eagerly, hoping for another trail to the killer.

Sigismundo looked blank again. "From no one, apparently," he said after a moment of thought to bring back to mind a subject patently unimportant to him. "She said she had found the clothes rolled up in her barrow but that she had not put them there."

Lucrezia did not doubt that the clothes vendor had been questioned straitly to wring from her the answer Sigismundo gave so briefly. Nor did she doubt that Correggio had truly made sure that the vendor did not know how the clothing had appeared in her barrow. She suspected it would be a work of utter futility to obtain more information from Sigismundo, and made a mental note to ask Alfonso to get the details from Correggio, to whose report Sigismundo had barely listened. Free of her questions, Sigismundo began to talk about Master Leonardo's suggestions for enhancing perspective. Lucrezia tried to stem the tide by suggesting that Sigismundo invite Giovanni Lateri to discuss the matter with him.

Sigismundo shook his head impatiently and said she did not

understand. He was explaining that he was questioning whether the rendering of perspective by a painter and the manner in which it is perceived in nature by the human eye are the same, when Ercole Strozzi limped in and promptly joined battle with him. Eventually, after several abortive attempts to divert the two from the subject of perspective, the musician was announced. Lucrezia, Angela, and Nicola greeted him with some relief until, hearing the word "perspective," he launched into the question of showing perspective in sound—a most necessary effect for masques and other entertainments in which a story is recounted accompanied by music and sometimes dance.

The ladies found this exquisitely funny and the party settled around the table in gales of laughter. Even after having the matter explained to them, the gentlemen did not seem to understand what was so funny, but they did abandon the subject of perspective, giving time to Ercole Strozzi to recall that Lucrezia had asked him about the family and political connections her ladies had.

Most of the information was not new, but it seemed that Bianca had kept up her friendship with the French ambassador and not infrequently arranged meetings for him in her apartment. One of the people who had been invited to meet Philip della Rocca Berti had been Teodora Angelini.

"Sweet Mother Mary," Lucrezia breathed, "could there have been more in those letters from Donna Teodora's uncle and aunt than family news and court gossip?"

"What?" Strozzi shrugged. "Nothing worth killing over. Duke Ercole is firm in his loyalty to French interests."

That was true enough, but Lucrezia was accustomed to the labyrinthine politics of the papal court and was certain that what was innocent *could* be bent to look treasonous . . . but by Bianca? Still, Teodora had tried to deny that her uncle and aunt wrote to her.

"And Beatrice Tisio's family is in a sad state. I have heard they will have to sell their last farm and perhaps the great house itself," Strozzi reported.

"Which might make Beatrice really desperate to get hold of the legacy from Bianca, but we know Beatrice did not kill Palagio. That does seem to absolve her of Bianca's death," Lucrezia said.

"Only if Palagio *was* killed because he tried to extort money from the murderer," Strozzi pointed out.

Lucrezia thought that over, her head cocked to the side. Then she straightened up and shook it. "No. And I cannot say why, except that there was really no other reason to kill him. He might have tried extortion on others for reasons unconnected with Bianca's death . . . but that *feels* wrong."

"And I have found nothing about Elizabetta Dossi that could involve her," was Strozzi's final statement. "She is poor but not destitute, I would say certainly not desperate enough to kill. She lives quietly with her daughter and a few old servants. So far as I can discover, she has no political connections, except a friendship with the duke's mistress, which, I suppose, is how she obtained her appointment among your ladies."

"Why are we talking only of the ladies?" Sigismundo asked rather plaintively.

"So far as I know, they are the only ones who could have any cause at all to kill Donna Bianca. Because of the way she was killed, anyone in the world could have had the means and the opportunity. Thus we are reduced to suspecting those who had a reason and trying to discover who filled that flask with poisoned lotion."

"And since we can go no further with that discovery until Madonna Lucrezia can talk to the woman who bought the bottle and cleaned it and then sold it, I think we should abandon this dismal talk," Angela said very firmly, her cupid's-bow lips in a pout. "Madonna, you promised! Master Menotti, will you not play for us, and I will sing."

Lucrezia had to laugh and, having noticed that Sigismundo was looking as bored as Angela, nodded to the musician and said, "Yes, do play."

18

 WHEN ALFONSO stormed into her bedchamber—although this time he did not open the door so forcefully that it bounced back and hit him—Lucrezia realized she should have paid more attention to Nicola's suggestion. Perhaps if she had considered what to say to him about inviting Ercole Strozzi to dine with her the very day after Alfonso had all but forbidden her to see so much of the Latinist, she would have been able to ask her husband the questions she had in mind.

As it was, he tore off his bedrobe and cast it away with such violence that it slid from bed to chest to the floor and turned on her with doubled fists. Lucrezia's mouth dried as he flung off her coverings . . . but not with fear; her nether lips were swollen and wet. He was naked and as ready as a man can be, and without pulling shut the bedcurtains, he threw himself upon her.

Face and body were rigid with a fury that would no doubt have erupted into heavy blows had she been another woman. With her, his hands opened to grab her wrists, as if he expected her to fight him, but she hardly felt his grip. Her eyes were fixed on his enraged face, all black lines and changing shadows in the uncertain light of the night candle, and the wiry hair on his chest brushed against her upstanding nipples; Lucrezia moaned softly with pleasure.

When they subsided, Alfonso was panting as if he had fought several hard rounds in the fencing salon, but after he withdrew and flopped onto his back, a small satisfied smile curved his lips. He doubted he could have drawn shrieks of equal fervor from his wife if he *had* beaten her—stubborn bitch that she was. And now, as her eyes fluttered open, there was admiration, not hate, in them. But he would not give her the satisfaction of knowing he was pleased. He schooled his lips to grimness and, as soon as he caught his breath, started to sit up.

"Wait, Alfonso," she begged, a hand on his arm.

"I need pay no courtesies to a disobedient wife," he snarled. "Yesterday I told you I did not like your companying Ercole Strozzi, and in defiance the very next day you invite him to dinner."

Lucrezia swallowed hard to control her impulse to laugh. Courtesies? What did he think he had been doing? She was pregnant already; his marital duty was done. If not for "courtesy," why visit her at all? But making Alfonso swallow his words was not important right now. The itch in her mind was growing more and more urgent. She had to find a way to soothe it.

"Pooh on your opinion of Ercole Strozzi! I needed information from him. Now I need information from you. If you know Strozzi was dining with me earlier tonight, you know that Sigismundo was there also—"

"Yes," he interrupted roughly, "and Menotti too. So?"

"So what did Correggio find out when he questioned the dealer in old clothes?"

"Didn't you ask Sigismundo?"

There was a moment of pregnant silence in which their glances met. Defying control, Alfonso's lips twitched. He had not really been thinking of what he was saying. Asking Sigismundo was not always a fruitful activity.

Lucrezia sighed and said softly, "Yes, I did. He wasn't interested. You know what kind of answers you get from Sigismundo when he isn't interested in something! He wanted to discuss whether there is any difference in the way the mind perceives perspective when applied to painting and to the human eye in nature."

Forgetting he was supposed to be angry with her, Alfonso groaned. "Yes, I know. It is his most recent madness and he *would* talk to me about it because he is sure it is important in aiming cannon!"

Lucrezia giggled. "So you understand why I could not discover any details about the clothing the killer wore under the cloak."

Alfonso shrugged. "There weren't any. The woman was questioned with . . . ah . . . rigor. If she had known anything, believe me, she would have told it. Correggio is sure that the clothing was simply left and she has no idea by whom."

"There was nothing in or on the clothing that could give a hint?"

"Like what?"

"Oh . . . a long hair, perhaps, to show that it had been worn by a woman? Remnants of face paint around the collar?"

"Hmmm. That is a clever thought. I don't know, but I will bring the idea to Correggio's attention."

He started to get up again, but Lucrezia held on to him and told him what they had learned about La Vecchia. "And now I am wondering again if I did right not to send for her yesterday. What if it was not Diana she was trying to get money from . . . well, she would not, would she, if she is living in Diana's house?"

"No, of course not. If she is living in Diana's house, she must be

Diana's mother. I cannot imagine an Altoviti giving house room to a bottle washer, not for any amount of convenience in business. That was an old, proud Florentine family."

For a moment Lucrezia was silent, recognizing that what Alfonso said must be true and feeling an utter fool. Now she remembered that on the day they had had dinner with Count Ugoccione, he had mentioned seeing Gabriella Altoviti in the Palazzo Cortile. He had mentioned how shabby she looked and how, pitying her discomfort, he had not detained her long or asked what she was doing there.

"But she *is* a bottle washer," Lucrezia said. "And she goes about in what amounts to rags. If she is Diana's mother and Diana can afford a decent house, why should her mother dress in rags?"

"Because it makes a good disguise? Because her clothing is not important, but Diana, who must appear at court, must be finely dressed? As to washing bottles . . . if Diana had to buy expensive bottles, her profit would be much less. She would do for her child things she would not do for herself."

That made sense. And then Lucrezia remembered the page saying that both *ladies* had gone out. She felt foolish again. Of course, Gabriella no doubt had better clothing into which she changed when her bottle-collecting chores were done. And there were servants in the house who no doubt did the actual cleaning. Gabriella wore the "rags" to collect her bottles, partly as a disguise and partly to plead that she could pay very little for them. Fine clothing would encourage the maids to ask more for their discards. Unfortunately, what she had done and would do for her daughter also made it more likely that Gabriella Altoviti would put pressure onto whomever she had sold that bottle.

"Oh, Alfonso, do you think that what she would do for her daughter might include . . . Palagio's trick? Trying to extort money from the person to whom she sold the bottle? Did you know that Teodora Angelini was not on duty today? And she has *never* missed a day before—at least not without informing me and appointing a temporary head lady."

He had sat up despite her restraining grip on his arm, but now he turned to look at her, frowning. "Do you mean that Gabriella threatened Angelini and she has fled? Good God, you do not mean Teodora killed Gabriella, do you?"

Lucrezia sat up too. "I don't know what I mean. I know all the pieces of the puzzle are in my head, but they will not fall together to make a picture. There is something I have heard that I cannot remember and that leaves a hole in the puzzle so it does not make sense. I must know what Gabriella Altoviti did with that bottle. Will you send some men to get Gabriella out of Diana's house, even if they must go in and search and remove her by force?"

"I can do that."

Alfonso was now out of the bed and groping for his bedrobe. When he had it in hand, he paused and Lucrezia found herself admiring his strong body, the muscles marked by candlelit shadows.

"Do you want me to go myself?" he asked as he drew the bedrobe on slowly, as if he knew she liked what she saw.

Lucrezia hurriedly looked away. "You have the most authority," she said. "I do not want to destroy these women's lives if it is not necessary. If you go with an armed guard, it might be just a visit. If the guardsmen go alone, it looks like an arrest."

"And Diana herself? Do you want her too?"

"Diana should be here. She is on duty tomorrow. I will have my page let you know if she does not arrive with the other ladies."

Alfonso stood, frowning. "Are you sure Diana did not fill that bottle herself and poison Bianca?"

"I know it would have been easiest for her, but she had the least reason to want Bianca dead. She did not need the money the way Beatrice and the others do. And I know she did not kill Palagio. I saw her dancing with a man dressed as a cook—of all things, a cook—just before Beatrice began screaming. It was too short a time for her to have run in and out and changed her costume."

"The woman was masked, was she not?"

"Yes, but I had seen the costume in my public reception room before we left for the ball. Most of the ladies had not bothered to put on their masks yet . . ." Her voice faded uncertainly.

"Yes?" Alfonso prodded.

"Teodora Angelini was masked. I recognized her because she was so tall and thin and the costume was not very becoming. It was . . . provocative."

"I do not think you should complain about provocative costumes," Alfonso said dryly. "You were all but naked."

Lucrezia shook her head at him but did not respond to his remark, only saying, "But Donna Teodora said she had not gone to the ball because immorality was encouraged by being masked."

Alfonso laughed, his expression turning the sound coarse, then turned to go out the door. "Perhaps she did not want to confess that no one had made any immoral propositions to her."

The door closed behind him and Lucrezia lay looking out of the open bedcurtains, which he had not bothered to pull shut. If screaming would have helped, she would have shrieked with frustration. Alfonso had put together one of the parts of the puzzle by pointing out that the bottle washer was Diana's mother. Diana could easily have killed Bianca, but she could not have killed Palagio. Lucrezia reached out and pulled the bedcurtain closed. Perhaps she would find her answer in her dreams.

When she slept, however, it seemed to Lucrezia that she did not dream at all. Certainly the identity of the killer was no clearer when she woke. She sent Lucia at once to discover whether Diana and Teodora were in the public reception room. Diana was there, talking indolently with Elizabetta Dossi about the emotional values of certain scents; Beatrice was sitting on a chest, staring out of a window at the hanging garden; Teodora Angelini was still missing.

"Black and silver," Lucrezia said to the maid as she got out of bed and went behind the screen to relieve herself. "And have my bath filled as quickly as possible," she called.

When she emerged she told Lucia to pin up her hair. She would not wash it today, she thought. When she had finished the business of the murder, she would spend a whole afternoon soaking in her tub and wash her hair and work out with Nicola all the ins and outs, all the reasons and unreasons. She bathed very quickly and dressed with equal speed, looking pale and severe when she emerged into her private reception room. Angela took one look at her and shrank back in her chair; Nicola's lips thinned.

"Was Teodora Angelini in my public reception room when you came in?" Lucrezia asked.

"No, madonna," Angela said.

"Send one of the older pages to her apartment. If she is ill and her maid says she has been abed for two days, have him give her my best wishes for a rapid recovery and ask if she wishes me to send Master dei Carri to her. If she is not there, he is to ask the maid on my authority where her mistress is and when she is expected back. If the apartment is closed, he is to come here at once and tell me."

Angela went out at once. Nicola busied herself with putting those items Lucrezia liked best on her plate and urging her to eat something. She nibbled on a slice of sausage followed by a bite of cheese, which she washed down with a few sips of a light, white wine. She picked up another piece of sausage, but never put it in her mouth.

"There is one connection I cannot make," she said, staring at nothing. "But it must be through Anna Peruzzi. It was she to whom Gabriella Altoviti brought the empty bottles and . . . and flasks of lotion and perfume. Could it be that Anna Peruzzi is not a perfumer herself but is the common outlet for Diana Altoviti's products?"

"Of course!" Nicola exclaimed. "How stupid I am not to have thought of that. We knew she had a decent house and money enough for clothing, even some jewelry. How could she make that much from selling only to the ladies of the Court?"

"Yes," Lucrezia agreed. "But she did not dare open a shop under her own name lest the ladies of the Court refuse to buy the same scents and lotions as were available to the common folk. But yesterday Lucia visited all the perfumers on the tax rolls. The better shops were interested in the fine flask, but denied they had been offered any like it to buy or to fill as did the more common shops. The one place Lucia did not go was Anna Peruzzi's shop because she already knew that Gabriella sold to Anna. Do you not think it likely that it was Anna who filled that bottle with lotion?"

"But I doubt she even knew Donna Bianca," Nicola said.

"I did not say Anna Peruzzi put poison in the flask. I said she may have put lotion, pure lotion, in it. The person for whom she filled it may have added her own touch. But if rumors of how Bianca died have circulated as widely as I expect, Peruzzi will deny ever seeing or handling such a flask—unless she is frightened enough to confess her part and name the guilty party."

"How will you frighten her? Will the duke arrest her on your suspicion?" Nicola looked rather frightened herself.

"I would rather not involve the duke until we have some more certain answers," Lucrezia said doubtfully, and then smiled as a hubbub filtered through the portiere. "I will not need to, I hope. That must be Alfonso bringing in Gabriella Altoviti." She started to rise, saying, "Oh, how stupid I am. I forgot to tell him to—"

Before she could get to her feet or finish saying she had forgotten to tell Alfonso to bring Donna Gabriella into her private reception room immediately, he was lifting the portiere and urging through it a tall, dignified woman. Aside from the gray hair there was not much to connect Donna Gabriella with La Vecchia. The hair that had been strained back into a tight, skimpy bun was now dressed high and fashionably, the patched and darned skirt replaced by a sober but quite elegant gown. She nodded regally to Lucrezia and then clasped her hands before her and waited silently. Glancing at her sidelong after returning her nod, Lucrezia saw that Donna Gabriella looked wary but not frightened. Instead of speaking to the woman, Lucrezia smiled at Alfonso.

"Thank you, Alfonso. How clever of you to take Donna Gabriella right though the outer chamber without letting her linger in talk. Would you do me another favor, my lord?"

"Let me hear what it is before I commit myself."

"Would you send some men—four or six in case there is some resistance—to Anna Peruzzi's shop in the alley off Santo Stefano, and have them bring Mistress Peruzzi here?"

"Why not?" Alfonso said, and stepped out again.

Lucrezia heard his voice rumbling without being able to make out the words, but she found it a trifle disquieting to see that although Donna Gabriella looked even more wary, she still showed no fear.

"Donna Gabriella, why did you not come to speak to me when my maid Lucia asked you to do so?" Lucrezia asked coldly.

"Because your maid never asked me to come and speak to you. Why should she?"

Lucrezia blinked. It had not occurred to her that Donna Gabriella would flatly deny buying and selling bottles. Then she nodded to Nicola, who rose and went to the bedchamber to summon Lucia. When the maid came in, she looked curiously at Donna Gabriella, then away, then back again with a puzzled expression as she curtsied to Lucrezia and asked how she could serve. Lucrezia controlled a sigh of relief. She had been afraid that Lucia would not see the similarities to La Vecchia at all.

"Is this the woman to whom you sold Madonna Isabella's bottle?" Lucrezia asked.

First Lucia looked surprised, but then she stared long and hard at Donna Gabriella. Finally she nodded. "Yes, madonna. Oh, her hair is done now and she is not wearing that old, patched skirt, but this is La Vecchia."

Lucrezia heard the faint sounds that marked Alfonso's return to the inner room, but he did not speak and Lucrezia's eyes never left Donna Gabriella's face.

"The little bitch is trying to curry favor. She is lying," Donna Gabriella said calmly.

"Lucia would not lie to me, Donna Gabriella. She has no need to do so. I do not dismiss or punish my servants for making a mistake."

"You will take the word of a common servant girl over mine?" Gabriella asked haughtily.

Lucrezia laughed. "I would take Lucia's word over that of many higher born liars."

She heard a faint sound but did not look away from Gabriella's face to see whether Alfonso was laughing also. However, when Gabriella did not respond except by a sniff of disdain, Lucrezia went on.

"Lucia is clever and honest . . . and she knows I am able to protect her. Why in the world should she lie about selling bottles to you? I have no objection to her doing so no matter to whom she sells."

"She has mistaken me for another," Gabriella said.

Lucrezia examined the woman's stubborn expression and sighed. "Donna Gabriella, will you make it necessary for me to call in the highborn ladies that sell to you? Shall I ask Alfonso to send a message to Count Ugoccione, who met you in the Palazzo Cortile wearing your disguise as La Vecchia? He recognized you."

That last shot hit hard. Donna Gabriella's gaze slid away from

Lucrezia's, and the hands she had clasped before her now showed white knuckles.

"So I buy and sell bottles," she said at last. "That is not a crime. And I prefer that no one knows how poor I am. Is that a crime?"

"Certainly not," Lucrezia said, "but murder is a crime and it was committed with the lotion that was in that little flask. I am not going to accuse you of the crime—although you might well be guilty. You could have sold that lotion to Donna Bianca—"

"I did not! I never saw or spoke to Donna Bianca. Her maid will answer to that—since you would rather believe a maid than me."

"Yes, well, there is an easier way to prove you did not sell the lotion to Bianca. You can tell me to whom you sold the bottle, and we can question that person."

Donna Gabriella burst out laughing. "I can tell you, but the person will answer no questions."

"Any person will answer questions if he or she is asked in the right way," Alfonso said quietly.

Lucrezia repressed a shiver, but Donna Gabriella laughed again.

"Not this person. I sold that bottle to Don Guido del Palagio."

19

THE PROFOUND silence that greeted Donna Gabriella's statement that she had sold the flask that carried the poison to Palagio was broken by Ascanio's frightened voice saying that Lucrezia was summoned to Duke Ercole's audience chamber. Lucrezia's gaze flew to Alfonso's face and met utter blankness there. Had she been wrong all along about Donna Bianca's murder? Had Correggio found some political reason for Palagio's death and caught the killer? But the duke's audience chamber? Would he summon her there to tell her that Palagio's murderer had been discovered?

Even as those thoughts scurried around in her head, Lucrezia nodded at Ascanio and said that she would attend the duke at once. The sound of her own voice, calm and indifferent, steadied her, and she realized that she did not believe Donna Gabriella. The woman had already lied to her. What would be easier to say than that she had sold the flask to the person who last had it, when that person was dead and could not deny her lie?

"I am very glad of the duke's summons," Lucrezia said. "It will save time, since I have this business of Donna Bianca's murder that I promised to solve. You will accompany us, Donna Gabriella. You too, Lucia. And Nicola, you and Angela, since Donna Teodora is not here, would you make sure that all my ladies-in-waiting come as well? Together, I think we can lay the matter of Donna Bianca's death to rest once and for all."

Ascanio had scurried back into the public reception chamber to give Lucrezia's message to whomever had come from the duke, and Alfonso politely lifted the portiere so that Donna Gabriella could pass through. As Lucrezia came up to him, he asked in a low voice whether she had heard anything in a private message from her father . . . or her brother.

She raised startled eyes to his, realizing how her concentration on the murder had warped her point of view. To her, Bianca's and Palagio's death were of paramount importance, but to Duke Ercole, it would be political considerations that came first, and she was still the daughter of the Pope and the sister of Cesare Borgia.

"Cesare?" she whispered to Alfonso. "Merciful Mary help me! What can he have done now?"

Her obvious shock and anxiety removed the black frown from Alfonso's face. "Come to visit you?" he suggested, almost smiling.

Even as she shook her head in denial, knowing that Cesare would not be far enough north to leave his troops midmarch for a casual visit, she understood a summons to the duke's audience chamber would indicate something like a visit. Ercole d'Este was too canny a politician to announce in his audience chamber a private sorrow, like the illness of the Pope, or a Cesare-created calamity, like the destruction of another friendly duchy.

Lucrezia followed the head shake with a shrug. "Possibly an emissary from my father," she said, and passed through the portiere into the public reception room.

This was far more crowded than Lucrezia had expected, but the nearest person to the portiere was Don Niccolò da Correggio and there was no smile of triumph on his face, so he had not solved the murder. In fact, Lucrezia thought, noting his frown and tight mouth, he looked troubled.

Oh, dear. Lucrezia stifled a sigh. Likely this was the Pope's response to the accusation of murder against her. No doubt whoever her father had sent had demanded the public venue and also demanded that the emissary speak to Lucrezia herself. She thought she had convinced the Pope to let the matter rest in her hands. This was just the wrong time . . . and then she had to tighten her mouth against a smile. Not the wrong time at all. If it was an emissary from her father, he would hear her clear herself. And these others who wanted gossip . . . they could hear too.

Lucrezia looked around the room with a broad smile. "I am going to the duke's audience chamber," she said. "My ladies must, of course, accompany me, but I cannot see why the rest of you cannot do so as well, for I have much to say about the murders in this Court."

She was not surprised when she heard Correggio make a small sound of distress and turned on him so bright a smile that his expression became more wary than concerned. She would have asked him whom her father had sent, but Alfonso stepped ahead of Don Niccolò and offered his arm.

"I do not think Don Niccolò wants to hear what I have to say," Lucrezia murmured, after a last glance at Correggio.

"I don't think my father will either," Alfonso rumbled. "Specially if one of the Borgia cardinals is here."

"Perhaps you should not walk with me," she offered.

"The nether millstone is a trifle softer than the upper."

Lucrezia was so surprised by that statement and it gave her so much to think about that she remained silent until they had mounted the outer marble staircase of the Palazzo Cortile, then another inner, broad marble staircase. Beyond the stair head were a pair of handsome double doors, which now stood open. The maestro di sala pounded his staff on the floor and announced them, and the crowd of courtiers and hangers-on parted to open a pathway toward the dais on which the duke stood. But it was no red-robed cardinal who stood beside Duke Ercole, it was the French ambassador and, a step behind him, Donna Teodora Angelini.

Fury made Lucrezia's hand close so hard on Alfonso's that the nails bit deep. He did not flinch but said, hardly moving his lips, "Softly goes the successful hunter."

The respite gave Lucrezia's mind time to make a leap to an entirely unexpected situation. Teodora had doubtless written to her uncle at the French court about Lucrezia's cruelty and the uncle had written to Philip della Rocca Berti to ask his intervention on behalf of his niece. Possibly the French ambassador had assumed Teodora's uncle had royal sanction for the request; equally possibly he wished to make a mischief that he could later soothe. And the duke . . . Lucrezia's generous mouth became thin and pinched . . . damn his hide, thought he could shame her into agreement to support his damned group of paupers.

She began to walk more quickly, giving every sign of an eagerness to reach the dais. Duke Ercole, who had been looking regretful but firm, began to look concerned when Lucrezia released Alfonso's arm and almost leapt up the step to the dais.

"Donna Teodora!" Lucrezia exclaimed. "How glad I am to see you here! I thought you were ill when you did not appear to manage the ladies-in-waiting yesterday and today. I sent my page to you to ask if you wished for a physician—"

"You found the ladies troublesome in my absence?" Donna Teodora asked, smirking in satisfaction.

"Oh, no, not at all. I hardly ever see them," Lucrezia said, watching sidelong with pleasure as the duke's expression of satisfaction over her seeming relief over seeing Donna Teodora changed to irritation as she continued, "I merely needed you to identify Donna Gabriella Altoviti as La Vecchia. My maid and others have done so and Count Ugoccione told me at his dinner that he had seen her, but she prefers to hear the identification from a gentlewoman."

Lucrezia gestured toward the group that had followed close behind her, and Nicola took Gabriella's arm to lead her forward while Angela stood close beside Diana. To spare both Diana and her mother embarrassment, Lucrezia had very carefully not identified La Vecchia as a woman who bought and sold used bottles.

"This lady," Lucrezia continued, now looking at the duke, "will be instrumental in solving the murders of Donna Bianca Tedaldo and Don Guido del Palagio."

Now she had Ercole d'Este in a cleft stick. He did not dare raise the petty question of her support of the ladies he had appointed to serve her in the face her statement that she was near the solution of the two murders that had plagued his Court. However, Lucrezia had to swallow hard when she noticed that Alfonso, instead of following her up on the dais, had melted back toward his guardsmen. Apparently the nether millstone was not soft enough to permit him to resist the upper. Nonetheless, Lucrezia had gone too far to retreat. She smiled at the duke and asked him if he would please send for Master Ludovico dei Carri.

"And ask him to bring with him the two bottles of poisoned lotion that he has had in his keeping."

The buzz of excitement that had started when Lucrezia said Gabriella would be instrumental in solving the murders increased substantially over this last statement. Until now, Lucrezia surmised, the use of poison had only been a rumor, and now there were *two* bottles of poison. Doubtless all wanted to know on whom the second bottle had been used. Everyone would wait patiently until Master dei Carri arrived.

Behind the comfort of that knowledge, however, was a nasty problem. Lucrezia needed Anna Peruzzi to say to whom she sold the flask filled with lotion, and Alfonso's guardsmen would bring the woman to her apartment. How was she going to instruct them to bring Peruzzi here to the duke's audience chamber now that Alfonso had disappeared? She exercised her not-inconsiderable willpower to prevent herself from grinding her teeth.

Alfonso was the most infuriating man! She could have sworn that he was taking pleasure in talking to her and helping her and was as interested as she in solving the murders . . . but possibly not in letting his father see his interest or cooperation. She would have to ask Duke Ercole to send one of his men to order Alfonso's men . . . The very thought made her feel pale. Perhaps Angela could find Alfonso.

The arrival of Master dei Carri steadied her frantic thoughts. She smiled at him as he mounted the dais and decided she would have to send Angela to find Alfonso and tell him to have his men bring Peruzzi here. Likely he was still in the audience chamber, watching from a less exposed position. She signaled Angela to come closer, but could not explain what she needed because the duke had referred dei Carri's question about why he had been summoned to her.

"Thank you for coming so promptly, Master dei Carri," Lucrezia said. "Would you be kind enough to tell the duke—and everyone else—how poor Donna Bianca Tedaldo was poisoned and from where you obtained that second bottle of lotion?"

"You know the answer, madonna?" dei Carri asked softly.

"I am very close," Lucrezia replied.

As the physician began to explain the workings of aconite, Lucrezia looked for Angela. She had obeyed and come to the very foot of the dais, but she had misunderstood what Lucrezia wanted and brought Diana Altoviti and Elizabetta Dossi with her. Now Diana was separated from her mother only by the bulk of Elizabetta Dossi, who, to Lucrezia's considerable surprise, stood, grim-faced, beside Diana.

Lucrezia bent to explain to Angela what she needed her to tell Alfonso just as Master dei Carri held up the flask that had contained the lotion that poisoned Bianca. From the group of noblewomen closest to the dais, the wife of Count Ugoccione cried out.

"But that flask is one that I am sure Madonna Isabella uses for her perfumes!"

"Lucrezia!" the duke thundered. "Are you trying to say my daughter sent a flask of poison—"

"Of course not!" Lucrezia interrupted forcibly. "Madonna Isabella has no more to do with the poisoned lotion in that flask than Don Alfonso has to do with the poisoned lotion that was delivered to me in the other flask Master dei Carri holds, although that bottle did originally contain a cream that Don Alfonso uses."

"What?" duke Ercole gasped, his eyes searching the crowd and fixing about the middle of the room on something that made him pale suddenly. "Alfonso!" he bellowed. "Why are you bringing guardsmen into my audience chamber? Why did you try to poison your wife?"

If Lucrezia had not had a more urgent need, she would have leapt down from the dais to embrace her husband. Far from abandoning her, Alfonso had understood the problem about bringing

Peruzzi to a new place. Apparently he had himself gone to get his guardsmen and was now preceding two of those guardsmen, one of whom had a firm grip on Anna Peruzzi and the other an even firmer grip on a young woman who looked familiar but whom Lucrezia could not place. Alfonso's mouth opened to reply to his father, but Lucrezia was quicker.

"Your Highness!" Lucrezia protested in a high, clear voice that easily filled the audience chamber. "Alfonso did not try to poison me or anyone else! And the guardsmen are to prevent the solution to this crime from running away. The flask that came holding perfume, which I indeed purchased from Madonna Isabella, was emptied of her wholesome perfume and sold, as was that bottle, which originally held a cream Master dei Carri made for Alfonso to put on his hands."

Shock was making the duke slow. "Dei Carri?" he turned to stare at his physician with bulging eyes, but Lucrezia's voice overrode whatever more he might have said.

"I assure you that Master dei Carri put no poison in his cream. Alfonso used and emptied the bottle—and as you can see is in the best of health. That bottle too was sold after it was emptied. And I believe both of them were purchased by Anna Peruzzi."

Lucrezia gestured to the older woman held by the guardsman. She paused and then added rather grimly, "Who will now tell us, or her daughter Paola will, to whom she sold the bottles she had filled with lotion."

"No!" the woman shrieked. "No! I never bought either of those bottles!" Then she twisted and leaned as far forward as the grip of the guardsman would permit and pointed toward Gabriella. "Tell them! Tell them, you proud bitch! Tell them you never sold me either of those bottles!"

Gabriella Altoviti stood silent as death and looked like death, too.

"God's curse on you, woman!" Anna Peruzzi spat. "Just because you were married to Donato Altoviti you think yourself so much better than I. He was in my bed more than in yours, even though I was only a poor shopkeeper. And my daughter Paola is as much his as your Diana. What have I to hide? You, you would have killed to keep your secret—that one of the ever-so-noble Altovitis was now no more than a peddler of old bottles."

Stony-faced, Gabriella stared straight ahead into nothing. Lucrezia felt sorry for her and then felt a quiver of uncertainty. Was it possible that Gabriella had killed to hide her secret? Had Bianca stumbled on it, perhaps through her maid. Bianca was the kind to babble everything. Could Gabriella have killed her to silence her?

"Tell them, damn you!" Anna Peruzzi screamed. "It wasn't me! I never saw those bottles! I never filled them!" There was a moment of silence and then Anna began to laugh. "No, you won't talk, will you, because you did it yourself! Your daughter makes the lotions. You filled that bottle and poisoned that girl, and you tried to poison Madonna Lucrezia when she came close to your secret too!"

But Lucrezia had come face-to-face with a new problem. Gabriella would not have been invited to the masked ball and thus could not have killed Palagio. About to point out that fact, she swallowed the words. Gabriella would not have needed an invitation. Masked and dressed in Sigismundo's clothing, no one would have prevented her from entering the ballroom. In the next moment, however, Correggio had put that doubt to rest.

Shaking his head, Correggio said, "No. Look at her. Gabriella Altoviti could not have killed Guido del Palagio, and there is no reason for his death except that he must have attempted to extort money from the poisoner. So it was the poisoner who killed him."

"Why could she not have killed Palagio?" the duke asked, sounding aggrieved; doubtless he would have preferred someone he hardly knew, someone not Ferrarese, to be guilty.

"Because Gabriella Altoviti could not have fit into the blood-stained clothing we found," Correggio replied.

"But Anna Peruzzi could have fit into that clothing," Lucrezia said, her clear voice dropping into the silence that followed Correggio's remark.

Lucrezia did not think that Anna Peruzzi had killed either Bianca or Palagio. Peruzzi had no reason to kill, not even so far-fetched a reason as hiding that she bought and sold bottles. All Lucrezia hoped to accomplish was to wring out of the woman whatever else she knew. But Peruzzi did not have any more to say; she burst into tears and sagged against the guardsman's hold, whimpering that because she was nothing she would die for a crime she had not even known had been committed.

"No!" Paola cried. "No! My mama did not even know what happened. I won't let her die to save that bitch Diana. It was Diana. She made the lotion. She made all the lotions we sell. And Gabriella never sold us the really fine flasks. She kept those for Diana to fill for her noble clients."

"But Diana could not have killed Palagio," Lucrezia said. "I saw her myself dancing with a man dressed as a cook when Beatrice Tisio began to scream."

"Not her!" Paola screamed. "She made me change into her costume in the garden and attend the ball in her place. It was me you saw! It was me dancing with the cook—and he wasn't a noble dressed as a cook, he *was* a cook! Your own cook! Innocenzio! He knew who I was too. Ask him. We thought it a great joke. The maid and the cook attending the duke's masked ball. I didn't know what Diana was going to do. And my mama didn't even know I was at the ball."

Tears were pouring down Paola's face, and Lucrezia swallowed, remembering that she had wondered why Diana Altoviti was sitting in a corner instead of being her usual lively and provocative self. She remembered feeling sorry for her, wondering whether she was still troubled by the incident on the stair. The incident where she had pretended to catch at Teodora Angelini . . . and had doubtless pushed her instead.

"And she killed that man!" the girl shrieked. "I didn't see her, but I know she did. When I heard the screaming, I didn't wait. I knew something terrible had happened. I ran away."

On the words, Paola wrenched herself free of the guardsman's increasingly lax grasp, but she did not try to escape. She only turned to where Diana had been standing. But Diana was not there, and Elizabetta Dossi was down on the floor, just getting to her knees.

Every pair of eyes in the room had been fixed on the screaming maid. No one had seen Diana slip away from Angela and push Elizabetta Dossi. Now all instinctively turned toward the door to see if she were trying to escape. By then it was too late. By then Diana had jumped up on the dais and drawn the knife that no one had found after Palagio's death.

"So clever. So clever," she hissed, stalking closer to Lucrezia, who was staring unmoving, wide-eyed with shock.

Then she struck. "I must go down to hell," Diana shrieked, "but I will take you with me."

20

TWO ROARS of equal volume and ferocity made both Diana and Lucrezia flinch. The knife still plunged down, but Diana had turned infinitesimally toward the the duke's bellow while Lucrezia shrank away toward Alfonso. The blade barely nicked Lucrezia's voluminous sleeve instead of plunging into her throat. In the next moment, Alfonso was on the dais and had seized Diana. Screaming, she tried to turn the knife on him. His two guardsmen rushed forward, abandoning their charges, who were no longer of any importance. Alfonso virtually flung Diana at them, while he reached out to catch Lucrezia, who, still staggering back away from the attack, was just about to topple off the dais.

Alfonso caught her to him and held her hard against his breast while the whole room erupted into chaos. Diana had eluded the guardsmen, pushing her mother into their path. A few onlookers rushed to seize her, accomplishing no more than to get into the guardsmen's way. Others shrank away from her and the wildly slashing knife, leaving a relatively open space in the center of the room. Through this Diana rushed, only to come up against the maestro di casa, who put his heavy staff across the doorway and shouted for the door guards. They appeared behind him, halberds leveled.

Gabriella Altoviti had regained her balance and rushed after her daughter, shouting, "Stop, Diana, stop!"

And Diana did stop and turn to face her mother, knife raised high. The maestro di casa shouted. Several men on the sidelines also shouted and began to surge forward. The knife came down—not in Gabriella's breast but in Diana's own throat. A collective moan, made up of little shrieks, sighs, groans, whispers, and other wordless sounds came from the appalled onlookers.

"Did she end it?" Lucrezia whispered, lifting her face just enough so she could speak.

"Yes," Alfonso replied, and his arms, which had been trembling as he held her, stilled. "You knew?"

"I should have, but I did not. Thank God she made an end." Lucrezia closed her eyes and tipped her head forward onto Alfonso's breast again.

"You idiot! She nearly made an end of you," Alfonso growled.

Lucrezia had no time to reply to that. The duke rushed over and pulled her from Alfonso's arms. "Daughter," he gasped, his voice shaking, "are you badly hurt?" And without waiting for an answer, he turned on the physician. "Master dei Carri, why are you standing there like a statue! Come and attend Madonna Lucrezia!"

The physician approached slowly, looking very frightened. He was a *physician*. He had no more skill at treating wounds than any common man, and less than most women, who ordinarily bandaged scratches and bruises for their menfolk. What they needed was a barber. But by then Nicola and Angela had converged on Lucrezia and eased her gently from the duke's grasp.

"We will care for her," Nicola said, "but we need a quiet place."

"Alfonso, carry her to my apartment, to my private closet," the duke ordered. "I will take care of what has happened here—not that I have the faintest idea what did happen, except that a woman is dead and I do not understand why. Why did that woman try to kill Lucrezia? Why did she kill herself?"

"Your Highness." Lucrezia's voice was soft but not faint. "Thanks to God, His Son, and Mary the Merciful, I am not hurt. But I am shocked, and I would like a quiet place to recover myself. What happened was that I have fulfilled my promise to you to find who murdered Donna Bianca and Don Guido del Palagio. If you would have your guards bring Anna Peruzzi and her daughter and Gabriella Altoviti to your apartment, I believe I will be able to explain everything."

Although she sounded quite calm and collected and she started out on her own feet, Lucrezia began to tremble as soon as they left the audience chamber. She was accustomed to preserving an appearance of indifference under verbal attack, but the physical reality of hate had shaken her. Once she no longer had to put on a good appearance before the duke's Court, she began to collapse.

Without comment Alfonso lifted her into his arms and carried her up the stairs to his father's apartment. He marched without hesitation through the public rooms back toward the duke's bedchamber. To one side was a small room, beautifully paneled and lined with shelves holding books and exquisite small statuary. There he set Lucrezia down on a daybed, where she burst into tears.

Angela and Nicola, who had followed on Alfonso's heels, both squeezed past him and embraced her. Angela wept with her, but after a moment Nicola busied herself with removing the sleeve that

324 Roberta Gellis

had been slashed. Alfonso shrugged and stepped out of the room to bellow for his father's servant, whom he ordered to bring wine and, after a moment's thought, sweetcakes also.

Having satisfied herself that Lucrezia had not even been scratched, Nicola sank down on the floor beside the daybed, her face gray because her dark complexion could not turn white.

"I thought you were dead," she breathed. "I still cannot believe you came away scatheless."

Lucrezia wiped her eyes and nose on a kerchief that Angela offered and uttered a shaken giggle. "I thought I was dead too. I saw her raise the knife and I could not do a thing. I just stood there like a graven image. What saved me was the duke and Alfonso shouting. It was as if the sound had pushed me back and to the side. Truly, I don't remember moving, but when the knife came down, I was out of the way."

"Thank God I didn't see it at all," Angela said. "The old woman—Gabriella Altoviti—made a noise and I looked around at her, and when I turned my head, Diana was gone! Well, I looked behind to see if she was trying to get to the door . . ." Suddenly her eyes rounded and she caught her breath. "Oh," she cried, "oh, it was *my* fault you were nearly killed. I should have been watching Diana. I should have been holding her. I should—"

"Don't be silly, Angela," Lucrezia said, her voice much stronger and steadier. "She would just have pulled away or knocked you down."

"But I would have screamed then, and—"

"It's all right, Angela," Nicola said, smiling and patting her fellow's shoulder. "It wouldn't have mattered no matter what you did. God had His hand over our lady and kept her safe."

On that propitious note, Alfonso reentered the room followed by two servants who poured wine and set out plates with tiny bonbons and sweetcakes.

"Now let us all have a glass or two of wine and some sweets and we will all feel much better," he said.

That prediction was true; however, they sipped their wine and nibbled on the sweetcakes in silence, none of them being able to think of any subject to talk about. No one wanted to mention Lucrezia's close escape, and everything else seemed too trivial— until suddenly Alfonso laughed aloud. All three women looked at him in shock.

"Sorry," he muttered, but he did not sound sorry.

Lucrezia said sharply, "If you have found something to laugh about, I would be grateful to hear it."

That made Alfonso laugh again and he said, "I was just thinking about how you rolled right over my father." He shook his head in wonderment. "Rolled him up, I say, horse, foot, and guns."

"What are you talking about?" Lucrezia asked. "Your father and I are not at war, and I have no army—"

"If you are not at war over that accursed appanage of yours, I do not know what war is, madonna. But you do not need any army. You not only defeated my father, but routed the French too!"

Lucrezia sipped at the glass that Nicola had refilled with wine and her lips twitched slightly. "Oh, you mean Teodora Angelini and the French ambassador. I did not set out to 'defeat' them. I simply did not have any time to waste on a fruitless argument."

Slight sounds came from the open doorway and Lucrezia's eyes flicked toward the it. She frowned and raised her voice a trifle.

"In fact, I am very sorry I was not able to discuss the matter of my appanage with the French ambassador. I think he would be shocked to hear how little I am allowed. Likely he would not be too happy to see a French bride treated so meanly."

"Well, Lucrezia, I see you are fully recovered," the duke said from the doorway.

Lucrezia smiled with great sweetness. "Perhaps not fully recovered, Your Highness. I would not like to need to stand for any length of time, but my mind is clear and I am ready to explain why Diana Altoviti killed first Donna Bianca Tedaldo and then Don Guido del Palagio."

"Unfortunately, this room is too small for all of those I wish to hear the explanation. Not," the duke added dryly, "that my entire Court does not understand clearly that you are innocent of those deaths. By evening there will not be a person in Ferrara who has not heard of the attack on you and the woman's suicide. You are a heroine, my dear. All Ferrara will be praising your name." The dry voice was emphasized by a hard glare.

"I am glad of it," Lucrezia said, widening her eyes to an innocent stare. "I wish to be well thought of in Ferrara, since this is now my home. And I will gladly go anywhere you say to explain why Diana committed murder, but I should hate to faint in the middle of my explanation."

Duke Ercole showed his teeth in what was not a smile, then shrugged. "I will have the daybed carried into my private reception room, if you can walk so far."

"Alfonso will give me his arm," Lucrezia said, smiling, and reached out toward her husband, who, to her surprise, did not respond except to shake his head as soon as his father had turned away.

He did lift her to her feet, a moment later, while Angela took the wine glass from her hand. Two sturdy servants came in and carried out the daybed. Alfonso said nothing and made no delay about leading her to the bed, now placed centrally in the reception room—and leaving her there. Lucrezia swallowed hard. He was incomprehensible! She had thought they were coming together, but now he was behaving as he had when she first came to Ferrara.

Her hurt and confusion were adequately covered, however, by Nicola, who brought a small table to the side of the bed, and

Angela, who set the glass of wine and a plate of rolled sweetcakes upon it. In the next moment, the duke's family and favorites were coming to the bedside—Sigismundo, who embraced her and kissed her, weeping with relief, Don Giulio, Don Ferrante, Don Niccolò da Correggio, Count Ugoccione dei Contrari, Don Gian Luca Castellini da Pontremoli—all to kiss her hands and speak fervently about how glad they were she was safe and unhurt.

Lucrezia did not doubt the sincerity of their sentiments at all. For one thing, she believed each of the men genuinely liked her; for another, far more important, she was sure none of them would have relished explaining to her father and her brother her injury or death.

With the initial greetings and well-wishings out of the way, all the gentlemen found seats, and the duke nodded at Correggio, who said, "Well, madonna, you were right and I was wrong. These deaths were a personal matter, I gather, not at all political."

"Oh, no," Lucrezia replied, "they were political—but for a personal reason. You remember, Don Niccolò, that the thing no one could understand was why Donna Bianca, who was as sweet and obliging . . . and silly . . . as any woman alive, should have been killed in the first place."

"I remember," Correggio said. "You say the matter was political. Perhaps it was because she had a very loose tongue. I should never have allowed her to touch any correspondence, vital or not."

"Probably not," Lucrezia said, smiling, "but you need feel no guilt over that. The correspondence she carried—either directly to the proper recipient or to Palagio for his examination—had nothing to do with her death. Diana Altoviti killed Donna Bianca because Palagio wanted to marry Bianca."

"For jealousy?" the duke's voice was redolent of disbelief. "You have been reading too many romances, Lucrezia."

"People do kill for jealousy," Lucrezia said bleakly.

There was some uneasy shifting around to ease discomfort as

most of the men recalled the rumors that Cesare Borgia had killed his own elder brother Juan over a woman. It was not the only reason, of course.

"Not," Lucrezia continued, "that Diana was not jealous of Bianca, who had everything she herself wanted, but she would not have killed her for that reason. Palagio had a greater significance to Diana than as a lover."

"My fault," Gabriella Altoviti moaned. "My fault. I spoke constantly of the glory of the Altovitis before we were cast out by the Medici. I spoke of how hopeless our situation was, without a man of family to speak for us." She covered her face and wept. "Ferrara is no friend to Firenze. How could I know that Guido del Palagio would come here and try to win favor with Madonna Lucrezia?"

"And when Diana first spoke to you of Palagio, she did not know he was Florentine, did she?" Lucrezia said. "To curry favor with me, Palagio claimed to be Neapolitan. I knew he was not, but because I had no interest in him—his poetry was simply dreadful—I did not bother to contest his statement or ask from where he really came."

"My fault. My fault," Gabriella moaned again. "I knew he was Florentine as soon as I met him and I told Diana." She sobbed for a moment and then added, "I told her about his family too. I warned her of how poor they were and warned her that he was more interested in her business than he was in her, but she only laughed and said it was better that way. Once they were married, he would be all the more interested in regaining the Altoviti property."

"How likely was it he could do that?" Correggio asked.

Gabriella looked at Don Niccolò blankly and he repeated his question more specifically, asking whether she thought the Palagios still had enough connections to get the Signory of Firenze to disgorge the Altoviti property.

"Connections or no connections," Gabriella said bitterly, "I doubt that anyone will wrest that property from whoever holds it . . . likely Giulio de Medici. When my husband went to Firenze to appeal for our restoration . . . he died. I do not know from what he died, but I doubt it was any natural illness. I told Diana that, but she would not listen."

"I suspect that soft-hearted lady thought that Palagio's death in her cause would be a small sacrifice if it would identify the person who was holding the Altoviti lands," Nicola muttered into Lucrezia's ear.

Lucrezia flashed a minatory glance at Nicola for her sarcasm about one recently dead and said, "So Diana expected Palagio would ask her to marry him. She intended to accept and then send him back to Firenze to begin negotiations for the return of the Altoviti property. When did Diana realize that Palagio was no longer interested in her?"

"I don't think she ever allowed herself to realize it," Anna Peruzzi's daughter said. "Like she only remembered I was her half-sister and noble on my father's side when she wanted me to go to the ball in her place. Otherwise I was just her maid, and a bastard too. But *I* knew Palagio would never try to get the Altovitis restored. I saw that in his face when she told him about the property. The next day he was kissing Bianca's hand and cuddling up to her."

"Surely not the next day," Lucrezia said, looking at Don Niccolò. "Surely he would have asked his father about the chance of obtaining the lands, or at least some of them?"

"So that was what those passages meant!" Correggio said with a certain amount of satisfaction. "Palagio's father did write about sequestered lands, but he never used the Altoviti name, nor the name of the man who 'oversaw' the property. All he said was that those dreams could never be fulfilled."

"So it would have been a week or two after Diana spoke about her hopes of Florentine restoration before Palagio began to respond to Bianca's flirtation." Lucrezia nodded at an idea confirmed.

"Diana would not have associated the two things, nor, likely, acknowledged that it was Palagio who was making the advances."

Paola Peruzzi uttered a harsh laugh. "No. Diana blamed Bianca, but at first she did not regard the flirtation as serious. She said Bianca would drop him as lightly as she picked him up, as lightly as she had dropped all the others. Palagio lied to her also. He said he was encouraging Bianca because she could bring him your letters, madonna, which would tell him what the Pope and Don Cesare were planning. It was while you were in the convent over Easter that Diana began to realize she had lost him."

"So then she killed Bianca, hoping that when Palagio was deprived of the hope of marrying a wife whose property would require no effort on his part, he would return to her."

Lucrezia looked at the duke and then around at the seated men. Sigismundo was looking horrified; Giulio and Ferrante nodded as if they had known all along and were approving of her statement. The duke's courtiers made her respectful bows of the head in acknowledgment. Alfonso alone did not return her glance. He stood by the window, looking out.

"And instead Palagio accused her of the murder and demanded money to keep silent." The duke's measured tones were a judgment. He shook his head. "Palagio deserved to die for stupidity alone. She had already killed once. Did he think she loved him so much that she would not take revenge . . . and ensure her safety?"

Lucrezia shrugged. "He was the most self-satisfied fool I have come across in a long time, and he thought very little of women. He imagined, for example, that I would not recognize all the lines he stole from other poets. But to be fair, he probably did take precautions against poison. He could not believe . . . well, I find it hard to believe myself, even though I saw it happen . . . that she would simply walk up to him and . . . and stick a knife in his throat."

"But why dressed as Sigismundo?" the duke asked, looking

angrily at Gabriella. "Was that an attempt to embroil our family in Florentine affairs?"

Gabriella, however, was staring into nothing, tears trickling down her face. She was beyond caring what anyone said, even the duke, and Lucrezia answered.

"No." She smiled at Sigismundo. "That was simply because no one expects to be harmed by Sigismundo. In his clothing, Diana could walk up to Palagio and even draw the 'toy' sword. Nor would Palagio think it strange that Sigismundo should gesture for him to remain seated; he would have known something was wrong if Don Giulio or Don Ferrante did so, but not Sigismundo."

"Perhaps for the safety of others I should cultivate a more ferocious reputation," Sigismundo said dryly.

"No, my son!" the duke exclaimed, looking alarmed. "*Please* let me have one male child that gives me no grief."

That drew laughter from everyone in the room except Gabriella and the Peruzzis. Slowly, as the questions had been answered and explanations given, the three women had come together. At first Anna Peruzzi and her daughter had stood shoulder to shoulder, their backs to Gabriella, Anna now and again glancing at Paola and away to the duke with trembling anxiety. However, as Paola's revelations came to an end and no angry words were directed at them from anyone, Anna had drawn closer to Gabriella, even once touched her arm.

Lucrezia was surprised at first, but she realized that these women had known each other for a very long time. It was not unusual for wife and mistress to accept each other—certainly Lady Eleanora, the duke's wife, and Don Giulio's mother, who had been her lady-in-waiting, had maintained civil relations. And Lady Eleanora had brought up Giulio like a mother when his own mother died.

Between Anna Peruzzi and Gabriella Altoviti there had clearly been some hard feelings, as Anna Peruzzi's calling Gabriella a proud bitch showed. But all in all they were relatively even;

Gabriella had the advantage of a legal marriage and a noble name, but Anna had had the majority of Donato Altoviti's affection. Both had had a daughter ... and now Gabriella's daughter was dead. Anna Peruzzi could easily forget her own injuries in light of that far greater disaster. And Gabriella would be completely alone now; perhaps she would welcome Anna's and Paola's company in her grief.

There had been a buzz of talk in the background while thoughts of the women passed through Lucrezia's mind. That was temporarily silenced when the duke asked if anyone had any further questions or doubts about the murders. If not, he said, he would send home Gabriella Altoviti and Anna Peruzzi and her daughter. He signaled a page to summon a guard to accompany them, and he recommended that they all remain together and not try to leave Ferrara until judgment on the murders had been formally passed.

When they were gone, he invited Lucrezia to take the midday meal with him, but she shook her head. Now that the whole sorry mess was over she felt exhausted and very sad—angry, too, at those who sat around gaping at her as if she were a clever beast trained to do tricks.

"I would like to return to my own apartment, Your Highness." She glanced again around at the men in the room and added bitterly, "I will leave you to explain to each other what kind of accidents allowed a silly woman to first discover the truth that *doubtless* you would have found in another hour or two."

"Never silly, Lucrezia," the duke replied. "I assure you I have not for some time thought you silly." His voice was grim, but suddenly he smiled. "I assure you also that if such a dreadful misfortune as an inexplicable death strikes this Court again, it is in your hands that I will place the investigation."

"I beg you will not, Your Highness," Lucrezia said, smiling in response. "For in this case I did have advantages that Don Niccolò did not, it being essentially a woman's crime."

With the words she stood up, just a trifle shakily, Angela and Nicola coming forward to give her support. But the duke barked, "Alfonso! See to your wife."

Alfonso turned from the window, his face unreadable, his black eyes blank, and came to take her arm. He did not speak a word all the way back to Castel Vecchio, where he brought her right into her bedchamber. A single glance at Angela and Nicola stopped them in the doorway. He closed the door.

"Do not be *too* clever, Lucrezia," he said, but he was not looking at her. He was looking at a blank wall that, had it been an open space, would have shown the Palazzo Cortile.